Also by Peter Straub
available from Random House Large Print

Black House **(with Stephen King)**

In the
Night
Room

In the
Night
Room

A NOVEL

PETER STRAUB

RANDOM HOUSE
LARGE PRINT

Published in the United States of America
by Random House Large Print in association
with Random House, New York.
Distributed by Random House, Inc., New York.

Library of Congress Cataloging-in-Publication Data
Straub, Peter, 1943–
In the night room: a novel/Peter Straub.
p. cm.
ISBN 0-375-43395-3
1. Young adult fiction—Authorship—Fiction.
2. Children—Death—Fiction. 3. Sisters—Death—
Fiction. 4. Women authors—Fiction.
5. Spiritualism—Fiction. 6. Large type books. I. Title.

FICTION PS3569.T6915I5 2004
813'.54—dc22
5/05   2004051570

www.randomlargeprint.com

FIRST LARGE PRINT EDITION

10 9 8 7 6 5 4 3 2 1

This Large Print edition published in accord
with the standards of the N.A.V.H.

For Gary K. Wolfe

I wanted to write, and just tell you that me **and**
my spirit **were fighting this morning. It is'nt known**
generally, and you must'nt tell anybody.
—EMILY DICKINSON,
letter to Emily Fowler, 1850

The consolation of imaginary things is not
imaginary consolation.
—ROGER SCRUTON

Acknowledgments

I owe much to many, foremost among them Emma and Ben Straub, Kathy Kinsner, Joy Andersen, Bill Sheehan, Gary Wolfe (to whom this book is dedicated), and Susan Straub. To Lee Boudreaux, whose brilliant and visionary editing helped me to see what I was doing and how to do it, I owe profound gratitude. My debt to Lila Kalinich, who in several ways saved my life, can be repaid only in love, memory, and thought.

Contents

Willy's Losing Her Mind Again/So Is Tim

PART ONE

1

About 9:45 on a Wednesday morning early in a rain-drenched September, a novelist named Timothy Underhill gave up, in more distress than he cared to acknowledge, on his ruined breakfast and the **New York Times** crossword puzzle and returned, far behind schedule, to his third-floor loft at 55 Grand Street. Closing his door behind him did nothing to calm his troubled heart. He clanked his streaming umbrella into an upright metal stand, transported a fresh cup of decaffeinated coffee to his desk, parked himself in a flexible mesh chair bristling with controls, double-clicked on Outlook Express's arrow-swathed envelope, and, with the sense of finally putting most of his problem behind him, called to the surface of his screen the day's first catch of e-mails, ten in all. Two of them were completely inexplicable. Because the messages seemed to come from strangers (with names unattached to specific domains, he would notice later), bore empty subject lines, and consisted of no more than a couple of disconnected words each, he promptly deleted them.

As soon as he had done so, he remembered dumping a couple of similar e-mails two days earlier. For a moment, what he had seen from the sidewalk outside the Fireside Diner flared again before him, wrapped in every bit of its old urgency and dread.

2

In a sudden shaft of brightness that fell some twenty miles northwest of Grand Street, a woman named Willy Bryce Patrick (soon to be Faber) was turning her slightly dinged little Mercedes away from the Pathmark store on the north side of Hendersonia, having succumbed to the compulsion, not that she had much choice, to drive two and two-tenths miles along Union Street's increasingly vacant blocks instead of proceeding directly home. When she reached a vast parking lot with two sedans trickling through its exit, she checked her rearview mirror and looked around before driving in. Irregular slicks of water gleamed on the black surface of the lot. The men waiting to drive out of the lot took in the blond, shaggy-haired woman moving through their field of vision at the wheel of a sleek, snub-nosed car; one of them thought he was looking at a teenaged boy.

Willy drifted along past the penitentiary-like building that dominated the far end of the parking lot. Her shoulders rode high and tight, and her upper arms seemed taut as cords. Like all serious compulsions, hers seemed both a necessary part of her character and to have been wished upon her by some indifferent deity. Willy pulled in to an empty space and, now at the heart of her problem, regarded what was before her: a long, shabby-looking brick structure, three stories high, with wide metal doors and ranks of filthy windows concealed behind cobwebs of mesh. Around the back, she knew, the dock that led into the loading bays protruded outward, like a pier over the surface of a lake. A row of grimy letters over the topmost row of windows spelled out MICHIGAN PRODUCE.

Somehow, that had been the start of her difficulties: MICHIGAN PRODUCE, the words, not the building, which appeared to be a wholesale fruit-and-vegetable warehouse. Two days earlier, driving along inattentively, in fact in one of her "dazes," her "trances"—Mitchell Faber's words—Willy had found herself here, on this desolate section of Union Street, and the two words atop the big grimy structure had all but peeled themselves off the warehouse, set themselves on fire, and floated aflame toward her through the slate-colored air.

Willy had the feeling that she had been led here, that her "trance" had been charged with purpose, and that she had been all along **meant** to come across this building.

She wondered if this kind of thing ever happened to someone else. Almost instantly, Willy dismissed the strange little vision that blazed abruptly in her mind, of a beautiful, dark-haired teenaged boy, skateboard in one hand, standing dumbstruck on a sunlit street before an empty, ordinary-looking building. Her imagination had always been far too willing to leap into service, whether or not at the time imagination was actually useful. That sometimes it had been supremely useful to Willy did not diminish her awareness that her imaginative faculty could also turn on her, savagely. Oh, yes. You never knew which was the case, either, until the dread began to crawl up your arms.

The image of a teenaged boy and an empty house added to the sum of disorder at large in the universe, and she sent it back to the mysterious realm from which it had emerged. Because: hey, what might **be** in that empty house?

3

The memory of the messages he had seen on Monday awakened Tim Underhill's curiosity, and before going on to answer the few of the day's e-mails that required responses, he clicked on **Deleted Items,** of which he seemed now to have accumulated in excess of two thousand, and looked for the ones that matched those he had just received. There they were, together in the order in which he had deleted them: Huffy and presten, with the blank subject lines that indicated a kind of indifference to protocol he wished he did not find mildly annoying. He clicked on the first message.

From: Huffy
To: tunderhill@nyc.rr.com
Sent: Monday, September 1, 2003 8:52 AM
Subject:

re member

That was the opposite of dis member, Tim supposed, and dis member was the guy standing next to dat member. He tried the second one.

From: presten
To: tunderhill@nyc.rr.com
Sent: Monday, September 1, 2003 9:01 AM
Subject:

no helo

Useless, meaningless, a nuisance. Huffy and presten were kids who had figured out how to hide their e-mail addresses. Presumably they had learned his from the website mentioned on the jacket of his latest book. He looked again at the two e-mails he had just dumped.

From: rudderless
To: tunderhill@nyc.rr.com
Sent: Wednesday, September 3, 2003
         6:32 AM
Subject:

no time

and

From: loumay
To: tunderhill@nyc.rr.com
Sent: Wednesday, September 3, 2003
　　　　6:41 AM
Subject:

there wuz

There wuz, wuz there? All of these enigmatic messages sounded as though their perpetrators were half asleep, or as though their hands had been snatched off the keyboard—maybe by the next customer at some Internet café, since the second messages came only minutes after the first ones.

What were the odds that four people savvy enough to delete the second half of their e-mail addresses would decide, more or less simultaneously, to send early-morning gibberish to the same person? And how much steeper were the odds against one of them writing "no helo," whatever that meant, and another deciding, with no prior agreement, upon the echo-phrase "no time"? Although he thought such a coincidence was impossible, he still felt mildly uneasy as he rejected it.

Because that left only two options, and both raised the ante. Either the four people who'd sent the e-mails to him were acting together in conspiracy, or the e-mails had all been sent by the same person using four names.

The names, Huffy, presten, rudderless, loumay, suggested no pattern. They were not familiar. A moment later, Tim remembered that back in his hometown, Millhaven, Illinois, a boy named Paul Resten had been his teammate on the Holy Sepulchre football team. Paulie Resten had been a chaotic little fireplug with greasy hair, a shop-lifting problem, and a tendency toward vio-lence. It seemed profoundly unlikely that after a silence of forty-odd years Paulie would send him a two-word e-mail.

Tim read the messages over again, thought for a second, then rearranged them:

    re member
    there wuz
    no helo
    no time

which could just as easily have been

    re member
    there wuz
    no time
    no helo

or

there wuz
no time
no helo
re member

Not much of an advance, was it? The possibility that "helo" could be a typo for "help" came to mind. **Remember, there was no time, no help.** Whatever the hell that was about, it was pretty depressing. Also depressing was the notion that four people had decided to send him that disjointed message. If Tim felt like getting depressed, he had merely to think of his brother, Philip, who, not much more than one year after his wife's suicide and the disappearance of his son, had announced his impending marriage to one China Beech, a born-again Christian whom Philip had met shortly after her emergence from the chrysalis of an exotic dancer. On the whole, Tim decided, he'd rather think about the inexplicable e-mails.

They had the stale, slightly staid aura of a Sherlock Holmes setup. Faintly, the rusty machinery of a hundred old detective novels could be heard, grinding into what passed for life. Nonetheless, in the twenty-first century any such thing had to be seen as a possible threat. At the very least, a malign hacker could have compromised the security of his system.

When his antivirus program discovered no loathsome substance hidden within his folders and files, Tim procrastinated a little further by calling his computer guru, Myron Dorot-Rivage. Myron looked like a Spaniard, and he spoke with a surprisingly musical German accent. He had rescued Tim and his companions at 55 Grand from multiple catastrophes.

Amazingly, Myron answered his phone on the second ring. "So, Tim," he said, being equipped with infallible caller ID as well as a headset, "tell me your problem. I am booked solid for **at least** the next three days, but perhaps we can solve it over the phone."

"It isn't exactly a computer problem."

"You are calling me about a **personal** problem, Tim?"

Momentarily, Tim considered telling his computer guru about what had happened that morning on West Broadway. Myron would have no sympathy for any problem that involved a ghost. He said, "I've been getting weird e-mails," and described the four messages. "My virus check came up clean, but I'm still a little worried."

"You probably won't get a virus unless you open an attachment. Are you bothered by the anonymity?"

"Well, yeah. How do they do that, leave out their addresses? Is that legal?"

"Legal schmegal. I could arrange the same thing for you, if you were willing to pay for it. But what I **cannot** do is trace such an e-mail back to its source. These people pay their fees for a reason, after all!"

Myron drew in his breath, and Tim heard the clatter of metal against metal. It was like talking to an obstetrician who was delivering a baby.

After hanging up, Tim noticed that three new e-mails had arrived since his last look at his in-box. The first, **Monster Oral Sex Week**, undoubtedly offered seven days' free access to a porn site; the second, **300,000 Customers**, almost certainly linked to an e-mail database; the third, nayrm, made the skin on his forearms prickle. The **Sex** and the **Customers** disappeared unopened into the landfill of deleted mail. As he had dreaded, nayrm proved, when clicked upon, to have arrived without the benefit of a filled-in subject line or identifiable e-mail address. It had been sent at 10:58 A.M. and consisted of three words:

hard death hard

4

Yo, Willy! You with the funny name! Are we interested in another journey back to the antiseptic corridors of western Massachusetts? An hour or two in the Institute's game room?

No.

Don't think about what might be hidden in empty buildings, okay?

That was the whole problem: what might be, could possibly be, and according to every variety of internal registration she possessed **actually was** at that very moment inside the warehouse located two and two-tenths of a mile north of the Union Street Pathmark. What she was thinking, what she unfortunately believed, was completely crazy. Her daughter, Holly, could not possibly be hiding or kept prisoner inside Michigan Produce. Her daughter was dead. Raw though it was, Holly's death was not actually all that recent. She had been dead for two years and four months. Along with James Patrick, Willy's husband, Holly had been gunned down in the back of a car, soaked with gasoline, and set on fire. That was that. No matter how deeply they were loved, children who had been shot to death and set on fire did not come back. As a doctor (whose name, Bollis, Willy wouldn't wish on a two-headed dwarf) in the Berkshires village of Stockwell could explain to any party in need of explanation, the belief that one's child had returned from the realm of the dead not as a ghost but a living being could be no more than the product of a wish bamboozled into mistaking itself for fact.

Willy took in the produce warehouse, saw the letters pulse above the high row of windows, and knew beyond any possibility of a doubt—apart, of course, from its not being true—that her daughter was in there. Holly cowered at the back of a storeroom, or she was hidden in a closet, or beneath the desk in an empty office. Or in some other clammy bardo from which her mother alone could rescue her.

Willy grasped the car's door handle, and sweat burst out across her forehead. If she opened the door, out she would go, her shaky control over her actions vanished altogether. Brainless as a falling meteor would she race toward the warehouse, brave little Willy, searching for a way to break in.

If she were ever to give in to this disastrous impulse, she realized, it would happen at night, when the warehouse was empty.

In the night would she pull the curved spoon of the door handle from its recessed pocket, releasing the catch, opening the door, thereby creating a space immediately to be filled by her body. As if scripted in advance, the whole doomed enterprise would follow. Half of her agony lay in its own uselessness; grief led people to do things they understood were hopelessly stupid. Even worse, she knew that should she succumb, her nighttime entry would trigger an alarm. She would attempt to conceal herself, would be discovered and taken to the police station, there to try to explain herself.

After his return from England, or France, or wherever his mysterious errands had taken him, maybe Mitchell Faber could talk her out of custody, but then she would have to face Mitchell. In almost every way, her husband-to-be was more threatening than the local cops.

Willy had no doubt that a brush with the police would have a dire effect on Mitchell. Given his capacity for well-banked fury, it would take her weeks to worm her way back into the sun-

light. Unlike her late husband, Mitchell was dark
of eye, dark of hair, dark dark dark of character.
His darkness protected her, she felt; it was **on
her side** and alert to threat, like a pet wolf. Far
better not to attract its dead-level glare. For a
person who appeared to wield a great deal of influence, Mitchell Faber refused the limelight
and demanded to live in the shadows at the side
of the stage.

Willy released the handle and grasped the
steering wheel with both hands. This felt like
progress, and at the same time like an unimaginable betrayal. Although the temperature had
dropped, slick moisture clung to her face like a
washcloth. She could all but hear Holly's clear,
high voice, calling out to her. How could she
turn her back on her daughter? Her left hand
drifted to the handle again. Only a massive effort of will permitted her to pull her hand back
to the wheel. For a second or two, she granted
herself leave from rationality and howled like
an animal stuck in a trap. Then she shut her
mouth, forced herself to turn the key, and put
the car in reverse. Without looking at the rearview mirror, she backed away from the building. On the lot, the surfaces of all the puddles
seemed to shiver in rebuke.

Driving too quickly, she bumped her tires
against the curb. When she shot forward, flee-

ing a sound audible only in her head, the front of her car crashed down onto the road, and she gave the inside of her cheek a quick, sharp bite. The pain in her mouth helped her through the dangerous two and two-tenths miles to the Pathmark. After that, each passing mile brought her a greater degree of clarity. It was as though she **had** been in a trance, no longer responsible for her thoughts and actions.

Willy drove the rest of the way home in a complicated mixture of relief and bright panicky alarm. Very narrowly, she had escaped craziness.

5

hard death hard

More than a little creeped out, Tim stared at the message on his screen. Narym had joined in with Huffy, presten, and the others to disrupt a stranger's day with what was either a joke or a threat. If it was supposed to be a joke, the disruption had been hideously mistimed. A little more than a year earlier, Tim's nephew, Mark, his brother's son, had vanished utterly from the face of the earth. Tim still felt the boy's loss with the original sick, vertiginous sharpness. His grief had only deepened, not lessened. How greatly he had loved Mark he understood only after it was too late to demonstrate that love. **Hard death hard,** yes, hard on the survivors.

Tim had wanted to bring his nephew to New

York City and advance his education by showing him a thousand beautiful things, the Ver-
meers at the Frick, an opera at the Met, little
hidden corners of the Village, the whole rough,
lively commerce of the street. He had wanted to
be a kind of father to the boy, and if he could
have seen Mark enrolled at Columbia or NYU,
he would have been a better father than Philip
ever was. Instead, after watching his brother almost immediately abandon hope for his son's
survival, Tim had written a novel that permitted
Mark the continued life a monster named
Ronald Lloyd-Jones had stolen from him—in
lost boy lost girl, to be published in a week,
Mark Underhill slipped away into an "Elsewhere" with a beautiful phantom named "Lucy
Cleveland," in reality Lily Kalendar, the daughter of a second homicidal monster, Joseph
Kalendar. **She** had almost certainly died at her
father's hands sometime in her fifth or sixth
year, although as with Mark, no remains were
ever found. In Tim's imagination, the two of
them, the lost boy and the lost girl, had escaped
their fates by fleeing into another world altogether, a world with the potentiality of cyber-
space, where they ran hand in hand along a
tropical beach below a darkening sky, conscious
always of the Dark Man hurrying after them.

Better that for his dear nephew, better by far, than monstrous Ronnie Lloyd-Jones's attentions.

There had to be a Dark Man, for otherwise nothing in their world would be real, least of all them.

Tim had known about the Dark Man since the day his older sister, April, had been murdered in an alleyway alongside the St. Alwyn Hotel and he, dimly seeing it happen and running toward her, was mowed down by a passing car on Livermore Avenue. Before thirty seconds had ticked away, April was dead, and he, too, had passed out of life. He seemed to be following her into a realm where darkness and light inhabited the same dazzling space. Then a sturdy, unexpected cord yanked him back into his mutilated body, and his education really took off.

His brother claimed not to remember anything about April, which may have been the truth. Mom and Pop never spoke of her, though from time to time Tim could see the subject of his sister's death glide into form between them, like a giant cloud both his parents pretended not to see. Could Philip have missed it altogether, their stifled grief? April had been nine at the time of her death, Tim seven. Philip had been three, so maybe he really did have no conscious memory of their sister. On the other hand, Philip possessed a massive talent for denial.

If Tim had ever thought he could forget April, her recurring ghost would soon have let him know otherwise. A year after her death, he had seen her seated four rows behind him on the Pulaski Avenue bus, her face turned to a window; three years later, he and his mother bunking off on the Lake Michigan ferry, Tim had looked down and with a gasp of shock and sorrow seen his sister's blond head tilted over the railing at the squared-off aft end of the lower deck. Later, he had seen her outside a grocery store in Berkeley, where he had been a student; on a truck with a lot of uniformed nurses in Camp Crandall, Vietnam, where he had been a pearl diver on the body squad; twice riding by in taxicabs, in New York, where he lived; and twice again in the first-class sections of airplanes, when he had been having a nice little drink.

On all but one of these occasions, Tim had understood that for a brief moment desire had transformed a convenient female child into his sister; but there had been no little girls in Camp Crandall. In Camp Crandall, the daily task of

rummaging through ruined corpses in search of
ID had affected Tim's consciousness in a number of extravagant ways, likewise the enforced
proximity to elaborately fucked-up grunts with
names like Ratman and Pirate. There he had
witnessed what he took to be the only true hallucination of his life.

Until this morning. What he had seen across
the street from the Fireside Diner on West
Broadway **had** to be a hallucination, for it could
be nothing else. Without benefit of sound effects or a premonitory shift in the lighting,
nine-year-old April Underhill had abruptly
entered his field of vision. She was wearing an
old blue-and-white thing she called her Alice
in Wonderland dress. At the time of her death,
Tim remembered, April had been obsessed
with **Alice's Adventures in Wonderland** and
Through the Looking-Glass, and she'd had on
that crazy dress because she usually refused to
wear anything else. Now she faced him, her
stare like a shout in the crowded street. Limp
blond hair in need of washing, the bodice of the
Alice dress darkened with raindrops, a figure so
distant from her proper time she should have
been in black and white, or two-dimensional—
this apparition struck him like a bolt of lightning and left him sizzling where he stood.

Two stubble-faced boys wearing black swerved to move around him.

For a time he was incapable of speech. He could tell himself, **April isn't really there, I'm hallucinating,** but what he was looking at seemed and felt like fact. Long-forgotten things returned laden with the gritty imperfections of the actual person his sister had been. The characteristic note of April's nine-year-old life had been frustration, he saw: she had the face of a child who, having grown used to being thwarted, was in a furious hurry to reach adulthood.

April's stubborn face, with its implacable cheekbones and tight mouth, reminded Tim of Pop's uncomprehending rages at what he perceived as April's defiance. No wonder she had fled into the mirror world of Alice and the Mad Hatter. A tavern-haunting elevator operator at the St. Alwyn Hotel supervised her life, and he found half of the things that ran through her mind unacceptable, irritating, obscurely insulting.

A second and a half later Tim was left with the fact of April's face, narrower than he remembered, and the smallness of her body, the true childishness of the sister he had lost. All his old love for nine-year-old April Underhill awakened in him—she who had defended him when he needed defending, stuck up for him when he needed a champion, entranced him with the best stories he had ever heard. She, he realized, she should have been the writer! April had been his **guide,** and **to the end.** On her last day, she had preceded him into the ultimate Alice-world, the one beyond death, where, unable any longer to follow his best, bravest, and most tender guide all the way to her unimaginable destination, he had yielded to the forces pulling him back.

He wanted to tell her to get out of the rain.

April stepped forward on the crowded sidewalk, and Tim's heart went cold with terror. His sister had swum back through the mirror to interrupt him on his way to breakfast. He feared that she intended to glide across the street, grasp his hand, and pull him into the SoHo traffic. She reached the edge of the pavement and raised her arms.

Oh no, she's going to call to me, he thought, **and I'll have to go.**

Instead of dragging him through the mirror, April brought her hands to the sides of her mouth, leaned forward, contracted her whole being, and, as loudly as she could, shouted through the megaphone of her hands. All Tim heard were the sounds of the traffic and the scraps of conversation spoken by the people walking past him.

His eyes stung, his vision blurred. By the time he raised his hands to flick away his tears, April had disappeared.

6

Guilderland Road, at the upper end of which lay Mitchell Faber's expansive, densely wooded property, traversed an area on the southwestern slopes (so to speak) of Alpine, New Jersey, where not long after the Civil War the nearly invisible village of Hendersonia had been surgically detached from the more public borough of Creskill. In all aspects of life save the naming of places, the Hendersons of Hendersonia had presumably cherished obscurity as thoroughly as Mitchell Faber, for they had passed through history leaving behind no more than a scattering of barely legible headstones in the postage-stamp graveyard at the lower end of the road. Farther down the hill, the cement-block bank, an abandoned Presbyterian church, a private house turned into an insurance agency, a video and DVD rental shop, and a bar and grill called Redtop's made up the center of town. The previous summer, a Foodtown grocery store had taken over an old bowling alley in a paved lot one block south, and Willy promised herself that from now on she would do her shopping there.

She was still finding her way around, still trying to get into a routine. It had been only two weeks since Mitchell had succeeded in persuading her to abandon her cozy one-bedroom apartment on East Seventy-seventh Street for the "estate." They were to be married in two months, why not start living together now? They were adults of thirty-eight and fifty-two (a young fifty-two), alone in the world. **Let's face it,** Mitchell said one night, **you need me.** She needed him, and he wanted her as extravagantly as someone like Mitchell Faber could ever want anything—dark, frowning Mitchell summoning her into his embrace, promising to make sure the bad things never got close to her again. The "estate" would be perfect for her, he said, a protective realm, as Mitchell himself was a kind of protective realm. And large enough to provide separate offices for both of them, because he wanted to spend more time at home and she needed what all women, especially women who wrote books, needed: A Room of Her Own.

When Willy had met Mitchell Faber, he

amazed her by knowing not only that her third YA novel, **In the Night Room,** had just won the Newbery Medal, but also that its setting, Mill Basin, was based on the city where she had been born, Millhaven, Illinois.

The prize had been announced four days earlier, but the party at Molly Harper's apartment was not in her honor, and Willy's triumph was so fresh, as yet still half unreal, that she felt as though it might be revoked. Willy herself, having yet to emerge from mad grieving darkness, would have run from anything as public as a celebration. She felt only barely capable of handling a dinner party. Some of the people present were aware that Willy had just been honored by the Newbery Committee, and some of those came up to congratulate her. Molly's friends tended to be too rich to be demonstrative; like Molly herself, many of the women were decades younger than their husbands, thereby generally obliged to exercise a kind of behavioral modification akin to the pushing of a "Mute" button. Added to their characteristic restraint was their response to Willy's appearance, that of a gorgeous lost child. Some women disliked her on sight. Others felt threatened when their husbands wandered, flirtatiously or not, into Willy's orbit.

Toward the end of the evening, or shortly after ten o'clock, for these silver-haired men and their gleaming wives never stayed up later than eleven, Lankford Harper, Molly's whispery husband, left the chair to Willy's left and within seconds was replaced by a sleek, smooth male animal remarkable for being older than most of the women and younger than all of the men. Energy hummed through his thick, shiny black hair and luxuriant black mustache. Black eyes and brilliant white teeth shone at Willy, and a wide, warm dark hand covered hers. That she did not find this intimacy discomfiting amazed her. Whatever was about to happen, would; instead of feeling offended, Willy relaxed.

—I want to congratulate you on your magnificent honor, Mrs. Patrick, the man said, leaning in. You must feel as though you've won the lottery.

—Hardly that, she said. Do you keep up with children's books then, Mr. . . . ?

—I'm Mitchell Faber. No, I can't say I'm an expert on children's books, but the Newbery's a great accolade, and I **have** heard wonderful things about your book. Your third, isn't it?

She opened her mouth. —Yes.

—Good title, **In the Night Room,** especially for a children's book.

—It's probably too close to Maurice Sendak, but he was writing for a younger audience.

Why am I explaining myself to this guy? she wondered.

His hand tightened on hers. —Please excuse me for what I'm about to say, Mrs. Patrick. I knew your husband. At times, our work brought us into contact. He was a fine, fine man.

For a moment, Willy's vision went grainy, and her heart hovered between beats. Ordinary conversation hummed on around her. She blinked and raised her napkin to her mouth, buying time.

—I'm sorry, the man said. I did that very badly.

—Not at all. I was just a bit startled. Do you work for the Baltic Group?

—From time to time, they call me in to make murky issues even murkier.

—I'm sure you bring clarity wherever you go, she said, and, in a way she hoped brought the conversation to a neat conclusion, thanked him for having approached her.

Mitchell Faber leaned in and patted her hand. —Mill Basin, the village in your book. Is it based on Millhaven? I understand that's where you're from.

Mitchell Faber was chockablock with little astonishments.

Flattered, puzzled, she smiled back at him. —

You must know Millhaven very well. Are you from there, too?

The question was absurd: Faber did not look, sound, or behave like a Millhaven native. Nor was he a product of the East Coast privilege-hatcheries responsible for Lankford Harper.

—Sometimes when I'm in Chicago I like to drive up to Millhaven, check in to the Pforzheimer for a night or two, wander along the river walk, have a drink in the old Green Woman. Do you know the Green Woman Taproom?

She had never heard of the Green Woman Taproom.

—Lovely old bar, fascinating history. Ought to be in encyclopedias. It has an interesting connection to criminal lore.

Criminal lore? She had no idea what he was talking about, and no intention of finding out. As far as Willy was concerned, the murders of her husband and daughter were more than enough crime for the rest of her life. The very idea of "criminal lore" struck her as a bad idea.

Mitchell Faber could have struck her the same way, but Willy found that she had not made up her mind so quickly. Calling Molly the next day to thank her, she found herself asking her friend about the man who had spoken to her about the

Newbery and Millhaven. Molly knew very little about him.

A day later, Willy called to report that the unknown dinner guest had asked if they might get together for a cup of coffee or a drink, or anything.

—I'd go straight for the anything, Molly told her. What have you got to lose? I thought he was pretty cute. Besides, he isn't a hundred years old.

—I don't know anything about him, Willy said. And I don't think I'm ready to start dating. I'm not even close.

—Willy, how long has it been?

—Two years. That's nothing.

—So's a cup of coffee.

—I'd have to tell him everything.

—If he works with Lanky, he knows everything already. These guys can find out whatever they want to, they can dig up **anything.** Lanky told me they're better than the CIA, and they should be! They have about ten times the money!

—Ah, Willy said. So that's how Mr. Faber found out about **In the Night Room** and Millhaven.

—He had Lanky!

—Lanky knows I won the Newbery? Excuse me, I didn't mean that the way it sounded.

Molly was laughing. —Of course Lanky knows. He even read **Night Room.**

Now Willy was stunned. —Lanky read my book? It's a YA!

—YA novels are Lanky's secret passion. When he was twenty-five years old, he read **The Greengage Summer,** and it changed his life. Now he's an expert on Rumer Godden.

Willy tried to picture Molly's gaunt, secretive, gray-haired husband in his blue pin-striped suit and gold watch, bending, in the light of a library lamp, over a copy of **Miss Happiness and Miss Flower.**

—He has a fabulous collection, Molly said. We're talking about Lankford Harper now, remember. There's a special vault with huge metal bookshelves. When you push this little button, they revolve. **Thousands** of books, most of them in great condition. When he gets a new one, he buys a bunch of copies, one to read and the rest to put in the vault. Philip Pullman— you wouldn't believe how much those Philip Pullmans are worth.

Willy should have known that Lanky Harper's interest in her fiction was primarily financial. —How many copies of **In the Night Room** are stashed away in that vault?

—Five. He bought three when it came out,

and as soon as the Newbery was announced, he bought two more.

—Five copies? I guess he liked it a lot. Her mind had returned to Mitchell Faber, whose intrusiveness had contained an unexpected quantity of appeal. At least Faber had been unafraid actually to talk to the tragic widow, instead of swaddling her in clichés. Secretly, dark Mitchell Faber rather thrilled Willy Patrick: he was the kind of man for whom everyone else's rules were merely guidelines.

7

So there he had been, Tim Underhill, in the good old Fireside, trying to act as though his hands weren't shaking so badly that the mush-rooms fell off his fork; and trying to look as ab-sorbed in the crossword puzzle as he was every other morning. The words kept blurring on the page, and none of the clues made sense; above all, Underhill was trying simultaneously to fig-ure out and ignore whatever his murdered nine-year-old sister had been shouting at him from the other side of West Broadway. Contradictory desires were difficult to fulfill, especially when wrapped in such urgency. April bending for-ward, shouting at him, bellowing, frantic to get her message across . . .

"Mr. Underhill?"

Tim turned to see the face of an eager black-haired man of forty or so, still boyish, and radi-ant with what looked like mingled pleasure and bravado. A fan. This kind of thing happened to him maybe three times a year.

"You got me," he said, dropping his hands to his lap to conceal their trembling.

"Timothy Underhill is right here, right smack in the Fireside. Just like a normal person."

"I am a normal person," Tim said, stretching a point.

"I yam what I yam, hah! Didn't you say that once? In print, I mean?"

He had quoted Popeye? It sounded remotely possible, but possible. Barely.

"Would you do a big favor for me? I'm a fan, obviously—who else would barge in on your little breakfast, right? But I'd really appreciate it if you signed some books for me. Would you do that, Mr. Underhill? Would you sign some books for me, Tim? Is it all right if I call you Tim?"

"You carry my books around with you?"

"Hey, that's funny. You're a funny guy, Tim! Ever think about going into comedy? No, the books are back in my apartment, I mean, where else would they be? If I had ESP, I'd have them with me, but no such luck, right? But I live right down the street, be back in five minutes, less, four minutes, time me with your watch, check it out, see if I'm wrong. Okay? We got a deal?"

"Go get the books," Tim said.

The fan made a pistol with his hand, pointed it at Tim, and dropped the hammer of his thumb. He whirled away and was out the door. Tim realized that he had never given his name. As fans went, this one seemed slightly off, but Tim wished to preserve an open mind about anyone who bought his books. Anyone who did that had earned his gratitude.

Today's admirer stretched his patience nearly to the breaking point. After twelve minutes, Tim began to simmer. He liked getting to his desk by ten, and it was already 9:40. If he gave up on the eggs he didn't want and abandoned the puzzle he couldn't concentrate on well enough to finish, he could avoid dealing with the fan, who had been overassertive, overintrusive, and was unlikely to be satisfied with merely a couple of signatures. He would want to talk, to swap phone numbers, to find out where Tim lived. He'd escalated from "Mr. Underhill" to "Tim" in less than a second. "Tim" did not want to encourage a fan who told him he was a funny guy—it gave him the willies. So did the shooting gesture with which the man had left him.

Again, he saw April before him, cupping her hands and shaping her mouth to shout . . .

Whistle to us? That could not be right.

Tim let his fork clatter to his plate, signaled

the waiter for the check, and returned his pen to his pocket. Rain streamed down the windows of the diner, and when the door swung open, a few drops spattered onto the tiles. Tim sighed. A wet hand swept the sodden hood of a sweatshirt off his admirer's glowing face. The fan held up a yellow bag bearing the likeness of Charles Dickens.

"Did you time me?"

Tim looked at his watch. "You were gone at least twenty minutes."

"No, six, at the outside. I would have been here earlier, but the rain slowed me down."

The fan pulled the books one by one from the shiny bag and stacked them about an inch north of Tim's plate. They were copies of **lost boy lost girl,** as yet unpublished. He had received his box of author's copies only a short while before. "These babies stayed dry, anyhow." The fan wiped his face and pushed the moisture back into his thick black hair. "Must be a great feeling to sign a book you wrote, huh? Like 'This is my baby, get a good look, 'cuz I'm one proud papa,' right?"

Tim wanted to get rid of this character as soon as possible. "Where did you get these books?"

The man slid the books nearer to Tim. "Why? I bought them, didn't I?"

Water dripped from his sleeves, and drops landed on the **Times** crossword puzzle. In a small number of squares, the ink melted into the paper.

"Okay," he said, and sat down in the chair opposite Tim. "Sign the first one to Jasper Kohle, that's Jasper the normal way, and Kohle is K-O-H-L-E. My full name is Jasper Dan Kohle, but I only use my middle name on checks and my driver's license, ha ha. Inscribe it however you like. Have fun. Use your imagination. You could say, 'To Jasper Kohle, I yam what I yam.' "

The only thing worse than someone ordering you to be inventive when you signed their book was someone telling you exactly what to write. This fan had managed to do both. Tim looked at Jasper Kohle, for the first time actually taking him in, and saw someone whose cheerfulness was laid on like paint. His eyes had no light, and his smile displayed too many teeth, all of them yellow. He was ten to fifteen years older than he had first appeared.

"You didn't go to your apartment," Tim said. "You ran all the way to the bookstore, and then you ran back. I don't understand it, but that's what you did. But the real problem is this book hasn't actually been published yet, and it's not supposed to be on sale. The copies aren't even supposed to have shipped to the book-stores."

"Come on," Kohle said. "You must have some kind of problem with trust."

"If I looked inside that bag, I bet I'd find a receipt with today's date on it."

Kohle glowered at him. "Let me ask you a question, Tim. Are you this pricky to all your fans?"

"No, I'm just interested in your explanation."

"I wanted more."

"More copies of the same book?"

"I have four at home. But since you're here, I thought I should get three more, so I'd have three signed, plus four backup copies. One of 'em I've read, but that's all, just one." He nudged the books still closer to Tim. "Don't in-scribe the second two, just flat sign them and put down the date. On the title page, please."

"You wanted seven copies of **lost boy lost girl**?"

Kohle showed his yellow teeth again. "If you want to know the truth, I'd like ten, but I'm not a fucking millionaire, am I?"

"Why would you want ten copies?"

"I collect books!"

"I guess you do," Tim said. He picked up his

pen, opened the topmost book to the title page, and thought for a second before writing:

To Jasper Kohle
a collector's collector
All Best,
Tim Underhill

After adding the date beneath this inscription, he handed the book, still opened to the title page, to Kohle, who was waiting to receive it like a child, both hands out. Gimme gimme gimme. He yanked the book from Underhill's hands, turned it around, and dipped his head toward the inscription. Odd, irregular white-gray streaks ran through the thick black pelt on the top of his head. When he snapped his head back up, his eyes held a dull, flat glare, and the skin at the corners of his mouth looked wrinkled and dark with grease.

"What happened to 'I yam what I yam'?"

"I'm not doing so well this morning, but I don't think I ever put that in a book," Tim said.

"Oh yes, you did. That cop, Esterhaz, says it in **The Divided Man.** 'I yam what I yam.' Right at the beginning, when he's hungover and getting out of bed. Just before he sees the dead people marching around."

At his worst moments, Hal Esterhaz, an alcoholic homicide detective in Tim's second novel,
had seen an army of the dead trudging aimlessly
through the streets. He had not once, however,
quoted Popeye.

"I see you don't believe me," Kohle said. "No
wonder, stupid me—you can't, because you
don't know. Okay, go ahead, sign the other
books, you probably got things you want to do."

Tim removed the second book from the pile
and opened it to the title page. He looked back
at Jasper Dan Kohle and found that he could
not resist. "I don't know what, exactly?"

"Mr. Underhill," Kohle said. "Tim. Let me
say this, Tim. And I'm saying this although I
know that you will have precisely no idea at all
what I'm talking about, because that is guaran-
teed one hundred percent certain. So first let me
ask you: do you have any idea **at all** why a guy
like me would want to collect twenty copies of
the same book? A hundred copies, if I had all
the money in the world, a likely story, thank
you very much?"

"As an investment?" Tim took his eyes off
Kohle long enough to sign the second book and
pick up the third.

Kohle went through a savage parody of yawn-
ing. "I don't even live in this neighborhood. But
I saw you doing your crossword puzzle, and I let

my whaddayacallit, my joie de vivre, get the better of me, and the next thing I know, I'm spending a whole lot more money than I should on your new book. Which to tell you the truth is a little lightweight, not to mention kind of rushed at the end."

"Glad you liked it," Tim said.

"So why do I want fifteen, twenty copies of a book that isn't really all that hot, if you don't mind my saying so?"

"That was my question, yes." Tim pushed the last two books across the table.

"Listen up now, here it comes." He leaned over and cupped his mouth with his hands, as April had done. **"One of them might be the real book."**

He pulled the three copies of Underhill's novel into the circle of his arms. "What, you ask, is the real book? The one you were supposed to write, only you screwed it up. Authors think every copy of a book is the same, but they're not. Every time a book goes through the presses, two, three, copies of the **real** book come out. **That's** the one you wanted to write when you started out, with everything perfect, no mistakes, nothing dumb, and all the dialogue and the details exactly right. People like me, that's what we're looking for. Investment? Don't make me laugh. It's the **reverse** of an investment. Once you find a real book, sell it to some-one? Give me a break."

"You're out of your mind," Tim said.

Kohle raised his hands chest-high in exaspera-tion. "You guys are all the same. Ninety percent of the time, you're just making things up. You act like a bunch of lazy, irresponsible gods. It wouldn't be so bad if you weren't basically deaf and blind, too. You don't listen."

"What are you talking about?" Tim asked, un-settled by the sudden reappearance on his men-tal screen of his sister, April.

"If you paid more attention, your real books wouldn't be all that different from the ones you wrote."

Kohle seemed wetter than he had been earlier. Greasy moisture covered his sunken cheeks. His filthy sweatshirt was on the verge of disinte-gration.

"Jasper, I signed your books, and now I'm just about through with this conversation. But if these 'real' books exist, how come no one ever showed me one?"

"**Authors** can't see them," Kohle said. "I can't imagine what the sight of a real book would do to one of you people—total meltdown, I sup-pose. Most people never get so much as a glimpse at a real book. The collectors manage to scoop 'em up almost as soon as they come out.

Once in a blue moon, a reviewer gets a copy. That can be pretty funny. The reviewer flips out over some book that's a piece of crap, and everyone wonders if he lost his mind. Come to think of it, that happened to one of your books."

"One of my books was an overpraised piece of crap?"

"Yeah, imagine that."

Smiling, Jasper Dan Kohle turned his head and watched rain bounce off the roofs of the cars inching down West Broadway.

"You didn't happen to look through that window and see me eating breakfast in here. You didn't just want me to sign a couple of books. Are you even a real collector?"

"I collect a lot of things," Kohle said, amused.

"Why are you here, Jasper? If that's your name."

"Don't worry about my name, Mr. Big-Time Author. Mr. Fifty-five Grand Street." In his dark, greasy face, the yellow teeth crowded his mouth. "I yam what I yam, and that's what I yam." He pushed the books into the bag, pulled the wet hood over his head, and rushed through the door. Tim watched him vanish into the gray street. This hostile being was walking away with samples of his handwriting. Tim felt a flicker of disquiet, as if his signature bore his DNA.

8

The author of **In the Night Room** was grateful for the medal it had won and the money it had earned, but she had written her third book as an act of rescue, not a means of achieving recognition. Thanks to James's various life insurance policies, plus the fortune the Baltic Group had paid him in income and bonuses during his lifetime, money, very much a concern during the writing of **Fairy Ring** and **The Golden Mountain,** had ceased to be an issue. Her husband's death payments had underwritten the months she had spent in western Massachusetts under the care of Dr. Bollis and the quiet attendants never less than determined to give their charges what they needed: a comforting book, a comforting hug, or a comforting jab in the upper arm with a needle. Back then, nothing but bloody shreds seemed to remain of the once-familiar Willy. The bloody shreds were usually too limp and wounded to think about reassembling themselves. Her conscious life, the life of her spirit, had been murdered along with her family. For her first two months at the Institute, Willy had groped in darkness at the bottom of a well, grateful for the absence of light, too depleted to commit suicide. She was not wounded, she was a wound.

In Massachusetts, she had no visitors but visiting phantoms.

One day she walked into the dayroom, saw a familiar shape occupying a folding chair, looked more closely as fear moved toward her empty heart, and froze in shock at the reappearance in her life of Tee Tee Rowley, a flinty, sharp-fisted girl who, as ever, held her ground, scowling at Willy.

She had come from the Millhaven Foundlings' Shelter, established in 1918 and everywhere referred to as either "the Children's Home" or, as its familiars knew it, "the Block." All in all, Willy had spent something like two and a half years "on the Block."

Tee Tee Rowley, who stood five feet tall and weighed perhaps eighty pounds, responded to challenges by squaring up to them and suggesting her readiness to do anything necessary to instill respect in her challenger. Unlike some of her peers, Tee Tee did not default to crazed violence at the first sign of difficulty, but the willingness to employ craziness and destruction spoke from her posture, her eyes, the set of her mouth.

That of all her acquaintances from the Block the one to pay a phantom call should have been Tee Tee made perfect sense to Willy. It was to Tee Tee that Willy, who had begun to enjoy a small reputation as a storyteller, had told the best story of her young life.

From the first, Willy Bryce half-sensed, half-suspected, and, she hoped, half-understood that she had not fully explored the dimensions of the inner life awakened by the books she devoured in the Block's library: that it contained some element, some enigmatic quality that was of immense importance to her. Deep within, this unknown element **shone.**

Willy's discovery of what the unknown element contained had led Tee Tee's shade to appear. Willy had discovered how to save her own life.

This was how it happened: one day, tough, ten-year-old Tee Tee Rowley materialized before eight-year-old Willy Bryce in the second-floor lounge and asked her what the fuck she thought she was doing there anyhow, you fucking piece of shit. Instead of backing away and slinking off, Willy said, Listen to this, Tee Tee. And told

her a story that almost instantly drew half a dozen other girls to that side of the lounge.

If she had stopped to think about what she was doing, doing it would have been impossible. But she did not **have** to think about the odd little tale. It spun itself out of the unknown element and gave her the right words, one after the other. She launched into the first real **story** of her life.

—**When Little Howie Small stood before the ancient wizard and wiped the tears from his eyes, the first thing he noticed was that a sharp-eyed bird was peering out at him from within the wizard's enormous beard.**

And an entire adventure followed, a story involving an eagle and a bear and a furious river and a prince who rescued his princess-to-be with the aid of a walnut discovered by the bird who had been hiding in the wizard's beard. The whole thing just rolled off Willy's tongue as if it had all been written out in advance. Whenever she needed some new information or a fresh development, the perfect thing arrived at the proper moment to be inserted into a blank space exactly its size and shape.

—**That was a real good story,** said an astonished Tee Tee. **You got any more like that?**

—**Tomorrow,** Willy said.

Tomorrow came, and the day after tomorrow,

and the day after that, and on each of them, day
after day until she walked out of the Block for
good, Willy entertained the Tee Tees and Ray-
lettes and Georginas with episodes from the adventurous life of Little Howie Small. As far as
she knew, the little person within her who had
come into her own, the secret Willy, always told
the truth. She was like Scheherazade, except at
the time she was not fighting for her life.

That came twenty-nine years later, after her
companion on the Block began calling on her in
Massachusetts.

—You're writing again, Willy? asked Dr. Bollis. I think that's excellent news. Is it a story, or
is it about yourself?

—You don't know anything about fiction,
Willy told him.

Dr. Bollis smiled at her. —I do know how important it is to you. Will this one be like your
others, or are you going to try something new?

Dr. Bollis had let her believe that he had read
her books. Willy thought he had probably read
perhaps half of both of them.

—Something new, she said.

Her doctor gave her a look of careful neutrality.

—It'll be good for me. It already is.

—Can you tell me what it's about?

She frowned.

—Who's the main character?

—A brave little person named Howie, she said, and immediately burst into tears. Willy had never told Dr. Bollis that when her daughter, Holly, was first beginning to speak, and then for a long time after, she spoke of herself as "Howie." In fact, Willy tried never to speak of Holly to Dr. Bollis.

Willy could remember writing very little of her third and most successful book. Much of what happened in the Institute had been a blur of smeary voices nattering on and on; the same blurriness took over when she thought about the beginning of her book, except that the incessant voices had been those of her characters. After she seemed to have recovered sufficiently from the shock of her great loss, she returned to New York feeling like an unpeeled egg. She settled herself back in her little apartment, where **In the Night Room** amplified itself into a kind of fever dream from which she awoke, dripping with sweat, pulse rocketing, only long enough to order Chinese food, do the crossword puzzle, or collapse into sleep. Once, on a slow day for both of them, she played Scrabble with her old, amusing college friend Tom Hartland, who wrote detective books for boys, and crushed him, pulverized him, left him gasping and bleeding on the board. She had met with her dead husband's lawyers and discovered that she was, by almost anybody's standards, wealthy; two or three times in that period, she had lunches or dinners with Molly Harper and Tom. (He had once told her that his greatest problem was keeping his boy hero from having sex with the other boys he met in the course of his investigations.) An utterly kind man, Tom came around four or five times to make sure Willy was eating—actually, he used his concern about her diet as his way of making sure she could keep herself together. And she was, largely due to her furious obsession with her book. Willy knew she was using the book as a kind of therapy, also as a way of shutting out the world, but it was as though she had no choice as to how these months were to be spent. **In the Night Room** had taken her over, demanding to be written. When people praised it to her, Willy felt as though she were being given credit for someone else's accomplishment.

During one of their lunches, Tom Hartland told her, I wish I could write a book that way sometime.

—No you don't, she said.

Tom knew nothing about Willy's background. The facts of her childhood would have horrified him. The facts of her childhood would have horrified most of the people she called her friends. But not all of Willy's childhood had been harsh and difficult: although the years from birth to the age of six, during which she had been a child living with her parents, had passed entirely from her memory, they had left behind a shimmer of warmth and vanished, never-to-be-replaced pleasure. Before her parents had been killed in an automobile accident, they had loved their daughter, they had cherished her. Willy knew this. As far as she was concerned, this shimmer—the glow of her earliest childhood—explained why, during the worst of her many wretched times, she had escaped descending into despair or madness.

9

Tim Underhill was like a kind of Scheherazade,
telling stories to save his life. Fiction gave him
entry into the worst and darkest places of his
life, and that entry put the pain and fear and
anger right in his own hands, where he could
transform them into pleasure. In his youth he
had been without direction, reckless, too loud,
a real pain in the neck. After he let himself get
drafted into Vietnam at the age of twenty-two,
he reinvented himself based on the more ob-
noxious aspects of his character and became
louder, profane, open to violence. He made a
point of taking as his lovers slight, girlish young
Vietnamese boys of eighteen or nineteen, whom
he referred to as his "flowers," daring anyone to
call him on it. He used drugs whenever they
were available, and the drugs gave him the toxic
gift of addiction. In these years, he told stories,
but he never wrote them down. Salvation came

after Vietnam, when he was living above the flower market in Bangkok and there began writing the dialogues with himself that eventually turned into stories and novels. And bit by bit the fiction let him straighten out his life. It allowed him to live many lives at once, all in the peace and seclusion of his little apartment.

After he had published half a dozen books and felt more or less healed, he left Thailand and moved to New York City. He had turned into a person for whom his younger self would have felt as much contempt as envy. He lived quietly and loved his friends, his nephew, his city. What this settled character felt for the desperate young man he had been was a mixture of pity, admiration, and regret so sharp it could nearly have drawn blood.

Throughout the war, Underhill's belief in his ability to tell a story that would knock the eyes out of his audience's heads had shaped his ambitions, and he had developed this talent in an ongoing tale he called "The Running Grunt." The characters of "The Running Grunt" had populated many otherwise boring hours in the tents and various wastelands of Camp Crandall. But his storytelling career had been born not in Vietnam, he knew, but in Millhaven, rather, and in completely mundane circumstances.

He had been a senior at Holy Sepulchre, eighteen years old, wasting time one evening in the house of a good-looking, lively neighbor, Esti Woodbridge, whom he liked because she read a lot of books and attracted mean-spirited gossip about which she cared not a whit. He liked her six-year-old daughter, Marin, too. Marin Woodbridge was a seriously cool kid. Esti had something going in the kitchen that required unblinking attention, and Marin, left alone in the living room with Tim, wandered up to him and said, "If you could tell me a story, I bet it'd be pretty good." He heard Marin's mother in the kitchen, laughing. "Well, let's give it a try," he said, and opened his mouth—and what came out amazed him at every step, a lengthy, complicated story about a prince and a magic horse and a girl with long golden hair. Everything fell into place; nothing was left over or unresolved at the end. When he was finished, Marin grinned at him and Esti popped out of the kitchen to say, "Wow! Great story, Tim!" **Wow** was what he thought, too. Where in the world had that come from?

Now he wondered if he would ever again know that surprised satisfaction. A great part of the reason Tim was wasting time on a lunatic book collector and fussing around with e-mails and virus protection had to do with avoiding actual work. Not only did he not feel comfortable with what he was writing, he was beginning to dislike it. Over the next few weeks, he hoped, this situation would change. When he found that he disliked what he was writing, he was writing the wrong things. He would be increasingly depressed until his story told him where it wanted to go.

He called up his document, but before a fresh sentence spoke itself in his mind, he saw Jasper Kohle seated across the table in the Fireside, saying, **You don't listen.**

Listen to what?

He shook off the question and began to advance words across his screen.

10

The big house behind the gated wall at the end of Guilderland Road had required significant repairs at the time of purchase, mainly to the roof and the wraparound porch, and Mitchell's current business trip had seemed to all parties an advantageous period in which to get as much done as possible. Perhaps rashly, Willy had supported this schedule, thinking that she would be able to keep an eye on things while she got a feel for the house she was going to share with her new husband. Now, as she drove through the gate to what might almost have been a construction site, Willy wished she had never agreed to camp out in the house while Mitchell cruised around Europe.

Two pickup trucks bristling with ladders and lengths of lumber stood on the patchy, soon-to-be-revitalized grass near the curving gravel drive. Short rows of roofing tiles lay near a tall ladder leaning against the left side of the house. A lot more lumber had been piled up on the far side of the house, and men with carpenter's belts roamed across the roof and beneath the porch, hammering as they went. The branches of a Japanese maple half-obscured a third pickup. It belonged to the Santolini brothers, whom Mitchell had hired to doctor his property's extensive trees, initially by hacking away the thick foliage that had grown up around them. Unlike Dellray Contractors—whose small army of worker ants had arrived in the other pickups—the Santolini Brothers had only two employees, themselves. The day before, Willy had glanced out the kitchen window just in time to see Rocky Santolini smashing Vincent Santolini's head into the trunk of the oak tree that dominated the great sweep of lawn to the right of the house. The Santolinis did that sort of thing all the time, it turned out; they got some kind of horrible pleasure from bloodying each other's faces. Willy derived none from the sight of it. The idea that it might be her responsibility to terminate their brawls made her feel doomed and twitchy.

Entering the scene through the open garage door at the moment Willy rolled up alongside one of the Dellray pickups came scowling Roman Richard Spilka, Mitchell's number two right-hand man, right behind lizardlike Giles Coverley. Spilka served as a sometime bodyguard and general—what was the word?—factotum. In his dark suits and T-shirts, Roman Richard looked as massive and sour as a bouncer at a Russian nightclub. The permanent three-day whiskers on his pasty jowls, his louring eyes, communicated intense moral authority. (Roman Richard had pulled the Santolinis apart within seconds.)

"Put your car in the garage," Spilka said. "It's gonna rain again. What were you doing, anyhow?"

I was going to liberate my dead daughter from a produce warehouse out on Union Street, she thought of saying. Then she considered telling him to mind his own business. Unfortunately, it had become clear that, in Roman Richard Spilka's mind, monitoring Willy's actions was one of his professional functions.

"I went shopping," she said. "Would you care to inspect my bags?"

"You should park in the garage," he said.

Willy drove past him and into the garage. Roman Richard watched as she got out of her car and moved around to the trunk to remove the grocery bags. For an awkward and uncomfortable moment, she imagined that he was going to offer to help her, but no, he was just having a Testosterone Moment. Roman Richard often glanced at her chest when he thought she wouldn't notice, usually with a puzzled air she understood all too well. Roman Richard was wondering how Mitchell could be attracted to a woman with such an unremarkable chest.

To put him in his place, she asked, "Heard anything from the boss lately?"

"He called while you were out. There's probably a voice mail on your line."

Shortly after buying the house, Mitchell had installed a complicated new telephone system. Willy had her own private line; they shared a joint line; Mitchell's assistant, Giles Coverley, had a line that rang in his office; and a fourth line that was dedicated to Mitchell's business calls rang everywhere in the house but Willy's office. She was forbidden to use this line, as she was forbidden to enter Mitchell's office, which took up most of the third floor. In the glimpse she had once been granted through a half-open door, the office looked old-fashioned, opulent in a leather-and-rosewood manner. That made perfect sense to Willy. If Mitchell Faber, who had the taste of someone who fears that he has no taste at all, were to redesign the world, he would make it look like one vast Polo advertisement.

Willy wasn't sure how she felt about being for-

bidden entry to her future husband's home office. Mitchell offered three excellent reasons for
the prohibition, but the motive beneath two of
the reasons sometimes troubled her. She did not
want to be troubled by Mitchell. And all three
reasons he had given her spoke to the protective
role he had so willingly taken on. She might
move papers around, thereby creating disorder;
he did not want women in there at all, because
women were distractions; having lived alone all
his life, he needed some corner of the house that
would be his alone. Without a private lair, he
feared he might grow restless, irritable, on edge.
So the first and third reasons had to do with
shielding Willy from the consequences of ne-
glecting Mitchell's need for a single-occupancy
foxhole, and the second was supposed to flat-
ter her.

   He had lived alone for his entire adult life,
without parents, siblings, ex-wives, or children.
Mitchell had invited only a small number of
working colleagues to their wedding, plus, of
course, Roman Richard and Giles Coverley. To
Willy, his life seemed bizarrely empty. Mitchell
had no friends, in the conventional sense. Maybe
you could not be as paranoid as Mitchell was
and maintain actual friendships.

   Mitchell trusted no one absolutely, and the
amount of provisional trust he was willing to

extend did not go far. This, she suspected, was the real reason his re-creation of a men's club lounge was closed to her. He did not trust her not to violate whatever confidentialities he kept in there, and his suspicion of her underlay the way in which he had concluded their single conversation about the matter.

He had intended to answer her still-lingering surprise at the prohibition with an inarguable case.

"Do you print out hard copies of your writing as you go along?" he asked.

"Every day," she said.

"Suppose you're working on a new book, and the manuscript is on your desk. Suppose I happen to walk in and discover that you're not there. How would you feel if I picked up the manuscript and started to read it?"

Knowing exactly what she would feel, she said nothing.

"I can see it in your face. You'd hate it."

"I don't know if 'hate' is the word I'd use."

"We understand each other," Mitchell said. "This topic is now closed. Giles, would you please make some tea for my bride-to-be and myself? We'll take it on the porch."

When the tea was steaming in the cups borne on the tray his assistant was carrying to the front door, Mitchell remembered that he had to field an important telephone call. He left her sitting on the porch by herself, the mistress of the wicker chair, a front yard festooned with pickup trucks, and two hot cups of English breakfast she had not wanted in the first place. Alone, she picked up the **Times** and blazed through the crossword in twenty minutes.

From the window in her second-floor office, Willy saw Roman Richard lumbering across the driveway to speak to one of the Dellray men, a carpenter with a beach-ball gut, a red mullet, and intricate tattoos on his arms. Soon they were laughing at a remark of Roman Richard's. Willy had a strong, unpleasant impression that the remark concerned her. The two men glanced upward at her window. When they saw her looking down, they turned their backs.

Mitchell's voice came through her voice mail, sounding a little weary, a little dutiful.

"Hi, this is me. Sorry you aren't picking up. Giles told me you're home, so I was expecting to talk to you.

"Let's see, what can I tell you? I'm in Nanterre, just west of Paris. From the way things are going, I'll be here another three, four days. The only thing that might keep me away is a development in Toledo. Spain, unfortunately, not Ohio. So, let's see—if you need me, I'm at the Hôtel Mercure Paris La Défense Parc, and if

I have to go to Toledo, I'll be at the Hotel Domenico.

"I talked to Giles about this, but I'll mention it to you too. The Santolini brothers were making noises about taking a couple of limbs off the oak tree at the side of the house. I don't want them to touch that tree until I get home. Okay, Willy? They're just making work to drive up their fee. Giles knows what to do, but I want you to back him up on this, okay? That oak is one of the reasons I bought the estate in the first place.

"And honey, listen, don't worry about the wedding, hear me? I know it's only two months away, but everything's taken care of, all you have to do is shop for something pretty to wear. I set up an appointment for you at Bergdorf's the day after tomorrow. Just drive into town, meet the lady, the personal shopper, buy whatever you like. Giles will give you all the details. Let him drive you in, if you feel like it. Enjoy yourself, Willy! Give yourself a treat."

She heard a low voice in the background. It sounded self-consciously confidential, as if the speaker regretted breaking into Mitchell's monologue. Against her wisest instincts, Willy suffered a brief mental vision of Mitchell Faber sitting up naked in bed while a good-looking woman, also naked, whispered in his ear.

"Okay, look, I have to go. Talk to you soon, baby. Stay beautiful for me. Lots of love, bye."

"Bye," she said into the phone.

It was the longest message she had ever received from Mitchell, and at the sound of his voice she had experienced a peculiar range of emotions. Warmth was the first of these— Mitchell Faber aroused a flush of warmth at the center of her body. He had turned out to be a tireless, inventive lover. And with beautiful timing, the sense of safety Mitchell brought to her came obediently into play. Where there was Mitchell, MICHIGAN PRODUCE offered no threat; the mere sound of his voice banished craziness, which he would not tolerate. Also, the chaos of workmen, their tools and vehicles, no longer seemed a threat to her inner balance. Before the wedding, all this would pass; the Dellray men and the Santolini brothers would finish their work and depart.

But along with these positive feelings came darker ones, and they were no less powerful. Among them was her old irritation at Mitchell's deliberate mystifications. He had told her he was in Nanterre, but not what he was doing there, nor why he might have to go to Spain. He had left the date of his return completely open, apart from mentioning that it might occur in four or five days, which could easily mean eight or nine. And making an appointment for her at Bergdorf's seemed unreasonably dictatorial, even for Mitchell. Willy knew he thought he was being helpful, but suppose she didn't want to buy her wedding dress at Bergdorf's? And all those little bullying interrogatives at the ends of his sentences, okay? That's an annoying habit, okay?

Willy supposed that throughout her life to come, the life with Mitchell, she would feel much the way she did at this moment. As long as warmth and gratitude outweighed irritation, she would enjoy a happy enough marriage. For Willy, "happy enough" sounded paradisal. It wasn't a phrase like "not all that rainy," which contradicted itself; in describing a situation one could easily live with, it was a good deal more like "fairly sunny." On the whole, did she feel fairly sunny? Yes, on the whole she did.

Also, Mitchell Faber frightened her, a little bit. Willy wanted her prospective husband never to know this, but at times, when regarding the smooth breadth of his back or the sheer weightiness of his hands, she experienced a little eroticized thrill of fear.

11

They marched across his screen, all right, the words, but he could not help feeling that, about half the time, in crucial ways, they were the wrong words. His bizarre admirer had thrown him farther off course than his visit from April.

Underhill shoved back his chair, groaned, and stood up. Habit brought him leaning back over the keyboard to save the dubious new paragraphs to his hard drive. When he released the mouse, he saw his hand execute a real aspen-leaf-in-the-wind flutter. His left hand was trembling, too. He registered his slightly elevated heartbeat and realized that the morning's adventures had touched him, so lightly he had not noticed until this moment, with fear. Funny—under his gaze, his hands ceased to tremble, but he could feel the remainder of his fear prickle his lungs. For the hundredth time, Timothy

Underhill observed that fear was a **cold** phenomenon.

Now that he was on his feet, he needed a diversion that might restore his concentration. He walked across the loft to his refrigerator, but the thought of putting food in his mouth made him queasy. Underhill wandered to one of the big windows and looked down on Grand Street. A huddle of stationary umbrellas at the corner of West Broadway belonged to people waiting for a break in the traffic. Then he noticed that one figure, a man in loose, dark clothing, had turned his back on the crowd to gaze across the street at Underhill's building. The oval blur of his face gleamed white beneath the hood of his sweatshirt. When the umbrellas began to drift across the street, the man moved down into the shelter of the corner building, keeping his eyes on the entrance to 55 Grand. Tim thought he was waiting for someone to come out of the Vietnamese restaurant on the ground floor. Then the figure shifted position, and his identity snapped into focus.

Hooded gray sweatshirt, jeans, a bright plastic bag clamped under one arm—Jasper Kohle had not, after all, left the neighborhood; he had circled around from wherever he had gone, and he was keeping watch on Tim's building. What was he doing out there, and what were his motives? Hunched and utterly still, he had the pure attentiveness of a hawk on a telephone pole. He made no effort to shelter himself from the rain, although he could easily have moved to an awning fifteen feet down the block.

Unless he wanted to spend the next few days hiding in his loft, Tim realized, he would have to deal with this character.

Abruptly, Kohle straightened his spine and swept the hood off his head. Any hopes that Tim might have been mistaken disappeared with the exposure of the man's face. Streaming with water, his dark hair flattened to seaweed on his forehead, Kohle's head pointed like a compass needle to the door at 55 Grand. Strange to remember now that when Tim had first seen him in the diner, Kohle had struck him as youthful, fresh, almost innocent. That freshness had been the first thing to go; with it had vanished the illusion of youth. Thinking back, Tim thought he remembered that Kohle's face had subtly darkened as the man's tone had changed from adulation to confrontation.

It happened so quietly that Tim had only barely noticed the deepening of the lines across the forehead, the spreading of a web of wrinkles around the man's eyes and mouth. The process he had noted in the diner had continued. The patient being beneath Tim Underhill's third-floor window looked like nothing so much as an implacable ex-con in the grip of a really lousy scheme. An embattled history of brutal triumphs and bitter defeats spoke from his unblinking acceptance of the rain streaming down his face, the set of his mouth.

Why me? Underhill thought. **How did I attract the Charlie Manson of fandom?**

The instant this thought appeared in Tim's head, Jasper Kohle stepped forward, raised his head, and with a sizzling glance found Tim's eyes across fifty feet of rainy space. Tim jumped back. He felt as though he'd just been exposed in the commission of a sordid crime. Jasper Dan Kohle continued to stare up. The situation brought back in roaring sound and color April's flashing out at him from the crowd on West Broadway. He saw the hands bracketing her mouth, her dear small body bending forward to hurl her message across the street. This time he could read her lips. April had not shouted some nonsense about whistling. Instead, she had bellowed, **Listen to us!**

When the memory-vision of bellowing April receded, Jasper Kohle no longer glared up at the Grand Street building; he was gone. No, he **was going,** for Tim saw his drenched, unhooded figure backing slowly down the sidewalk in the di-

rection of Wooster Street, still looking up but
no longer quite managing to hold Tim's eyes
with his own. **Enough,** Tim thought, and gestured sharply three times with a down-pointing
index finger. He had no idea what he intended
to say to Kohle, but he would start by demanding an explanation.

Kohle looked away and thrust his hands in his
pockets. He still appeared brutal and crazy, but
also a little bored, as if he were waiting for some
petty functionary to unlock his office and get
to business. On his way out of the loft, Tim
grabbed a WBGO cap and a raincoat and wind-
milled himself into them as he bypassed the elevator and trotted down the stairs. He charged
through the big door at the bottom and felt bulletlike raindrops pummel the top and the bill of
his cap. The shoulders of his ancient Burberry
were instantly soaked.

Down on the street, rain spattered and
sprayed from every surface, creating a mist in
which reflected points of light swam and flashed.
In a fume of yellow headlights, Tim thought he
saw Kohle's thick dark figure standing motionless twenty or thirty feet down on the other side
of the street. He had moved on, but not very far.
His body seemed to shimmer in the haze, and
for a second it seemed almost to inflate, as if

Tim's odd admirer had grown two inches and added twenty pounds.

In the few seconds Tim had been on the staircase, the rain had intensified into one of those New York downpours that reminded him of Vietnam. Water battered down in sheets and bounced off everything it struck. Before he had gone three feet, water had penetrated his cap and made a rag of his raincoat. The frayed threads at the ends of his sleeves wound over his wrists like hair. On Grand Street, the traffic crept along at five miles an hour, and the conical headlights illuminated thick slashes of rain.

When Tim stepped off the curb, his foot descended into a fast-moving streamlet of ice water. A taxi horn jeered at him. For a moment or two, he was forced to take his eyes off Kohle's gauzy form and concentrate on weaving through the slow-moving cars without getting injured. When next he looked up the block, he made out a few men and women trotting along beneath their umbrellas, but Kohle had disappeared. Another car honked, and another driver yelled. Underhill was standing still as a post in Grand Street's uptown lane, trying to make out a figure that was not there. His shoes felt as though they might float off his feet, like little boats.

Tim pushed through a rank of waist-high plastic news boxes, felt something tumble to the sidewalk, and jogged down the pavement, wishing he had grabbed an umbrella. Three people were moving along the sidewalk, two of them coming toward him, and the third, a short, almost dwarfish person who could have been either male or female, heading away, toward Wooster Street. In the thick rain, they looked like wraiths, like phantoms.

Neither of the men drawing near to him was Kohle. The dwarf-like creature scuttling off appeared to be picking up steam as he went, in his haste almost hydroplaning across the surface of the pavement. A young man with black hair and furious eyes stood beneath the awning of an entrance to a drugstore, but he was not Kohle, and neither was the girl in jeans and a black tank top hugging her arms over her chest under the next awning down the block.

Rainwater seemed now to pass directly through the fabric of his cap. His raincoat adhered to his shirt, and his shirt adhered to his chest. He no longer understood why he was doing this to himself. Running outside had been a spectacularly bad idea from the first. If he ever saw Kohle staked out on Grand Street again, he would call the police. The man had taken him by surprise; to be honest, Kohle had frightened him, and his fear had flashed into sudden anger, with the ridiculous result that here he was out on the street, asking for pneumonia.

He turned around, thinking only of getting back to his loft. The girl in the tank top gave him a sympathetic smile as he went squelching by. Under the next awning, the boy with furious eyes was peeling off his tight-fitting black shirt. He gave Tim the resentful glare due a voyeur, then bent to take off his boots. After he had tucked the boots under his arm, the boy undid his belt and shoved his pants down to his ankles. He wore no underwear, and his long body was a single streak of shining white. Tim stared at the boy's smooth, hairless groin, as blank as a Ken doll's. The young man stepped forward, and Tim stepped back.

That was . . . now, there was some mistake here, he couldn't see right, the rain was screwing with his vision . . .

With a sound like the crackling of heavy canvas sails, immense wings folded out from the young man's back. He stepped forward on a beautiful naked foot. Tim thought, **I have seen what it is to tread.** The being was much taller than he had at first appeared, six-seven or six-eight. Instantly, water ran in shining rivulets down its gleaming and hairless chest. When it glanced at Tim, its eyes, though entirely liquid black, conveyed what Tim's old Latin teacher would have called "severe displeasure." Tim had no idea if his heart had gone into overdrive or stopped working altogether. The inside of his mouth tasted like blood and old brass. Creaking, the great wings unfolded another five or six feet and nearly met at their highest point.

The angel was going to kill him, he knew.

Instead of truly stopping his heart, the angel swept past Tim Underhill, turned toward West Broadway, and took two long, muscular strides. The world at large failed to notice this extraordinary event. The traffic crawled by. A man in a parka and a fishing hat ducked out of an apartment building and walked past the angel without a sign of surprise.

Can't you see that? Tim wanted to yell, then realized, no, he couldn't see that; he had seen nothing at all.

Two more steps up the street, the angel jettisoned its clothes onto the sidewalk in front of the news boxes, took one more majestic stride forward, raised a knee, and with a great unfolding and unfurling of its wings lifted off the pavement and ascended into the air. Up and up, open-mouthed Tim watched it go, until it dwindled to the size of a white sparrow, and—instantly, as if translated to another realm—disappeared. Tim kept watching the place in the air where it had been, then realized that the man in the fishing hat, who had come almost level with him, was looking at him oddly.

"I thought I saw something unusual up there," he said.

"Get any more water in your mouth, you'll drown." The man shook his head and moved on.

Tim squelched over to the rack of news boxes and saw, between the **Village Voice** and the **New York Press,** a yellow plastic bag bearing a cartoonlike caricature of Charles Dickens. The angel's clothing had, like its owner, traveled elsewhere.

With the half-conscious sense that the bag seemed familiar, he bent down and picked it up. Cold and slippery to the touch, it contained a number of books. Tim's first impulse was to protect the books, then to see if he might somehow be able to return them to their owner. Carrying the bag, he waited a moment for a break in the traffic, and when one came he moved down off the curb and remembered where he had seen such a bag earlier that morning.

Tim reached the other side of the street and opened the top of the bag as he trotted toward the entrance to his building. When he peered in, a small amount of rain fell through the opening and beaded on the glossy jacket of **lost boy lost girl.** Two other copies were stacked beneath it.

Tim stepped inside the entry of 55 Grand. Too small to be called a lobby, it held only a row of metal mailboxes, a cracked marble floor, a hanging light fixture that worked half of the time, and, to one side of the stairs, a wooden school chair. This was one of the light fixture's off days. Tim spun around to prop the door open a couple of inches so that he would be better able to see the condition of the books.

He opened the cover, turned to the front matter, and gasped at what he saw. In spiky, slashing letters three inches high, Kohle had printed FRAUD and LIES all over the page. Tim's inscription had been crossed out and covered over with UNTRUE AND OUTRAGEOUS. Tim slid the book back into the bag and removed the next. He discovered the same furious graffiti scrawled over the front matter. In the text, individual phrases and paragraphs, sometimes whole pages, had been x-ed out.

A fast-moving thread of water slipped from the bill of his cap onto a violated page, and the R in FRAUD softened and ran into the adjacent letters on both sides. The book seemed to be dissolving in his hands. In horror, Tim slammed it shut, making a soft splatting sound, as if some big insect had been squashed between the pages. The books went back into the shiny bag, and he trotted out into the fierce rain and, with a swooping gesture of his right arm, threw the bag into a garbage bin.

12

In Hendersonia, the rain predicted by Roman Richard Spilka came and went in under an hour, never amounting to much more than a sprinkle. (There was something suspiciously overdetermined about that storm over SoHo.) The sun shone the entire time it rained. The workmen who wore shirts shed them to enjoy the sensation of mild, warm rain falling on their upper bodies. Willy envied them. She wished she could strip naked to the waist and stroll through the sun-gilded rain.

Suddenly, she felt like talking to Mitchell, not just listening to his voice on the answering machine. Mitchell disliked intrusions of his personal life into his work world, and probably wouldn't like being called back. He especially wouldn't like it if he were in bed with some woman who worked for the Baltic Group. The thought of her husband-to-be in the embrace of one of his female colleagues gave Willy an entirely unwelcome pang. Sometimes she wondered why he had chosen her, Willy Bryce, Willy Patrick, with her funny little gamine body and clementine breasts. Gently, in a series of little nibbles, despair attempted to draw her downward through a psychic drain. She really did want to talk to Mitchell, and at first hand, not through an exchange of recorded messages.

The Internet soon found the telephone number of the hotel in Nanterre. She dialed for what seemed a frustratingly long time, but was then rewarded with a series of rings that sounded like the wake-up signal of a portable alarm clock. A male, wonderfully clear French voice said something she had no hope of understanding.

"Excuse me," she said, "but do you speak English?"

"Of course, madame. How may I help you?"

"I'd like to speak to one of your guests, please, a Mr. Mitchell Faber."

"Moment." Soon he was back on the line. "I am sorry, madame, Monsieur Fay-bear is no longer a guest of the Mercure Paris La Défense Parc."

"I must have just missed him. When did he check out?"

"Monsieur Fay-bear checked out this morning, madame."

"He couldn't have," Willy said. "He just left a message on my voice mail, and he was speaking from your hotel."

"There is some mistake. Unless he called you from a telephone in the lobby?"

"He said he was in his room." She hesitated. "You said he checked out this morning? What time was that?"

"Shortly before ten, madame."

"And what time is it there now?"

"It is 4:45 P.M., madame."

Mitchell had left the hotel almost seven hours earlier. Willy hesitated again, then asked, "I'm calling from New York with a message for his wife. Was Mrs. Faber with him, or did she go ahead to Toledo?"

"We have no record of a Mrs. Faber."

She thanked him and hung up. Back to the Internet for more information, then back to the telephone to dial another endless series of numbers. When she was connected to the Hotel Domenico in Toledo, she had trouble communicating with the man on the other end of the line, and finally succeeded in replacing him with a hotel employee whose English was less like Spanish.

"Mr. Faber? No, no Mr. Faber is registered here. I am sorry."

"What time do you expect him?"

"There is no record of a Mr. Faber reserving a room in this hotel, I regret."

She thanked him, hung up, and pushed the intercom button that connected her to Giles Coverley's telephone. His bland drawl asked, "Can I help you with something, Willy?" A light on his phone told him where the intercom message had originated. "Hold on there, Giles," she said. "I'll be right in."

"I believe the boss left a message for you. Did you hear it?"

"Roman Richard told me as soon as I drove in, and yes, I did hear it. You two don't want me to miss anything, do you?"

"We want Mitchell to have whatever he pleases, you could put it that way. And you, too, of course. Did he mention a trip into the city?"

"I'll be there in a second, Giles."

That last-minute bit of diplomacy was typical of Coverley. From Willy's first meeting with her future husband's assistant, she had understood that Giles Coverley would always be delighted to perform any tasks she might assign him, as long as they coincided with his employer's desires. Occasionally, as she had begun to settle into the house and arrange a few insignificant things to her liking, a taut, short-lived expression on Giles Coverley's smooth face had reminded Willy of Mrs. Danvers in **Rebecca.**

Giles's office, a long narrow alcove Mitchell had partitioned off what he called the "morning room," was only slightly more familiar to Willy than her husband's office upstairs, but she had far less curiosity about what it contained. Her presence in his lair tended to make Coverley speak even more slowly than usual and consider his words with greater care. This deliberation struck Willy as both self-protective and pretentious. Giles always dressed in loose, elegant overshirts and collared tops, handsomely draped trousers, and beautiful shoes. As far as Willy knew, he had no sexual interest at all in either gender. Giles seemed perfectly self-sufficient, like a spoiled cat neutered early in kittenhood.

The door to the alcove stood half open; Willy assumed Giles had positioned it like that, in an ambiguous gesture of welcome. As she approached, he offered the therapeutic smile of a man behind a complaints counter. Giles's desk was extraordinarily neat, as it had been on every other occasion when Willy had stood before it. His flat-screen monitor looked like a modernist sculpture. Instead of using a telephone, Giles wore a headset and spoke into a little button.

"Good morning, Willy. I didn't realize you'd gone out. Didn't get you into any difficulty, I hope, did I?"

"I went out for groceries, Giles, I didn't run off with anybody."

"Of course, of course, it's just . . . well, you know. If Mitchell thinks somebody's going to be there, he can get a little heated when they're not."

"Then you'll be happy to hear that Mitchell seemed perfectly rational."

"Yes. In the future, we might do ourselves a favor by keeping in better communication about your comings and goings. Is that something you'd be willing to think about?"

"I'm willing to think about anything, Giles, but I'm not sure I want to feel obliged to tell you every time I go to Pathmark or Foodtown."

Giles held up his hands in mock surrender. "Willy, please. I don't want you to feel **obliged** to do anything. I just want things to go as smoothly as possible. That's my job." He nodded his head, letting her see that his job was a serious matter. "Anything else you'd like from me?"

"Do you know where Mitchell is right now?"

Coverley tilted forward and looked at her over the top of an imaginary pair of glasses. "Right now? As in, this moment?"

Willy nodded.

Giles continued to stare at her, without blinking, over the tops of his imaginary glasses. A couple of seconds went by.

"From the information I have, Mitchell is in France today. And is expected to stay there for perhaps three more days. To be more specific, he's in a suburb of Paris called Nanterre."

"He told my voice mail he was in Nanterre."

"I thought he might have done, you see. That is why your question rather took me by surprise."

The reason your question sounded so stupid was what she thought he meant.

"He said he was staying at the Hôtel Mercure Paris something-or-other Parc."

"Mercure Paris La Défense Parc."

"That's it, yes. I called them as soon as I listened to his message, and the man I talked to said Mitchell checked out almost seven hours earlier. That's like five in the morning here."

"Well, then, he checked out without telling me. He'll be in touch later today or tomorrow, I'm sure."

"But he told me he was still checked into that hotel." For a moment, their eyes met again. Coverley did not blink. "You can see why I would be a little concerned."

Coverley pressed the fingers of one hand to his lips and, without any change of expression, lifted his head and gazed at the ceiling. Then he looked back down at Willy. "Let us clarify this situation. I'll get the hotel's telephone number."

"I already talked to them," Willy said.

"It never hurts to get a second opinion."

For a little while Coverley moved his mouse around and watched what was happening on his screen. "All right," he said at last, and punched in numbers on his keypad. Then he held up an index finger, telling her to wait. The finger came down. **"Bonjour,"** he said. Then came a long sentence she did not understand that ended with the word **Fay-bear.**

Pause.

"Oui," he said.

Pause.

"Je comprends."

Pause.

"Très bien, monsieur." Then, in English: "Would you please repeat that in English, sir? Mr. Fay-bear's wife asked me to inquire about his status at the hotel."

He clicked a button or flipped a switch, Willy could not tell which.

Through the speakers on either side of the monitor came a heavily accented male voice saying, "Mrs. Fay-bear, can you hear me?"

"Yes," Willy said. "Are you the man I spoke to earlier?"

"Madame, I have never spoken to you before

we do it now. You were inquiring about your husband's residence in our hotel?"

"Yes," Willy said.

"Mr. Fay-bear is still registered as a guest. He arrived three days ago and is expected to remain with us yet two days."

"Somebody else just told me he checked out at ten this morning."

"But you see, he is very much still here. His room is 437, if you would care to speak to him. No—excuse me, he is not in his room at this time."

"He's there."

"No, madame, as I explained—"

"He's staying in your hotel, I mean."

"As I have said, madame."

"Is he . . ." Willy could not finish this sentence in the presence of Giles Coverley. "Thank you."

"À bientôt."

Coverley raised his hands and shrugged. "All right?"

"I don't know what happened."

"You got through to some other hotel with a similar name, Willy. It's the only explanation."

"I should have asked to leave a message."

"Would you like me to call him back? It would be no trouble at all."

"No, Giles, thanks," she said. "I guess I'll wait

for him to call me back. Or I'll try again to-morrow."

"You do that," Coverley said.

That night, again in the grip of her compulsion, Willy drove back to Union Street. All the way she asked herself why she was doing it and told herself to turn back. But she knew why she was doing it, and she could not turn back. Already she could hear her daughter's cries.

Her headlights picked out the entrance to the parking lot and the huge dark ascent of the warehouse's facade, and without intending to do so, she swerved into the lot. Her heart fluttered, birdlike, behind the wall of her chest.

She had known what she was going to do ever since she had realized that she really was backing her little car out onto Guilderland Road. She was going to break into the warehouse.

Holly's high, clear, penetrating voice pealed out from behind the massive brick wall. Sweating with impatience, Willy drove around to the back of the building. Her headlights stretched out across the asphalt. A voice in her head said, **This is a mistake.**

"I still have to do it," she said.

A high-pitched wail of despair like that of a princess imprisoned in a tower sailed out from the wall and passed directly through Willy's body, leaving behind a ghostly electrical tremble. In her haste, Willy struggled with the handle until muscle memory came to her aid. Her body seemed to flow out of the car by itself, and she took her first steps toward the loading dock in the haze of light that spilled through the open door. Her headlights cast a theatrical brightness over the loading bay.

There it was again: Holly's song of despair, the wail of a child lost and without hope. Willy's feet stuck to the asphalt; her legs could no longer move.

The long platform emerged from a wide, concrete-floored bay that opened up the back of the building like an arcade. At the rear of the bay, a series of doors and padlocked metal gates led into the building itself.

I can't deal with the fact that she's dead right now, Willy thought. **First I have to get her out of this damned building.**

Holly screamed again.

Willy opened her trunk, rooted around the concealed well, and discovered a crowbar Mitchell had forgotten to remove. She picked it up and went toward the stairs. Again she was halted in midstride, but by nothing more alarming than a meandering thought. With the memory of Mitchell borrowing her car had come the strange recognition that while she had imagined him bailing her out of jail, she had never considered his reaction to being presented with his fiancée's living daughter. Holly and Mitchell seemed to inhabit separate universes—

For the first time in her life, Willy saw literal stars. She seemed on the verge of falling backward into a limitless darkness. What she was doing was crazy. Mitchell and Holly could not be thought of in the same room because they did live in different universes, those of the living and the dead. Even in his absence, the sheer irrefutability of Mitchell's physical presence pushed Holly back into the past, the only country where she could still be alive.

Willy felt like a death-row inmate given a last-minute reprieve. A cruel madness had left her, driven away by the appearance within its boundaries of Mitchell Faber.

She went back to the car, dropped the crowbar in the trunk, slammed the lid, and collapsed into the driver's seat. During the last few minutes, she felt, her life had changed, and she had moved into clarity for the first time since her tragedy. And the agent of that change had not been herself, but Mitchell. His sleek, brooding image had led her out of the shadows. She felt a

wave of love and longing for him. That there
had been a mix-up at some hotel in a Parisian
suburb meant nothing. A serious question remained, however: what had convinced her,
against all she knew, that her daughter was crying out for her in the ugly old building? At
some point in the future, that would have to be
thought about, **deeply considered,** probably
with professional help.

Light exploded from her rearview mirror, and
there came the peremptory **bip!** of a siren an-
nouncing its presence. Startled, Willy looked
over her shoulder and saw the headlights of
a police car immediately behind her. Guilt
washed through her body, and even after she realized that she had done nothing criminal, its
residue affected her demeanor when the officer
came up to her window.

"Identification?" He held the flashlight on
her face.

She fished around for her wallet and produced
her license.

"This is your name, **Willy**?"

"Yes, it is."

"I see you live in Manhattan, Willy. What are
you doing parked in a warehouse lot in New
Jersey at this time of night?"

She tried to smile. "I moved here about two

weeks ago, and I haven't done anything about my license yet. Sorry."

He ignored her apology. The flashlight shone directly onto her face. "How old are you, Willy?"

"Thirty-eight," she said.

"You've gotta be kidding me." The officer played the light on her driver's license, checking the date of her birth. "Yep, born in 1965. You must have very few worries, Willy. What is your new address, please?"

She gave him the number on Guilderland Road.

The policeman lowered the flashlight, appearing to be occupied by his own thoughts. He was a decade younger than she. "That's the big house with the gate. And all those trees."

"You got it."

He smiled at her. "Brighten up my evening and tell me why you're sitting here in this parking lot."

"I had something to think about," she said. "I'm sorry, I know it must look suspicious."

The officer looked away, still smiling, and rapped the flashlight against his thigh. "Willy, I recommend that you start up this gorgeous little vehicle and get yourself back to Guilderland Road."

"Thank you," she said.

He moved back, holding his eyes on her face. "Don't thank me, Willy, thank Mr. Faber."

"What? Do you know Mitchell?"

The young officer turned away. "Have a nice night, Willy."

13

For Tim Underhill that night, periods of unhappy wakefulness alternated with alarming
dreams in which everything around him, including the ground he stood on, proved, when
scrutinized, to be a collection of CGI effects.
He fled across fields, he wandered through vast
empty buildings, he walked slowly through a
haunted city, but all of it was as unreal as a mi-
rage. The cobbles and mosaics beneath his feet,
the long slope of the hill, the sconces and the
walls on which they hung were shiny, cartoonlike computer effects.

He got out of bed feeling worse than when he
had climbed in. A shower, usually an infallible
cure for the disorders that afflicted him on aris-
ing, left him feeling only partially restored.
Groaning, he toweled himself dry, pulled
clothes out of various drawers, and sat on the
edge of his bed. At that entirely ordinary mo-

ment, his memory finally delivered to him the events of the previous morning.

He was holding open a sock with both hands. The sock made no sense at all. It was only a tube of cloth. The angel's foot had come down on the sidewalk, and that foot had been astonishingly beautiful. And he had seen that smooth passage of white flesh at the groin, the giant wings creaking open, the bright and powerful ascent. Sudden, stinging tears leaped to the surface of Underhill's eyes. When he had tugged the sock onto his foot, he ran to the windows on Grand Street and looked down. Between rain showers on a dark gray morning, people holding folded or upright umbrellas hurried this way and that on the pavement. He saw no lurking angel, no feral Jasper Kohle. A glimpse of yellow in the refuse bin on the corner reminded him of Kohle's discarded books.

I couldn't have seen all that, he told himself. He knew what had happened: Jasper Kohle had affected him more than he had known. Soaked through, anxious, angrier than he had wanted to be, Tim had let his mind pull him into the surreal. No wonder he had dreamed of wandering lost through slippery landscapes made entirely of illusion. Tim wanted to think that yesterday's vision of an angel was the product of an overdeveloped imagination.

He decided to eat breakfast at home for once, and to avoid looking out the window.

But when he sat down before his computer, he immediately found himself in trouble. On the preceding day, he had needed the amnesia produced by concentrated absorption in his story and covered page after page with his heroine's difficulties. Now his language had turned leaden and clumsy, and her problems seemed contrived.

Abandoning the struggle, he brought up his e-mail. By now, this was a dubious act, akin to talking to shiny-eyed fans who metamorphosed into aging, unclean madmen. As he'd feared, a number of letters without return addresses had appeared in his electronic mailbox. Tim deleted the spam, read his real e-mail, answered what had to be answered, and only then retrieved the messages from Nowhere.

Byrne615 wished to communicate the following:

not rite, not fair, you pansy
i dont know where i AM

Sorry, but I know less than you do, Tim thought. (But something about Byrne615 snagged in his mind.)

Cyrax told him:

b patient. u will know all soon.
watch listn. i wl b yr gide.

And kalicokitty weighed in with:

breth was taken frum my bodee
I see only veils of fog or smok
with sounds of greatr engines

som never liked u
I did

The last message, in some way the most disturbing, came from phoorow:

u aint soch
bastrd no
mor ha ha

"Phoorow"—how many Phoorows could there
be? The only one Underhill had ever known had
been a fellow grunt in Lieutenant Beevers's
band of merry men, his real name being Philip
Footler, but known everywhere as Phoorow, a
sweet-faced young redneck who had participated in Lieutenant Beevers's second-greatest
fuckup, a military exercise that took place in

Dragon Valley, or down in Dragon Valley, as they used to say, them what was there. Phoorow had disliked Tim, but having seen what Tim did to a very few others who objected to his "flowers," he kept his objections to himself. Maybe he had been a bastard, Tim allowed. For sure he had been a loudmouth show-off, and a country boy like Phoorow would never have met anyone like him.

Unfortunately for him at the time, and unfortunately now for Tim Underhill, Phoorow had been cut in half, literally, by machine-gun fire during their platoon's sixth or seventh hour under fire down in Dragon Valley.

Tim stood up, a number of internal organs trembling slightly, and walked from his desk to his fake fireplace with a gas fixture capable of making it look exactly like a real fireplace, should he ever turn it on, and thence to the handsome bookcases to its right. There he drew comfort from the rows of familiar titles and names. Martin Amis, Kingsley Amis. Raymond Chandler, Stephen King. Hermann Broch, Muriel Spark, Robert Musil. A couple of yards of the black Library of America volumes. Then more fiction, imperfectly alphabetized: Crowley, Connelly, Lehane, Lethem, Erickson, Oates, Iris Murdoch. Iris was dead; so were Kingley Amis, Chandler, and Hermann Broch. Dawn

Powell, you're gone, too. Are you folks going to start getting in touch? Where Phoorow rushes in, will you fear to tread?

He moved to the window and gazed, unseeing, down. How could the Phoorow of today be the barely remembered Phoorow of 1968? He couldn't.

In the hitherto semipeaceable kingdom of Timothy Underhill, things appeared to be falling apart. Yesterday he had hallucinated seeing his sister and a gigantic, pissed-off angel; yesterday he had been rattled by a crazed stalker posing as a fan; today a dead man had sent him an e-mail. Down on the street, cars and trucks crawled eastward through rain as vertical as a plumb line.

There could actually be another person called Phoorow, he supposed. According to the person called Cyrax, Tim would know what was going on fairly soon. Cyrax, it could be, had orchestrated all these messages. Tim could not persuade himself that this Cyrax was capable of arranging everything that had happened in the Fireside and on the street, but undoubtedly a single, deeply misguided individual could send out tons of bizarre e-mails under a variety of names.

Tim had largely succeeded in calming himself down, and as he returned to his desk he re-

membered what had struck him about the first
of today's crop of mystery e-mails. The center
on the Holy Sepulchre football team had been
one Bill Byrne, a 250-pound sociopath who
from time to time had referred to Tim Underhill in the terms of today's e-mail. "Pansy,"
"queer," all of that. At seventeen, Underhill had
not known himself well enough to be angry; instead, he had felt embarrassed, filled with an in-
coherent sense of shame. He had not wanted to
be those things. Acceptance had come only after
his first experience of sex, with, as it happened,
the spookily sophisticated, Japanese-American
seventeen-year-old Yukio Eto, who had become
the template for the "flowers." After Yukio, he
had done his best to feel guilty and ashamed,
but the effort had been doomed from the start.
The experience had been so joyous that Tim
was totally incapable of convincing himself of
its wickedness.

Bill Byrne, on the other hand, had no problem in accepting his natural bigotry, and during
the whole of their years at Holy Sepulchre, Tim
had never heard any utterance from his teammate that did not contain a sneer. Was Bill
Byrne still alive? Of course, Tim had no proof
that Byrne615 was his old adversary of the high
school locker room, yet he did want to know
what had happened to Byrne. His best friend in

Millhaven, the great private investigator Tom Pasmore, could have told him in a minute or less, but Tim did not want to waste his friend's time on a question like this. Surely he could discover Bill Byrne's fate by himself.

The name of the one person in the world who could tell him exactly what had become of his high school class, Chester Finnegan, floated into consciousness. Many high school graduating classes contain one person for whom the previous four years represent an idyllic period never to be equaled in adult life, and those persons often take on the role of class secretary. They went to different schools than the rest of their classmates, and in their imaginations they want to stroll through their beloved corridors as often as possible. Chester Finnegan was the self-appointed Class Secretary for Life of Tim's year at Holy Sepulchre, a man generally to be avoided, but not now.

Information gave him the telephone number, which he promptly dialed. After retiring from State Farm Insurance a couple of years ago, Chester Finnegan had turned to the full-time organization of his Holy Sepulchre "archive." Tim imagined him sitting at home day after day, screening other people's home movies of football games and commencement exercises.

(Despite Tim's attitude, it should be noted

here that Finnegan had enjoyed a long career as an insurance executive, a loving marriage of thirty-four years, and was the father of three grown children, two of whom were graduates of excellent medical schools. The third, Seamus, reckoned a failure within the family, had taken the handsome face he had inherited from his father to Los Angeles, where he worked as a massage therapist in between acting jobs. All three children had graduated from Holy Sepulchre. On the other hand, Chester Finnegan talked like this:)

"Hey, Tim! It's great to hear from you, really great! Gosh, this is like ESP or something, because I was just thinking about you and that stunt you pulled in chemistry class our junior year. I mean, talk about stink! Whoa! Worser'n a family of skunks. So how are things, anyhow? Written any good books lately? You're probably our most famous alum, you know that? Jeez, I remember seeing you on the **Today** show, when was that, last year?"

"The year before," Tim said.

"Cripes, I looked at you and I said to myself, Boy that's the same guy who damn near asphyxiated Father Locksley. The good father passed away this March, did you see that? I put it in the class newsletter."

"Oh, yes," Tim said.

"Eighty-nine, he was, you know, and his health was all shot to hell. But if he caught you talking to Katie Couric, not saying he did of course, I sure know what went through his mind!"

"In a way, that has something to do with the reason I called."

"Oh, I'm sorry, Tim. You missed the memorial. We had ten, twelve of us there. You were mentioned, I can say that. Oh, yes."

"Actually, I was wondering about Bill Byrne, and it occurred to me that you could probably fill me in."

Finnegan said nothing for a moment that seemed longer than it was. "The colorful Bill Byrne. I suppose you were wondering about how that happened."

Tim closed his eyes.

"Tim?"

"Well, I wasn't sure."

"The obituary in the **Ledger** ran only two days ago. What, you saw it online, I guess?"

"Something like that."

"The **Ledger** couldn't say much about how Bill died. Of course, I won't be able to be much **more** specific in the online newsletter. You do get those, don't you?"

Tim assured Finnegan that he received his online newsletter, without mentioning that he always deleted it unread.

"Well, you want to know about old Wild Bill. Well, it was pretty bad. He was in this bar downtown, Izzy's. A lot of lawyers hang out there, because it's near the Federal Building and the courthouse. This is about one, two in the morning, Friday night. Leland Rose comes up to Bill and says, 'I believe you're messing around with my wife.' Leland Rose is some fancy financial adviser, big office downtown. Bill tells him he's crazy, and he completely denies having anything to do with this guy's wife, who by the way is of the trophy variety and pure trouble from top to bottom.

"So they get into an argument and by and by this Leland Rose, this pillar of society, pulls out a gun. Before anybody can stop him, he takes a shot at Bill. Even though he's about two feet away, he misses Bill completely, only Bill doesn't know it. He thinks he was shot! He throws a punch at Rose and knocks him out cold. Then he falls down, too. This is pure Bill Byrne. He's at least as drunk as Rose, and he imagines he's wounded, which is because in his fall, he smashed the hell out of one of his elbows. Bill got up to about three hundred pounds there toward the end.

"An ambulance shows up and takes both of them to Shady Mount Hospital. They're strapped onto gurneys. This whole time, Bill is carrying on, trying to get at Rose, who's still out. They get to Shady Mount and unload Bill first, only he's rolling around so much that they actually drop him, and that's the last straw. Poof! Whammo! Massive heart attack, **huge** heart attack, a heart explosion. No way they could revive him."

"So he died drunk, on a gurney outside the emergency entrance of Shady Mount."

"Actually, at that point he wasn't on the gurney."

"Was Rose right? Was Byrne having an affair with his wife?"

"That fat little Irishman was always screwing someone else's wife. Women ate him up, don't ask me why."

Tim thought of Phoorow and had the sudden desire to stop talking to Chester Finnegan.

"I was just remembering that day you and I drove up to Random Lake," Finnegan said. "Remember? Boy, that was one of the best days of my life. Did Turner come with us? Yes, he did, because Dicky Stockwell pushed him off the pier, remember?"

Tim not only failed to remember the great excursion to Random Lake, he had no idea who Turner and Dicky Stockwell were. Unchecked, Finnegan could fill another hour with golden moments only he remembered, and Tim began making noises indicative of the conversation's end.

Then he remembered that Finnegan could, for once and all, banish the specter that had shimmered into view. "I suppose Byrne was on your newsletter list."

"Naturally."

"So you have his e-mail address."

"Not that I'll ever use it anymore."

"Could you please tell me what it was, Ches?"

"Why would you want a thing like that?"

"It has to do with my work," he said. "I'm ruling out some possibilities."

"Oh, I see," said Finnegan. "Hold on, I'll get my database. . . . All right, here we are. Wild Bill's e-mail address was Byrne, capital **B,** 615 at aol.com."

"Ah," Tim said. "Yes. Well. How unusual."

"Not really," Finnegan told him. "A lot of AOL addresses are like that."

The specter had come shimmering back into view, and Bill Byrne, who had died of not being shot to death, had a fairness issue on his chest. Besides that, Bill felt lost.

"Ches, if I give you the first part of some e-mail addresses, can you see if they are in your database?"

"You mean the names, right?"

"I'm just testing something out here."

"Hey, if I help you, I expect a cut of your royalties!"

"Talk to my agent," Tim said. He went to his e-mail screen. "How about Huffy? Do you have a Huffy? Capital **H**?"

"I don't even have to look for that one—Bob Huffman. Huffy at verizon.net. Nice guy. Cancer got him about three months ago. Had two remissions, and then it went nuclear on him. This is a dangerous age, my friend."

Tim remembered Bob Huffman, a lanky red-haired boy who looked as if he would remain sixteen forever. "Is there a Presten?" He spelled it.

"Presten at mindspring.com, sure. That's Paul Resten. You have to remember him. Strange story. Paul died right around New Year's. Gunshot wound. Poor guy, he was an innocent bystander in a liquor store holdup, wrong place, wrong time. Paul was a very successful guy! Every year, he gave a generous contribution to the school."

The remark contained a quantity of reproach,

but Finnegan's attention had shifted to another point.

"These e-mail addresses are all for dead people, Tim. What's going on?"

"Someone must be messing with my head. In the past few days, I got some e-mail that was supposedly sent by these people."

"I'd call that obscene," Finnegan said. "Using our classmates' names like that."

"I just figured out another one," Tim said. "Rudderless must be Les Rudder. Don't tell me he's dead, too."

"Les died in a car crash on September 11, 2001. I'm not surprised you never heard about that one. Anyone else?"

"Loumay, nayrm, kalicokitty, and someone called Cyrax."

"I know two of those right off, but let me look up. . . . Okay. This guy's a real bastard, whoever he is. Kalicokitty was Katie Finucan, year behind us, remember? Cutest little thing you ever saw. God, I used to have the hots for Katie Finucan. Better not let my wife hear me say that, hey? Katie died in a fire last February. She was visiting her grandkids in New Jersey, and no one knows what happened. Everyone got out but her. Smoke inhalation, I'd say, but hey, I was in the insurance business, what do I know?"

Tim was appalled by the ease with which death had moved through the ranks of his classmates at a mediocre little Catholic school in Millhaven.

"Okay, same deal goes for loumay and nayrm, Lou Mayer and Mike Ryan. Ryan died in Ireland last year, and Lou Mayer drowned in a sailing accident off Cape Cod."

"Oh, Christ," Tim said.

"I hear he was a lousy sailor. What was that last name?"

"Cyrax."

"He doesn't seem to be here. Nope. So maybe that one's real."

"He said he wanted to be my guide."

"That's your joker, right there." Finnegan's voice rose. "Here's the guy who's sending you this crap. It has to be someone we went to school with. Who else would know about these people? He's picking the names of people you cared about."

Except I didn't, Tim thought. "That crossed my mind, too."

"There has to be someone who can pin down this creep."

"I know a couple of people who might be able to do something," Tim said. "Thank you for your help."

———

Now his computer seemed like a hostile entity, exuding toxins as it crouched atop his desk. If Cyrax was sending him e-mails using the Internet names of dead classmates because Cyrax had been a classmate himself, how did he know about Philip Footler? No one in Tim's life was familiar with both his life in high school and his Vietnam tour. The one and only intersection on earth of Bill Byrne and Phoorow was Timothy Underhill.

He went back and started over. Someone calling himself Cyrax had been rooting through his past and using what he found there to send these crazy e-mails. Tim could see no other explanation. Cyrax had already appointed himself as guide, so let him make the next move. Since without full addresses these e-mail conversations could be only one-way, he would make the next move anyhow. When Cyrax showed himself again, Tim would decide how he wanted to respond. He could always start deleting any e-mail that came without an @ sign and domain name.

He remembered the astonishing sight of his sister, a little Alice in Wonderland girl leaning forward to hurl the words **Listen to us** at him, and for the first time connected April's command with the e-mails. An uncontrollable shiver went through his body. Helplessly, he looked at the computer, squatting on his desk like a sleek black toad. From below it, the voices of the dead bubbled up to print their inchoate words on the screen, one after another, emerging from a bottomless well.

He had to get outside.

But when Tim Underhill left his building to walk aimlessly down Grand, then turn left on Wooster Street, then right on Broome, his hands in the pockets of his still-damp Burberry, his head covered by his still-damp WBGO cap, he felt no release from the phantoms that had driven him into the streets. In the passing cars, the drivers scowled like the officers of the secret police in a totalitarian state; on the sidewalks, the people who passed gazed downward, sloping along mute and alone.

Down Crosby he went, that street of cobblestones and sudden windy spaces, now as empty as it had been twenty years before, when he had first moved into the neighborhood. Loneliness suddenly bit into him, and he welcomed it back, for the loneliness was a true part of him, real, not a fearful phantom.

A few days before, Tim had been leafing through his volume of Emily Dickinson's letters, and for some reason a phrase from one of the "Master" letters—written to a man never identified—came into his head: **I used to think when I died—I could see you—so I died as fast as I could.** It had been a long time since he had loved someone that way. This gloomy recognition came to him wrapped in the unhappiness that seemed to leak from every blank window and closed door on the street. Underhill tried to reject it and the unhappiness both. Because he thought he would fail, he failed, and loneliness and sorrow thickened around him.

Something set him off, and after that he was, for all purposes, back in his generation's war. Phoorow, phoorow, Private Philip Footler had been the trigger. Gliding toward him, shifting back, sliding under his defenses, a particularly unhappy vision had flooded Tim's mind, whether or not he could actually see it at any given moment. Tim Underhill had been something like six feet from Phoorow's grotesque separation from himself. It had been granted him to witness every one of the four or five seconds it had taken the boy to die—reaching down to pull his body back into connection, his mouth opening and closing like that of an infant seeking the nipple. Tim was grateful not to have seen Phoorow's eyes.

He longed for the reassuring sound of other people's voices. He could have gone to the Fireside—okay, not the Fireside, but any one of the little bars and restaurants scattered throughout his village: for over the previous two decades that was what the territory bounded by West Broadway, Broome Street, Broadway, and Canal Street had inevitably become: his hometown, the one place where he felt truly comfortable.

He turned around, and a hint of movement caught his eye. On a street where only he was in motion, the idea of movement seemed a little spooky. Tim Underhill turned back, then spun his head again, scanning the sidewalks and the anonymous facades. It was as if the street had been evacuated, specifically for the purpose of stranding him in it.

Thin, foggy, impenetrable veils hung like sheets of cloud-colored iron at both ends of the block. The ordinary sounds of the city were muted and distant, walled out. If he looked hard at the cobblestones, he thought, he would see unreality's slick, cartoonish sheen. Everything that had happened to him over the past two days had been designed to get him here, to this empty block on a false Crosby Street.

Now it had happened for real, Tim thought. His mind had rolled past its own edge. Even the gray air seemed to resist him as he turned around once again to face north: uptown, the direction that would take him back to Broome Street. And as he turned, he thought he detected a hint of movement closer to him than the first time. Tim scanned the storefronts and windows and this time really noticed that every one of them was dark. The hypothetical movement had been off to his right and behind the large plate-glass windows of a vanished art gallery. He looked more closely at the window and saw only the murk of an empty room.

Once, the gallery had been dedicated to minimalist installations that featured simulated body parts, piles of dirt, and reams of text. Behind the scrim of the dirty enormous window, the bare walls receded into darkness. When he shifted his glance to the cloud-gate at the top end of Crosby, something in the gloom at the rear of the empty gallery revealed itself, then slid back into invisibility. Whatever it was had been **looking** at him. He snapped his head back and stared into the window. Then he moved forward across the sidewalk, bringing more of the interior into view.

At the far end of the room, a dim shape materialized out of the darkness and seemed to move forward, matching his movements.

Jeez, he thought, stung by a recollection, **didn't I write this somewhere?**

He took another reluctant step forward. In either mockery or challenge, the figure inside matched him again. In the darkness and obscurity at the back of the immense room, its shape, which was not human, seemed to waver, swelling and shifting like smoke. A long, wide body lowered itself a few inches, as if crouching. There was the suggestion of ears. A silvery pair of eyes swam into view and focused intently on him. A kind of blunt force streamed toward him. Tim gasped and stepped back. He felt as though he had been pinned by a pair of flashlights. Unrelenting and soulless, made entirely of will and antipathy, the creature's eyes hung in the gloomy air.

He found himself moving backward and off the sidewalk, into the middle of the cobbled street. It seemed important not to turn his back.

Knowing that his terror was ridiculous did nothing to tame it. He continued to move across the street, eyes locked with the creature's, pushed himself up onto the far sidewalk, and whirled to sprint north toward Broome Street. Around him, the atmosphere tingled and snapped. He once again became aware of the rain. Before he had taken two long strides, a door opened in what had seemed a blank wall, and a couple emerged from a tall iron-fronted building. The world around him had solidified into its old unreliable self. He reached Broome with the sense of having broken through an invisible but palpable barrier.

Because the people who had reappeared on the sidewalk were staring at him, he slowed his pace. By the time he was crossing Broadway, he had brought himself down to a walk. His heart was knocking in his chest, and he could hear his own ragged breathing. A pair of shiny young men with rain-resistant hair turned their heads to see how much trouble he was in.

"I'm okay," he said.

The young men snapped their heads forward and began walking a little faster, leaking disdain.

Strange, how normal the world seemed to him now, after Crosby Street. Those young men, what would they say if they knew he was getting e-mail from dead classmates? No more. Underhill was turning his back on all that nonsense. He resolved to concentrate on his work. From here on out, he would delete, unread, all e-mails without domain names. He wanted order and productivity.

He reached this decision with the sense of having established the ground rules for the next six months of his life. He would create a clearing, and in that clearing, free of uncertainty and disorder, he would write his book. Within imagination's protective confines, he would set his heroine in motion. **She** was supposed to be in emotional extremity, not he. He needed to get in balance again.

With this resolve in mind, Tim turned the corner of Wooster and Grand, looked through the drizzle to the entrance of his building, and noticed a tall man in jeans and a hooded sweatshirt emerging through the open door. **Oh, no,** he thought, without being entirely certain why he should react this way. Then he looked more closely beneath the edge of the hood and saw what part of him had already registered, the face of Jasper Kohle. Kohle was grinning at him.

Tim stopped moving. For a second or two, Kohle's face seemed to slide over its bones, and the bones themselves to shift. All that remained steady was the grin. Kohle's face disappeared when his body turned, and he began to move in a deliberate slow jog toward West Broadway, where a wet young woman with green hair and facial piercings slouched past a steady stream of cars.

"Hey!" Tim shouted. "What are you doing?"

Kohle jogged around the corner, and Tim followed. For a moment he saw Kohle's back moving purposefully away from him; then it slipped around a group of policemen staring at the entrance of a shop, and was gone. Tim thought of calling out to the cops, but he realized that he had no crime to report.

"Oh, shit," he said. "Oh, hell." One of the

cops turned his head and gave him a look that said, **Do you really want to mess up my day?**

He spun around and raced back to the entrance of 55 Grand, as if haste could alter whatever he was going to find in his loft. The key jittered in the lock, demanding extra body English before it slid home. Though Tim's mind was empty of nearly everything but anxiety, he managed to wonder how Kohle had gotten inside without a key. Callers could not be buzzed in: loft holders had to go downstairs and open two sets of doors for their visitors. This reality created a possibility for hope. Maybe Kohle's visit had been no more than the act of a stalker pushing the envelope.

Tim ran past the elevator and charged up the staircase. His heels rang on the metal steps. He was breathing hard by the time he reached his door, and he had a sharp stitch in his side. He placed his left hand over the pain, with his right inserted his second key into the slot, and the door swung open by itself. Instead of unlocking it, he had almost locked it.

"Bloody hell," he said, trying to remember if he had locked the door on his way out. The memory would not come. In fact, he could not even remember if he had taken the elevator or walked down the stairs, but he could not imagine forgetting to lock his door when he left the building.

Holding his breath, he pushed the door open, stepped inside, and flattened his back against the wall. From this position, at the end of a long, narrow corridor lined on one side with framed photographs and a row of coat hooks on the other, he could see only a small vertical slice of the loft itself. He realized that he was being absurdly cautious. Tim unpeeled himself from the photographs and called out, "Anybody here?" He moved to the end of the narrow corridor and surveyed his loft. No furniture had been overturned, and nothing seemed to have been destroyed.

Then he noticed that ten to fifteen feet of the floor in front of the wall of books at the rear of his loft was covered with ripped papers. When he moved closer, he saw lines of type on the papers. They were pages ripped from books. He took in that about half of the sheets were scattered throughout a shining yellow pool a half second before he registered the stink of urine.

Underhill walked up to the ruined pages and saw familiar words in familiar sentences. The pages had all been torn from copies of his most recent book. Groaning, he placed his hands on the sides of his head and looked up at the shelves. The five copies of **lost boy lost girl** still

on hand to be given out as gifts were more or
less in their proper places, but looked rumpled
and hard used. Tim moved gingerly around the
pool of urine and pulled down two of the
copies. Long runs of pages had been ripped out
of each book.

"I don't believe this," he said. He went to his
phone and dialed Maggie's number.

"Maggie, did you let someone in the building
a little while ago?"

"Funny question. Ask another one."

"I'm sure you didn't let anyone into my loft."

"Uh-oh, this isn't sounding good."

"I had a break-in," he said. "A guy ripped up
some books and pissed on the floor."

"You think **I** let him in?"

"No, no. It's possible I even left my door unlocked. I just wondered if you saw anything."

"What are you going to do?"

"Go out and get some cops," he said.
She laughed. "You going to buy them at the
deli?"

"I just saw a bunch of policemen around the
corner. I'd rather talk to them than call the station. It'll work faster."

"Ride 'em, cowboy," Maggie said.

Tim ran back down the stairs and discovered
that the rain had stopped. The streets had already begun to dry, and damp patches of dark

gray lay across the sidewalk. He made an end run around a group of Japanese men and women consulting an astonishing number of guidebooks and trotted around the corner. The policemen were just beginning to disperse. The first one to notice him was the cop who had given him the warning look.

"Officer," he said. "Excuse me, but I could use your help."

The plate on the policeman's uniform said BORCA. "What's the problem, sir?"

"Someone broke into my loft and did some damage. He pissed on the floor. I know who did it, I can tell you his name. He was leaving the building when I came up."

"This is another resident at your building?"

"No, it's someone I barely know."

Borca motioned to an officer who looked much too fat to be effective, and the man waddled up to him. Tim always wondered where policemen like that bought their uniforms. "Your name, sir?" Borca asked.

Tim told him his name.

"This is my partner, Officer Beck. Let's go have a look."

After making the call to the precinct, Beck produced a battered little notebook and wrote down various details on the walk back to 55 Grand.

"K-O-H-L-E," Tim said, "and no, he isn't a friend of mine. I'm not sure what he is."

"How did he get in the building?" Borca asked.

"You got me."

Inside, Tim automatically went to the staircase. When he put his foot on the first step, Officer Beck asked him, "What floor are you on?"

"Three."

"We're taking the elevator," Beck said. He pushed the button.

The three men stood in silence until the elevator arrived and the doors opened. They stepped in.

"What's your relationship to this Kohle?" Borca asked.

"I'm a writer. Kohle presented himself as a fan. He brought some books for me to sign. That was the same book he ripped up and urinated on."

Simultaneously, Borca said, "I guess he didn't think much of your writing," and Beck said, "Everybody's a critic." They were still laughing at each other's wit when the elevator doors opened to reveal Maggie Lah standing in the darkness of the hallway, her weight balanced on one leg and her arms folded in front of her. Both officers fell silent.

"How bad is it?" she asked.

"Mostly, it's embarrassing," Tim said.

The policemen were staring at Maggie. She said, "At least we have these handsome officers to keep us safe from riffraff."

Borca switched his gaze to Tim. "You're a writer, huh? My wife reads books. Would she know your name?"

"It's not impossible," Tim said. He unlocked the door.

"You can smell it, all right," Borca said. "Actually, it stinks pretty good."

"Like tiger piss," Beck said.

Tim led them down the corridor.

"I remember that smell from the zoo when I was a kid," Beck said, walking sideways to avoid rubbing against the coat hooks.

The odor had doubled and redoubled upon itself in the past few minutes; now it had become so intense that it stung the eyes.

Maggie groaned when she saw the damage.

Borca and Beck strolled around the loft, writing in their notebooks, examining the books, looking at everything they found curious.

"Don't worry," Maggie said. "I know a great cleaning service. They practically specialize in tiger piss."

Borca had been eyeing her. "Where are you from, anyway?"

"Where do you think I'm from?" Maggie asked.

"Well, not from here. China or Japan, some Oriental country. Asian, you're supposed to say now."

"Actually, I was born in a small town in rural France."

Borca was nonplussed by this information. "Uhhh . . . do you have any idea who might have done this? Did you see anyone enter or leave the building?"

"Mais non," she said.

He turned to Tim. "Presumably, you can give us a description."

"I can try. White male, about six feet tall, a hundred and eighty pounds. I have no idea how old he is. The guy kept getting older every time I looked at him."

The policemen exchanged glances.

"Can you remember what he was wearing?"

"A gray sweatshirt with a hood. Blue jeans. Sneakers, I guess."

"What do you mean, sir, he kept getting older every time you looked at him?" Beck asked.

"In the beginning, I thought he was a young guy, in his early forties, say."

Beck and Borca, who were in their early thirties, glanced at each other again.

"But every time I looked at him after that, he seemed to be older. I mean, I saw wrinkles I hadn't seen before."

"We have his name," Borca said. "Mr. Kohle won't be hard to find." He handed Tim a card, paused for a second, and gave another to Maggie. "Give me a call if you think of anything else. We'll be back in touch when we locate your perp. He didn't steal anything, did he?"

"Apart from my peace of mind?" Tim said.

"Look, it's not so bad. Get a cleaning company in here, you'll be good as new. All you lost was a couple of your own books."

"But how did he get in?" Tim asked.

"When we find your guy, we'll ask him," Beck said.

"You should be hearing from us soon," Borca said.

"Not to make any promises," said Beck. "But this sort of stuff usually gets cleared up in a day or two." Like Borca, he was having trouble not staring at beautiful little Maggie. Unlike his partner, he was no longer struggling with the impulse.

The elevator doors closed, and before Tim could say anything, Maggie said, "If I were Mrs. Officer Beck, I could live out on Long Island and give French lessons."

"Marriage might not be what he had in mind," Tim said.

"Dommage," Maggie said. "Now let's get up as much of that stuff as we can, okay?"

They mopped up what they could with paper towels, and when they ran out, they went to the deli for more. When eight rolls of Bounty and Brawny had been stuffed into a black plastic garbage bag, and the bag sealed up to keep in the stink, they brought out a mop and a bucket and washed the floor in front of the book-shelves, over and over, for half an hour. Tim sprinkled white wine and baking soda—an anodyne of his own invention—over the infected area and scrubbed that into the wood before rinsing it off. The ruined books went into another black bag.

"What do you think?" Maggie asked.

"I can still smell it."

"Should I call the super-duper-A1 cleaning service?"

"Please do."

Maggie floated away to the loft she shared with Michael Poole, leaving him attempting to ignore the lingering odor of feline urine, now compounded with the aroma of spilled chardonnay, while he summoned the courage to face his computer. He made himself a cup of peppermint tea. He removed a low-carb no-fat cookie from a container of puritan design and took both to his desk. A flashing little icon at the lower-right-hand corner of his screen informed him that he had received one or more e-mails. Not now, thanks, nope. Dutifully, he evoked his document, clicked to the last page he had written, and did his best to continue. His heroine was about to reach a great turning point in both the book and her life, and to discover the details that would bring breath, air, and light to the scene, Tim had to work with unalloyed concentration.

Over the next hour and a half, he succeeded in writing two paragraphs. The unseen e-mails ticked away at the back of his consciousness, interfering with the process of magical detail discovery. **All right,** he thought, **I give up.** He minimized his document and called up the day's eight new arrivals. Two were from writer-editors inviting him to contribute to theme anthologies. Three were spam; he deleted these. He also deleted the three e-mails from encoded strangers that had arrived bereft of subject lines and domain names. One new e-mail remained in his in-box. Also absent subject line and domain name, it had nonetheless been sent by Cyrax, the most authoritative of all his phantom correspondents. Tim clicked it open and read Cyrax's message:

> now are u ready 2 listn
> 2 yr gide?

Experimentally, he moved his cursor to **Reply** and clicked on it. Instead of the conventional e-mail reply form, a large blank rectangle, pale blue in color, appeared at the center of his screen. It reminded Tim of the instant-message windows he had seen on other people's computers.
All right, he said to himself, **let's give it a whirl.** Within the blue box he typed "yes."
In less than a second these words appeared beneath his acceptance:

> Cyrax: good deshizn, student myn, u stpd buttsecks!
> (LOLOL!) ok. let me tell u abt deth, fax u will need 2—
>
> or, to speak YOUR language, little buddy, and your language is a bit closer to what mine used to be, it's time you learned a few facts about death!

Two Voices
from a Cloud

PART TWO

14

Merlin L'Duith:

Minor deity though I may be, I am nonetheless the god of Millhaven, Illinois, the god of Hendersonia, New Jersey, and the god of all points in between. Where my gaze happens to fall, there I make the rules. It is I who decides who ends their days on silken sheets surrounded by a competent medical staff, and who expires in a cell, miserable, starving, and alone. And my name is not Merlin L'Duith; rather, **within** Merlin L'Duith I confine myself.

It is my pleasure now to recount certain latter-day episodes in the life of Willy Patrick, the better to advance the dear girl's progress toward her great challenge, which is of recognition.

On the day of her appointment at Bergdorf Goodman, Willy spoke to Tom Hartland, her writer friend, and agreed to meet him for a glass of wine at the King Cole Bar at the St. Regis. Tom sounded unusually serious when he suggested their get-together and told her that he had been thinking hard about something that concerned her. Willy assumed that it had to do with her agent or her publisher. When, like his boss's obedient girlfriend, she informed Giles Coverley of this appointment, he suggested that he do the driving for this excursion. One glass of wine could easily lead to two, and there was no sense in courting trouble. In the end, she gave in.

The previous day, the Santolini Brothers had informed her that they really felt they ought to amputate the limb of the big oak tree at the side of the house. Damage suffered years ago could bring it down any day, causing injury to the house—how much they could not say, nor could they guarantee that the limb would fall, but still. Lady, you wanna save money I can't blame you, but it could wind up costing you a whole lot more later. Is all I'm saying. Following the boss's orders, Willy deflected them, and off they sloped, shrugging as they went.

She went over and looked at the oak after the Santolinis had wandered away, and although she could not, in fact, see all of it, the long, sculptural limb extending toward, then curving away from the roof of Mitchell's office did not look damaged to her. Probably Mitchell was right about the Santolinis.

With the feeling that Faber had once again proved his worth in absentia, Willy prepared a light, nearly gravity-free lunch of two table-spoons of tuna salad smoothed along a piece of crispbread, half an heirloom tomato cut into tiny wedges, and a can of caffeine-free Diet Coke. She dined upon this feast while watching **One Life to Live** on the little TV from her for-mer apartment, now installed on the kitchen counter. To a narrative-drenched mind, **One Life to Live** presented an astonishing banquet. Each new course was richer and more florid than the last; and the banquet went on forever, endlessly, at the rate of one hour per day. In the past, the day's installment had often returned Willy to her desk with the sense that a river of story flowed through her, ready always to be tapped.

Unfortunately, the spell cast by her soap opera seemed not to have survived the move from East Seventy-seventh Street to Guilderland Road; and Willy spent hours pushing at stubborn sen-tences that trickled along until they dried up.

That evening, the two glasses of wine she had with dinner put her to sleep somewhere in the

middle of the first chapter of **The Ambas-
sadors.** (Willy typically read English novelists,
A. N. Wilson, A. S. Byatt, Iris Murdoch, Muriel
Spark. When out of sorts, she devoured crime
novels; when depressed, she enjoyed Tim Underhill's books, which were not crime novels,
exactly, except that they always had crimes, usually appalling ones, in them; in exceptionally
good moods, she picked up nonfiction books
with titles like **The Origin of Consciousness
in the Breakdown of the Bicameral Mind.**)

At 11:00 P.M. she came awake and decanted
herself into her bed, almost immediately to
suffer through one of the worst nightmares of
her life.

From a point about eight feet off the ground,
she was observing, camera-like, the back of a
teenaged boy staring at an abandoned house.
He had short, dark hair and wore floppy jeans
and layered T-shirts. His posture struck her as
oddly poised, even graceful, and she thought
he must have a nice-looking face. With the
unquestioned conviction of dreams, another
thought came to her: the boy's face would be a
more youthful, more masculine, but otherwise
virtually identical version of her own. The boy
took a tentative step toward the empty house.
As soon as he moved forward, Willy understood

that the house, which was empty only technically, represented a mortal danger to this boy. If he went through that door, the house would close around him like a trap; the filthy, ravenous spirit that looked out from the front windows would claim him forever. Willy's consciousness of his danger did not slow the boy in his steady progress toward the door. Inwardly, the entire building trembled to devour him—she could feel the bottomlessness of its hunger. She could not move; she could not speak. Her dread redoubled itself, and the dread deepened her paralysis.

The boy took another step forward on the little broken path leading to the porch and the awaiting door. As if within a snow globe emptied of its snow, the house and the boy stood isolated in a no-place defined entirely by themselves. Within the globe, intolerably to our watching Willy, a sick desire fattened upon itself. As it whispered to the boy, his hesitant footsteps carried him nearer and nearer to the porch. At last she could bear it no longer: the sheer pitch of her dread let her overflow her confinement and fly, out of control, deep into the sacred space. She sped toward the advancing boy as if on a silver rail, and when she was within the minutest possible time fraction of somehow not knocking him over but **gliding into his body** she jolted into wakefulness, the scream in her throat already fading to a gasp.

For hours that night Willy alternated between pitching back and forth on her sheets and lying still. When she rode into Manhattan the next day, seated in the passenger seat of Mitchell's car while Giles Coverley chatted about trivia of no interest to either of them, she felt nearly as dislocated and displaced as Tim Underhill on a difficult day. Thanks to Kimberley Todhunter, the helpful young woman conjured up by her fiancé, Bergdorf Goodman folded itself around her like a velvet purse. Under Ms. Todhunter's guidance, Willy pared down a dozen dazzling choices to a final two, and finally chose the shimmering Prada garment over its counterpart from Oscar de la Renta, then moved on to a pair of terrific sexpot shoes from Jimmy Choo and a number of other accessories previously voted in by her tactful guide. Having spent an astonishing amount of Mitchell Faber's money, Willy got back into the car and told Giles to take her to the Metropolitan Museum.

Willy meandered through the impressionist rooms, only half-seeing the paintings as she speculated about what Tom Hartland thought was so serious. Coverley had dropped her off at the entrance and driven away to perform sundry mysterious duties. On reflection, Tom's subject probably had nothing to do with publishing. Tom seldom talked shop with her. It kept occurring to her that Tom had never been entirely supportive about Mitchell Faber, and that it seemed likely that he had arranged this meeting, this date between two old friends, to try to dissuade her from getting married.

Monet's views of haystacks and Rouen cathedral, once sources of almost infinite pleasure, today seemed merely pictorial. It was predictable that Tom should have turned against Mitchell, she thought. Not only did they have nothing in common, Tom's political views automatically made anyone who worked for outfits like the Baltic Group a dupe or a villain. What had Mitchell said, at their first meeting? **From time to time, they call me in to make murky issues even murkier.** She had thought he was telling her he was a kind of corporate lawyer. (It was, she realized, the first and last time she had heard Mitchell say anything that sounded witty.)

Willy found herself before a painting by Corot. She had always loved this painting. About the size of a window, it depicted the onset of a storm in a rural landscape. The air was a luminous gray and, like everything else in the painting, hummed with anticipation. Beneath a great tree on the banks of a river, a cowherd huddled beside his charge. Overshadowing the cow, its attendant, and the riverbank, claiming center stage, the enormous tree—a linden, Willy thought—threw up its arms in the gathering wind. Its hands shook, and the leaves were blown backward on their stems. That was the painting's center, its heart. The undersides of the leaves gleamed gray-green, beautiful to behold. Undoubtedly they rattled as they shook. Something sacred, an inhuman force deep within and beneath the rind of the physical world, spoke from the flipped-over, gleaming, vibrant leaves. They had been **seen,** those leaves, and in the midst of her turmoil Willy was able to think, I, too, have **seen** you, leaves, and feel the onset of the storm.

Later, she thought the painting had driven her from the museum. The storm it promised to the French countryside had arrived in New York City, and Willy's body had known it before she reached the top of the immense staircase and looked down to the tide of wet jackets and umbrellas streaming in past the guards. The Dellray men scrambling across the roof, the Santolinis and their concerns about the oak tree . . . it seemed wrong to keep Giles Coverley from his job, and she nearly decided to cancel her drinks date with Tom Hartland. But if any problems came up, Roman Richard had only to use his cell phone for a consultation; and she found herself unwilling to give up her hour with Tom.

The interval between the Met and the St. Regis seemed to pass in an instant, and when Willy, who had arrived in advance of her friend, took her seat on the banquette and waved away the hovering waiter, it was with literally no memory of how this period had been spent. Two and a half hours had gone by, leaving not even the memory of rain bouncing off the windshield of Giles Coverley's car. She could, just, remember leaving the car and moving toward the hotel's marquee under the shelter of a uniformed doorman's immense black umbrella. Even that had the slightly dreamy, black-and-white quality of something remembered from an old movie.

It was true, she was going crazy. How could all that time have disappeared? The missing hours felt as though they had been carved from her body like Shylock's pound of flesh. Looking back to what remained in her memory from the museum, Willy came across another inexplicable lapse. She retained a clear picture of three paintings only: a Monet haystack, a Monet rendering of the Rouen cathedral, and the Corot.

On either side of all three of these pictures hung fuzzy daubs like paintings seen through a layer of Vaseline—this gauzy stuff had filled whole galleries. The only real paintings in the Met had been the ones she had paused to look at.

A familiar voice inquired why Willy was looking so incredibly grim, and she looked up to see handsome, kind Tom Hartland bending down toward her. As her heart surprised her by knocking in her chest, Willy resolved to keep these indications of mental chaos to herself. Instead, she blurted, Oh, Tom, please don't tell me you wanted me to come here so you could say terrible things about Mitchell. Then she apologized for this outburst; then tears flew from her eyes, and an ugly sound of distress escaped her lips. The nearest patrons of the King Cole Bar slid a few inches away on the banquette.

Tom Hartland conjured up a glass of white wine and a vodka martini, and under his tactful guidance Willy tried to describe the afternoon's bizarre experiences.

—Well, Tom said, it sounds like a kind of temporary, stress-related amnesia. You're not going crazy, Willy. You've just been drifting along, letting other people tell you what to do, and now that you are coming to an irrevocable moment in your life, part of you is starting to rebel. I think that is a very positive sign.

—Oh no, Willy said. I was right, and you want to talk me out of getting married. This is so unsupportive of you. Can't you be happy for me?

—I wish I could, Tom said. Look, people who write detective books, even ones for boys, learn how to get all kinds of information. Because I was worried about you, I did some research into Mitchell Faber and the Baltic Group. What I found out distressed me, and I have to at least discuss it with you.

—You're a snoop. You went prying around into corners and you found some dirt. Very noble of you.

—Willy, please shut up and listen to me. Let's begin with the wedding, okay? Don't you want to spend more time deciding what to wear? And what about the flowers, the food, the music? Where was this hypothetical wedding going to take place, anyhow?

Mitchell had arranged for a private ceremony on the grounds of a magnificent estate, like a country house, a Brideshead kind of place, called Blackwoods, she thought, somewhere up around New Paltz, or maybe Woodstock, but in the mountains, anyhow. If it rained, the ceremony would be held in the library, which was supposed to be gorgeous.

Tom informed Willy that she was talking

about a gigantic Baltic Group property called Nightwood, stuck up in the mountains halfway between Woodstock and New Paltz. It was used for top-secret, hush-hush conferences. Cigars, single-malt whiskeys, business suits.

—So the problem is what, exactly?

Well, this wasn't the sort of place usually used for weddings, that was all. But wedding invitations usually got sent out right about this time—what about hers? And had Mitchell obtained the marriage license and hired the clergyman, or the judge, or whatever? She didn't know, she didn't care, she was a passive partner in her own wedding!

She couldn't think of anything better, Willy said. Who wanted to worry about table settings and flowers and invitations anyhow? She was going to show up at her wedding and get married. Besides, the only person she was inviting was Tom. Why get bent out of shape over details Mitchell could handle better than any wedding planner ever born? Passivity was underrated.

—So Mitchell makes it possible for you to avoid thinking much about this wedding you're about to have.

If he wanted to see it that way, sure, he should go right ahead. Mitchell made it possible for her to concentrate on her work.

—Is your work going well?

Well, no. It wasn't going at all, unfortunately. Kind of a settling-in period. Getting used to the new house, adjusting to the idea of being married again, that sort of thing.

—Sometimes I get the feeling, Tom said, that I'll be lucky to see you again after the happy day.

Willy shook her head in vehement denial. How could Tom say that?

—What does this boyfriend of yours do for a living?

—Mitchell works for the Baltic Group.

—And what does the Baltic Group do? Was Willy up on their happy little empire?

They make money all over the world, that was what they did. How should she know? What was she, a financial journalist?

—Are you aware that you sound a little defensive?

All right, all right. She was smiling at him. Tom Hartland had the gift of telling her the truth in a way that improved her mood. Which meant **he** was a gift. For a moment Willy wondered if she should not marry someone like Tom Hartland instead. Being married to Tom would be fun, apart, of course, from the absence of sex. But maybe they could improvise something. Whoops, I'm out of wine already!

As Willy ordered a second glass for herself, Tom explained what he knew about the Baltic Group: a vast, multifarious development company with headquarters in Switzerland, South Africa, Saudi Arabia, Washington, D.C., and the Bahamas. Tied to governments all over the world and staffed by ex-ministers, ex-senators, ex-generals, retired statesmen. Its banking division propped up dictatorships in half a dozen countries. When big overseas contracts were to be awarded, Baltic accepted most of them as if by sacred right.

Okay, he didn't like them. We already knew this. But what, she wanted to know, did he actually **make** of them?

—Maybe I'm a paranoid left-wing conspiracy junkie, but companies like that are my definition of evil. They interfere with politics wherever they want to gain advantage, they buy cooperation, they ruin the environment, they get up to dirty deals all over the world. You should consider, Willy, that your first husband might have been murdered because of his connection to Baltic.

For a second, Willy heard the ghostly wail of her daughter's voice. The loss of her husband and daughter swarmed over her, and she began to shake. —Thanks very much, she said. This is hardly news. Whose side are you on, anyhow?

—I'm on your side, but I am concerned about you. No, hold on, don't get all worked up, Willy.

So what did he want to tell her about Mitchell? It was the reason they were there, he might as well get it out.

—Nobody wants to see you drift into a marriage with a man who isn't right for you. And that **is** what you seem to be doing, at least to me. Because, forgive me for what I'm about to say, but you don't really know this man very well, and even worse, what he represents is absolutely counter to your values.

My values?

—Your boyfriend was in Special Forces before being taken on by the CIA, and when he blotted his copybook there, the Baltic Group was more than willing to snap him up. Are you hearing me? Mitchell Faber did something so bad that he had to be drummed out of the CIA. They're **really** not talking about whatever he did, but it was something special, that's for sure. Like a massacre, Willy, and I'm not exaggerating. To be buried so deep, it **had** to be something like that. Now he's a kind of mercenary, except he has only one client and he gets paid really well.

Was he actually saying that Mitchell was responsible for the deaths of her husband

and daughter? Was **that** what he was trying to tell her?

—Maybe indirectly, yes.

Now, to her horror, Tom's life opened before her as a series of broad, sunlit avenues, while hers looked to be spiraling down into a cave, a cell, a speck.

She became aware that Tom had stopped talking. He was looking at her through narrowed eyes, and beneath his well-mannered blond hair his forehead looked corrugated.

—Willy, did you hear any of what I just said?

Everything important, yes.

—Because when you start telling me things about your daughter, I know you need professional assistance.

Willy shot to her feet in a flutter of limbs and other people's scarves and jackets. It was time to get back, she had things to do on the estate, and the roads would be terrible. Could she call Tom for advice, or for help . . . ?

—I want you to call, he said. Willy?

She was already maneuvering through the crowd between the bar and the tables.

Then it was if she had fallen asleep the instant she entered Giles Coverley's car, for without transition she went from running through a downpour toward the open back seat to the recognition that she was standing beneath an umbrella held by Rocky Santolini, as he pointed, in the torrential rain battering down on Hendersonia, to a messy obscurity of branches and limbs where the gable over Mitchell's office window should have been. Beneath his own, double-sized, plaid umbrella, Giles was staring up at the same place, swearing with an astonishing eloquence. The Dellray men stood huddled at the front of the garage. Unprotected from the deluge, Roman Richard was yelling at Vincent Santolini. With his soaked clothing and streaming hair, he looked like a manatee. Willy thought she was going to faint, then that she would scream. She wanted to scream: screaming would make what was happening to her everyone else's problem instead of hers. She flattened her hands over her mouth.

—We told you this could happen, Rocky said. He thought her horror had been caused by damage to her house.

Roman Richard swung his body sideways, extended an arm, and bellowed something at Rocky.

—I can't deal with that guy. This is the deal. Out of respect for your husband, we could go up to that room, clear out the wreckage, and staple a sheet of plastic over the opening. Maybe we could save the carpet and whatever else in there ain't already ruined. Only we need the key, on account of that room is locked right now.

Willy could barely hear him. She was still reeling from the hours subtracted from her day. Everything else was an irrelevance, a minor problem. Hours had not been taken from her; she had lost them, because she was cuckoo, bats, looney tunes.

Giles had wandered over. Mud was spattered across his beautiful shoes. —And it's locked for a reason, Santolini. Mr. Faber values his privacy very highly. Can't you do something from the outside?

—What, you want me to **pull** that shit out? Sorry, missus.

—Go in and open the door, Giles, Willy said, wanting to put an end to all this blather.

—I'm sorry, but I can't do that without authorization from Mr. Faber.

—Mr. Faber won't be very happy with you if you let his office get wrecked any more than it already is. Let's get out of the rain.

—This is on your head, Willy.

He spun around and proceeded toward the garage with Willy immediately behind him. Rocky and Vince Santolini trotted off to pick up power saws and rolls of plastic sheeting.

Willy whispered, Did I fall asleep in the car?

—How would I know? Ask yourself how much you had to drink.

Expressing his opinion of the enterprise by leaving muddy footprints on the carpets, Coverley refused to say any more as he marched up the big central staircase, wheeled across the landing, took the next, narrower flight up, and positioned himself in front of the office door. Through its thick, dark wood came the sound of a high wind and the rattling of leaves. He pulled a baseball-sized key ring from his coat pocket, selected a key, held it up in front of Willy, and challenged her with a glare.

—I take no responsibility for this. Coverley inserted the key into the lock and twisted it. The door flung itself open on a blast of wind and struck the startled Coverley full in the face. Rainwater and torn leaves flew past him.

—Christ. Blood dripped from behind the hand Coverley held over his nose. I'm not going to stand here and bleed to death. He moved aside, with an ironic gesture of welcome.

The Santolinis brushed past Willy and went immediately to work in the chaos of Faber's lair. Saws roaring like motorboat engines, they climbed over the tangle of branches protruding through the roof and the destroyed window frame. Wood chips and sawdust flew up around them as they worked.

—This was your idea, **you** deal with it, Coverley said. A fat streamlet of blood was running down over his chin and dripping onto his shirt.

—I'll drive you to the hospital, if you like.

—Just make sure these clowns don't steal anything. He slipped away.

Willy entered Mitchell's office with hesitant footsteps and a distinct feeling of trespass. A smell of burnt wood that somehow reminded her of Christmas came from the Santolinis' side of the room. The floor and huge rectangular Persian rug were covered with wet and far-flung papers, and in the absence of anything else to do, Willy began picking these up. Hunkering down to scoop up a long, spilled-out sheaf of documents, she groaned at the mess before her and put out a hand to steady herself. Then her eyes fell upon a flat, intricately carved wooden box propped open on its hinged top. Either the wind or one of the invading branches had wiped it from its accustomed surface and sent it flying. Beneath the box lay a scattering of photographs. Willy duckwalked over to the box, closed its top, and set it down next to her right foot. When she reached out for the photographs, a stray breeze caused them to stir and flutter as if suddenly come to life. Willy caught one in its ascent from the deep reds and inky blues of the densely patterned rug and turned it over to look at its surface. **What in the world is Mitchell doing with a picture of Jim Patrick?** she wondered, only mildly intrigued by the mystery of her first husband's photograph turning up in her fiancé's office.

It was not until her surprise at the unexpected sight of her first husband's face began to recede that she was able to take in what had happened to his body. In the photograph, Jim Patrick's corpse lay on stony soil beside the car in which his charred body, and Holly's, had been found. Three bullets had entered his body, and a great deal of blood lay pooled around it. Then she saw that his hands had been cut off. The picture, it came to her, represented a kind of trophy.

She must have made some kind of noise, because Rocky and Vince raised their heads and looked at her, curious as dogs. Trembling violently, Willy waved them off.

That night, she locked herself in her office and tried to sleep as she lay shaking on the floor. She feared for her life: she feared that Giles Coverley would overcome his scruples, enter his boss's office, and see the photographs scattered on the floor. She was terrified of a knock on her door, but no knock came, and no one knew what she had seen.

The next morning, she managed to avoid being seen by Coverley and Roman Richard as she crept down the stairs, passed from the kitchen into the garage, and drove at a reckless speed down the hill and into Hendersonia, where she had an appointment with her banker.

And at nine-thirty that night, following a most adventurous day, she gave her car keys to a valet in front of the Milford Plaza hotel, took the escalator to the lobby, rolled her suitcase up to the front desk, and checked in under the name James Patrick had wanted her to use on her Gold AmEx card, W. Bryce.

15

Cyrax:

it is an endless <omplexity and u will never undrstnd
it, buttsecks, but here we r & I must try.

oh, y do I call u buttsecks? is that wht u ask? 8e<uz
u don't GEDDIT! u r a IGNORAMUS on the subject
of death. (LOLOL!)

And why am I writing that way, you ask, Underhand? I was writing that way, and I will write that
way whenever I feel like it, which is to say when
you're acting like a jackass, for the simple reason
that it is a pleasure for an ancient laddie-buck (so to
speak) like myself to learn a new language every
now and again, and presently I am feeling my way
around HAXXOR, a language exclusive to juveniles
addicted to mIRC and other chat programs. Of
course it isn't a real language, merely a system of

jokes and substitutions, but it's a hoot, **n'est-ce pas**? Between my birth in Byzantium during the reign of Michael II, known as the Stammerer, and my premature (by your standards) but not all that untimely (by mine) death under Michael III, known as the Drunkard, I acquired a good working knowledge of six languages, a matter quite useful to me in my work as a gatherer and disseminator of information. (Since my disappearance from the surface of the Earth and gradual introduction to eternal realms, I have learned perhaps six hundred, including a great many "lost" dialects.) You could say, I was a journalist of sorts. A gossip columnist, to be specific, though of course we did not call it gossip at the time. What we did call it was "news," and to come up with this commodity on a steady basis I dragged myself here and there about the empire, dropping in on the local satraps and princelings ever eager to have their accomplishments publicized at court.

& y 4m I 73lling u thi5?

Because like you I was a writer, and they felt that you needed One who could communicate with you in a familiar manner. So I, Cyrax, will be your Familiar Spirit.

Underdog, it is necessary for you to LISTEN! Acting recklessly and ignorantly, you have sent winds of disorder, tides of resentment, waves of confusion through the Eternal Realms, or the Other World, or the Other Side, or whatever you want to call it. You have created DIFFICULTY & TROUBLE! You have given a **WEDGE** to **CHAOS**.

Oh how, you ask, as if any such answer can be simple, can be even what your kind would call Answer. But let me try, Underdown, let me try. My enormous pleasure at the possibility of communicating directly with a 21st Century man—and having him communicate with me!—much outweighs the irritation of having to deal with such obdurate material as yourself.

For the sake of clarity, I will employ the vulgar typographical device known as the "bullet":

* 7 years after the dawn of your life, your wings brushed this REALM—April your Sister preceded your spirit here as its Guide, and you were CALLED BACK, but only after you had established a FRAGILE CONTACT with HIGHER POWERS, THE WORLD BEYOND, the fringes of THE GREAT HIERARCHY.
* Since that day, Intimations of Connectedness, Coherence & Secret Order have sweetened your existence: suggestions of a GRAND FORMALITY. These Intimations have proceeded directly from your near Approach to the REALM.

- April your Sister is ever your guide and will be for a time after your Entrance to the Mysteries, for which you may and should thank the PRIME.

- Alas, yours was the 1 case in 1,000,000 in which Proximity = Influence, so that what You did in your Realm could, were the correct conditions to prevail, affect us Here, particularly Those of Recent Induction still learning what you call "the ropes." Recent = within roughly the past 80 years.

- We Figures & Spirits of the Formerly Living are of 2 Kinds. What I next shall tell you is a cruel simplification, but for our Purposes it will have to do.

- Those Recently Deceased are of the category **sasha. Sasha** are the Living Dead, Remembered still by those whose time on Earth overlapped with theirs. When the last living person to know a **sasha** departs into Death, the **sasha** enters the category of the **zamani.** (I use a category system of the Kiswahili peoples.) **Sasha** retain sharp memories, cling to urgent lusts & passions, fret & worry abt. their reputations and those of people once known. **Zamani** let such baubles drop from their hands. The **Zamani**'s task is to understand, to see, to Inhabit the correct Position in the GREAT HIERARCHY, and to serve the PRIME.

Oh how duz this rel8 to u?

Fool Underground, & yet I have grown fond & fonder of you. Hold on, here comes a bullet with your name on it.

- No HELL or Infernal Region exists within the Infinite Space of the REALM. The wicked & sindeformed have their Places, too, as do the Mad & Criminal, & within their Places endure the **sasha** term in a Kind of Suffering of Recognition. Their Crimes & Misdeeds & Lunacies come back endlessly to them in sharp Relief, & thru their Torment they cleanse their eyes, properly to see.

- As the **sasha** draws nearer the condition of **zamani,** he is givn knowledge of our great Libraries & allowed access to the Beauty & Wisdom gathered therein. Our Libraries contain every volume written by mankind lost and unlost & Completed if left unfinished by the Author at the time of his/her death. Each volume is as its Author wisht it to be & dreamt it might be, in its Perfect State. Unflawed, Uncorrupted, Undamaged by the fevers & intoxications & hastes & forgetfulnesses of the human Author, Raised Up to the individual Perfection of its Kind. And yes, some few of these Perfect Books have transported or have been transported across the Border, thru the Curtain or VEIL, into yr Fallen & Corrupt world, there to Shine.

◆ Wandring dazed within the Treasures of a great Library of the REALM, a particular **sasha** encountered a particular tome, and upon reading same, the which named LOST BOY LOST GIRL, the **sasha** grew maddened and enraged. Ancient Passions & fevers again took hold, and the crack-wit **sasha** roared wild through those small portions of the REALM known to it, howling for justice & retribution & revenge. The name of the **sasha** should be known well to you: on Earth, he was Joseph Kalendar.

◆ Spirits as yet barred access to **zamani** may betimes slip from REALM to Realm and enter the plane from which their death had lifted them. There, they may be witnessed, described, and identified as GHOSTS.

◆ GHOSTS are of many kinds & arrayed along a continuum from entirely insubstantial (a haze, a wisp, a curl of smoke, and how how how I wish I could smoke, 4 I know I wd a-door it) to entirely substantial & corporeal, at least as to sight, touch, taste & smell, & tho this latter is quite rare, such is the case with yr Mr. Kalendar.

◆ For this u have only yrself to blame, Underdone. GHOST-KALENDAR HAS ALL THE ATTRIBUTES

YOU PERMITTED HIM IN YR SILLY FLAWD BOOK! Thus: He can change his Form & appear in various Guises, he is in Possession of Great Strength & Subtlety & may show Himself as a savage Beast neither Swine nor Canine but a creature Hideous in-between. He possesses the Power of Invisibility!

If u had never brushed against our REALM, yes, u r right, Undercooked, JK your angry reader wd still be angry but his anger would be confined to This Side, where easily it wd be contained, Suff'red Through, Endured & Understood. BUT!!!!!!!!!! U BUTTSECKS, U OPENED THE WEDGE!!!!!!!!!!

Wht can I doo, poor poor me?
Oho u are looking for Advice frum Cyrax? Okey-dokey, artichokey, Cyrax Sez: U will know the Right Thing when the Time comes. We hope. We trust. We must Nipp this Intrusion in the Budd, and u will be Aided Toward that End.

by whom Aided?
By one of the HIGHER BEINGS, u stupidity, a representative of the class known to u as Angels, beings made Visible in the Class 3 Manifestation, a CLERESYTE (or approximately that) to us, by name in your tongue WCHWHLLDN . . . He is impatient

of success in his most unwelcome mission, and u must be wary of his wrath, for WCHWHLLDN's morality is not yours & in no way prohibits him from inflicting upon you an agonizing death. In his appearance before u on Grand Street u saw how great WCHWHLLDN dislikes detests loathes the tight & unclean surround of Earth. His Task is to CLEANSE.

what is our structure, here, within the REALM??????

u ask what cannot be answered bcuz u r not capable of comprehension & arrogant besides. But this is what we enjoy about your kind & what I in particular like about u in particular, buttsecks. A kind of Valor—blind, unconscious, oft-foolish, never without greed, but of value nonetheless, for are not u in all your measures and qualities the raw material of the REALM, even as to its Upper Reaches? So try this on for size. U have yr Holy Books, Scripture, the Koran, the Hebrew Bible, the Upanishads, necessary to you all & Images of the True and the PRIME, and within Scripture there exist the Gospels, and within the Gospels exists a wise passage about many mansions. Picture each mansion as a Plane or Level, and u will have som idea. With Plane Upon Plane, Level Upon Level, until Mathematics scarce can encompass them all. Of suchlike is the Structure of the REALM, tho of course it is really not.

& why have u received e-mails from departed classmates?

Becuz, as u should have figured out by now, those who knew u and r not long dead, the newest of the **sasha,** being confused and dis-located unlocated, perceived immediately the opportunity to establish thru u contact with their lost world, thence to complain, to beg for help, to ask for directions & mouth off in the lisping baby-babble that is their only mode of speech. Ignore these & leave them 2 find their way or not. For in time, all will find their way, if over millennia. I myself have attained but Level 4, and in this Station I know bliss.

now keep your hands off the keyboard, stop interrupting, and take a few more bullets 2 yr brain:

• Yr sister April, a tender GHOST in Alice-garb, will manifest herself be4 u when she can, but April cannot act against yr enemy Kalendar 4 they r of the same KIND.

• WCHWHLLDN the CLERESYTE **can** oppose Kalendar on yr behalf, but in his outrage may destroy u as well as he. He is yr Guardian, yes, but more so he is the Guardian, a Guardian, one of many, of the Lower Realm.

• U MUST CO-RECK AN ERROR, U MUST MAKE IT RITE! it is what u wr0te that opened the **WEDGE** to **CHAOS,** 4 Kalendar saw the ER-

ROR in yr book & ran am0ck & now u must stay alive although u face a 2ble peril now becuz u created a 2nd Dark Man, did u not? Kalendar was not threat enuf & so u MERGED him with the dark dark villain almost instantly to b in pursuit of yr lovely gamine & now a problem U MUST FACE.

◆ Becuz the shite is about to hit the fan the wall the floor the ceiling 2, buttsecks, and u will have 2 b nimble & imaginative & brave as u have never been be4!

what, u ask, is the great ERROR discovered by the madman Joseph Kalendar in yr book & which enraged him so that he found entrance to yr Lower Realm?
What do u think it was? U accused the stupid beast of repeatedly raping & eventually murdering his own daughter, Lily, and HE DID NOT DO IT!!!! Mr. Kalendar is MIGHTILY PISSED OFF, IN FACT U CD SAY HE IS TIGER-PISSED OFF, which is why he wishes to deface the errant book, not to mention its libelous author!

and what then is yr task?
buttsecks, you disappoint old Cyrax, you must do better than this! Yr task, as u should already KNOW, podner, is to get on yore cayuse, hit the trail & go west 2 yr own Byzantium & the begin-

nings of this story. To Lily Kalendar's real fate, which has been much on yr mind, after all.

& as if by magick, are u not being sent out very soon to perform the odd & self-referential act u call "Readings"? & is not 1 "Reading" in yr own Byzantium? & is not yr brother to wed beauteous China Beech? GO! ATTEND yr brother's nuptials! Have u lost all civility and kindness along with yr poor Wits?

& deer buttsecks, if you do, u will have a chance of achieving something extraordinary & incestuous & ravishing unto heart-melt & impossible for every crack-brain author but u!

& know this also: a terrible terrible thrice-terrible price must be paid & paid by u—a great sacrifice, as if the heart were to be torn from yr body & yr brain crackt & yr spirit engulfed. yrs wuz the crime, yrs will be the punishment.

4 now I say no mor.

The Role of
Tom Hartland

PART THREE

16

"I don't **know** what I'm going to do, Tom," Willy said. "I don't even know if I'm thinking straight. Shit, shit, shit, shit, **shit.** The only thing I do know, did know, was that I had to get out of that house, and in a hurry. You know, you're the only person I swear in front of, but when I talk to you, I swear all the time. I wonder why that is?"

"You're swearing because you're angry. You're not used to that, so you barely know how to act."

"No, no, no," she said. "I'm too shook up to be angry."

Willy had called Tom Hartland as soon as she had locked the door behind the departing bellman. It had been one of those moments when her life felt pathetic and insubstantial, for whom could she have called but Tom? By some dire, remote-control variety of magic, Mitchell

Faber seemed to have driven away most of the
people she had once thought of as her friends.
Her isolation made her feel like locking herself
in the bathroom and weeping. What had kept
her from giving in to self-pity was the thought
that if Tom Hartland was the one person whom
she could telephone at such a moment, at least
he was one of her oldest and dearest friends.

"It's more like shock than anger," she said.
"The only way you and Molly went wrong was,
you were too easy on him!"

"Are your hands trembling?"

"Like crazy. I don't know how I managed to
drive across the bridge."

"You're way past anger, Willy. Sure you're in
shock, but on top of that, you're furious."

"I HAVE A RIGHT TO BE FURIOUS!
THAT CREEP KILLED MY HUSBAND
AND MY DAUGHTER!" She held the phone
out at arm's length and discovered that, by
means of tiny internal adjustments, she could
graduate from mere yelling to gorgeous, all-
stops-out screaming. **"HE TALKED ME
INTO ALMOST GETTING MARRIED TO
HIM! THAT PSYCHO FUCK WAS SUP-
POSED TO REPRESENT SAFETY!"**

Willy gripped the receiver as if trying to choke
it to death. Although she had not known that
she was crying, tears covered her face. Her body

seemed to be breathing by itself in great ragged inhalations and exhalations. She sagged over, letting it go on. Her hot, sparkly face felt as if it had been electrified. Tom's voice leaked from the phone, but Willy could not make out his words. In every important sense, her life seemed over. She had nowhere to go. Pretty soon, an evil creep who had been intimate with every part of her body was going to be hunting for her. Willy felt irredeemably contaminated. After a little while she became aware that she was, after all, still breathing. She straightened up and brought the receiver to her ear.

"Okay, you're right on the money," she said. "I'd like to kill Mitchell Faber. But the problem is, I think he'll probably want to do the same to me."

"Willy, you're going to have to explain all this stuff about killing people. What makes you think he killed your husband? Why would he want to kill you?"

"God, there's so much you don't know." Willy told him about the storm, and the tree limb crashing through the office window. "When I went inside there, I sort of started to clean things up, and I saw all these photographs lying on the floor. Right next to them was this upside-down ornamental wooden box, like a fancy cigar box, that must have been knocked off a shelf. All those photographs were of dead people, and one of them was Jim. They cut his hands off! He was shot to death, and he was lying next to the car they found him in."

"Do you still have that picture?"

"Are you crazy? He was **dead**! Please help me figure out what to do. I'm shaking all over, like I have a fever. I don't seem to be able to stop. Giles knows I saw the picture, and Mitchell is going to be coming for me as soon as he gets off the plane."

He asked for her room number.

"Room 1427."

"I'll be there in fifteen minutes."

"I can **sort of** tell you what I did." Willy lay on her king-sized bed, her arms folded in front of her. Tom Hartland's sweet, serious face stared at her from a nubbly upholstered chair across from the desk.

Tom had been at Haverford when Willy Bryce and Molly Witherspoon were students at Bryn Mawr, and not long after meeting at a mixer the three of them had become close friends. In the summer after their junior year, they had traveled through France in a heady bubble of van Gogh, Gauguin, Bonnard, Loire châteaux, Rimbaud and the **Tel quel** poets, Gauloise smoke, intense conversation, sleepness nights, bistro meals, **le fromage du pays,** and **vin du pays.** One night after too much **vin rouge** they had all piled into a big bed on the third floor of a cheap hotel in Blois, but nothing much had happened except for fumbling and laughter and Willy's silent observation that Tom Hartland's kisses tasted of honey and salt. Tom and Willy had been reading each other's work for years, and they had their first acceptances—he with Scholastic, she with Little, Brown—within the same two-month period.

Now, leaning forward in the ugly hotel chair with his elbows on his knees and his fingers steepled before him, he resembled the grown-up version of Teddy Barton, his brave and clever boy detective, steadfast, concerned, ready to be of use.

"For example," Willy said, "I know I spent the rest of the night in my office with the door locked. For a while I couldn't really **think.** I just paced around the room, scared out of my mind, trying to work out some kind of plan. On their way out the Santolinis yelled through the door that they had to come back the next day. All I really wanted to do was get in my car and run away, but I only had about thirty dollars on me. I needed more cash, because I thought I'd have to be wary about using ATM machines."

"Good thinking," Tom said. "If you're going

to run away, never use cash machines and throw away your cell phone. But flight isn't a solution, it's a delaying action."

"You said the Baltic Group was the definition of evil!"

"They line their pockets in corrupt ways; they're not a cabal of serial killers."

"You didn't see those pictures."

"There could be a lot of explanations for them, Willy." She turned her head on the pillows to give him a dark look. Tom said, "Of course, one of the explanations would be that he is a sick, homicidal fuck."

"That's more like it."

"Another one would be that he was involved in internal investigations of those incidents."

" 'Incidents'? They were **murders,** Tom."

"All the more reason for Baltic to cover itself." This time the look in Willy's eye was of a gloomy intensity. He said, "One thing I can do for you is to play devil's advocate here. But as you must know, basically I'll do anything you want. However, I do have something to say to you, and you're going to have to listen to me."

"What is it?"

"I'll tell you when you're done."

"It's important?"

"Yes. It is to me."

"Tell me now."

"When you're through with your story, Willy."

"Okay, but you're a jerk. All right. I told you I spent the night in my office, right?"

He nodded.

"Have you ever tried to fall asleep when you're scared out of your mind? Besides that, I realized that I'd trapped myself in that office, so stupid stupid stupid. I could have run out as soon as I saw the pictures, but after that, Giles would know I'd probably seen them, know what I mean? And he wouldn't **dream** of letting me leave the estate until Mitchell got home. So I had to get out early in the morning, when those two creeps might not be waiting for me. Anyhow, at least I had plenty of time to think.

"Mitchell and I had our own checkbooks, naturally, but he had just had me transfer most of my accounts to the little bank in Hendersonia, and I had no idea what kind of cash I had available. What I wanted to do was clean him out, if I could, and take his money with me. I didn't think I really **could** do that, but anyhow. It was worth a try, wasn't it?"

"What did you do?" Tom asked.

"I managed to get out, for one thing. I had a little suitcase with some clothes in it, and this white leather bag, like a duffel bag, that Mitchell gave me once, that I was going to use for the money. It was like five-thirty in the morning. I went downstairs without seeing a soul. Then I got in my car and took off for Hendersonia. **They** weren't following me; they weren't even up yet. I drove into the Pathmark parking lot and fell asleep, out of sheer exhaustion. Just before the bank opened, I called and asked for Mr. Bender, the president. I told him my husband was out of town and I needed a lot of cash in a hurry, so what could he do for me? You have to understand, all this time I am barely keeping myself under control."

"You were beginning to feel how angry you were."

"And **scared**! I was just improvising, I don't really know what I wanted to do." She scooted backward on the bed and sat up with her back against the headboard. "So this Bender guy tells me that he's been thinking of arranging a meeting between us for some time, and he'd like me to come in that morning."

Willy gave Tom a look he could feel at the base of his spine.

"And the next thing I know, I'm **there,** in his office. Remember when I said that I knew I locked myself in my office? Well, that's why I said it."

"I don't quite get you."

"Tom, it's just like yesterday. Don't you remember **anything**? I lost two and a half hours between the Met and the St. Regis! And afterward, the whole trip back to New Jersey disappeared. I'm getting in the car, boom, I'm standing on our lawn in Hendersonia. There's no transition—East Fifty-fifth Street, Guilderland Road, one right after the other."

Tom's gaze deepened.

"Weird, huh? As if I needed any more **weird** shit in my life. So the same thing happens all over again, and I'm not in my car anymore, I'm in Mr. Bender's office, and evidently I just got there, because he's waving me toward a chair and telling me he's glad I could come in on such short notice."

"It's your selective amnesia."

"It's more like the in-between stuff never happened. Like it was just left out. Anyhow, here's this portly guy with glasses and a bald head, and it strikes me that he looks a little nervous. Right away, I know—**Mitchell** makes him nervous. And the first thing he says to me is that he's very happy I brought Mitch Faber back to his hometown."

For it turned out that Mitchell Faber had been born and raised in Hendersonia. He had been on the local high school's football team, and after graduation he'd gone to Seton Hall, but college had not worked out all that well, and in his second year he had enlisted in the army and qualified for Special Forces. His father, Henderson Faber, one of **the** Hendersons and a very, very important man in not only the town but that whole section of New Jersey, was happy to see him launched in a career in the military. Because Mitch had always been a bit wild. If truth be told, his father's influence was the reason some of the boy's escapades never went any farther than they did. Military service channeled his aggression and made a man of him.

What did the father do? Oh, he owned an auto-repair shop, but that didn't cover half of it. Mr. Faber was a powerful man. He had a hand in almost every business in the county. In fact, Mr. Faber had been instrumental in founding the Continental Trust of New Jersey, the very bank they were in at that moment. Unfortunately, Mitch's dad had died of a gunshot wound six, seven years back. Unknown assailant.

"His father was murdered?" Tom said. "Was he some kind of gangster?"

"Hang on," Willy said. "We're still getting to the good stuff."

The bank was very grateful for all the business Mr. Faber and Ms. Patrick had brought to it, Mr. Bender said. Of course, with the gentleman's connections to the institution a great degree of trust came into play, mutual trust he hoped he could say, and excellent customers such as Ms. Patrick, soon to be wed to the son of a sort of "silent partner" at the inception of that institution, could be granted a degree of latitude not permitted the general public. With that said, and Mr. Bender wished most heartily that his concerns should not be taken amiss, it would be less than perfectly responsible if the chief officer of a banking institution did not seek independent verification of financial arrangements said to be established between account-holding couples. For example. Let us say a significant sum of money has been transferred between accounts, and agreements exist to establish similar transfers of funds at regular intervals, said agreement to have been signed right on Mr. Bender's desk here by one of the parties, then taken away by that party for the secondary signature to be affixed at a separate location. In such a case, Mr. Bender trusted that the question of verification would be seen as a simple formality entered into for the purpose of dotting all the **i**'s and crossing all the **t**'s.

And with that verbal flourish, the nervous Mr. Bender withdrew from a file on his desk an agreement that transferred an immediate $200,000 from various of Willy's shiny new accounts into Mitchell's savings account, and thereafter moved half that amount from hers to his on the first of each month for the next eight months. This document bore two signatures, Mitchell's and one that came pretty close to Willy's hasty scribble.

"I don't believe it," Tom said.

"He forged my signature on a document that moved one million dollars from my accounts into his over the next eight months."

"I mean, I do believe it, but it's incredible. How did he explain it to the banker?"

"He told him that I was nervous about investing money, and wanted him to do it for me. He said after we were married, we were going to have joint accounts anyhow."

"Were you?"

"Do you think Mitchell ever discussed finances with me? It was taken for granted that he had tons of money. He certainly acted like a rich man—he bought me a Mercedes! With my money, it looks like. I guess I bought his Mercedes, too."

"Willy, how much money do you have in that crappy little bank, anyhow?"

"Around three million," she said. "Most of it was from Jim's estate. If Baltic paid that kind of money to Jim, I thought Mitchell would earn pretty much the same thing."

"Mitchell must be a long way down the totem pole. What did the banker do when you told him your signature was forged?"

"I thought he was going to commit hari-kari. You know the funny thing? He always knew there was something fishy about that agreement. He was afraid of Mitchell. Mitchell intimidated him. I bet Mitchell intimidated everyone in Hendersonia. And the arrangement didn't take any money away from his bank, it just moved it around a little, so he didn't ask any questions. He apologized for about half an hour and begged me to let him make things right."

Tom laughed. "He's been 'making things right' all afternoon. I bet his shredder's seen a lot of use."

Willy drew up her knees and wrapped her arms around them. To Tom, in the low light of the bedside lamp, she looked, at first, only a few years older than the mysterious girl he had met in 1985; then he saw the fine lines around her mouth and the faint tracery under her eyes and, although he had never before thought of her in these terms, that she was one of the most distinguished women he knew.

"And of course another way he could make things right was to grease the wheels for your withdrawal. How much money did you walk out with?"

"A hundred thousand."

"Jesus Christ." He half-rose from the chair and looked at the floor on the other side of the bed, then at the closet door.

"It's in the closet. I didn't know where else to put it. A thousand hundred-dollar bills makes a pretty big stack."

"I've never been in a room with that much money before."

"Mr. Bender told me I could come back tomorrow and get another hundred thousand, but I don't think I should do that."

"No," Tom said. "What did you do after you left the bank?"

"I almost killed Roman Richard Spilka, that's what I did. I got out of the bank, and I was walking toward my car, holding one of my bags and rolling the other one along behind me, and in pulls Mitchell's car, with Giles driving and Roman Richard sitting beside him. All of a sudden, I felt like this horrible, reeking cloud of **villainy** was all around me. . . . I couldn't **see,** I could barely **breathe**. . . . Aah!"

Willy threw out her arms and waved them violently in front of her, as if she were trying to shake off spiderwebs or frighten away a bat. Her eyes were wild and out of focus. She kept uttering **aah!** in a small, stifled voice that went higher and higher. Scattered tears flew from her eyes.

Tom jumped off the chair, stretched out on the bed beside her, and put his arms around her. At first, it was like holding a trapped animal, but after a few terrible seconds in which Tom felt his own self-control begin to waver under her assault, Willy ceased to thrash in his arms and pound her fists against his back. He stroked her head, saying her name over and over. Eventually, she sagged against him, as limp as if she were boneless. She said, "Ooooooohh, just hold me for a while, okay?"

"Try and stop me," he said.

Sometime later, Willy groaned and separated herself from him. "I said something about a cloud of evil, and all of a sudden it was literal, a literal cloud, all sticky and foul. . . ." She chafed her hands together, wiping off imagined gumminess.

"It was 'villainy,' not 'evil,'" Tom said. "A 'reeking cloud of villainy.' I thought that was pretty good. You know, you have a certain way with words. Ever think about becoming a writer?"

She groaned again, this time with a touch of self-mimicry. "I never got to the part where I almost killed that fat pig, Roman Richard. So they're in the car, and I'm close to mine, right?"

"Right."

"Giles puts on his brakes, but I keep going. When I'm tossing my bags into the back seat, Giles and Roman Richard are both getting out of the car. Giles says, 'You left home pretty early this morning, Willy.' I say, 'Isn't that allowed these days?' They're both walking toward me, but slow, like this is just an ordinary conversation on an ordinary day. I didn't know if Giles had gone in and seen the pictures, and if he did, he doesn't know if **I** did. 'No need to worry about me,' I said, and I got in behind the wheel. Now they're walking a little faster. Giles says, 'Hold on, Willy,' and we look at each other, and bang, he sees that I know, and I see that he sees, and now we're not playing games anymore. Giles yells, 'Stop her!' to Roman Richard, and they both come running. I got my car started just in time, and I turned the wheel and jammed the pedal, and the car just **shot** forward. Then Roman Richard was right in front of me, and there was a kind of a soft thump, and off he flew to the side. I hit him, all right."

"How do you know you didn't kill him?"

"I don't even think I hurt him all that much. I looked in the rearview mirror and saw him getting up. He sure was mad, though."

She pushed herself a bit farther away on the bed, picked up his right hand with both of hers, raised it to her mouth, and kissed it. She flattened the palm of his hand against her cheek. "You were wonderful to come here and tend to me. I hope you won't mind if I tell you I love you."

"I was just thinking the same," Tom said.

Willy placed his hand on the bedspread and patted it. "Now I have to go into the bathroom and wash my face."

He patted her hip as she swiveled sideways to get off the bed. For a second, sexual interest raised its head, and Tom was astonished for the second it took him to imagine that, at one level below consciousness, she had just reminded him of his first lover, slight, brilliant Hiro, who had relieved him of his virginity in his sophomore year. Then he thought, **No, it's Willy, I can't believe it, she's turning me on. What's happening to me?**

Sounds of running water came from the bathroom. "Really, Tom, I'm so grateful you're here," she called out.

"Me, too. Willy, didn't they follow you?"

"I got away too fast. The bank is only half a block from the expressway, and by the time they got themselves organized, I could have gone in either direction. They probably guessed that I came to New York, but I don't see how they could know where I am." She appeared in the bathroom doorway, wiping her face with a small white towel. "I just hope I'm not getting you into any trouble."

"Don't worry about me. I don't suppose there's any way he can find out you're in this hotel, is there?"

"Molly once told me that the Baltic people can find anything out, but after all, we're talking about Mitchell, not the whole company. And he's still in France."

"How did you check in here? Did you use a credit card?"

"As far as the hotel is concerned, I'm W. Bryce. That's the name on my AmEx card. Jim Patrick told me to do that when I applied for the card. Actually, Jim made out the application, and he told me that was the name he wanted me to use. We hardly ever took the AmEx cards out of our wallets, though. When we paid with plastic, we usually used Master-Card."

Willy was drawing the towel over first one hand, then the other, staring at the moving towel, as if she expected something to slip out from beneath it. She glanced at Tom.

"I figured it was about some accounting riga-marole, because we got the American Express cards through a service division of his company. It was like we got reduced rates, or something like that."

"Did the bills come through the company, or directly to you?"

"They came straight to us. I used to write the checks. But like I said, we almost never used those cards." She stopped moving the towel across her hands. "That wasn't an idle question, was it?"

Tom shook his head.

"You think he was trying to protect me."

"I think he was probably covering his ass."

"My ass, you mean." Willy flipped the towel into the bathroom. "He knew something was wrong. **Damn** him. What kind of company are they, anyhow? Oh, as if that hasn't become transparently clear. But Jim was such a nice man, and such a smart man, too—he was kind, you know? Do you suppose he had Holly with him to keep her safe? To protect her from being kidnapped?"

Tom was looking straight at her, giving nothing away.

"All this **stuff** is going through my head! Did I tell you that I almost broke into a produce warehouse because I was sure Holly was imprisoned inside it? I could hear her calling for me! I knew my daughter was dead, but I couldn't stop myself—I got out of the car, fully intending to break a window and climb in. I swear to you, Tom, sometimes it feels as though I am being **made** to do things. Like I'm a marionette, and someone else is pulling the strings."

Wild-eyed again, she held her arms straight up and wiggled them as though they were controlled by puppet strings. Tom stood up, hesitated, then saw from the tragic expression on her face that she was close to losing herself again. He moved across the room and pulled her to his chest.

"I think you should have a little vodka," he said. "While you're at it, I'll have one, too."

He opened the minibar, removed two miniature bottles of Absolut, took two lowball glasses from the top of the cabinet, set them down on the table, and told Willy he would be back in a minute with some ice. "You're like Superman," she said. "No, I think you are Superman."

He returned almost as quickly as he had promised, and in another minute they were seated across from each other, Willy on the side of the bed and Tom back in the nubbly chair, raising glasses filled with ice cubes and a clear liquid.

"To you," Willy said. "My anchorage, my port in the storm."

"To us," Tom said. "We'll go crazy together."

Willy took a sip of the vodka, winced, and shook her head. "My port in the storm has a terrible effect on my character. I hardly ever drink, except for when I'm with you. Then there's the swearing. What's next, we take up smoking?"

He took a swallow. "What's next is, we figure out a way to go to the police. What would Teddy Barton do? We need proof that you're being followed, assuming that you are. Good old Teddy would round up a little band of boys, and some of them would create a diversion while another one takes a picture of the bad guys. We can't organize the little band, but there's a cheap little camera in the minibar. If someone's following you, I could take a photograph of them and we could take it to the police. And just to be safe, you ought to leave this hotel in the morning and check in somewhere else. Somewhere a little obscure, like the Mayflower."

"The Mayflower?"

"It's a nice little hotel near the foot of Central Park West. What time did you get here, anyhow?"

"About nine-thirty."

"And when did you leave Hendersonia?"

"Something like ten in the morning. You

know, I haven't had a thing to eat all day. This vodka is going to do me in." She placed her glass on the bedside table.

"And the time in between ten in the morning and nine at night?"

"Gone, mainly. I can remember driving across the G.W. bridge, but that's it. It was daytime, and then it was night. I was on the bridge, I was parked in front of this hotel. It's not that I forgot the time in between, it's that it never happened. Those hours happened in your life, but they didn't in mine."

"I don't know what to say to that."

"Then don't say anything. I want to order some room service. Are you hungry? Could you eat anything?"

"No, but please order something, Willy. You have to eat."

She called room service and ordered a hamburger without French fries and a Diet Coke. "I guess I can start to relax now, sort of. It's strange, I don't have the faintest beginning of a plan of what to do next, but for some reason I'm not really worried about it. I think the next thing will happen, and then the thing after that, and I'll find out where I'm going when I get there."

She collapsed back on the bed and gave him a

look of flat inquiry. "Didn't you have something you were going to say to me?"

"I did, yes," Tom said. "But I'm going to hold off. This isn't the time to bring it up."

" 'Bring it **up**'? Uh-oh. This is pretty serious, isn't it, pretty grim."

"Well, it's serious. Tomorrow, maybe. If you want to see me tomorrow, that is."

"Want to see you tomorrow? I don't want you to leave, Tom. I want you to spend the night here. With me. Please."

"That's probably a good idea," he said. "I'll sleep on the floor."

"No, you won't," Willy said. "You're going to sleep in this bed, right alongside me. That way, if time gets taken away again, it'll happen to you, too."

17

From Timothy Underhill's journal

Before I deal with my unhappiness with what I've been doing in my new book, I really have to write about what has been going on around here. In the midst of all this stuff I'm about to describe, I somehow feel a kind of gathering clarity—the sense is not that I'm beginning to understand it all, because I'm not, rather that one day I am **going to** understand it, and that feels like enough. Enough, certainly, to keep me from another visit to the Austen Riggs therapeutic community in Stockbridge, Mass., and kindly Dr. B., although after 9/11/01, I was entirely grateful to spend sixty days in their care.

Ever since "Cyrax" filled the mysterious blue box on my screen with page after page of instruction, advice, and what he thought of as explanations, events have been conspiring to make me imagine, very much against my will, that some of what he told me might be true. And if I can feel part of a larger pattern, a **huge** pattern, incorporating a multiplicity of worlds filled with entities like sasha, zamani, and towering angels with names like WCHWHLLDN, the individual events themselves become less inexplicable. Hardly less threatening, though, because I am about 90% sure that yesterday afternoon, while I was taking a long, slow walk back from Ground Zero after my first visit there, Jasper Kohle tried to murder me.

I eventually noticed that I had wandered over to West Broadway. As always, it was crowded with people young, middle-aged, and old hastening up and down the sidewalks, crossing the street in the middle of the block, lingering in the doorways of shops, and haranguing someone just out of sight. Great vivid balloons of color sparked and floated by, advertisements, the sides of buses, neon flashing, an unforgettable face seen through a taxi window, all the usual riot south of Canal Street. As ever, Manhattan seemed to have produced an inexplicable number of men whose jobs involved surging along the pavement and yelling into mobile phones. I was glowering at one of these Masters of the Universe when I caught a quick, furtive movement reflected in the window of the little

Thai restaurant behind him. Whatever it was, it seemed **wrong**—a sudden, sneaky dodge into concealment, a movement that had no real beginning and no real end, only an abrupt lateral shift from one obscurity into another. Then the asshole shouting into his hand moved on, and the restaurant window reflected only the kids from NYU and a homeless guy and the bright taxis rushing down West Broadway. When I stepped forward, so did the homeless guy, and with a flash of shock I realized that I was looking at myself. Evidently, I hadn't paid much attention to what I was wearing when I left home. My old gray sweatshirt looked all wrong under the blazer I had wrestled myself into on my way out the door. The blazer itself appeared to have come from some charitable agency. The blue jeans, the sweatshirt, and the soft, almost shapeless loafers on my feet were the most comfortable clothes I owned, and on days when I wanted to get through a lot of work, they sort of slipped onto my body by mutual agreement, as if they, too, had a job to do. When the shock of recognition faded, I looked again for what was **wrong,** but it had concealed itself within the scene around me.

It seemed probable that Jasper Dan Kohle was still intent on punishing me for failing to write "I yam what I yam" in his book, or for the flaws in my writing, or whatever was bugging him. I kept glancing over my shoulder and looking at the reflections in plate-glass windows as I proceeded up the street. To draw him out of cover, I turned corners and crossed streets in the middle of the block.

I turned off Sixth Avenue at Thompson Street, still with the feeling that someone was following me. I quickened my pace. At my back, it seemed, an unclean spirit capered along, dancing, jigging, bopping in its glee at having me so close at hand. Not looking over my shoulder was one of the most difficult things I've ever done. When I could, I shot brief glances into the ghostly mirrors provided by windows, and saw only the ordinary street traffic of the Village. Mothers pushed strollers that looked like either phaetons or **Jetsons** vehicles, fiftyish New York frizz-heads waved their hands in conversation as they ambled along, a few underfed kids lip-synched to their iPods. The feeling of being shadowed clung to me as I hastened toward home.

At Grand Street I turned right and moved toward West Broadway. More people filled the sidewalks, and all of them looked as though they had been born to appear on Grand Street at precisely that moment. I mean, they looked **at home** in a way I knew I did not. I realized

that I no longer had the feeling of being followed, but neither did I feel at ease.

Before I reached the corner, a slash of the blue
of a Wedgwood plate—a mild English blue, an
Adams blue, an Alice blue!—caught my eye,
and my heart surged into my throat even before
I realized that I was looking across the street at
my sister, gorgeous unbeautiful April. Fists on
her hips, she stood glaring at me within a small
circular space of her own making. The people
who approached her made an unconscious ad-
justment at about four feet away and swerved to
pass behind her. She was a little blue fire, a blaze
of blue and yellow. If you got too close, she'd
singe your eyebrows off. I stopped moving
so abruptly that a woman with a nose ring, a
sleeveless black leather jacket that showed a
lot of tattoos, and Paki-basher boots bumped
against my back. She called me an ignorant turd
and tried to dust me off the pavement with her
fingertips. Without taking my eyes from April,
I said, "Sorry." Acting on an impulse I neither
understood nor questioned, I placed my hand
just above her hip and pushed her away. She
flailed back, swearing at me.

April was on the verge of spitting out lightning bolts. She took her right hand from her
hip, held it out fingers extended, and swept it
two decisive feet to her left, telling me to move

backward. After I had taken two steps back, then another, April returned her hand to her hip and lifted her chin. She appeared to be gazing at the sky above my side of the street.

I looked up and saw a speck tumbling through the air. The speck got bigger as it fell. Far overhead, a dark little head peered down from the top of the nearest building. I staggered backward another couple of steps and yelled, "Look out!" Six feet away, the woman with the nose ring whirled around and opened her mouth to screech something at me. An object moving too fast to be identified cut through the air between us and smacked into the pavement with a hard, flat, ringing sound over a dull undertone faintly like cannon fire. Stony chips flew upward in a gritty haze.

"Fucking hell!" the woman yelled. "Are you **kidding** me?"

I looked across the street at the place where April had been, then up at the edge of the roof, where the dark little head was pulling back out of sight. On the sidewalk, a broken concrete block rested in the pothole it had made on impact. Cracks and fractures crazed the entire section of pavement where the block had fallen.

"Did you actually **hear** that?" the woman shouted at me.

I said nothing.

"Did you? Is that why you pushed me away?" For the first time I realized that she had an English accent.

"Something like that," I said. People had started to crowd in, pointing at the sidewalk, pointing at the sky.

She pulled a cell phone from a zippered pocket. "I'm calling 911. We'd be dead now, if you didn't have ears like a fucking bat."

An hour later, a bored police lieutenant named McMenamin was telling me Jasper Dan Kohle had never served in the armed forces, never voted, never taken out a library card, never bought property or contracted to use the services of a telephone company. He had no passport or driver's license. He didn't have an address or any credit cards. He didn't own a car. He'd never been arrested, or even fingerprinted. It also appeared that he had never been born. With that, Lieutenant McMenamin ordered me out of his station.

18

From Timothy Underhill's journal

Yesterday I spent so much time on an entry about what happened after I left Ground Zero that I never got around to what I thought was going to be my principal topic, what's happening with my work. Today I am determined to put some of this down on paper, because doing that should help me think about what I'm doing—really, what my protagonist is doing, and how I am handling it—but before I get to the main subject, I ought to describe my recent dealings with my brother.

My brother's reaction to his son's disappearance damn near drove me crazy. At the earliest possible moment, he gave up all hope. He resigned himself to the **supposition** that Mark was dead. In another person, that might have been realistic; for Philip, the murder of hope was self-protective. He couldn't bear to live with anxiety and uncertainty, so he willingly embraced devastation, thereby killing his son in his own heart. I **couldn't take that,** I **hated** it. It felt like a betrayal. Philip **chose** to give up on the boy, and I wasn't sure I could ever forgive him for the sheer lazy selfishness of his choice. I certainly had no interest in talking to him or spending time with him during the months when my grief was at its peak. The two times he called me—amazingly, for I can't remember his ever doing this before—instead of talking about anything personal, he wanted to tell me about certain errors and inconsistencies he had discovered in the bound galleys of my new book. Maybe for him that was personal.

Then came the news that in mid-September, he was going to marry a woman named China Beech, a born-again Christian behind whose previous job description of "exotic dancer" I was sure I discerned a stripper. In a way, it was touching. This tedious, pot-bellied, fifty-three-year-old man with thinning hair and a boring job had been so hypnotized by his tawdry girlfriend that he wanted to seize happiness with both hands and clasp it to his intoxicated breast. What erotic feats China Beech must have inspired in him, what unexplored territories must have opened up before him, all moist, yielding, ready to be conquered! For these services, Ms. Beech would be compensated with the use of an unspectacular but sturdy little house, access to a vice principal's salary, and the kind of respectability valued by the newly Born-Again.

I had always liked and respected Nancy, Mark's mother. Her suicide had felt like a wound. My brother should have taken more time before deciding to remarry. In typical Philip fashion, he had wrapped up his grief in resentment and tossed the whole package overboard. With the onset of China Beech, nice, kind, loyal Nancy Underhill had been escorted deeper into the Underworld, a kind of premature zamani. In fact, I thought this was exactly what Pop had done after April was killed. He wanted to forget her, to erase her traces from his life, and after the funeral, he never spoke her name or acknowledged that she had existed.

My book tour brings me to Millhaven right around the time of Philip's wedding, September 12, and if I am to attend the ceremony, as I suppose I must, I have only to extend my stay there a couple of days, but I cannot say that I feel particularly well-disposed toward the bride and groom.

The first of my telephone calls from Philip came three days ago, that is, about a month after the receipt of the typo-riddled e-mail that announced his upcoming marriage. The message from Cyrax berating me for having lost all civility and kindness had prompted me to think about calling my brother, in fact to gaze at the telephone for extended periods when I should have been working, and when I picked up the receiver and heard his voice speaking my name I had a second's worth of resentment that he had beaten me to the punch.

"Hey, Tim," he said. "How are you doing? I just wanted to check in. How's the new book coming along?"

With these harmless words, Philip broke two lifelong traditions: he spontaneously inquired about my well-being, and he displayed or at least feigned an interest in my work. It threw me so far off balance that my first response was to suspect that he wanted to ask me for money. Philip has never asked me for money, not once, not even in the years when my income must have been ten times his.

I mumbled something innocuous.

"Yesterday I saw your name in print. New Leaf Books sends out a newsletter once a month, and they have you down for a reading two days before the wedding. China and I sure hope you'll be able to come see us get hitched."

Come see us get hitched? Who was this stranger? My brother didn't talk like that.

"Of course I'll be there. I changed my tickets so I fly out the day after the ceremony." When the moment had come, I discovered myself incapable of saying "your wedding." "I thought you already knew."

"Well, I don't think you were ever very specific about it. But I know, your schedule must get pretty complicated when you're out on tour and all that. We're just really happy to hear that you'll be able to make it. After all, you're my only brother. In fact, you're all the family I've got, Tim, and I want you to know how important that is to me."

"Philip, is that really you? I don't know who the hell I'm talking to."

He laughed. "We're not getting any younger, bro. We gotta get straight with ourselves, with our families, and with God."

All of this had to be decoded. **We're not getting any younger** was pure Philip, who cherished clichés. **Bro,** on the other hand, came from some other planet. Where the part about getting straight with God came from was no mystery.

"This girl seems to have had a tremendous effect on you," I said.

"Why China's willing to marry a dull old fogy like me I'll never know, but I guess she saw something in me! And of course she pulled me out of the worst year I've ever had. After you went back to New York, I more or less fell apart. It was terrible. Nancy and Mark both gone. My life, wow, it was a smoking ruin. I reacted so badly to everything, I made the situation worse. I don't know if you picked up on this, but I was very, very angry at Nancy."

"That would have been hard to miss," I told him.

"I'm sorry for the way I must have acted. I can hardly remember any of that time now. It was so dark! Was I awful to be with? I'm sure I was. Please, if you can, forgive me for being such a selfish pig."

He had so astonished me that I hardly knew how to reply. All sorts of internal calibrations had to happen before words that seemed at least reasonably suited to the situation came to me. "Philip, you don't need my forgiveness, but I find it very moving that you should ask for it. Of course I forgive you, if that's what you want."

"Thank you," he said. "Now say hello to China. Here she is."

Immediately, a warm alto voice seemed to fill the receiver. "Tim, is that really you? It's such a pleasure to talk to you! And we're both so happy that you'll come to our wedding."

"Well, I wouldn't miss it," I said.

"All your brother needed was for someone to look past the lobster act and find the real person in there," she continued.

In the background, I could hear Philip shouting, "Hell, I hardly knew I **was** a real person!"

To which I can only reply, Hell, I hardly knew you were, either. For years and years I've been kind of going on faith that something like "a real person" was lurking under Philip's terrible persona, but that faith had been eroded almost to the point of disappearance. If this China Beech can unearth the happier, more sensitive man I hoped lived within my brother, I've been misjudging her ever since the first time I heard her name.

Now to get to the other topic, the one I've been avoiding.

I fear I'm on the verge of letting the crazy events in my life leak into my fiction. Jasper Kohle, my sister, Cyrax . . . if I put this stuff into the book no one on earth is going to think it comes straight out of my life; the real challenge is to make it fit in with the material already present. Surely there would be some way to insert WCHWHLLDN and little Alice in Wonderland into my girl's adventures, especially once she hits the road. Maybe that's what I'm supposed to do!—feed the whole mishmash of e-mail from dead people, along with a pissed-off angel, pissed-off Jasper Kohle (the Dark Man?), and Cyrax into this flight-from-Bluebeard narrative. It wouldn't be the book I set out to write, but I've begun to lose faith in that book anyhow.

When I look again at the chapter I finished last week, its information seems to come out in too great a rush—within a space of fifteen pages, two separate kinds of treachery are revealed. We have to get this information, it sets up her flight from the villain & her discovery of the truth behind what she imagines to have been her life, but I have the unhappy feeling that the download time is too fast here. The fault may lie in the presentation, which consists nearly 100% of conversation. How far can I push the conventions that automatically come into play when you have two people talking alone in a room? That is, how much of the scene has to be about **them,** and how much of it can it be stretched out to accommodate the information they bring into that room? Drag in too much exterior stuff, and you've got a soap opera on your hands.

Or maybe it's just that the scene is inert, and I'll have to go back and write the whole thing out in chronological order. The storm, the photos, the bank, the return to the house, the lost hours, and the arrival at the hotel. **Then** the conversation with Tom—but if we've already seen what our heroine has been through, why have the scene at all? The whole point of getting Tom into the hotel room was to set him up for the scene that comes immediately after this one. And **there** I thought I got things right, for a change.

The elements seemed to fall together in a way that created a lot of emotion, as well as tension, if I say so myself. We've established the love between Willy and Tom (and, in fact, for some reason I found myself noticing a little sexual attraction between them, a kind of spark that surprises the two of them only a little more than it surprised me), which I think adds something to Tom in our eyes, so that we are swayed by his opinions—or at least want his view of things to be accurate. Tom is generous, loving, attentive, he has a sense of humor, and—most important of all—he's slightly skeptical when Willy goes into one of her rants about Mitchell.

At the same time, the possibility that Giles might have tracked her to the hotel quietly speeds up the pace while Willy and Tom wind up deciding to relocate to the hotel Tom had mentioned the previous night, the Mayflower, on Central Park West.

Another bit of unresolved business also keeps

the scene taut—along with Willy, we're wondering what this dire **thing** is that Tom says he
has to tell Willy. It must be important, it must
even be crucial, but Tom clearly feels that his
message, to call it that, will have an unhappy effect on Willy, and he's waiting for the proper
moment. Tom was even hoping she had forgotten about this thing he wanted to say to her, but
no such luck; at some level she's wondering
about this matter throughout their morning together, and therefore our reader wonders, too.
What in the world is Tom being so cautious
about telling Willy?

And I have to say that I am pleased with the
way the sexual tension, also completely unresolved, plays through the scene. At first we
think, Okay, they're handling it very well, especially since it can't really go anywhere. Anyhow,
this hardly seems like the optimum moment
for the kind of sexual exploration that would
necessarily have to go on. But, aha, Willy is
too wound up to fall asleep. She's anxious and
frightened, and she is quite aware that her pal
Tom is only faking sleep, and, what's worse, doing it for her sake. And how can she know that
he is also having hours of time subtracted from
his life unless she and Tom are more or less
holding hands?

So they reach out and grasp each other's hand,

which immediately feels like a tremendous, almost shocking intimacy. And although Willy soon tells Tom that she is so frightened that she would like him to put his arms around her, if he wouldn't object too much, that is, and Tom replies, "Oh, sweetie, no problem," and slides across to meet her in the middle of the bed and folds her into his arms so that her lovely head weighs lightly on his chest, the moment when their hands first touched so greatly retains its startling erotic power that this greater, in fact far more intimate, contact seems merely an extension of that first moment of touching. They are both in their underwear, and cannot but be intensely conscious of each other's body. Tom feels that his primary duty is to keep his beloved friend warm, for he believes that warmth will calm her fears, and he circles her small torso with his arms, her slim, straight left leg brushing his thicker, more solid right. From Tom's body, which indeed is warm, Willy absorbs peace, comfort, quietude; the slow, measured quality of his breathing, the sweet rise and fall of his chest bring her a degree of relaxation indistinguishable from a slow, spreading, involuntary physical pleasure. What she had needed all along, it came to her, was not a sexual dynamo like Mitchell but someone capable of giving her what Tom Hartland was so wholeheartedly supplying right now: a purring sensation, a feeling of slow, gentle, rhythmic humming that begins in the pit of her stomach and radiates out in all directions, delivering little blessings wherever it goes.

(I have to go back and insert some of this. It belongs in the book, not my journal.)

Anyhow, after all of that, Tom's murder in the next chapter should come as a real shock.

The reader should be anticipating some trouble at the Mayflower, I'm still not quite sure what, but I think it could begin with Monday morning and their exit from the new hotel. Tom H. is still present, of course. He wants to do everything he can to help Willy through what strikes him as a great, paranoid confusion, and if that involves shifting her from hotel to hotel, so be it, he'll shift with her and hold her hand. Along the way he'll do his damnedest to talk her into getting help.

They take the stairs, I think, although Tom says she's being absurdly overcautious.

They make their way down to the lobby, carrying their bags (Willy's bags), Willy starting at every noise and clutching Tom's arm whenever a door opens or closes elsewhere on the staircase. When they reach the bottom, they patrol through the lobby and turn the corner to the café. Willy abruptly comes to a stop, grabs his arm, and nods her head back toward the lobby, where an arm encased in a plaster cast and a wide, straight back that could well belong to Roman Richard Spilka is vanishing through an arch.

So the first thing Tom does is walk her to the back of the café and through the service doors into the kitchen. It's relatively calm in there, after breakfast and before lunch, and Tom explains that his friend Willy here has to hide from someone she doesn't want to see, someone like a stalker, while he goes and deals with the situation, is that okay?

"Certainly, sir, and while your friend is under our protection we'll show her how to make a really good veal Bolognese, one of our lunch specials today." And "Don't worry, she is in good hands, sir." The chef and line cooks are happy to have Willy in their realm. Or not. It doesn't matter very much; all I have to do is get her in the kitchen so that she can sneak out by a service door.

Tom says that he will go out and hail a cab. In the meantime, Willy should wait at the street entrance to the kitchen, and when she hears his taxi honk its horn, race out of the building and scramble into the cab. Then he'll figure out somewhere else to go. His place first, probably.

Out into the lobby he goes. Uh-oh, Roman Richard Spilka is planted on a couch, watching both the elevators and the hotel's entrance. Spilka gives him a glance and goes back to waiting for Willy. Tom checks out. (It's not important, but he'd used his credit card to check in, and they had called themselves Mr. and Mrs. Thomas Hartland.) Spilka ignores him.

Out on the sidewalk, Tom sees a languid-looking blond man in a silk sweater the color of a robin's egg engaged in deep conversation with a pair of uniformed policemen. If the man in the sweater is Giles Coverley, and Tom is pretty sure he is (for one thing, this dude looks exactly like he'd be named Giles Coverley; and for another, he matches her description of the guy more closely than an Identi-Kit image), Willy was all wrong about Giles being asexual—it's obvious to Tom that he's queer as a coot. Far more to the point, the cops are on **his** side, which probably means they are on Faber's. Maybe Faber is already back in America, back in New York! All of a sudden, the stakes are much higher. Tom thinks he'd better take Willy to the airport and get her on a flight to where, South America, as Mrs. Hartland? No, she'd need her passport, and flights are out of the question because you can't get on a plane these days without showing your driver's license to everybody but the pilot.

The cops and Giles Coverley glance at Tom without paying him any more attention than did Roman Richard. He steps up to the curb and raises his arm. It's pointless, there isn't a cab in sight, but the three men near the hotel's entrance make him nervous. He keeps imagining that they are staring at his back. He checks over his shoulder while trying to be nonchalant, but there's no way to be nonchalant and peer over your shoulder at the same time. When he looks back up the street, four cabs are coming toward him, three of them containing passengers and the fourth with its off-duty lights glowing.

The cabs go by and sweep into Columbus Circle. Tom looks back up the street and finds that two blocks away an old woman with a three-footed metal walker has appeared out of nowhere and parked herself, right arm raised, on the corner of Sixty-third Street. She is about four foot ten, and the top of the walker comes up to her breastbone.

He says, "Damn."

When he looks back over his shoulder, the policemen conferring with Giles Coverley take a moment to inspect him. Their interest still seems merely reflexive, but it spooks him. He's let them know that he is nervous, impatient, under stress, and consequently they have filed his image away in their mental circuits. He's sure that the panic radiating out of him will begin to tickle the cops' antennae in about a second and a half.

The ancient female midget two blocks up lowers her arm out of weariness. Arm up, arm down, it makes no difference, because there are no empty cabs rolling down Central Park West. If Tom could summon a taxi for the midget, he'd do it in a nanosec, almost as much for her sake as for his, but mostly to eliminate his competition.

Now he's afraid to look back and check out the policemen, but in a way he's also afraid not to, in case they might be strolling toward him.

Would you mind opening that bag, sir?

Excuse me, sir, but we couldn't help noticing that we seem to make you uncomfortable.

He can't find a taxi and he's afraid to look back—it's time to move along, Sunny Jim. With only the smallest of glances at the cops and Giles Coverley, who seems to be wrapping things up and on the verge of rejoining the bouncer-type guy in the cast, Tom spins around, glances at his watch to suggest that he is a traveler looking for a ride to La Guardia or

JFK, and marches down past the front of the hotel, crosses the street, walks straight past the much grander entrance to the Trump International Hotel, and turns right at the traffic-jammed edge of Columbus Circle. There he reverses direction and walks north on Broadway, backward, with his arm held up in the air. Flowing past him is a constant stream of private cars, interspersed with black Town Cars bearing wealthy gentlemen to their mysterious destinations, and many, many taxicabs charging uptown in search of handsome tips.

Sixty-second Street runs one-way in the wrong direction, west toward the Hudson River, not east toward Central Park. But halfway up the block a small miracle occurs, that of the arrival at the curb about ten feet south of his position of a new, SUV-like taxi, a Toyota Sienna with sliding doors, from one of which emerges a beautiful but stern young woman cradling the most bored-looking pussycat Tom Hartland has ever seen. The light goes on even before the door slides shut, and Tom trots forward, smiling. Both the beautiful young woman and the pussycat frown at him.

By now, he hopes, the cooks will have conducted Willy to the kitchen's back entrance.

The young woman completes closing the door even while Tom approaches, but she does not retreat. Nor does she alter the expression on her face, which hovers between dismay and disdain. The cat hisses, and squirms in her arms.

"I'm sorry," she says. "I'm in your way, aren't I?"

"Just a bit," Tom says. "Do you mind?"

The woman moves backward. As Tom opens the door, he is aware of her continuing scrutiny. She's still looking at him through the window when he has pulled himself onto the seat and closed the door.

"Go down Central Park West and turn right on Sixty-first Street," Tom says to the driver. The cab does not move. Tom waits, willing himself not to say, "Come on, come on."

They finally get through the light at Sixty-second Street, only to become mired in a tangle of taxis, cars, and moving vans oozing up Broadway with the alacrity of a slug crawling down a garden path. Tom pounds his knees, knowing the driver is not to blame. The people on the sidewalk move faster than the traffic.

These people make him feel uneasy, too. Some of them may be part of the plot against Willy; they may have been hired by Mitchell Faber to act as scouts and lookouts; Faber could have saturated the neighborhood with people hired to capture his runaway fiancée. It's too much, it's dizzying. Suddenly, Tom feels far out of his depth: he should be back in his apartment, working away at his new book about Teddy Barton and the suspicious goings-on in and behind the Time & Motion building on Fremont Avenue, Haleyville's commercial center. Teddy is getting close to understanding why Mr. Capstone was digging in his backyard at 11:00 P.M., and after he and Angel Morales sneak into the Time & Motion building and pick Mr. Capstone's lock, everything is going to come together in a hurry, meaning that in about six weeks, Tom will be able to send the 300-odd pages of **The Moon-Bird Menace** to his editor. Yet he must do whatever he can for Willy; he has to snatch her out of that hotel before Coverley and the guy with the broken arm get their hands on her. He must pull her out like a tooth, in one swift, powerful movement.

He'll have to get her out the service door, across the sidewalk, and into the taxi when Faber's goons and the police are looking in another direction. He should have set up a diversion, that's what clever Teddy Barton would have done, but he hadn't had enough time to plan anything, and now it is too late. He should never have left Willy's side. Instead of racing off to get a cab, he should have taken Willy over the rooftops or through the Mayflower's basement, or swapped clothes with two of the cooks and escaped that way.

Finally, the cab reaches Sixty-fourth Street, turns the corner, and navigates past a row of double-parked trucks. Next comes a heap of broken glass and twisted metal that appears to have fallen from the sky. That can't be true. It looks a little like it used to be a car. The men in dark suits and actual hats standing around it could easily be from Roswell or Quantico. These men check out the cab as it slides past. Tim is intensely aware of their scrutiny, which has the same stony neutrality as the masklike gaze of the woman carrying the inert pussycat. Such neutrality does not seem really neutral to him. It's like watching people cross an item off a list they have in their heads.

All right, there's that one, let's draw a line through his name.

It seems to him that the men examining his taxi have grouped themselves together to conceal the twisted heap behind them.

The driver turns onto Central Park West and says, "Did you see that, sir?" He is an Indian, and he has a musical accent. "I can promise you one thing, that you will never read a word about it in the newspapers. And yet it is an event I believe that would be of serious interest to a great many people in this country."

"That's the truth," Tom says. "Keep going until you get to Sixty-first Street, then turn right and go about thirty feet, I'll tell you exactly where. Stop and honk your horn. We're picking somebody up."

"Because do you understand why, sir? Because it is a conspiracy of silence!" the driver tells him. "I was born in Hyderabad, in India, sir, and I came to this country twenty-one years ago, and neither in India nor in this country are things what they appear to be. I am telling my wife every day, 'What you read in your newspaper is not true!' " He looks at Tom in the rearview mirror. "There will not be much waiting time, I hope."

"I hope there won't be any," Tom says.

"Now, those men we saw were government officials," the cabbie says. "But the names used by such men are never their real names. And when they die, it is as if they have disappeared completely from the face of the earth. What a thing it is, to live a life of lies and pass from the earth unrecognized. But the evil that they do amongst us in this life is repaid a thousandfold in the next."

In front of the Mayflower, the sidewalk is completely empty.

"Okay, here's where we turn," Tom says.

"Do you think I do not remember that you

wanted to turn right on Sixty-first Street? Do you think I have forgotten that I am to stop and honk my horn?" While he is making the turn, the cabbie twists sideways and glares at his thoughtless passenger.

"No, sorry," Tom says, scanning the street before them. Way up the block, a couple of guys he cannot quite make out are talking in front of one of the Florentine-style apartment buildings. The usual knot of pedestrians streams across the intersection with Broadway. A northbound patrol car zips by in a flash of white. The conditions look about as good as they could be.

"Where is it, exactly, that I am to stop, sir?"

Tom is keeping his eye on the dark, scratched-up surface of the service door. He imagines Willy crouched behind it with her ear cocked, fearful that he will never return.

"Okay, stop," Tom says.

"And I am to honk my horn now?"

"Yes," Tom says, a little more loudly than he intends.

The cabbie taps his horn, which emits a brief blatting noise.

"That's not much of a sound," Tom says. "Do it again." He slides open the heavy door and steps down out of the cab. He leans over and speaks through the opening he has made. "I mean it. Do it again."

The driver really leans on his horn, and the service door flies open. Out onto West Sixty-first Street tumbles Willy Patrick, scrambling to stay on her feet. She is carrying her suitcase and the duffel, and her white shirt glares like a flag.

"Oh, thank God," she says. "I was so **worried.**" She wobbles toward him. "Did you see them? Are they still around?"

"We'd better hurry." He grabs her arm to hold her steady, and reaches down with his other hand for the suitcase. The cab driver is watching all of this with glum, gathering suspicion.

"You won't believe this," Willy says, "but they really did teach me how to make veal Bolognese in there."

Tom pitches the money bag into the back of the cab and waits for Willy to step up and in. Now the cabbie is looking straight ahead and pointing toward the windshield.

When Tom looks up the street, he sees the two men who had been standing in front of an apartment entrance running pell-mell toward them, the larger of the two reaching under his jacket for what is probably not his wallet. It's an awkward business, because the man has a cast on his right arm, and he is forced to use his left hand, which makes reaching his holster difficult.

Standing beside Tom, Willy freezes. Tom tries

to push her into the cab, but has no luck until Roman Richard at last has extracted his pistol from its holster and begins to take aim. At the sight of the weapon in Roman Richard's massive hand, Willy vaults into the spacious back of the taxi, taking her suitcase with her.

"Come on, get in!" she screams, reaching out for Tom.

"Tom Hartland!" yells Giles Coverley. "Stop right now! If you do, my friend won't shoot. You're never going to get away, so you might as well cooperate."

The cab driver rams his vehicle into reverse, and Tom sees Willy lurching, bent over, toward the opening in the side of the vehicle. Her face seems to widen with panic.

Twenty feet down the otherwise empty street, Roman Richard Spilka steadies his left arm upon his plaster-encased right and squeezes the trigger. Flame seems to jump from the end of the barrel, and a low, flat **crack** widens out around the two running men and the reversing taxi. Tom Hartland sees a spatter of blood appear on Willy's dazzling shirtfront at the same moment what feels like a horse's hoof slams into his chest. Then the cab has flown backward past him, and he realizes that he is lying flat on his back with the impression that the taxi's door slid shut at the moment he hit the deck.

Another soft, minimalist explosion goes off in the air above him, and he says to himself, **Oh, a silencer, that makes a lot of sense.** Tom Hartland has written about silencers but never seen one, and he's sorry he did not get a better look. Willy's screaming, and the driver is cursing, presumably in some Indian dialect. Or would it be Gujarati? Tom has no idea. He regrets never having gone to Bombay or Hyderabad, he's sorry that he never learned even a little bit of the language. If he had, over the past ten or fifteen years he could have had lots of interesting conversations with cab drivers.

Directly above him, Roman Richard Spilka's immense body moves into the frame of unclouded sky and looms over him. Giles Coverley strolls into view. A lopsided frown disturbs the symmetry of his sleek face. "Did you really think we didn't know who you were?" he asks, as if this were a perfectly reasonable question.

"Dumb fuck," says Spilka, glaring down.

"Shoot him in the head, and we'll get his body off the street," Coverley says.

The entire top of Spilka's body tilts over like a derrick, and the pistol comes abruptly, enormously into view, allowing Tom Hartland to observe that the silencer has a decidedly homemade look about it. It occurs to him that he is miraculously not afraid, for which he is deeply grateful. He hopes Willy can get away from these monstrous men. The silencer flickers and jumps back, but Tom does not see it move, for he is already elsewhere, confused and astounded, trying to find his way, like all new sasha.

19

In a town called Haleyville, which is located in a kind of generic midwestern landscape with woods and streams and distant farms, a sixteen-year-old boy named Teddy Barton awakens to a world that has been altered in some subtle yet unmistakable fashion. The air seems somehow dull, the colors of his walls and bedclothes a tone darker than they had been. The big round clock on the table beside his bed says 6:10, so his parents are still asleep. Teddy wonders what his mom and dad will make of this peculiar change, which now that he has been taking it in for a minute or two seems not to be merely a matter of color and tone but of substance itself. Maybe the change doesn't go very deep, maybe it's more a matter of perception than anything external. In that case, Mom and Dad won't notice a thing. Teddy sort of hopes it will turn out that way. He has always been sharper, better at noticing things, than anyone around him, and he has noticed that in time people get so accustomed to new situations, new contexts, new furniture that they no longer register them, and life eventually seems unchanged all over again.

On the other hand, if his first impression is right, and the actual substance of the world has somehow changed, become quieter, duller, softer, less vital, Mom and Dad are going to notice it, too, and then something will have to be done. Mom is going to go around the house polishing and waxing like a demon (for although most of his friends' mothers have jobs that take them into downtown Haleyville every weekday, Mom, although once a famous stage actress in New York City, has settled down as an old-fashioned homemaker, albeit one with a lot of glamorous friends who drop in all the time), and Dad will charge down to the offices of the **Haleyville Daily,** where he is both editor and star reporter, and try to get to the bottom of this strange phenomenon.

Ordinarily, Teddy would feel that any new disturbance that enters his universe is bound to wind up in his hands. That's how it has always been: no sooner does something shady rear its head in Haleyville than Teddy Barton's fabulous intuition catches wind of it, and he's off like a shot, let the wicked beware! But it is a sacred law of life that disturbances enter Haleyville either one at a time or in secretly joined pairs, and for the past two weeks, Teddy has been working full-time on a baffling puzzle involving an enormous truck with the words MOON-BIRD painted on its flanks that has been appearing out back of the Time & Motion building at odd times of the day and that building's newest renter, a man named Mr. Capstone, who late at night goes out of his house on Marymount Street and digs a big hole in his backyard. This case already involves two elements, and they are **obviously** connected. There isn't room for a puzzle involving a sudden and universal decrease of energy.

Because that's what this feels like, Teddy realizes. It's as though electricity started running backward through all the wires in the world and went dribbling out of all the world's empty plugs.

He gets out of bed to look through his window, and it's true: everything in his neighborhood seems slightly drained of color and energy. He is looking at a weeping willow and wondering if the tree is saggier than it was yesterday when a tremendous reality, an enormous **fact,** occurs to him—that in some sense the world around him just died, and he must return to a previous world, one that until this moment he had always assumed to be identical to this and separated from it by only the passage of time.

In fact, Teddy realizes, nothing new is ever going to happen to him again. He will never figure out what Mr. Capstone was up to in his backyard, and the Moon-Bird truck will go forever unexplained. That door, and those beyond, are forever closed to him. From now on, he can go only backward, through older worlds, solving mysteries that have already been solved, and as if for the first time.

20

From Timothy Underhill's journal

Quivering with shock and terror, Willy is on her way across the Upper West Side of Manhattan, vibrating on one of the two back seats in the boxy Sienna piloted by Kalpesh Patel, a native of Hyderabad who refuses to stop or find a policeman because 1) he's scared and excited by the obvious connections between the FBI dudes and those guys who came running down West Sixty-first Street, shooting at his previous fare, and 2) well, Kalpesh Patel was borderline crazy to begin with, and now he's in overdrive. The woman weeping and trembling in the back of his cab has not given him a destination. If she did, he wouldn't go there on a bet—unless, of course, she were to say, "I'll give you a thousand dollars to take me to a top-secret government installation in the Sierra Nevadas," or something similar, in which case he would flip on his off-duty lights and rocket straight for the Lincoln Tunnel.

At last, Willy wails, "I don't know where to **go**!" She plasters her hand over her face and says, "They killed Tom! He's dead!"

After that, the funny noises emanating from behind her hands disturb Patel so greatly that he considers personally ejecting this woman from his cab, by force if necessary. She calms down, however, and begins to look about her, which Patel takes to be an excellent sign. And since he, like his distraught passenger, has no idea where he has taken them, he begins to check around for landmarks, too.

"Where **are** we?" Willy asks.

"Yes, in several senses," says Patel, trying to catch sight of a street sign. "Riverside Drive, I'd say, and about 103rd. Yes, there is the sign, miss. We are at 103rd Street. The question is, where do we go from here? The government agents will be mobilizing soon, and the police, too, will be massed against you. If you wish me to continue helping you, it is necessary that you explain the entirety of your situation to me."

"The police, too?" Willy asks.

"I have no doubt of that, miss. From what I saw, the police are in league with the forces against you. Nothing is as it seems, and those who pretend to act in the name of good in fact serve dark and evil masters."

"The evil master is my fiancé," Willy says. "His name is Mitchell Faber, and **he** isn't what he seems to be, that's for sure. He murdered my first husband, and my daughter, too."

"This is your story. It was given to you, and now you must repeat it. I understand. You are supposed to imitate a parrot. But now your story has reminded me of something I read this morning. It was that name—your fiancé's name. I am sure of it. Let me check on this, miss."

"Mitchell's name was in the paper?"

This seems so unlikely, also so foreign to Mitchell's character, that Willy cannot believe the driver's words. Besides that, this driver, although very polite, is also a screwball. She'd known people in the Institute who, like him, were convinced that they had the inside dope on governmental or military conspiracies. The problem with such people was that their theories almost always incorporated a good deal of the truth, as you learned every time governmental officials were caught telling whoppers, and this occasional (even fundamental) accuracy served only to buttress their faith in the wilder branches of their conspiracies.

Kalpesh Patel has pulled up in front of an un-

usually beautiful brownstone on the corner of
103rd Street, and he is bending over, evidently
shuffling through a stack of newspapers on the
seat beside his.

"Yes, that was the name. Undoubtedly, we are
talking about a bit of disinformation planted by
government agents." Willy hears the sound of
pages being turned. Then Patel's arm stops
moving, and his mouth stretches out in a smile.
"Oh, my, the lies these people are willing to tell
their own citizens. It is shameful. Do you know
you have been accused of bank robbery, Miz
Patrick?"

"Bank robbery?"

"And your name is Willy? You were given a
man's name? Not even a true, dignified name,
but a mere nickname? How did your mother explain this decision to you?"

"My parents were killed when I was a child—
I never had a chance to ask her. I want to see
that newspaper, please."

"You must read about your alleged crime,"
Patel says, and passes a folded-over copy of
the **Daily News** over the seat and through
the rectangle cut into the plastic divider between them.

Willy sees it instantly: a smudgy photograph,
lifted from film taken out of a surveillance video

camera, of herself seated before the desk of Mr. Robert Bender, president of the Continental Trust of New Jersey. She is dressed in the jeans and cotton sweater she had been wearing that day, and in the hand that rests on Mr. Bender's handsome desk is a pistol that looks a little too large for her grip. The headline reads **Imaginative Newcomer Breaks New Jersey Bank.**

"I wasn't holding a gun," Will says. "I don't even own a gun!"

"Photoshop," says Patel. "The maker of miracles. I believe this kind of thing happens nearly every day. Look how much money you are alleged to have stolen."

"I didn't steal, he stole from me!" Willy yelps, and scans the article running down the page alongside the photograph.

In an act that had puzzled both bank officials and New Jersey law officers, Willy Patrick, thirty-eight, a prizewinning author of novels for young adults and the fiancée of well-known area figure Mitchell Faber, had pointed a 9mm pistol at bank president Robert Bender during a private consultation requested by Ms. Patrick, and ordered Bender to give her $150,000 in cash from her future husband's accounts. "For the safety of my employees, I did as the lady requested," Mr. Bender was quoted as saying. A "troubleshooter" for the Baltic Group, Mr. Faber was said to be hurrying back from meetings in European capitals to offer support to his troubled bride-to-be and aid to area law enforcement officers. Aldo Pinochet, a spokesman for the Baltic Group, described Ms. Patrick as an "unstable woman with a history of mental problems and in desperate need of help."

"Aldo Pinochet," Patel says. "See how they work? Everything is connected. You need only take a few steps back, and the pattern comes clear."

" 'Troubleshooter,' " Willy says. "That's literally what he is."

"Will he want to shoot you?"

"Oh, shooting wouldn't be nearly good enough," she says. "First he'll want to break most of my bones, and after that he'll start cutting off little bits of me."

"Is there someplace safe I can take you? The meter will stay off, that should go without saying. However, I must soon return to my duties. You have a headquarters in this city, do you not?"

"I don't have a headquarters, no. Why would I?"

"Then perhaps you wish me to go to a police station and report your friend's murder. Or perhaps I should go to the offices of the **New York Times** and tell them what I saw."

"I don't know what to do. Maybe they're looking for this cab."

And it goes on from there—Willy is right: a police officer driving up the West Side Highway sees the cab, there's a cop anyhow, and we know he's calling in their location. Patel shoots around the corner, gets to Broadway, and drops her off. It is no longer safe for her to stay in his taxi; she must fend for herself. For the rest of the book, Willy is on the road, running toward knowledge she has been kept from all her life.

Now I must reluctantly climb out of my sandbox and begin to prepare for tonight's reading at the Upper West Side B&N, which is on 82nd and Broadway, about a million miles from here. My publicist and the bookstore event managers work out these decisions between them; nobody ever asks me where I'd like to read. How about the Astor Place store, that's pretty hip? How about Union Square, with that nice big reading space? For that matter, what's wrong with the one on Broadway in the East Village? But 82nd and Broadway is where they want me to read, so that's where I'll go.

For about five minutes I'll pander shamelessly for laughter, then read bits and pieces of **lost boy lost girl** for about twenty minutes, the maximum length of time **I** can bear to listen to someone else read from his own work. After that there'll be the good old Q&A, which I enjoy, and I'll sign books for as long as there's still someone in line.

Right after I saved my document and checked my e-mail—three new messages from mixed-up, unhappy dead people, deleted the way you'd wipe a stain off a wall—who should walk in but Cyrax, frend & gide, appearing as usual in a big blank blue rectangle on my screen. Apparently Cyrax expects unusual things to happen at my reading, and he wants me to brace myself.

> Underdone, yr gr8 moment comes 2nite
> u must do rite & b strong & brave
> tho
> it is not e-z 4 a slug like u
> (LOLOL!)
> rede yr boke, rede the 1 with-in
> the 1 u wrote
> & hear the brush of gr8 WINGS!
> u have no choice, my deer,
> yr time is come to make re-pair,

& re-pair u must!!! the lyfe u knew
is no mor b-cuz U MUST CO-RECK THE ERROR!!

What in the world does this gabby busybody expect to happen? Jasper Kohle, probably—I'll warn the staff to keep an eye out for him.

Tim Underhill Sails
to Byzantium/
So Does Willy

PART FOUR

21

On the second floor of the big Barnes & Noble bookstore on Broadway and Eighty-second Street, Katherine Hyndman from the community-relations department glanced up from the podium before her and said, "And after all that, I'm sure you are as eager as I am to hear tonight's guest, so here he is . . . Timothy Underhill."

She looked to her side and smiled at him through her outsized black-framed glasses, and Underhill walked out from cover and into full view of the thirty or forty people occupying the rows of chairs in front of him. Katherine Hyndman stepped back and motioned him toward the podium with a comically exaggerated sweeping gesture that got a few laughs.

It was a few minutes past 8:00 P.M. The enormous windows on the street side of the readings area showed a thorough darkness washed by light upon light. Cars swept up and down the length of Broadway. The few people standing on that side of the room could look down to see pedestrians wearing sweaters and jackets. Autumn—or at least this presage of the autumn and winter to come—seemed to have arrived overnight.

"Wasn't it just summer?" Underhill asked. He was rewarded by a little more laughter than had greeted his presenter's parodic courtliness— which had masked a real courtliness, he knew, designed to soothe the touch of anxiety Ms. Hyndman had mistakenly perceived as stage fright. Underhill had been doing readings, panels, symposia, and public talks for so long he had forgotten what stage fright felt like.

"I mean, like yesterday?" he said, to renewed laughter. "All of a sudden, the world turned harsh on us. I think we should try an experiment. Stick with me on this. I know, I know, you came here for a reading, and I **am** here to read, but first we are going to make a concerted group effort to influence the weather around here. It's going to sound like **Alice in Wonderland,** but deep in my heart I believe it's worth a try."

Tim was improvising. He'd had no idea he was going to say these things, but he figured he might as well keep rolling. Most of the people looking up seemed amused, expectant, interested in what he would ask them to do.

As he let the words come out of his mouth, Underhill scanned the audience, row by row, for Jasper Kohle. He would be peering out from beneath his ratty hood, or leaning forward in his chair; standing hunched against the window; peering out goblinlike from behind a rank of bookshelves. He might be gripping a heavy-looking brown bag, and the weight in that bag could be anything at all: a book, a Chinese take-out dinner, a gun.

"Let's clap our heels together and see if we can get another month of nice weather. It rained all of June, so we were cheated out of the best month of the year in New York. August was the usual fish fry. This month, it really **poured** a couple of times. We're coping with a fundamental structural maladjustment, and you and I have an opportunity to step in and make a difference. Not so much for our own sakes, of course, but think of the street musicians. Think of the people who live on the sidewalks. **They're** in no hurry to see winter come."

For some reason, two people in the middle rows had raised their arms and seemed to be trying to attract his attention. Underhill went on scanning his audience, moving from face to face.

"I'm warning you, if you don't go along with me on this, you risk putting us in a kind of Evil Punxsutawney Phil situation, with arctic gales around Halloween. So all together now, let's click our heels together three times and say—"

"It's the **Wizard of Oz,**" said a middle-aged man in the second row.

Behind him, one of the women with her arm in the air flapped her hand at him, smiled, and said, "That's what I was going to say. You're talking about **The Wizard of Oz.**"

"That's what I said, isn't it?" Tim asked. "**The Wizard of Oz.** Clicking your heels together, what else can it be? Apart from 'Springtime for Hitler.' "

"No," the woman said, "you said—"

But Timothy Underhill did not need these people to remind him of what he had said. In the form of his sister, April, little Alice Blue-Gown was watching him from the seat on the far left end of the last row. In the gap between two nouveau hippies, only her head and trunk were visible. April had made another trip back through the rabbit hole or the mirror, but her gaze lacked the ferocious urgency of her most recent appearance on Grand Street and the silent clamor of her first. He wondered what she had come to tell him. Undoubtedly, it had something to do with Cyrax's gr8 moment, and his utter ignorance of whatever that might be made him stand for a moment in openmouthed foolish silence at the microphone. The words **Alice in Wonderland** were still decaying in the atmosphere about him.

He had to say something, so he said, "You're absolutely right. I really must be getting senile. Thank you for correcting me—the truth is, I've had **Alice in Wonderland** on my mind lately."

In the little ripple of response, he glanced again at the chink of space between the curly-headed hippies, and was relieved to find April Underhill still keeping her watchful eye upon him.

"Let's carry on as if nothing had happened. We'll all feel better, especially me. Like you-know-who in **The Wizard of Oz,** not the heroine of **Alice in Wonderland,** let's all click our heels together three times and say, 'More warm weather. More warm weather. More warm weather.' "

Sweetly, almost all of the people in the audience did exactly what they were told, and most of them were smiling. Three times each, thirty to forty pairs of heels clicked together and made a staccato blur. A ragged chorus repeated the three words three times, leaving those who had spoken them with the mysterious satisfaction of people who have participated in a communal rite.

Instantly, glowing tracers of lightning sizzled across the night sky, igniting an enormous rumble of thunder that worked its way toward an end-of-the-world explosion. When a wall of rain smashed against the window, the lightning turned fat and gauzy and hung in the air.

"Wow," Underhill said. Everybody in the room was staring at the window. "Can I take it back?"

Another gigantic fork made of lightning noisily divided the sky.

Even before he looked back at the last row, Tim Underhill knew that his sister had departed. The new-wave hippies stared at the window like everybody else, but no one occupied the chair behind them.

"I guess I'd better stop talking and start reading," Underhill said. Some quiet laughter, caused more by alarm than humor, rippled flamelike here and there, and came to an end the moment he picked up his book.

Twenty-five minutes later, he thought he had managed to give a pretty good reading, despite

the Götterdämmerung beginning and the ty-
phoonlike rain that had never ceased to batter
the big windows on Broadway. Happy to be in-
doors, his audience responded as though they
were huddled around a campfire.

The last section Underhill read described the
entrance—into the book and into the life of
its adolescent hero—of a young woman who
may or may not have existed but offered the
teenaged hero an imaginative way out of the
grave dug for him by loathsome Ronnie Lloyd-
Jones. This young woman, who called herself
Lucy Cleveland, was in fact Joseph Kalendar's
daughter, Lily. According to Cyrax, Tim's as-
sumptions about Lily had brought down upon
him all the bizarre and threatening troubles of
the past week. In his book, however, although
after having been both sexually abused and
murdered by her father Lily was in fact indisputably dead, she nonetheless had something
like a beautiful life, forever in love, forever
loved, forever in flight. The circle around Underhill's campfire had seemed to be moved, and
if not moved then intrigued, by the series of
paragraphs that ended with the words **A slight
figure slipped into the room.**

"Wherever that is, that's where we are," Underhill said. "Thank you for listening."

After the applause and the invitation for questions, a couple of arms rose up like tulips, shyly, and for the first time since the onset of the storm, he permitted himself to look back at the place where April had been. The hippies smiled at him, bestowing the gift of infantile hippie love. Between them, in the last row, Underhill glimpsed a young person of indeterminate gender who appeared to be soaked through, staring at him with disconcerting intensity. He or she was halfheartedly wiping his or her arms with a wad of paper towels from the restroom. Obviously, this person had run into the bookstore to get out of the rain and camped here at the edge of his reading to try to dry off.

"You, sir," he said, nodding at a skinny, bearded man off to the right who was executing one-armed semaphores.

The man floated to his feet and said, "This is a two-part question. How hard is it to get an agent, and does anybody actually read the slush pile? I mean, how hard is it to get your work noticed?"

Groaning inwardly, Underhill gave a paint-by-numbers answer balanced between realism and optimism. As he spoke, he looked back between the marveling hippies and discovered that the drenched person was a she. Through her white shirt, dabbled with a sort of watercolor abstract red pattern, shone the X-ray outline of a brassiere. She was wiping her hair with another wad of paper towels, still staring at him as if he presented a puzzle some ruthless master had commanded her to solve.

The intensity of her interest compelled his own. Just sitting there, at the end of the last row of seats, she exerted what felt like a claim upon him.

Once begun, the questions washed toward him. Most of them were old acquaintances, more to be batted away with a stock response than to be answered. Where do you get your ideas? What was it like to work with another writer? What scares **you**? The woman in the last row never lost focus or looked away.

"I think that's enough," said Katherine Hyndman. "Mr. Underhill will now sign books at the table to your right. Please form a line, and those of you who have come with bags or suitcases filled with books, please wait at the end of the line."

A quarter of the audience stood up and left; another quarter came up to the podium to talk to him. For forty minutes, Tim Underhill signed books. Every couple of minutes, he looked at the woman in the last row, who seemed prepared to wait him out. Inscribing books to Tam-

mie, Joe, David, and Emsie, he began at last to
wonder if this woman had come as an emissary
from Jasper Kohle. He gestured to Katherine
Hyndman, and when she came to his side he
asked her to go over and start a conversation
with that woman in the wet clothes for the purpose of coming back and reporting how dangerous or crazy she might be.

Katherine wandered toward the young woman,
sat down beside her, and said something. Signing books, Tim now and then glanced over to
see how things were going. It looked like an ordinary conversation, though the young woman
seemed a little dazed. Katherine Hyndman stood
up, glanced at him, and instead of returning to
the desk disappeared into the back of the store.
In her absence, the woman alternated between
looking at the ground and taking peeks at him.
Now she was the only person still seated in the
reading area, and Tim could see that she had
brought two bags with her, one a rolling case of
the sort people take on airplanes, and the other
a kind of medium-sized leather duffel bag. Both
of these were off-white in color, almost ivory,
and looked expensive.

Katherine Hyndman came back carrying a
towel and gave it to the young woman, who
pressed it to her face, then wiped it back over

the top of her head and down to the back of her neck. Only three people remained in line, but the first two carried a pair of shopping bags laden with books, and the third man had a large suitcase.

"She's not going to be any trouble," Katherine Hyndman said, leaning down to whisper into his ear. "I couldn't quite figure out what her story is, and she does seem a little disoriented. Basically, all she told me is that she wants to talk to you. Do you want us to do anything about her, or are you okay with the situation?"

"I'd like to talk to her, too," Tim whispered back. "She seems sort of familiar to me, but I can't place her. Did she tell you her name?"

"Sorry, I don't remember it."

Tim went back to signing. The last man in line thumped his suitcase, a battered old Samsonite, on the desk, and opened it to begin removing multiple copies of each of Tim's books, plus a lot of pamphlets, bound galleys, and magazines. He looked about seventy or seventy-five, and as hard used as his old suitcase. His brown, wrinkly face disappeared into a wispy Confucian beard, and his recessed eyes were wary. An invisible cloud of cigarette smoke surrounded him, as did a faint undercurrent of dried sweat.

While this unlikely collector was still dipping into his stash, he said, "Your first book was the best one you ever wrote. **A Beast in View.** Want to know the truth, it's been downhill ever since."

Underhill laughed, genuinely amused by the things people thought they ought to share with authors at signings.

"I'm glad you liked it," he said, and began signing. Before him on the desk stood five copies of **The Divided Man** and six of **Blood Orchid.** The collector was stacking up a great many copies of **A Beast in View.** "But if you don't like these other books, why did you buy so many of them?"

The man's eyes seemed to retreat farther into his head. "Maybe I shouldn't buy these four copies of your new one, is that what you're saying?"

"No, I don't have any problem with you buying my books. I'm all for it, believe me."

"People do things for all kinds of reasons," the man said. "And maybe other people don't know enough to understand those reasons."

"Hold on." Tim stopped signing his name and looked up at the collector. At the side of his vision, the drenched girl stood up, collected her bags, and began to move toward him through the rows of empty chairs. Katherine Hyndman floated into view. "You're not an ordinary collector, are you?" Tim said. "And you're not a book dealer, either."

"What's it to you?"

"I think you're part of a special breed," Tim said. "I think you know about things other people don't."

The old man looked caught between pride and suspicion. "It doesn't matter what I am."

Katherine Hyndman and the girl who had come in from the rain stood about fifteen feet off to his right, conferring in front of the empty chairs.

"Have you ever found one?" Tim asked. "You must have, or you wouldn't keep looking."

The man shrugged. The narrow slits of his eyes shone.

"It's like the Maltese falcon, isn't it, except there are more than one of them. You're obsessed. Getting your hands on one is all you care about. Jasper Kohle was pretending, but you're the real thing." For a moment, Tim felt a kind of exaltation.

"I never heard of Jasper Kohle, and you're not supposed to talk about this. You're not even supposed to know we exist. Because if you know that, then you know . . . what you know,

I guess." The old man was bending over the table, grabbing books, and stuffing them into his suitcase, signed and unsigned alike.

"Do you know where they come from?"

"**Nobody** talks about that, bub. But let me tell you something." He bent closer to Underhill. He had tiger breath. "There are lots of contacts between here and there, right? Moments of passage. So every now and then, a book slips through."

"Slips through," Underhill said, taken with what seemed the lovely effortlessness of the process.

"Ever see a perfect thing? Ever hold one in your hand? Can you imagine how that feels? You want to talk about a rush, they don't get any deeper than that." His grin revealed sparse, rotting teeth. "I'm talking about **perfection.**"

Tim pulled his head back and noticed the girl with the white bags, standing exactly where Katherine Hyndman had left her. A chill tingle rippled across his skin.

"How many?" the old man said. "Three. That's how many. I'll get another before I'm done, too." He slammed down the lid of the suitcase and slid its locks into place.

"But why do you have to buy so many books? Why go through trial and error?"

"Sometimes, you have to stare at perfection

for a long, long time before you see it." He
leaned back over his suitcase, eyes shining, and
gave Underhill a good look at the horror in his
mouth. "But once you see it, it's yours forever."

Grinning, he pulled the suitcase off the table,
stepped back, and saluted Underhill by tapping
a finger against his forehead. Then he whirled
around and set off for the escalator.

Underhill watched him go and realized that
for a second he had forgotten all about the girl.
She stood ten feet away, between her bags, her
wrinkled skirt soaked through, her blouse still
adhering to her skin. He saw that she was a
woman, not a girl, a woman probably in her
mid-thirties, though at first glance she appeared
to be much younger. Her short hair had been
ruffed by the towel. She was extraordinarily
good-looking, he thought, though not in any
ordinary way. With her slightness, her coltish,
slightly androgynous air, she was a true gamine.
Then he realized that the red pattern on her
blouse was water-soaked blood spatter.

She took an uncertain step toward him, and
the planet seemed to wobble on its course. His
stomach dropped to the floor, but the floor
wasn't there anymore. He was floating in midair, with all the hair on his arms sticking straight
up. He recognized her, and for a moment the

recognition brought him into the purest fear he had known since Vietnam.

"This can't be happening," he said. "Is your name Willy?"

"I think I need your help," Willy said. "Do we know each other?"

22

Poor Willy—she was looking for an explanation of the strangest experience of her life, and she thought she had come to the right place. Kalpesh Patel had stopped at the corner of 103rd Street and Broadway, helped her get the bags out of his taxi, refused to take any money, and sped off in the general direction of Columbus Avenue and Central Park. She began aimlessly to walk down Broadway, trying to figure out how she could get out of town. New York represented the dual threat of Mitchell's henchmen and the NYPD, all of whom had probably been shown pictures of her face before being sent out to find its owner. Money was no problem: she could get in a cab and tell the driver to take her to Boston, or Pittsburgh, or any large city where she could hide out until Mitchell got tired of looking for her. But she didn't trust the driver of her hypothetical taxicab. One night he might tune in to **America's Most Wanted** and run straight to the police.

By the time she reached Ninety-sixth Street, she was thinking about long-distance buses. Buses went everywhere, and no one ever paid any attention to them, basically because they carried poor people from one place to another. If she got to Port Authority, she could pay cash for a ticket and travel anywhere she wanted. Willy did not think you had to keep validating your identity to get on a bus. She wished she had asked Kalpesh Patel to take her to the Port Authority building—the way that man drove, she could be there in minutes.

Willy moved to the curb and stuck out her right hand. With her left, she kept a good grip on the handle of the white leather bag stuffed with hundred-dollar bills and on the rolling case. Traffic flowed past her. The only cabs she saw already had passengers. The air grew darker and cool enough to make her wish she were wearing a jacket. A jacket would conceal the bloodstains, too—she had received a few curious stares. Then she thought of Tom again, and a molten current of panic, guilt, and despair ran through her.

A cold wind whistled down Broadway, and Willy shivered as she tilted forward to scan the approaching traffic. In the untimely darkness, a yellow light glowing from the top of a cab two blocks up had the brightness of a beacon. A menacing roll of thunder filled the sky, and distant lightning flashed. Willy hoped the cab would arrive in advance of the rain.

The lights changed again.

One block away, a pale car that looked exactly like Mitchell Faber's Mercedes turned the corner into Broadway. It could not be Mitchell's car. Like Mitchell's car, however, it seemed to move down the block with the swift, elegant shiver of a predator. A walnut-sized knot of fear located in the middle of her chest dialed up the volume of her general panic. She could not keep standing there as the Mercedes shimmered and shivered toward her.

Willy was bending over to pick up her bags when she looked back up the street at the Mercedes that could not be Mitchell Faber's and saw, with a terrible clarity, Giles Coverley at the wheel and Roman Richard beside him. Her only thought was to get far enough ahead of them to avoid being seen, and, one bag in each hand, she started running down the sidewalk.

Under a long barrage of thunder, the sky darkened by another degree. Willy darted across the sidewalk, and when her hand touched the door of a nearby shop, she heard the blasting of horns and the slamming of car doors. Her fear widened its wings and touched her heart. She heard clattering footsteps, looked to her left, and saw Coverley and Roman Richard running toward her through the traffic.

Willy took off—like an antelope sprinting for its life. Her suitcase weighed little, but the bag of money dragged at her right side. All of the sky split into incandescent, swiftly moving bolts of lightning. Thunder exploded overhead and echoed off the buildings on both sides of Broadway. Everywhere, people began to run.

Bulletlike rain shattered down. Instantly, Willy was soaked to the skin. Then her right foot skidded out before her, and she felt her balance begin to go. Inevitably and with shocking swiftness came the moment when her body obeyed gravity, not her will. She readied herself for a rough landing. Both of her legs unfolded before her. Instead of hitting the sidewalk, Willy felt herself propelled, supine and feet-first, along the Broadway sidewalk, which had become a canyon of roaring wind and slashing rain. She was **passing through** the canyon, and what indisputably had been Broadway was no more. Like a cork in rapid water, Willy shot forward, accelerating with every heartbeat. Borne along by a great force, she seemed to cover great distances in her skidding flight down the canyon made of darkness, wind, and rain. An incandescent vibration took hold of her and rattled her until she felt battered and limp. The world darkened and contracted, then expanded into a brief, brilliant burst of light and threw her forward like a rag.

Then again she was in the world of big buildings with lighted windows, and her feet skidded across solid pavement. She realized she was upright again, her legs beneath her. Momentum staggered her forward through the monsoon downpour toward the brightest window in sight, one of a row on the ground floor of a supersized Barnes & Noble. A great many books hung in the window, as did a modest placard featuring a photograph of an author who was scheduled to read from his work.

Beneath the photograph was printed:

TONIGHT 8:00

TIMOTHY UNDERHILL

READING FROM LOST BOY LOST GIRL.

The author she read when depressed seemed almost ridiculously appropriate for her circumstances. She needed to get out of the rain. She

needed to sit down and recover, to the extent re-
covery was possible, from Tom's murder and her
extraordinary flight through the darkness and
the wind. Her head felt as though it was literally
spinning, and the center of her body seemed
still to be traveling at great speed through a kind
of cosmic rabbit hole. It was the only time in
her life that Willy Bryce Patrick had ever felt she
had anything in common with Alice in Wonderland.

She wobbled to the door, barely able to see
through the curtain of water, and realized that
she did not know if Coverley and Roman
Richard had followed her through that violent
passageway. Her final, most comforting thought
before getting out of the rain was that a bookstore reading was the last place Mitchell's henchmen would think to look for her.

On the other side of the revolving door, a
security guard in a blue blazer looked her up
and down. Water streamed down her legs and
pooled on the carpeted floor.

Willy said, "The Underhill reading?"

"Second floor, top of the escalators, turn right.
First, though, you might want to go through
the children's section and dry off in the ladies'
room."

"Thank you." Willy smiled at him and stepped

backward out of her puddle. Water continued
to slide off her hair, her clothes, her legs.

"Please tell me that's not blood on your shirt,
ma'am."

"Just stage blood," Willy said, forcing a
brighter smile, and moved smartly toward the
escalator.

In the bathroom, she peeled off her blouse
and rubbed little paper towels over her arms,
neck, and torso. Her jeans were so wet that to
remove them, she had to yank down and wrig-
gle at the same time. She swabbed her legs with
paper towels that turned dark and useless.
When she had done as much as she could, she
still looked like a drowning victim, but a more
recent one. Willy pulled another handful of
sheets from the dispenser, gave her face a last
blotting, and left the bathroom.

A winding path through the bookshelves
brought her to the reading area, where she collapsed onto an empty chair and peered at Timothy Underhill through the space between the
heads of an emaciated hippie boy and a roly-
poly hippie girl. Underhill was leaning on the
podium and calling for questions. The sight of
this middle-aged man at the other end of the
reading space had a startling effect on her. Immediately, she felt as though everything that

had happened to her during this terrible day
had been designed to lead her precisely to this
point, and she had somehow come out at the
place where she was all along intended now to
be. That place—and the utter weirdness of this
circumstance can hardly be expressed—was in
the proximity of Timothy Underhill, a novelist
she liked, pretty much, but whose concerns
seemed to speak to her most clearly when she
wasn't feeling all that great. Timothy Underhill, it came to her, had something to give
her; he had something to tell her; he would
draw a map that she alone could read. What
gripped Willy as she peered at Tim Underhill
through the gap created by the heads and bodies of the people in front of her was the loony
conviction that without this man she would
be lost.

He looked at her—their eyes met without any
particular urgency—looked away, and said,
"You, sir," to a bearded man who asked a boring
question about getting published. While Timothy Underhill answered the man's question with
a series of anodyne banalities, he glanced back
at Willy, this time with real interest and something like recognition in his eyes. A lot of questions followed, and as Underhill answered them,
now and then moving his hands through the air,
sometimes laughing at himself, he kept glancing

back at Willy, as if to reassure himself that she was still there.

After the question period, a knot of people surrounded Underhill and the podium. Willy stayed pinned to her seat. She did not know what she would say when her time came, but she did know that what she would say had to be private.

He reminded her of Tom Hartland, she realized. Fifteen to twenty years older than Tom, a little heavier, shaggy hair going gray, Timothy Underhill did not so much look like her friend as suggest him. Much more than Tom, Underhill had the air of having **survived** something at which she could not even guess.

Underhill shot her another look, and she thought, No, there's more to it than being reminded of Tom. It's **him.**

Underhill whispered to the young woman who seemed to be in charge of the event, who then approached her with tactful concern, sat down beside her, and asked if she needed any help.

Yes, but not from you, Willy said to herself. Aloud, she said, "I got caught in the rain on my way here, and, well, look! I used up all these paper towels and I'm still soaked."

"I'll get you a towel from the back of the store," the woman said, and went off. When she returned with a big red towel printed with GREAT BEACH READING FROM GLADSTONE BOOKS!, Willy threw it over her head and rubbed her head until both her hair and her scalp felt as though they might at last be dry, mostly. She pulled the towel off her head and ran it over her arms. Her shirt no longer stuck so conspicuously to her body. Like watercolor on wet paper, the blood spatter had softened and fuzzed out, and now had an almost Manet-like quality.

When the last person in the line had reached the desk, Willy stood up and carried her bags down the row of empty chairs. The woman in charge sauntered up to her and asked if she wanted to have a book signed.

"Not really," Willy said. "It's just that . . . I want to meet that man."

A look of concern marred the perfect face. "You're not going to cause any trouble here, are you?"

"None at all," Willy said.

The wonder held out a small, smooth hand with sparkling nails. "I'm Katherine Hyndman, by the way. Community relations. I'm the person who invited Mr. Underhill here tonight."

"Willy Bryce Patrick," Willy said, expecting to see a spark of surprised recognition. None came. "I write YA novels. One of them won the Newbery Medal. **In the Night Room**?"

"In the what?"

"**In the Night Room.** That was the title of my book."

"I'm sorry, I don't think I know it. But, I gather you want to speak to Mr. Underhill author to author."

"Pretty much."

"It looks as though you'll have your chance fairly soon." They both looked at the signing table and the disheveled old man standing before it. While stuffing a good many Timothy Underhill books back into an old suitcase that resembled a battered clamshell, he was ranting.

"Book collectors," said Katherine Hyndman. "When they come out of the woodwork, you never know what to expect. We've seen some of the strangest people, I mean really the **oddest** people."

She smiled at Willy. "I'm surprised that I don't know your name. We do a great YA business in this store, and I do my best to keep up with all the authors. You know what? If you won the Newbery, we have multiple copies of your books. Would you mind signing some of them? I'll just run over to the children's section and bring you a nice little stack, all right?"

Willy had been fearing that her new friend Katherine would intrude herself into the conversation she had to have with Tim Underhill, and she embraced the opportunity of sending her off to another part of the store.

"Sure," she said. "Take as long as you like."

Katherine Hyndman strode off.

Willy watched Underhill stare at the receding back of the peculiar book collector and wished that he would look instead at her. As if she had touched his mind with hers, Underhill turned slowly in his chair and gazed at her in a way that combined close observation with appreciation. He seemed to measure and weigh her, to calculate her age, nearly to count her teeth. His warmth and good humor turned what could have been objectionable or even insulting into a kind of affectionate, observant approval. It seemed to Willy that being looked at in exactly this way was one of the things she truly needed, and he had given it to her unasked.

Then she saw him take in the blurry blood-stains on her shirt. He understood what they were, and that final detail seemed to lock some other understanding into place. Willy moved forward, now beyond wondering what she might say to him, and saw an amazing series of expressions flow across his face: disbelief, shock, love, fear, and total recognition. He said, **This can't be happening. Is your name Willy?**

He knew her name. By extraordinary, unrepeatable means, Willy had found her way to the one person who could both make sense of her life and save it, and when she spoke, it was from the center of her soul. "I think I need your help. Do we know each other?"

23

From Timothy Underhill's journal

Cyrax told me yr gr8 moment comes 2nite, but he never said that it would scare me silly. Well, he added that I would have to do rite & b strong & brave, so I guess he knew what he was talking about. Two completely contradictory impulses fought for control of my body: I wanted to put my arms around her, and I wanted to scram, to get out of there as fast as possible. Then Reason intervened to inform me that I was being ridiculous. This, Reason insisted, was merely a coincidence, albeit a coincidence of a very high order. Willy, this Willy, if that in fact was her name, had slipped into the room at the same moment that "Lucy Cleveland" slipped into the pages of my book. And because I had never imagined my heroine's face in specific detail, this woman's resemblance to fictional Willy Bryce Patrick was all in my head.

Reason, of course, had no idea what it was talking about.

It's 4:30 in the morning. Willy finally fell asleep about half an hour ago. As far as I can tell, we're safe here. A discreet look around the motel's parking lot found not a trace of Faber's silver-gray Mercedes. (About this, more later.)

To go back to the bookstore: after our first words, Willy said, "You seem like someone I've known for a long time. It's the strangest thing— as soon as I saw you, I felt that you were of enormous importance to me."

This did nothing to support my shaky belief that her appearance, in both senses, was no more than a kind of coincidence.

"You know my name," she said. "Willy. You said it."

"Is that really your name?"

"Maybe you know me from my work?" she said. Her next words demolished all hope that the world was still ticking on in the old manner. "Willy Patrick. Willy **Bryce** Patrick?"

She looked utterly charming, which made things much worse. I could just about feel the earth separating beneath me. In a second I was going to be in free fall.

"This is very embarrassing," she said, and hesitated. "I don't usually go up to other authors and say crazy things to them. Actually, I hardly ever meet other authors. Except, well, for . . ."

Instead of a name, what came out of her mouth was a muffled whisper. "I'm sorry," she said in a voice only slightly more intelligible, and raised her clasped hands to her eyes.

I guess that was my moment of decision, right then—when she stopped talking and let that name hang in silence before both of us. I could say what I did say, or I could have pretended that I didn't know what she was talking about. In the end, though, I had no choice at all.

"Except for Tom Hartland," I said. The building around me, the miles of books in that building, the cars and streetlamps on Broadway quietly held their breath.

Willy dropped her hands and gave me a look so overflowing with mingled relief and sorrow that it was all I could do not to take her in my arms.

"Did you know him?"

The walls of the building had not collapsed, the floor was still beneath my feet, and the traffic continued to move up and down Broadway. Everything and everybody breathed on, and so, with a breath of my own, I stepped deeper into the fiction I would eventually have to unmake.

"I knew Tom Hartland," I told her. "And I know he was close to you." For the moment, that was as far as I could go. "We shouldn't talk about this here."

She turned her head at the arrival within our charged perimeter of Katherine Hyndman, who broke in with an aggressive mimicry of harmless confusion that was clearly nothing of the kind.

"There seems to be some kind of problem," she told Willy. "I can't find your books. Nor can I find your name in our database. Where it ought to be, don't you think?"

"I don't understand," Willy said. "Maybe you're not spelling my name right."

"B-R-Y-C-E P-A-T-R-I-C-K? Willy, W-I-L-L-Y?"

"That's right, but—"

"And the title was **In the Night Room**? Which supposedly won the Newbery Medal?"

The expression on her face summoned Willy's strength. "This is absurd. I have written three books. They're all in print. The last one won the Newbery. If you don't have my books on your shelves, you're not doing your business very well, and if they're not in your database, your computer needs to be brought up to date."

Katherine turned to me. "I looked both in **Books in Print** and at the Newbery website—"

"I'm **on** the Newbery website!" Willy said. "What are you trying to say?"

"Ms. Hyndman looked in the wrong books," I said. "We're leaving."

I grabbed the bag full of money with one hand and Willy Bryce Patrick's elbow with the other.

When we reached the escalator, Willy a foot or two before me, she said, "I have to ask: how did you know Tom was dead? You said you **knew** him."

I gestured for her to get on the escalator. When she did, she looked up at me and, both giving information and asking it, said, "You should know that the men who killed him are out there looking for me."

"I know all about them," I said. "You can pretty much take for granted that I understand what's going on."

"Tom called you on his cell phone, didn't he? It's so strange that he never told me he knew you so well."

Instead of responding to that, I pulled out my cell phone, dialed 411, and asked for my publicist's home telephone number.

"Who's Brian Jeckyll?"

I shushed her. At home in Larchmont, Jeckyll answered. He was not entirely pleased to hear from me. Authors who call publicists, especially authors who call publicists who are at home in Larchmont, almost always want to complain about some fresh insult to their egos. Authors tend to be demanding, selfish, and easily wounded—just ask anyone in publishing. Brian Jeckyll became even less pleased with me when he heard what I had to say.

"You want to skip the reading in Boston and reschedule all those radio interviews? Are you out of your mind?"

"Probably," I said. "And if I told you what is going on, you'd certainly think so. But what you have to know is that I'm going to drive to Mill-haven, and I'm leaving tonight."

In unison, Willy and Brian Jeckyll said, "Mill-haven?" I was as surprised as they by what I'd said.

"I have that reading at New Leaf Books, re-member, on Wednesday the tenth? My brother is getting married on Friday the twelfth, and I'll stay over for that. Everything after the thir-teenth can stay the way it is. And that's about ninety percent of the tour you set up."

In the end I agreed to do the most important of the radio interviews, scheduled for the morning of Thursday the eleventh, by phone from the Pforzheimer Hotel, which was where I always stayed when I was in my hometown.

Willy was staring at me the way a new immigrant stares at the Statue of Liberty. I opened my arms, let her step into me, and closed them around her. Nestled against me, her head resting on my breastbone, her arms embracing me light as foam, hair fluffed by the towel, shirt still damp enough to print dark stains on my own, was a person to whom I had given life. No matter how impossible the situation, **here she was,** as predicted by Cyrax, and I had to deal with her.

So I have these questions: can fictional characters live out ordinary human lives, or does their existence have a term of some kind? What happens when they die? Does their entry into our world mean that their histories are now part of our history? (What happened in the bookstore indicates that it doesn't. Willy's name isn't in **Books in Print,** and her only Newbery Medal is the one I gave her.) And according to Cyrax, I have to take her back to Millhaven, but what am I supposed to do with her when I get there? Cyrax also said something about a great sacrifice—I don't like this. It seems obvious, but I can't stand the conclusion Cyrax seems to be leading me toward.

And my God, do I introduce Willy to Philip?

What else did Cyrax tell me? From what I remember, that I had created a second Dark Man and merged him with Kalendar—true enough, since I thought of Mitchell Faber as a sort of more presentable, less psychotic Kalendar.

My biggest question, though, was how I was to let Willy know exactly what she was. If she'd understood our relationship, her appearance in my life would have been even scarier and more unsettling than it was. As things are, I have to take care of her while slowly letting her figure things out.

"It's uncanny, how much you remind me of Tom," she said as we stood wrapped together to the right of the escalator on the ground floor.

"We had a lot in common," I said.

"Look, Mr. Underhill, you have to tell me how you knew he was dead. You **have** to. It's scary—can't you understand that?"

"I sort of figured it out when I saw you."

And she stepped in and abetted the lie I had just told her. "Oh, you were expecting **him.** No wonder you looked so dumbfounded. If you recognized me right away, he must have talked about me a lot." A tremendous range of expressions crossed her face. "I'm still in such **shock.** I saw these two men who work for my fiancé, his name is Mitchell Faber—I saw these men,

Giles Coverley and Roman Richard Spilka, running down the street, and Roman Richard had a gun, and right after I got into the taxi, he **shot** Tom. Tom's blood got on my shirt. The cab took off, took off, it took off like a rocket . . ." She started to sob.

"I bet it did," I said, and held her more tightly. My heart hurt for her; I felt like weeping, too.

"It just feels like I can trust you with everything . . . with anything. . . . You make me feel so much safer."

"Good," I said. "I want you to feel safe with me." At that moment, I would have run into a burning building to rescue Willy Patrick.

"My fiancé killed my husband," she said. "And he killed my little girl, too. How's that for a nasty surprise? Mitchell Faber. Did Tom ever mention him to you?"

"Once or twice. But please tell me this, Willy: how did you get from . . ." I realized that I could not say 103rd Street, not now. "From wherever you were with your cab driver to here? It happened during that storm, didn't it?"

"What happened doesn't make any **sense.** They were chasing me, Giles and Roman Richard—they got out of Mitchell's car and started running down the street—I got blown over, and I flew **through** the wind—and my feet hit the sidewalk right in front of your poster."

That was the best answer I was likely to get: she was blown out of one world and into another. It must have happened when that gigantic thunderclap sounded—right after I did my dumb stunt and had everyone click their heels together. It occurred to me that April had somehow opened a space for Willy, and that she had done it for my sake. In some sense, April had **given** Willy to me. Then I saw the hand, or at least the style, of Cyrax in all this, and wished I hadn't.

"I felt like a leaf being shot through a tunnel." Her body went extraordinarily still, as a bird's does when it is cupped in your hand. "I was crazy for a while, you know. Maybe I'm going crazy all over again."

Willy leaned back without losing contact. Her short, scrappy blond hair looked as though a Madison Avenue hairdresser had devoted hours to it, and her face filled with emotion. Early in my book, I had written that she looked like a gorgeous lost child, but I had not understood how beautiful she actually was. What could have been superficial prettiness had been deepened by sorrow, fear, intelligence, effort, imagination, and steadfast, steady application of her capacity for response and engagement. I knew that kind of work; I also knew that I had not done right by her. She was a more considerable being than I had taken her for. When I looked down at her face and into her eyes, I also understood part of the reason why I had to take her with me—this lost girl was supposed to be lost in Millhaven. Once I took her there, she was not supposed to come out again.

So I can never pretend, can never say, that I didn't understand that from the beginning.

"I feel as though I've known you for the longest time," she said. "Is that true for you?"

"Yes, like I've been living with you for months."

Her shaggy head dropped to the center of my chest again, and she tightened her embrace around me. I could feel the tremble in her arms.

Then she released me and backed away. "You want to hear another weird thing? You're the author I read when I'm—"

"Depressed?"

I had surprised her again. "How did you know that?"

"I hear that a lot. I'm literary Zoloft, I guess."

She shook her head. "I don't read you because you're going to cheer me up. It's another condition altogether."

While I was speculating about what that might be, which included wondering why I did not already know, I noticed something related to the most important question I'd asked earlier, about the term of her existence.

"Willy," I said. "Look at your shirt."

She looked down. Her shirt had dried to the extent that her bra was no longer visible beneath it, and its color was the bright, unbroken white of a movie star's smile.

"What happened to Tom's blood? It was right there!" She spread her neat little hand over the front of the shirt. "Where'd it go?"

"Good question."

"Tom's blood," she said, and shock and fear rose to the surface of her face again. "I want it back. This isn't fair." She struggled with her emotions. "No. At least, this way I won't be so conspicuous to the police. They're after me, too." She threw me a look of challenge, asking, **Are you up for this, pal?** "I don't get it," she said, staring back down at the brilliant white of her shirt. "I guess now I'm in Timothy Underhill's world."

I had to turn my head to keep her from seeing the tears in my eyes. "We'd better be sure your pursuers aren't lurking outside when we get into the car."

"Where's your car?"

"Mine is in a garage on Canal Street. The one that's going to take us there is parked right out in front." She looked a little confused. "My publishers arranged for a car to pick me up and drive me home afterward. Brian's very good about things like that."

Willy gave me an odd, dark look. "You didn't ask me why the police are looking for me. You didn't even blink."

Of course I could not tell her that I already knew about the falsified criminal charge. "Things have moved so fast, it never occurred to me."

"I was accused of something. Bank robbery. It's ridiculous, but the police are looking for me. I mean, I might as well go to Millhaven—I can hide out there until the charge is dismissed." She sighed. "The evidence is a Photoshopped picture of me holding a gun on the bank president. It's all a setup, but I do have a lot of money in that bag between your legs. If we're caught, that won't look too good, will it?"

I began to lead her out of the narrow passage into which I had drawn her and toward the door. "It might be misinterpreted. Let's go up to the doors, and I'll take a good look around. If everything seems safe, I'll wave to you."

She gripped my arm, nodded, and released me. "Make it fast. I don't want to let go of you."

Willy moved to the front of the store next to a case full of computer games, and I carried the long white bag through the tables and past the lounging guard. After I had pushed through two sets of doors and got outside, the air felt as though it had been washed, and the street and the pavement sent up that clean, stony fragrance that is one of the delights of city life. The black-suited driver of the Town Car leaned over the wheel and questioned me with a look. **In a minute,** I gestured. Something had occurred to me.

In its abruptness and violence, the storm had been far too much like the downpour over SoHo the afternoon I'd chased Jasper Kohle down Grand Street. The barrage of rain, all that noise and rampaging electricity, had expressed Kohle's rage.

I believed, I **knew,** that he was hiding somewhere among the pedestrians across the street, in the entry of a Thai restaurant, behind a shop window, keeping his eye on me. I could feel his presence, the concentration of his gaze. I had a duty to perform, and if he could keep himself from killing me, he would insist on satisfaction. Kohle was the world's most focused sasha. Probably his whole life had been a violation of the borders, an electrical storm, a thing of damps and shocks and visions.

Although I could **feel** Kohle, I could not see him; nor could I spot the terrible, displaced men in search of Willy. She was still posted by the window. I made a come-to-me gesture with my right hand, and in a second she was outside the store and moving quickly beside me, her hand in my hand, toward the Town Car. The driver scrambled out of his seat and around the back of the car.

"Can I take your bag, sir?" he asked.

"We're going to keep this one," I told him, "but please put the lady's bag in the trunk."

Willy and I sat in the roomy back seat of the Town Car with the white bag between us like a big dog. At least, I thought, we wouldn't have to worry about leaving a credit card trail. The driver looked at us in the rearview mirror and said, "Are we going directly back to Grand Street, Mr. Underhill?" **For a little roll in the hay with your attractive female admirer?** he meant.

"No, we are going directly to the Golden Mountain Parking Garage on Canal Street," I said. "Please tell me if you have the feeling that we're being followed by . . ." I caught myself just in time, and questioned Willy with a sideways look.

"A silver-gray Mercedes sedan," she said. "With two men in it." Her two-second pause radiated hesitancy. "It sort of **shivers** when it moves, it sort of **glides.**"

"I've seen cars like that," said the driver. "I always figured athletes were driving 'em."

As we drove south through the city, Willy kept alternating between making comments to me and turning to look through the rear window. "I can't **believe** you knew who I was as soon as I came up to you."

Nor should you, I thought.

She looked back at the endless, shining traffic writhing down Broadway. "I guess Tom called you when he went out to find us a cab. And he never told me he knew you!"

He didn't know he knew me.

"And the first thing I see after I get blown through the tunnel is a poster with your name on it! Don't you find that kind of staggering?"

More than you can imagine.

"We'll stay together when we get to Millhaven, won't we?"

I nodded, thinking, **Just like you and Tom at the Milford.**

"I want to tell you something else." She gave me a look full of worry about my reaction to what she was about to say. "In the past couple of days, a really disturbing thing has been happening to me. Whole hours, usually transitions of some kind, are sort of deleted from my life. They just don't happen. I get in a car and drive out onto the street, boom, instantly I'm at my destination. Sometimes I don't even get **out** of my car, I'm already in a building, talking to someone." She placed her hand on my wrist. "Listen, I'm probably falling apart."

"This started happening a couple of days ago?"

Another prolonged backward look. "I think so. But you know? Maybe it's been going on for a long time, and I just became aware of it. It's like having whole parts of my life **skipped over**—it's not like they were deleted, but like they never happened."

"We could take you to a doctor, have you examined."

"It's not happening now, though, and this is just a transition, isn't it? We're going to pick up your car, that's all. Maybe you cured me!"

If a bloodstain fades away in about an hour, how long does it take a human being to disappear?

"Oh my God, I have to tell you about how I really got this money—and the picture of Jim Patrick's body—and how I escaped from the house on Guilderland Road—and my poor baby—and the Baltic Group—and . . ." She fell back against the seat and leaned her head on my arm. Her mouth was open, as if she had been struck dumb by the immensity of all she had to tell me.

"In time, Willy. I already know some of it."

"That's so, so strange," she said. "Of all the writers in all the bookstores in all the world . . ." Willy held out her hand, and I took it. "And I had this terrible feeling of being manipulated, of being shoved around like a marionette and forced to do all these things I wouldn't really do. Can you imagine?"

She turned around again, pulling her hand from mine, looked out at the traffic, and gasped. Her head went down, and she slid to the edge of the seat to peer out. "I think I saw them! Tim! They're back there!"

"Did you see anything?" I asked the driver.

"Not a thing," he said. "But I can't be lookin' in my rearview mirror all the time."

Willy moaned. "Ooooh, I can't be sure. How could a car like that be blown through a wind tunnel, anyhow?" She slipped to the floor and kneeled in the seat well, with her arms resting on the cushions. "Tim, I know this isn't fair, but what we're doing now makes me feels like a puppet, too. I mean, why am I here, in the back of this limousine—with **you**? I never met you before tonight, and the second I lay eyes on you, it's like you're the most important person in my world. It makes a lot more sense that Giles and Roman Richard should be looking for me than for you to be helping me get away from them.

But here I am, and there you are, and we're about to drive to Millhaven!"

"Doesn't that seem the right thing to do?"

"That's what's so screwed up!"

"That it seems right?"

"That it seems right because **you** said it was what we were going to do. It'd be the same thing if you said we were going to, I don't know, anywhere. Charleston. Kraków. Chicago. My sense of agency seems a lot more doubtful than it should be. And you? You seem to take all this for granted!"

My sense of agency? I wondered. This is not the sort of expression I ever use.

"Willy, I have never taken anything, at any time, less for granted. The whole world seems like one vast confusion, and everything is out of place."

"Mr. Underhill," said the driver. "I'm pretty sure that Mercedes you asked me to look for just cut in, about four cars back."

"Oh, crap." Willy grabbed my hand and tried to shrink down into invisibility.

"Get rid of them," I said, and the driver squeaked through the last of a yellow traffic light at the next corner and for ten minutes zigzagged from street to street until he came to Ninth Avenue, where he turned south again. He drove with the bravado of a getaway man, shouldering his big car through gaps that did not exist until he created them and shooting through red lights at clear intersections. Every now and then Willy peeked out at our wake, and I kept a steady lookout. The Mercedes ducked into view a couple of times, always in the midst of an awkward spot—caught in grid-lock, blocked from a turn by a huge double-jointed bus, stalled by a wave of people moving across the street.

When we got to Canal Street, the driver said, "I think we're winning, Mr. Underhill. I haven't seen them for ten, twelve blocks."

Willy thanked her god, and I thanked mine. When we pulled up in front of the Golden Mountain garage, I tipped the driver fifty bucks. A car just like the one we had left came down the ramp, and we got in, and with Willy Bryce Patrick beside me I drove across the Hudson River in a night suddenly glittering with a thousand points of distant illumination.

I **might** have seen Mitchell Faber's sharklike ve-hicle emerging from a rest stop on the New Jer-sey Turnpike, and it is possible that just before she fell asleep, Willy spotted it coming over a hill about half a mile behind us. That's why I

made a quick tour of the parking lot before going back to our room.

We are in Room 119 of the Lost Echoes
Lodge, located nine or ten miles from the free-
way in Restitution, Ohio. We're a long, long
way from New York. It would be a miracle if
they found us here, and I don't think they will.
There has already been a kind of miracle in the
Lost Echoes Lodge, and one is enough.

I had been going to take two adjoining rooms,
but Willy told me there was no sense in throwing money away, and besides, she had no intention of sleeping alone this night. "I want a warm
body beside me, and since Tom is dead and we
don't have a golden retriever, you're elected," she
told me.

We were still standing outside the lodge, taking in the astonishing structure before us. It
looked like an infinitely ramifying Bavarian
hunting lodge built in the 1920s for a timber
millionaire. Gewgaws and rickrack ornamented
the facade, which included complicated turrets
and window embrasures. Every inch of the
building seemed to be decorated with something, giant ivy sprigs carved from a dark wood,
wooden ducks in flight and owls on branches,
big clamshells half-embedded in cement. Once

every sixty minutes, a giant cuckoo should have popped out of the heavy, cross-braced front door. Warm light shone through most of the windows. Dense trees edged in from the near side of the parking lot and crowded the back and sides of the building.

When we checked in, the desk clerk (a sweet little man named Roulon Davy, who turned out to be the owner of the Lost Echoes Lodge) nodded at our request for a room overlooking the parking lot, signed us in under the first name that came into my head, accepted a cash payment for one night, and led us up to Room 119.

"Most of our folks want a forest view," he said, marching past the enormous bed to reach the set of windows at the far end of the room, "but if you fancy a prospect of the parking lot, here it is." He pulled aside the heavy brocade curtains and let us look out. Over the tops of the trees, we could see the back half of the lot. Beyond it, thousands of trees blanketed the side of a steep hill.

Willy yawned. "Sorry. I can't stay awake much longer."

The little man twinkled to the middle of the room—there is no other way to describe his retreat. It looked like tap dancing, but his feet barely touched the floor. "Then, Mr. and Mrs.

Halleden, I beg you to enjoy the perfection of your bed, the pleasures of your dreams, and the company of one another."

He saluted us and was gone before I could offer him a tip.

"Methinks our gracious host is of the fairy folk," Willy said.

"No," I said, "I'm of the fairy folk."

"Then let's get in bed and be brother and sister." She yawned again, and stretched her back. I thought it was one of the best things I'd ever seen. "You want to go in the bathroom first? You can use my toothbrush, if you like."

I went into the bathroom, washed up, and used her toothbrush; then she went into the bathroom, washed up, and used her toothbrush. There was no top sheet on the bed, only a soft, daisy-patterned comforter that seemed to tuck itself around my shoulders. The bed felt cool, slightly yielding, unconnected to anything as solid as the floor.

Willy's head poked out of the bathroom door, and she laughed at the sight of me. "You look pretty good, for an old dude. Or shouldn't I say that?"

"Keep talking. Everything you say surprises me."

"Lights out."

The switch for the overhead light was between

the bathroom and the door, and I saw a bare
arm and a bare leg emerge into the room as she
reached out. Her hand found the switch, and
the room filled with purple shadows and silver
moonlight. A small, pale body with white strips
across its chest and beneath its smooth belly slid
through the bright darkness and slipped into
the bed.

"Oh, I love this bed," Willy said. "I think this
is the perfect bed, the one all other beds aspire
to be. I'm too tired to think about agency and
too fuzzy to contemplate the imponderables of
our situation. Here I am, in a bed with Timothy
Underhill. Everything is crazy, and nothing
makes any sense, not even the slightest, faintest
trace. At least I had a complete day, with no
parts skipped over."

She scooted a bit toward me, and I a bit
toward her.

"You'll hold me, won't you? I think that would
be heavenly, and I'm not even going to question
why. I'm too bushed. But one thing I will say:
in about an hour and a half I'm going to get up
and prowl around the parking lot to see if that
miserable fucking car is anywhere in sight."

Her head fell gently on my chest, and I put
my arms around her. I stroked her back, her
shoulder, the cool, soft, silken length of the arm
lying across my torso. Her slim straight leg nes-

tled against my leg, and we lay like that for what seemed an eternity built up of one second after another. My hand moved to the small of her back and stroked the cool skin there. She did not feel like a fictional character; she felt like a lovely human being with a boy's hips and a woman's soft, duck-tail bottom, only smaller than most. It had been a long, long time since I had been in bed with a woman, and that had been nothing like this. I wanted to touch every inch of Willy Patrick, to slide into Willy Patrick's tender body, and I wanted that with a depth of passion I had probably not felt since my twenties.

Her hand slipped down to the band of my undershorts, and my leg moved between hers.

"Oh, God," she said, and I said, "I know. This is so odd."

"Where are you?" she said. "Are you there? Ah, I see, you are there. My goodness. Don't you think you should sort of wiggle out of that stupid thing you're wearing? You're so **huge,** you're going to strangle yourself."

I wiggled out of the stupid thing, my panting organ even harder for having been so blatantly flattered, and she shed her bra and her little tighty-whity with what seemed one fluid motion, and after that a kind of paradise opened before us. When I entered her, it **was** like entering paradise. Within her, I felt miraculously, blissfully at home—in the perfect place at last. I fell in love—that's the corniest, most banal, and truest way to say it. Before, I had felt as though I was falling in love, and now I had completed the journey. I was **there.** I wanted to hold her, cherish her, celebrate her for the rest of my life. It happened that quickly: I felt cleaved to Willy Patrick, as if we had one soul. We were like the gods depicted in erotic transport on half-ruined temples lost in the middle of great jungles. In the end, we seemed to flow together, to wear each other's skin and find ecstatic release as one four-legged, four-armed, two-headed organism.

"God," Willy breathed. "You're the author I want when I'm depressed, all right. I'm going to stop fretting about agency. I don't care, I've never been fucked like that before, and I want more of it."

"I have no idea how this is going to work out," I said, and kissed the palm of her hand, "but I don't ever want to lose you."

"Why should you lose me?" Willy asked. "I'm yours, aren't I?"

Soon after, she fell asleep. I slipped into my shirt and trousers and went the back way down to the parking lot, where something like a dozen cars, none of them silver Mercedes sedans, slept under the shelter of the looming trees.

What happened in this room is what Cyrax meant when he sent across my monitor in his Arial ten-point font u will have a chance of achieving something extraordinary & incestuous & ravishing unto heart-melt & impossible for every crack-brain author but u!

Now, ravishing unto heart-melt, Willy is raising her head and groping the pillow beside hers, and this crack-brain author is going to put down his pen and let her find me.

24

Willy kneeling on the bed, rummaging in smiling concentration through her bag and offering various items of clothing for his contemplation: she had crammed a lot of stuff into that bag. Blouses, shirts, sweaters, underwear, dresses, skirts, and jeans were displayed to him for comment, then placed beside the suitcase on the bed. "I should wear something comfortable," she said. "Especially since we're going to spend all day in the car. How about this sweater and a pair of shorts?" She held up for his approval a little cream-colored cotton-and-silk sweater with long sleeves and a boat neck. It probably weighed as much as a packet of stamps.

"I'd love to see you wear that," he said, and offered her a fragment of the mosaic she would eventually have to assemble. "Where's it from?"

"Hmmm." She held out the sweater, glanced puzzled at Tim, then checked the back of the collar for a label. "I don't remember where I got it. The label says 'Grand Street,' but that must be the brand name. I don't know of any shop called Grand Street."

She could not remember where she bought the sweater because it had come into existence only at the moment she had opened her closet and pulled it from a shelf.

"I don't either," he said, "and I live on Grand Street."

"In a loft?"

He nodded.

"That's nice. I always wanted to live in a loft. If Mitchell Faber hadn't scooped me up, I think I would probably have left the apartment I had on East Seventy-seventh and looked for a nice loft space downtown." She began putting her clothes back into her case.

"Would you?" In a way that was quickly becoming familiar, she had surprised him. The woman who had appeared in his life exhibited certain subtle differences from her representation on the page. **His** Willy would never have thought to leave her Upper East Side apartment, but only because he had not understood her well enough. As he had seen in the bookstore, he had underrated his heroine.

"Sure, as long as I felt stable enough to move," Willy said. "But I was feeling pretty well put together before Mitchell relocated me to Hendersonia. I mean, on the **night** I met him, I wasn't all that secure, but in general I was recovering pretty well. Once I got to Hendersonia, though, wow, it was like I was in some weird slow-motion dream. I thought I needed Mitchell to protect me, and look how that turned out."

"We're going to have to keep an eye out for Mitchell," Tim said, remembering again that Cyrax had written of a 2ble peril created by Kalendar's merging with a 2nd Dark Man, a dark dark villain almost instantly to b in pursuit of yr lovely gamine.

"How much do you know about all that?" Willy asked him. "Mitchell, and Hendersonia, and Roman Richard and Giles, and the Baltic Group."

"A surprising amount, considering that we'd never met until last night. Tom kept me pretty well filled in."

"Boy, I never realized what a gossip he was," Willy said.

"He knew I was getting very fond of you."

"You were? Just from hearing about me?" She smiled at him, then closed her repacked suitcase and swung her legs down on his side of the bed. "How nice. What do you think, do I come up to your expectations?"

"You surpass my expectations," he said.

"I do?" She slid off the bed, moved quickly across the gleaming dark floorboards, and slipped into his lap. Her body felt as if she were made of balsa wood and foam. She kissed him. "I don't know about you, but what happened between us last night was extraordinary. People talk about out-of-body experiences, but I think my body left **me.** Talk about surpassing expectations! It was like some kind of religious experience."

"Maybe it was a religious experience."

"My whole body feels so **light**—really, I've never felt anything like it."

For a time, he held her with the fierce protectiveness that came from the knowledge that he was going to lose her—as if in her lightness she would float away from him on the spot.

"You must have had thousands of women," she said.

"Not really." He smiled, although she could not see it. "Tom Hartland and I have a number of things in common. I haven't had thousands of anything, but the people I have gone to bed with tended to be men."

She was already looking up at him with a mixture of disbelief and astonishment. "You? But you—you're not kidding, are you? You're actually gay? You can't be that gay, though. If you weren't incredibly turned on, I have no idea of what's going on, anywhere. You were like, I don't know, like Zeus coming down in a shower of gold."

She slid around on his lap, straddled him, and moved her head close to his and looked deep into his eyes.

"I thought so, too," he said. "It was exactly like that. I'm astoundingly attached to you." He spoke with all the frankness the moment would allow. "There's a reason for all this, Willy, and you're going to find out what it is."

"I certainly hope so."

She had taken his remark as an attempt at general encouragement. He said, "I'm not speaking loosely, Willy. You do have something to find out, and it's extremely important."

She pulled her head back. "Is this whatever Tom kept saying he had to tell me, only the time was never right?"

"No. They're related, but what Tom was talking about is something else."

"And you know what that was, that secret, or whatever."

He nodded.

"So he told you, but he didn't tell me?"

"Not exactly."

She cocked her head. "What does that mean? Either he told you, or he didn't. Which one was it?"

"He didn't, Willy. It's just something I know."

"So this is like general knowledge? If I put in the right terms, I could look it up on Google?"

"It's nothing like that."

"But now there are two big secrets. I don't like this. It's skeevy."

Skeevy? Tim thought. Like **agency,** it was a word he would never use.

"What makes Timothy Underhill willing to risk injury, death, and imprisonment on behalf of a woman he just met? Why would he even consider driving her halfway across the country?"

"Timothy doesn't feel he has much choice."

He put his arms around her, and the moment of tension passed. They clung to each other as if they were stranded on a rock. Tim kissed her forehead, and she sighed and tightened her grip.

"Do you want anything to eat?" he asked.

"I guess." She nestled into him, pressed the side of her head to his chest, drew in her legs. She weighed nothing, and her bones seemed made of water. "Will we get to Mill-haven today?"

"I think so, yes. We'll get to Indiana, then drive north. I want to get there in time to do a couple of things before the reading." Also, Tim could feel Cyrax as though he were present in the room, and he was saying, **Get to Millhaven, buttsecks, and do yr job! You caused this mess, now you SOLVE it!** It was time for another fragment of the mosaic: Willy had to understand everything before they got to Millhaven.

"What was the name of your second-grade teacher?"

"Who cares?" She unhooked the bra she was wearing and tossed it toward her suitcase. "I don't even think I remember."

"Mine was named Mrs. Gross. I remember that, and I'm a lot older than you are. You should be able to remember her name, Willy."

Willy closed her eyes and put her hands on the sides of her head. Her face tightened into a grimace. "Okay, okay," she said. "I think my second-grade teacher's name was Mrs. Gross, too. Maybe we had the same one. Did you go to . . ." Again, she squinched up her face and pressed her hands to the sides of her head. "Ahhh . . . Freeman? Lawrence Freeman Elementary School?"

"Yes, I did," he said.

"Well, there's your answer! We went to the same school, we probably had a lot of the same teachers."

"Kind of funny, though, isn't it, that the

school is right behind the St. Alwyn Hotel, in Pigtown, and the Children's Home is way over on the north side of town."

"I'm going into the shower, sorry. Come on, you're getting hard again, let's get this guy in the shower and see what he does when he's wet."

Tim found both amusement and a kind of wonder in having so underestimated his heroine's sexual frankness and appetite. They forgot their worries until their hunger brought them back to the world. For Tim Underhill, every time he made love to Willy, his darling and his invention, he became more attached and involved, deepening the process that had started when he had placed her, like a figure on a chessboard, in front of the Michigan Produce warehouse.

At the end of their breakfast in the Swan Room, Mr. Davy told them that he had been visited by the police. Willy had displayed an amazing appetite, eating all four of her pancakes and all of her bacon, and following that with the two pancakes Tim still had left on his plate.

"They were wondering, do you see, if I might have checked in a woman who robbed a bank in New Jersey. They showed me a picture, but I don't think it really looked like Mrs. Halleden, and I certainly don't think that Mrs. Halleden ever robbed a bank in New Jersey!"

"I don't think she did, either," Willy said. "Will they be coming back?"

"Not until lunchtime. Our police officers have a distinct taste for our sauerbraten and Wiener schniztel."

"We'll be checking out in a couple of minutes," Tim said. "And thank you, Mr. Davy."

Willy excused herself and stood up. While Tim calculated a tip, the total to be added to his hotel bill, he noticed that his host was closely watching "Mrs. Halleden" on her way to the restroom. In his admiration, he had forgotten that Tim was present. While Tim watched Mr. Davy watching Willy, the little man registered some sort of quick, fleeting shock: his body clenched, and he thrust his head forward. Tim glanced past him at Willy, who was disappearing around the door to the ladies' room.

Suddenly realizing that he had been observed, Mr. Davy twitched around to face Tim. A faint blush, a faint smile enlivened his cherubic face.

"What?" Tim asked.

"Mrs. Halleden is a striking presence. If I may, sir."

Tim gestured for him to go on.

"If I might say this without being impertinent, sir, the lady is somehow more beautiful than one takes in at first glance. And I believe she looks younger than when the two of you arrived last night."

"There's more. There's something you're not saying. What startled you?"

Mr. Davy looked at him sharply. "Startled me, Mr. Halleden?"

"Something made you do a double take. I'm curious about what it was."

"It was just a mistake, a trick of the eye," Mr. Davy said. "I'll be at the desk, sir, should you wish your bags taken down." He whirled around and was gone.

Tim examined Willy for signs of youthfulness as, evidently considering something she found troubling, she wove her way back to the table. She had always seemed essentially young to him, but he wondered if she did in fact seem a bit younger than she had the day before.

Abruptly, she said, "I have that 'light' feeling again. I don't mean hunger. That's emptiness. This is **lightness.** It's like a buzz or a hum going through my whole body. It's like a thousand hummingbird wings, all beating at once."

Upstairs, Tim called the Pforzheimer in Millhaven and was assured that he could secure a junior suite for as long as he liked through the end of September. He was a valued customer, and they would treat him right. Then he called Maggie Lah and asked her to FedEx some of his shirts, pants, jackets, and socks to the hotel.

When he put down the phone, Willy said, "Let me pay for our hotels, okay? I won't feel like such a parasite."

When he protested, Willy said, "You shouldn't have to pay for me, I should be paying for you! We could probably live off this money for a couple of years. Let me show it to you."

As Willy dragged the long, white gym bag toward the bed, the telephone rang. Tim picked up the receiver and heard Mr. Davy say, "Mr. Halleden, please take a look out of your window. It appears that someone is extremely interested in your car."

"Willy, take a look at the parking lot, will you?" He thanked Mr. Davy and watched her go to the window.

"De nada," Mr. Davy said. "Tell me if you or Mrs. Halleden recognize the gentleman. He's too elegant to be a police officer."

"Shit," Willy said. "It's Coverley. How did he ever find us here?"

Tim moved to the window and looked over Willy's shoulder. A tall, slender man in a sweater the blue of a gas flame and pale gray trousers was walking back and forth beside Tim's black Town Car. He had long, well-combed blond hair and the face of a bored priest, and he was stroking his chin as he peered through the windows. The man straightened up and looked around the lot, then checked his watch.

"He's waiting for Roman Richard," Willy said. "That soulless murdering prick."

"Mrs. Halleden does not harbor friendly feelings toward the gentleman," said Mr. Davy.

"No," Tim said.

"Would he have any connection to the gray Mercedes sedan parked in front of the hotel?"

"What are you doing?" Willy asked.

"Yes, that's his partner," Tim said. "Willy, Mr. Davy and I are working something out."

"Mr. **Davy**?"

"Listen to me, now," said Mr. Davy. "For Mrs. Halleden's sake, I am going to act against type. That lady not only never robbed a bank, she never did a wrong thing in her life. And that man in the parking lot is a scoundrel. When you hear a loud noise, or you see that blond-haired creature start to run out of the lot, leave your room. Three doors to your right, you'll find a maid's staircase that will take you down to the back of the hotel. Get in your car as quickly as possible and take off. Pay no attention to the fracas when you drive by."

"The fracas?"

"Don't worry about me." He hung up before Tim could reply.

"Now what?" Willy asked.

Coverley was pacing beside Tim's car, growing more impatient with every second. He pulled a yellow pack of cigarettes from his shirt pocket, lit one with a match, and exhaled a plume of smoke.

"Giles **smokes**?" Willy sounded almost shocked. Every bit as startled as his beloved by this display of character treachery, Tim once again felt that loosening of the ground beneath his feet that occurred whenever Willy acted independently of the template he had made for her. An elegant character like Giles Coverley wouldn't smoke, but here he was, puffing away anyhow, acting like a human being instead of a character in a novel.

Below, Coverley spotted something hidden from the occupants of Room 119 by the trees on the near side of the lot. He threw away his cigarette, gesticulated, pointed at the hotel, raised his arms in an angry query.

"Uh-oh."

"What's wrong?" she asked him.

"Our friend Mr. Davy was counting on Roman Richard staying in the Mercedes. He was going to create a diversion, and I think this one-armed creep was supposed to play some kind of role in it."

On cue, Roman Richard Spilka strolled into view, suit jacket slung over his left shoulder, right arm encased in a plaster cast supported by a broad white sling. He was making conciliatory gestures to Coverley, half-turning to nod at the hotel. Again, there was a slight disconnect between the way Tim's characters actually looked and the way he had imagined them when depicting them on the page. Where Giles Coverley was slimmer, taller, and more decadent-looking than the man bearing his name in **In the Night Room,** Roman Richard was heavier, more solid, more obviously a thug. From the back, his close-cropped head resembled a bowling ball.

"You know he had a broken arm? Tom told you?"

"I guess," said Tim, wishing he hadn't mentioned it.

"That's incredibly interesting." Willy turned her head to look over her shoulder. A hint of suspicion darkened her eyes. "Tom knew that I knocked him down with my car, but he didn't know about the cast until a minute or two before he was killed."

"Then I knew about it some other way."

"There is no way at all you could know about

it," Willy said. She turned her head back to the window.

Tim and Willy watched Roman Richard moving across the lot toward Coverley. Both of the men indulged in a good deal of pointing and arm waving. Whatever camaraderie they might once have enjoyed had shredded under their multiplying frustrations, and now they were just two guys trying to make the best of a bad deal.

Then two things happened at once: a good-sized explosion at the front of the hotel rattled their window and shook the pictures in their frames, and Roman Richard and Coverley looked at each other and sprinted off across the parking lot with the reflexes of former soldiers. Roman Richard had worked out a more efficient way to wear his pistol, which was in his hand before he disappeared beneath the trees.

Tim took Willy by the elbow, spun her around, picked up the bags, and pushed her into the hallway. Three doors down to the right, he opened a door marked FOR STAFF ONLY and clattered down the dark, narrow set of stairs with Willy close behind. A door opened by pressing on a metal bar swung out onto a little paved area with uncapped garbage cans lined up on both sides of a dumpster.

"What'd he **do**?" Willy shouted behind him.

The sunlight drenching the parking lot shimmered on the tops of the cars. Underhill pounded toward the Lincoln. He was only ten feet away when the button on his key ring unlocked the door, honked the horn, and made the lights flash.

"Get in and duck down," he called, and heard her footsteps coming along behind him instead of separating off to the other side of the car, as he had expected. He grasped the door handle and asked, "What the hell are you doing?" But he was asking the air, and already understood that she was going to get into the back seat. She opened her door a fraction of a second after he opened his, and as he threw the bags inside and slid behind the wheel, he heard her climb onto the back seat and close the door behind her. The ovenlike heat made him pant; his skin instantly felt sandblasted. Blurry features and a flash of blond hair swam across his rearview mirror as Willy Patrick sank out of sight.

He turned the key and hit the accelerator. After a moment's rumination, the big car shot across the lot and into the narrow, tree-lined drive that led to the front of the hotel. On the left-hand side, the drive widened into the entry court; on its right, it continued on to the street. Tim clicked his seat belt into place, and felt

Willy pulling herself up on the back of his headrest.

They came around the side of the hotel into expanding chaos. On the lawn between the edge of the forecourt and the sidewalk, a ruined silver-gray car sent up six-foot flames from its shredded rear end. Uniformed hotel staff milled around the burning Mercedes. Most of them looked like college students. Tim glimpsed a familiar-looking boy in a tight-fitting black T-shirt and black hair staring at him in inexplicable annoyance. People from the neighborhood walked or trotted toward the front of the hotel. In the middle of the street, two boys on bicycles stared at the car in shared fascination.

Roulon Davy stood alone on the sidewalk, watching a pair of police cars race toward the hotel. Roman Richard and Giles Coverley had posted themselves on the lawn between Mr. Davy and their boss's former vehicle, keeping an eye on the hotel while they watched the conflagration. Roman Richard's back looked stony with fury, and Coverley's slouch expressed an elegant despair.

"Is your head down?" Tim asked.

"Just drive," Willy said, meaning that it was not, entirely.

At the moment the Town Car zipped past the

short lawn and was a second or two from shooting into the street, Coverley's blond head
snapped sideways, and his spoiled face hardened
in concentration. He followed the car's progress
as it sailed over the sidewalk and raced away
down the block. In his rearview mirror, Tim saw
Coverley step out in front of the police cars and
watch them go. Behind him, the boy in the
black T-shirt walked away from the scene: he
had taken two long steps before Tim realized
who he was, and why Roulon Davy's "diversion"
had been so successful. His forearms prickled;
his scalp tingled.

"He's talking to the cops, all right," Willy
said, kneeling on the back seat. "He isn't even
letting them go up to the car. I wonder what
good old Roulon actually **did**?"

Thinking of WCHWLLDN throwing off his
clothes, unfurling his great wings, and leaping
into the vastness of the sky, Tim turned toward
the middle of Restitution. Beyond its white
houses and thick green hedges lay the long, long
unspooling of the highway. Quick tears filled
his eyes, and he wiped them away before Willy
could turn around.

"Pull over so I can get into the front seat."

He drew up at the side of the street, and she
got out of the rear door and advanced toward
the side mirror and the passenger door. Just be-

fore her right hand moved out of the mirror's range, Tim realized that from midpalm to the tips of her fingers, it was a gauzy haze outlined by the grass and sky behind it. Then the hand slipped from view, and the passenger door opened.

Willy threw herself into the seat. As she closed the door, he tilted his head to look at her right hand, which was small, intact, and solid.

"What are you looking at?"

"I'm not sure," he said, and took a breath, remembering Mr. Davy's double take.

25

From Timothy Underhill's journal

Good old 224 took us across the state of Ohio. Ohio is a big state, and we saw mile after mile of farmland. I didn't see any suspicious-looking cars following us, but neither was I watching with any real degree of care. The police were my main concern, but the state troopers and local cops who had the chance to pull us over blew right on by.

"I still can't figure out how Mr. Davy managed to create so much damage in so short a time," Willy said. "You must have a guardian angel, or something."

Then she started to complain about being ravenous again, and I said I would stop at the nearest thing that looked like a grocery store. "How can you have a grocery store when you don't

have a town? I've seen so many fields, I'm sick
of the color green. But really, what did that
man **do**?"

"Mr. Davy must have hidden talents," I said.

"He's not the only one. How did you know
Roman Richard's arm was in a cast? Tom didn't
tell you, so don't lie to me about that."

"Do you think I lie to you, Willy?"

"You're not perfect, you know. You snore. You
refuse to explain things to me. Sometimes you
act like you're my father or something. . . . Explain about the cast."

I told her I couldn't, and she went into a sulk.
For the next fifteen miles of dead-ahead driving,
Willy simply crossed her arms in front of her
and stared out the window. It was like being
with a grumpy twelve-year-old. I don't think she
paid any attention to the landscape. Of course,
the landscape was nothing special. Once, a man
on a tractor waved at us. Willy growled. She
would rather have put a bullet in his heart than
wave back.

"You could explain," she finally said, "but you
won't."

"Have it your way."

"You're the kind of person who likes secrets,"
she said. "I hate secrets. Mitchell Faber **loved** secrets, so you're like him."

"Not really."

"Okay, have it **your** way," she said, and slumped back into angry silence.

Fives miles on, she said, "I can't believe how hungry I am." She placed her hands on her stomach. "I'm so hungry, it hurts." For the first time in about half an hour, she turned her head to look at me. "By the way, although I am talking to you, we are not having a conversation. I am telling you something, and that's different from having a conversation."

A gas station appeared in the distance, and she pointed at it and said, "Pull in there. Pull in there. Pull in there."

"You want me to stop at that gas station?"

Now her eyes were bright with fury. "If you so much as **try** to drive past that gas station, I'll murder you, dump your corpse onto the road, and drive over it on my way in."

I asked her what she thought she was going to get at the gas station.

"Candy bars," she said. "Oh, God. Just the thought of them . . ."

When we approached the station, she gave me a dead-level look of warning.

"I could use some gas," I told her, and turned in.

She had her hand on the door handle before I pulled up to the self-serve tanks. By the time I stopped, she already had a leg out the door. I watched her moving toward the low, white, cement-block building, where the attendant sat behind his counter. Willy was walking as fast as she could. As I looked on, she stopped moving so abruptly she almost lost her balance. She appeared to be staring at her right hand, which her body blocked me from seeing. Then she bent over to get a closer look.

This is going to shake things up, I thought.

With the violence of a released force, Willy whirled around, held out her arm, and yelled, "Look!" For a second or two, the thumb and first two fingers of her right hand were transparent, and the last two fingers looked hazy and opaque. Then, without transition, her hand became solid again. Willy lowered it slowly, glancing from it to me—she had seen something in my response, and I would have to account for it—before she turned around again and walked, at nothing like her earlier velocity, into the station.

Gasoline pumped into the Town Car, and the numbers on the dial rolled upward.

In a couple of minutes, Willy popped out of the station empty-handed and came trotting toward me. Panic shone in her eyes. "Can you give me some money, Tim? Like twenty bucks? Please?"

I fished a twenty out of my pants pocket. She took it from me, then leaned forward and in a low, urgent voice said, "We're going to talk about what happened to my hand. We both saw that, so it wasn't some kind of optical illusion. **Right**?" This last word meant: **You know something, and you are going to let me know, too.**

"Right," I said.

She sprinted off, no longer able to concern herself with an abstraction like dignity, and I went back to pumping gas. When the tank was full, I moved toward the little white box of the station, expecting to see Willy come through the door carrying a bag containing twenty dollars' worth of candy bars. She still had not emerged by the time I reached the entrance, and I didn't see her at the counter when I walked in. The boy at the cash register had H. R. Giger tattoos on his arms and short, dyed-blond hair that he wanted to look artificially colored. Willy was puttering around in the aisles at the back of the store. The boy took his eyes off her to register my entrance.

"Hey, dude," he said. "Is that girl with you?"

"Yes," I said, and went to the counter to hand over a credit card.

"Planning on a long trip?"

At the back of the store, Willy ducked out of sight. I heard the rustle of bags. Her head popped up above the top shelf, and my heart thumped in my chest at this sudden vision— Willy's floating head. In spite of everything, all my love for her, which had been a bit subsumed under both concern and a kind of mild irritation, returned to me. She said, "I need more money. Come back here, Tim." At least I had a name again.

She was trying to keep a grip on about a dozen loose candy bars, individual Reese's Pieces, a container of Fiddle Faddle, bags of peanut M&M's, and larger bags of potato chips. My arrival in her aisle caused a lot of Hershey's bars to slither out of her grasp and land on the floor. Her hands seemed reassuringly solid, but her temperament was sizzling toward hysteria. "Shit!" she whispered to me, once again ducking out of sight of the attendant. "I'm so hungry I can't hang on to this stuff."

"Eat one now," I said. "Save the wrapper, and we'll pay for it later." As I spoke, I started unwrapping one of the Hershey's bars that had fallen to the floor. Before I finished, she tore it from my hands. The end of the bar disappeared into her mouth, and she bit off about three inches of almonds and milk chocolate.

"Oh, boy," she said. She chewed with her eyes closed, and I could see some of the hysteria leave her. It was like watching her pulse slow down. "Dark chocolate would be better, but this is really, really okay."

"I'll get a basket," I said, and in a moment was back beside her, tossing candy and junk food into a plastic supermarket basket. Willy squatted on her haunches, taking giant, irregular bites out of the Hershey bar almost faster than she could chew.

"Get me two more Score bars," she said around a mouthful of chocolate. "Those little deals are wicked, wicked good."

"We should get some real food in you," I said.

"Yeah, I need a meal. But for some reason, this crap is what I need most right now. That **lightness** is beginning to go away."

"Do you guys need any help?" the boy called out.

Up at the counter, I unloaded the basket under the increasingly skeptical eyes of the tattooed boy. He dug one hand into his bleached hair and shook his head, half-smiling. I signed a MasterCard slip for $73.37, a nice palindromic number.

Willy was looking at me with a stony intensity that promised a serious interrogation as soon as we got back in the car, and I asked the boy about the nearest town that had both a decent restaurant and a library.

"A library?" Willy interrupted the boy's response.

"Before we can talk, I have to show you something." I folded the credit card slip into my wallet and picked up our bag.

"In a book?"

"In an atlas."

"You still want to know about the library?" the boy asked. "Just stay on 224 out there all the way to Willard. Like the rat movie. It has a library, and you could eat at Chicago Station. They're famous for their pies."

"Ahh, pies," Willy said.

Off we go to Willard, which turned out to be a lot nicer than I'd expected. Willard is the sort of place people would retire to, if they had any sense. Like all small cities, it's on a human scale, and there is more to it than you at first imagine. The streets are spotless, the shop windows shine, and the people say hello to strangers. The only problem in Willard, by which I also mean the drive to Willard, was Willy Patrick. She gobbled down three candy bars in a row—another Hershey's bar, a Mounds bar, and an Oh Henry!—while all but holding up a finger to let me know I wasn't getting off the hook this time.

Then she tossed the wrappers into the seat well, took out a packet of M&M's, and while peeling it open said, "Now talk to me, lover boy. No games and no kidding around."

"I thought that Hershey's bar at the gas station made you feel better," I said.

"It did, but it wasn't enough, not by a long shot. Don't worry about me getting sick, or anything. I **need** this gunk, and as soon as I finish these M&M's, I'll have had enough. For a while. And then I'll start feeling light again, and after that, well, I guess, after that . . ."

Her eyes narrowed; she aimed a finger at my chest. "And after that I guess I'LL START TO DISAPPEAR! I GUESS PIECES OF ME WILL SUDDENLY BE TRANSPARENT!"

She rammed four or five M&M's into her mouth and chewed them furiously. A trickle of chocolate drool slipped down the left side of her chin. She smeared it away while keeping her eyes fixed on mine. She swallowed. "I looked at you, and you **knew** about it. It shocked the hell out of me, but you weren't even all that surprised. You'd seen it before. So I guess this BIG SECRET of yours turns out to be that I am DISAPPEARING, and now I need an explanation!"

I took a deep breath and hoped we would

soon be driving into Willard. "I did see it once before. Back in Restitution, when you were shifting into the front seat. All of a sudden, I could see through the top part of your right hand. I'm pretty sure Mr. Davy saw the same thing a little bit earlier."

"And you didn't **tell** me? You decided you needed another **secret**?"

"I didn't know how to tell you," I said.

She shook her head in disgust. "I just realized something—you're weak. That's why you didn't tell me. You were afraid."

"It kind of took me by surprise," I said.

"Me, too! Don't you think I would have **appreciated** being told about something like that? 'Honey, I don't know how to tell you this, but it looks like you're turning into a **window,** because I just saw right through the top of your right hand'?"

Willy balled up the empty M&M's packet and threw it into the back seat. "And do you know something? I still want lunch. This isn't about hunger, it's about staving off the **lightness.** It's like putting gas in the car, that's what it's like. Except when I run out of gas, I won't be there anymore."

She stared into my eyes with a complicated mixture of fear, bravado, desperation, anger,

and trust that filled me with the impossible desire to hold her forever and keep her safe from
harm. "How did this happen to me?"

That was her real cry from the heart. Although she was by no means ready for the truth,
I had no choice but to answer in a way faithful
to her trust.

"Do you remember the bloodstains you had
on your shirt when you showed up at my
reading?"

"Of course." Because the blood had been Tom
Hartland's, the question irritated her.

"And you remember what happened to them."

"They disappeared."

"Bloodstains don't just disappear, Willy. Not
even bloodstains that go through a downpour."

"So first the bloodstains, then me? Is that it?"
She gazed at me for a moment, thinking. "Are
you saying that Giles and Roman Richard are
going to start to disappear, too?"

That, at last, gave me an opening I could use.
I could have kissed her hand. "Think about
this, Willy: why did you ask about **them**?"

She frowned. "They followed me."

"Through what? **From** what, **to** what?"

Her frown deepened, and her eyes burrowed
into mine. She leaned toward me, trying to remember every detail of that strange passage.
"Through that thunderstorm. I thought I . . . It

sounds crazy. I thought I was flying through a tunnel. Because they were chasing me, they came through the tunnel, too. I guess that's what happened."

"And on this side of the tunnel, Willy, do things look the same as they did on the other?"

We passed a little airport on our left, where prop planes sat outside hangars in the sun. I paused at a stop sign, then turned right on Euclid Avenue, waiting for her answer.

"It seems to me that everything's a little brighter now."

"Brighter," I said, stung.

"Hold on. Are you trying to insinuate that . . . No. I won't even say it."

She wouldn't say it, but I knew what it was. The first seed of recognition had just fallen on ground prepared for it by whatever it is you feel when half of your hand disappears and you need six candy bars to bring it back.

"How much brighter?" I asked, unable to let this go.

"Only a little. You want to know the biggest difference? Before I wound up in that bookstore, I had the feeling that someone or something was pulling my strings and making me do things I didn't actually **want** to do. And now, I still feel that way, but I know who's pulling my strings and moving me around. You."

"Do you like it better this way?"

"Yes. I do like it better this way." She checked her hands for signs of transparency. "Do you think I'm going to disappear, like the blood-stains?"

"Unless we can fix a mistake I made in Mill-haven last year."

"We're going to Millhaven to **fix** something?"

"I know none of this makes sense, Willy, and when it does, if that ever happens, you're not going to like it much."

"But why? What are we doing?" Her face be-gan to tremble, and she looked in my eyes for a reassurance she did not find. For about thirty seconds, she fell apart. I would have embraced her, but she fended me off by every now and then removing one of her hands from her eyes and clouting me in the chest. I pulled over to the side of the road.

"I don't know why I believe you." Willy wiped her eyes and cleaned her palms by smearing them over the sleeve of my jacket.

"I do, Willy," I said. "Before we get to Mill-haven, you will, too, probably. If I explained it to you now, it would be the one thing you would refuse to believe."

"I couldn't have anything to do with a mistake you made last year in Millhaven. I never went near Millhaven last year, and I didn't know you."

"What did you do last year, Willy? Can you remember a single thing you did in 2002?"

She shook her shoulders and gave me a scowling, insulted glance. "In 2002, I wrote **In the Night Room.** That's what I did that year. You probably don't know this, but I started the book in a place, a psychiatric community you could call it, known as the Institute, in Stockwell, Massachusetts."

Now she was daring me to find fault with her, and self-doubt turned her confidence brazen. "It's a wonderful place, and it did me a lot of good. There was this doctor there, Dr. Bollis. I used to call him Dr. Bollocks, but he was great. Because of him, I could write again."

"In 2001, I went to a psychiatric community that sounds very similar," I said. "And the treatment I had there was wonderful for me, too. I could sort of put myself back together."

She grew a shade less defensive. "So you should understand. What was the reason you came unglued, or wasn't there anything specific?"

"On September 11, I saw people jump from the World Trade Center. And then the ruin and all the death you could feel around you. It brought back too many traumatic things from Vietnam, and I couldn't cope anymore."

"Oh, poor Tim," she said. Tears glittered in

her eyes again. "My poor honey." She shifted sideways and put her arms around me. "I'm sorry I wiped my slimy hands on your beautiful jacket." She rested her hand on my shoulder for a moment.

"What happened to me was, my family got killed—my husband and my daughter." She was speaking in a low, soft voice now, and she held one hand cupped against the side of my face. Very faintly, I could feel her pulse beating in the tips of her fingers. "My whole world disappeared. I don't even remember how I got to the Institute, but it did me a lot of good. It's funny, you ask about what I remember from 2002, and that's all there is. Everything else is just darkness, it's a room I'm locked out of."

"My place was called the Austen Riggs Center, and it's in Stockbridge, Massachusetts. My doctor, my main doctor, the one who did me the most good, was named Dr. B——"

She sat up and looked at me in wonder. "That's almost the same name!"

"And the town, Stockbridge, was home for most of his life to a famous magazine illustrator named—"

"So was Stockwell! I can't believe this! Our guy was—"

"Norman Rockwell."

"Norton Postman," Willy said, and her eyes underwent a subtle change. "This is an amazing coincidence."

"It certainly is. Norman Rockwell painted hundreds of covers for the **Saturday Evening Post,** so in a way, you could call him the **Post** man."

"But so did Postman," Willy said. "I didn't know there were two of these guys."

"Not to mention two world-famous mental-health facilities in little towns in the Berkshires, and two excellent psychiatrists who practically have the same name."

Willy tucked her lower lip between her teeth, a gesture that for some reason I would never imagine her making. Maybe I thought it was too girlish for her, but there she was, biting her lower lip, and it didn't look at all girlish. Willy unpeeled a Mounds bar and began to fend off another attack of lightness.

Ten minutes later, we were walking into the pleasant, air-conditioned space of the Willard Memorial Library, a modern-looking building on West Emerald Street, just two blocks off the main drag. **Oh, Emerald Street,** I thought, and began to sense the close, hovering presence of my sister. Ever since my stunt in the Barnes &

Noble, **The Wizard of Oz** had been as implicated in her appearances as **Alice in Wonderland.**

"Atlases?" said the librarian. "Right over there, in our reference room. The atlas shelves are directly to the left of the door as you enter."

A couple of men read newspapers at a blond wooden desk; two girls in their preteens plowed through copies of the same Harry Potter book in a dead-serious race to the end. Diffuse light filtered in through the high windows and hung evenly throughout the large room. Separated by four empty seats, an old man and a high school student leaned over the keyboards of computers as if listening to voices.

I swung open the glass door to the reference room, and Willy followed me in. To my left, three tall shelves of outsized atlases stretched off to the far wall. We were alone in the room.

"Do you have a favorite atlas?" I asked Willy.

"The Oxford, I guess," she said. It was the one I used.

I pulled the Oxford **Atlas of the World** from the lowest of the three shelves and slid it onto the nearest table. "Let's get one more, for backup."

"Backup?"

"You're going to want a second opinion."

After a little searching I found the National

Geographic **Concise Atlas of the World** and placed it beside the Oxford. Balanced on one hip, Willy watched me with her hands behind her back, seeming to glow with the light of her own curiosity.

I gestured to the chair placed before the books, and she sat down and tilted her head to look up. The expression on her face made me feel as though I was just about to strangle a puppy. I leaned over the table and pushed the National Geographic toward the center of the table, leaving the Oxford **Atlas of the World** in front of her.

I asked Willy where she had been living before she fled to New York.

"Hendersonia, New Jersey."

"See if you can find it."

Giving me a suspicious glance, she flipped to the index on the last pages of the atlas. I saw her trace her finger down the long list of the **H**'s, going from Hampshire, UK, quickly down to the place names beginning with **He.** And here were Henderson, AR, Henderson, GA, Henderson, KY, and Henderson, NV. Where Hendersonia should have been, she found only Hendersonville, TN, and its namesake in North Carolina.

She frowned at me. "It must be too small to put in the index."

"Oh," I said.

She held up a finger, this time telling me that inspiration had struck, and flipped backward to the **A**'s. Her finger went down the list to Alpine, NJ, and when she had the page and coordinates she turned more pages until she came to the one she wanted and moved her finger along the lettered squares until it intersected with the proper numerical one.

"It'll be in here," she said, and motioned me forward.

I put a hand on her shoulder and bent down. Willy's finger circled around until it hit upon Alpine, from whence she drew it in a southerly direction, apparently without any significant success. She leaned over, put her face an inch from the complex, colorful map, and scoured it with her eyes.

Willy looked back around at me and pulled down the corners of her mouth. "This is nuts. Give me another one of those books."

I slid the National Geographic in front of her.

"That first atlas was stupid. It'll be in here." Her eyes skittered over my face, looking for clues. "Won't it?"

"Do you think I'd ask you to look if I thought it would be?"

She pulled back her head and frowned. With the same expression on her face, she opened the book at the index and flipped pages until she came to the **H**'s. The frown increased as she once again had the experience of moving from Henderson to Hendersonville with no stop at a place called Hendersonia.

"This is impossible," she said, without modulating her voice. "It's absurd. They erased an entire town from these atlases."

Back in the general part of the library, Willy looked at the computers and said, "Hold on." She went up to the desk. "May I use one of those computers?"

"Be my guest," said the librarian. "By law I am required to inform you that using the Internet to violate any state or federal laws is prohibited. Now that I've done that, I'll have to see a driver's license and have you sign this form."

It was a limitation of liability form, and I signed it as soon as I produced my driver's license.

Willy pulled me toward the seat beside the teenaged boy. When she sat down, he gave her a classic double take. Then he noticed me and turned back to the images of severed limbs on his monitor. Willy motioned me closer and whispered, "I know it's on MapQuest, because I've looked at it a couple of times since I moved there."

"Give it a whirl," I said.

Willy quickly reached MapQuest.com and typed "Hendersonia" and "NJ" into the address boxes. She clicked on Search. In seconds, the screen displayed a message reading, "Your search for **Hendersonia** in **NJ** didn't match any locations."

While she was busy being frustrated, I sat down at the computer next to the old man, logged on, and waited only a second before a blue rectangle appeared on my screen. As I'd feared, Cyrax wanted to let me know what was on his mind.

u must tell her what she is & speed to yr Byzantium, 4 u must pay the dredful price in sacrifice of the being u made. CO-RECK yr error & yr crime. it will b terrible & yet it must b done & U MUST DO IT! as I luv u, buttsecks, I cannot ignor the CHAOS u brought to our REALM and yrs & for this U MUST PAY IN KIND—U OPENED THE WEDGE, NOW U MUST CLOSE IT!

oh, what does gentle Cyrax demand of u?
FIND the real Lily Kalendar! See what she is! Understand the deep complexity of her self & her position, so u know what u got WRONG! payment must be made!

I logged off and slumped in the chair. Payment must be made, he said. Wasn't it being made, in full measure, by the heartbreaking woman at my side?

"No, that's wrong," Willy said. I heard real distress in her voice. The boy risked another peek at her. "It was there before!" She shook her head. "What's happening to me?" She stared at the screen for a moment, then said, "Hold on, hold on, I'm going to try one more thing."

This time, she typed in "Stockwell" and "MA." The same "Your search" message appeared on the monitor. "It isn't there? There's no Stockwell? Okay, I'm trying one more thing, and then I quit."

She went to Google and typed in "Charles Bollis, MD," and told the service to search the Web. What came back was the question "Do you mean Charles Boli's, MD?" and a link to a site that provided oncology information from somewhere called Charles County.

Her face had turned white.

"Let's get out of here, Willy," I said. "You need about three candy bars and a bag of M&M's, and both of us should have lunch."

"What were you looking at?" she asked me.

I told her I was checking my messages.

—

When we got back into the car, Willy dove into the bag and pulled out a handful of candy bars. After she wolfed the first one down and had gone through half of the second, she said, "I'm learning how to handle this condition, whatever you call it, and I can keep it under control. I **think.**" She demolished the rest of her candy bar, picked up a third—a 100 Grand bar—and removed the wrapper with a single downward stroke. "But I also think it is time for you to let me in on these big secrets of yours, because I really have to know what the HELL is going on."

I turned the key in the ignition. "I'll try to explain over lunch. This isn't going to be easy for either of us, but after what just happened, there's a chance that you'll believe me." I looked at her and started driving back to the center of town, which is where I thought I probably would find the restaurant mentioned by the boy at the gas station. Willy was chewing a cud of chocolate, peanuts, and caramel and regarding me with a mixture of confusion, anger, and hopefulness that I felt penetrate into my viscera, if not my soul. "Because, and this is a promise, you wouldn't have believed me before this."

"The town I live in doesn't exist—at least not in **this** universe! I remember stuff that **you** remember! I didn't go Lawrence Freeman Elementary School, and I didn't have Mrs. Gross as my second-grade teacher. You did, but I didn't. What would happen if I tried to call the Institute? It wouldn't have a number, would it? Because it isn't there. Just like Dr. Bollis."

"To look on the bright side, there isn't any Baltic Group, either."

"But Giles Coverley and Roman Richard still exist, and I'm sure they're still trying to find us."

"I bet they're running into a lot of problems right about now."

"I bet they're scarfing down a lot of sugar right about now. But I guess I don't have to worry about Mitchell anymore."

"Unfortunately, that's not exactly true," I said.

"Save it. Is this the place?"

A tall, vertical sign outlined in lights spelled out CHICAGO STATION above a long, rectangular building faced with stone. I drove into the lot and parked under the only tree in sight.

"You're not paying for lunch. I should split everything with you. Do you know how much money is in that bag back there?"

"A hundred thousand dollars, in hundred-dollar bills."

Her face went soft and confused, almost wounded. I was afraid she would start to weep.

"Did I tell you that? Don't answer."

She got out of the car and opened the back

door. The long white bag lay across the seat, and she pulled it toward her and unzipped the top. Curious about what all that money looked like, I stood behind her as she reached in and lifted a neat, banded bundle of bills out of the bag. "Let's just take two of them," she said. "You carry them."

Willy tugged two of the hundreds out of the pack and handed them to me. She leaned back into the car to replace the rest of the bundle, and I looked at the topmost bill in my hand. What I saw made me gasp. For a hideous moment it struck me as funny. It was a hundred-dollar bill of the usual size, color, and texture. The numbers were all in the right places. Just left of the center, in the big oval frame where Benjamin Franklin should have been, was what looked like an old-fashioned steel engraving of me, in three-quarter profile, from the top of my head to the base of my neck. I did not look anything like as clever as Franklin, and I appeared to be wearing my old blazer and a button-down shirt with a frayed collar. The little scroll beneath the portrait gave my name as L'Duith.

"Your money's no good in this town," I said, settling at the end for a cheap joke. "Take a look."

Willy stared at the front of the bill, glanced up

at me, then back at the bill. "That's your picture on there."

"So it seems," I said.

Now she was so dumbfounded she seemed hypnotized. "How did that happen? How did you **do** that?"

"It's a long story," I said. "Let's go into the restaurant and get some real food in you."

Willy took my arm like a wounded child. "Look, do I actually exist?"

26

From Timothy Underhill's journal

"Of course you exist," I told her. "You're here, aren't you?"

Willy leaned out of our booth and waved to a waitress taking orders at one of the tables in the middle of the room.

"But as you have noticed, you don't quite exist in the normal way."

"How come the town I live in and the Institute I went to aren't real anymore, when they used to be? How come the stuff I remember seems to come from you? What the hell happened, did you make me up or something?"

The waitress appeared at our booth and gave us each a laminated menu. "Oh, aren't those cute?" she said, pointing at the hundred-dollar bills Willy had left on the table. "They almost look real. Can I pick one up?"

"You can keep it, if you like," Willy said. "I gather they're not exactly—what's the word?—fungible. I want a hamburger, medium. With fries. Make that two hamburgers, with fries."

The waitress said, "Wow, it even feels real. So your name is L'Duith? What is that, French?" She was a comfortable woman in her mid-forties who looked as though she had been born wearing a hairnet.

"It's part of an anagram," I said. Willy was staring at me intently. "I'll have a medium burger, too. And a Diet Coke."

The waitress went off to the kitchen, and Willy focused on me in a way I found extravagantly painful.

I looked down at my hands, then back at her. Her eyes concentrated on mine, and I knew she was watching for signs of evasiveness or duplicity. She would have spotted a lie or a deliberate ambiguity before the words left my mouth.

"Right after we sat down, you asked me if I made you up. I don't suppose you were being completely serious, but you hit the truth right bang on the head. Everything you know and everything that ever happened to you—in fact, everything you ever did before you showed up at that reading—came out of my head. As far as you're concerned, I might as well be God."

"You know, when I first saw you, I did think

you were kind of godlike. I worshipped you. And you were certainly pretty godlike in bed!"

The waitress chose that moment to place two glasses of water on our table. Her face made it clear that she'd heard Willy's last remark and had interpreted it to mean that I was a lecherous pig. She wheeled away.

"Oops," Willy said.

"I worship you, too," I said. "These simple words, all this deep feeling. I hope this is what God feels for his creatures."

I moved my hand to the center of the table, and she placed hers in it. We were both on the verge of tears.

"Say more," Willy said. "This is going to be the bad part, I know, but you have to tell me. Don't be weak now. How could you make me up?"

She was right. I had to tell her the truth. "Before you showed up, I was writing a book. Its first sentence was something like, **'In a sudden shaft of brightness, a woman named Willy Bryce Patrick turned her slightly dinged Mercedes away from the Pathmark store on the north side of Hendersonia, having succumbed to the temptation'**— no, it was 'compulsion'—**'having succumbed to the compulsion, not that she had much choice,'** I forget what comes next, something about driving a little more than two miles on Union Street, which I also happened to make up."

"Your first sentence was about me."

"You didn't exist until I wrote that sentence. That's where you were born. Hendersonia was born then, too, and Michigan Produce, and the Baltic Group, and everything else."

"That's nuts. I was born in Millhaven."

"Should we call the Births and Deaths office, or whatever it's called, and ask them to find your birth certificate?"

She looked uncomfortable.

"Willy, the reason you couldn't find Hendersonia in the atlases is that Hendersonia only exists in the book I was writing. I named it after a book about Fletcher Henderson."

"In your book, you named a town after another book?"

"The name of the book is **Hendersonia.** A man named Walter C. Allen wrote it. It's a wonderful book, if you're obsessively interested in Fletcher Henderson. Do you know who he was?"

"A great bandleader and arranger. In the twenties, he hired Louis Armstrong and Coleman Hawkins. Big influence on Benny Goodman."

"See? You're not a geeky jazz fan, Willy. You know that because I know it. Stuff from my head, at least the kind of stuff I think is important, gets into yours. Your memory is really my memory."

"This is . . . Even with the things that have been happening, it's still hard for me to believe that . . ." She removed her hand from mine and made a vague shape in the air.

"Let me tell you some things about yourself that I couldn't have learned from Tom Hartland, who was, by the way, another fictional character of mine."

Willy sat back in the booth, her hands in her lap, looking like a schoolgirl about to enter the principal's office.

I closed my eyes and tried to remember what I had written about her. The events of the previous two days had made some of the details recede. "You almost broke into a produce warehouse, but the thought of Mitchell Faber snapped you back into the real world. You realized that Mitchell Faber and your daughter couldn't exist in the same world because your daughter was dead, so she couldn't possibly be in that building."

Her eyes widened.

"And it's a good thing you changed your mind, because shortly after you got back into your car, a young policeman drove up behind you. He didn't believe how old you were until you showed him your driver's license. He told

you that you couldn't have too many worries—
to look so young, he meant. And when he saw
your address on Guilderland Road, he knew
your house right away. When you tried to thank
him, he told you to thank Mitchell Faber instead."

"How do you know that?"

"I **wrote** it. I put that part in to indicate that
the police were not going to be very helpful
later on, when you escaped into Manhattan. In
this book, you were supposed to be hunted by
the police as well as Faber's goons. Which is exactly the situation you're in now, except I'm
with you."

"What was the name of this book?"

"In the Night Room."

She absorbed that silently.

"There is a real night room," I said with a sudden recognition. "It's in Millhaven."

"A real night room. I don't even know what
that means."

"It's a room where it is always night. Because
of the terrible things that happened there." I
took a leap into the dark. "To you."

"When was this supposed to happen?"

"In your early childhood—the years you can't
remember. You don't really remember anything
that happened before you were sent to the
Block. All you have of your first six or seven

years is the sense that your parents loved you. That is a fantasy, a false memory. You use it to conceal what your life was actually like in those years."

"That's a goddamn lie."

"Willy, none of this happened in real life. I made it all up. It's fiction, and I know what I wrote—I don't blame you for not believing me, and I can't blame you for getting angry, but I know your history better than you do."

She took that, too, in silence. For the first time in our conversation, I had used the word "fiction."

"What else can I tell you? When you started to rearrange things in the house on Guilderland Road, sometimes an expression on Coverley's face reminded you of Mrs. Danvers in **Rebecca.**"

She was concentrating so hard that she didn't notice the arrival of our waitress, who to get her attention had to say, "Excuse me, miss, your hamburgers are ready." The woman put the plates on the table, and the glasses, and a bottle of ketchup, and Willy did not take her eyes from me for a second.

When the waitress had left, Willy immediately picked up one of her hamburgers and took an enormous bite out of it. She groaned with pleasure. Then she glanced at me and spoke a mushy, "Sorry."

I watched her eat for a time, unwilling to make further demands on her attention. It was like watching a wolf devour a lamb. Every now and then she pushed French fries into her mouth; every now and then she sipped at her Coke.

After vaporizing the first hamburger, Willy wiped her mouth with her napkin and said, "You can't imagine how much I needed that. I need this one, too."

"How's the lightness?"

"I don't think I'm going to start disappearing anytime soon. We're just talking about hunger now, basic hunger." She attacked another batch of French fries. "Look. Part of me thinks it's really creepy that you know these things about me. It's like you went around peering through the windows and rummaging through the drawers, like you listened to my phone calls. I don't like it. But another part of me, the part that loves you, is thrilled that you know so much."

She bit into the second hamburger. Chewing, she said, "You shouldn't know these things. But your face shouldn't be on that money, either, and there it is." She leveled a French fry at my

handsome portrait. "What's this L'Duith business, anyhow? You said it was part of an anagram."

"The full version is Merlin L'Duith. Can you
figure that out? You're very good at Scrabble and
crossword puzzles, so it should be easy for you."

Willy popped the french fry into her mouth
and stared at the altered banknote. "Um. Two
L's. An **N** and a **D-E-R.** That's easy. It's an anagram for Tim Underhill."

"I started Part Two of my book with a message
from Merlin L'Duith, in other words myself,
who said that he was the god of your part of the
world, plus Millhaven. Merlin, who's a magician, wanted to speed the plot along, so he sum-
marized the day you met Tom Hartland at the
King Cole Bar."

"Why is your face on that money?"

"Probably because I didn't bother to say anything about Benjamin Franklin, and when the
bills came through, there I was."

She pondered that.

"Merlin did something a little strange in his
section. He let you notice the bits that he
dropped out of your life. The lost hours, the
transitions that never happened. He's a god and
a magician—he can do anything he likes."

Willy stopped eating and, in an almost bel-
ligerent way, stared at me for a couple of

beats. She resumed chewing. She swallowed; she sucked Coke into her system. "That was in your book? You did that? Hiding behind this Merlin anagram."

"I had you notice the gaps that people in novels can never be aware of, because if they did, they'd begin to realize that they are fictional characters. I didn't have any particular reason for doing it, I just thought it would be interesting. I wanted to see what would happen. As it turned out, that was probably one of the things that let you leave the book and wind up in my life."

Her stare darkened. She wasn't blinking now.

"I hated those gaps. They made me feel that I really was losing my mind."

She shoved her plate away, and the waitress, hoping to get us out of her territory very soon, instantly materialized at our booth and asked if we wanted anything else.

"Pie," Willy said. "We heard you're famous for your pies."

"Today we have cherry and rhubarb," the waitress said.

"I'll have two slices of each, please."

Willy waved her off and pointed a lovely finger at me. "Okay, you, or Merlin L'Duith, deliberately let me notice that these transitions had been left out of my life. But why did you have me leave Hendersonia in the morning and arrive in New York nine hours later? What was the point of that?"

Willy had turned a crucial corner, though she did not know it. She had already bought what I was selling. I wondered how long it would take her acceptance to catch up with her.

"You had to get there at night so that it would be night when Tom Hartland came to your room."

"Why?"

"So that he could sleep in the same bed with you. At your invitation. It was the quickest solution—make it night instead of day. Whoops, nine hours gone."

"Do you know how disconcerting that is?"

"Probably not," I admitted.

"You wanted Tom Hartland in bed with me because **you** wanted to be in bed with me. I'm right, aren't I? If you invented me, you didn't understand me very well, and no wonder, because you don't understand yourself, either."

"In the way you mean, I do," I said.

"If you invented me, you did a BAD JOB!"

Before scurrying away, the waitress put two plates in front of Willy and, unasked, a cup of coffee. It was as though she had never been there at all.

"I didn't **want** to go to Michigan Produce,"

Willy said. "I didn't **want** to hear my daughter screaming for help. How could you do that to me?" She levered a big section of cherry pie onto her fork and pushed it into her mouth. "You never understood what kind of person I was. I'm so much better, so much stronger than you thought. All you saw was this weak little woman being pushed around by men." Her voice wobbled, and she brushed tears away from her eyes. "I suppose I'm not even a writer anymore. I suppose I didn't have any talent."

"Not at all. I gave you a beautiful talent, and an imagination so strong that twice you used it to rescue yourself."

"On the Block and then in the Institute, you mean." For at least a minute and a half, she ate big forkfuls of pie while crying steadily. Then she wiped her eyes again and looked over at me. "Would you care to know why I'm willing to believe all this bullshit of yours?"

"Please," I said.

"Do you remember when I went to the bathroom in the Lost Echoes Lodge? After breakfast this morning? It's nothing out of the ordinary for you, is it? But when I got into the bathroom, it was like I had to tell myself what to do. I couldn't remember ever using a toilet before in my life. And every time I go to the bathroom now, I marvel at how strange it all seems to me.

For the first thirty-eight years of my life, I never used a toilet!"

It was true. She never had, and I had never thought about that. In all of fiction, probably, urination scenes are specific to men.

"I have to sit somewhere else for a while," Willy said. Her cheeks were shiny with tears, and her eyes seemed half again as large. "Whatever you do, don't bother me."

She carried the plate of half-eaten rhubarb pie to the last booth in the line across from the bar. Because just about everybody in the room watched her go, I realized that they had been eyeing us ever since Willy had shouted that I had done a BAD JOB.

The waitress slipped into Willy's booth and started talking in that earnest manner people adopt when they think they are telling difficult truths. I thought Willy would get rid of her in about ten seconds. It took five. The waitress came scuttling out of the booth, looking like a hen trying to stay ahead of a fox, and everyone else pretended to ignore the drama we had brought to Chicago Station.

It took Willy something like twenty minutes to collect herself and make her way back through the tables in a gunfire of glances questioning and dismissive. (Some of those older ladies thought she deserved every bit of the punishment they assumed I was giving her.) She slid in, extended her arms over the table, and let herself tilt limply back against the dark wood behind her. "I give up," she said in a defeated voice. "I'm a fictional character. There isn't any other explanation. You created me. I don't belong in this world, which is the reason I feel this way—the reason I'm in danger of fading away. Fading **out.** Put me back in the world where I belong, crummy as it was. In that world I was a person, at least."

"I can't," I said. "That world doesn't exist anymore. You're here, and I can't finish the book."

"So I'm just going to eat a hundred candy bars every day until unreality finally catches up with me and I disappear."

I signaled for the check. The waitress moved up to the booth with the deliberation of an ocean liner coming into a narrow port. She slapped the slip of paper down on the table and backed away. I looked at the total and started counting out bills.

"I trust that we have dealt with the big secret," Willy said. "And I have to admit, it's a doozy. What's the little one, the one Tom didn't want to tell me?"

"Brace yourself," I said. "Tom knew something that made him worried and unhappy every time you mentioned your daughter. He didn't want to tell it to you because he thought you'd hate him, or fall apart, or both. He was on the verge of suggesting that you see a good psychiatrist."

"I'm waiting." And she was: under the limpness and the weariness she was communicating enough tension to make the air crackle.

"Remember that Holly wasn't in that photograph of your husband's body you found in Mitchell's office?"

She nodded.

"There's a good reason Holly wasn't in the photograph. You didn't have a daughter. You and Jim were childless."

Willy looked for signs that this preposterous chain of sentences was somehow supposed to be funny, or a trick, or anything but a statement of fact. When she saw no such sign, she got angry with me.

"That's unspeakable. It's obscene."

"I'm sorry," I said.

"I don't love you anymore. I never did—how could I love someone capable of saying that to me?"

"What was Holly's birthday?"

"What difference does that make?" Willy started to scramble out of the booth, and I caught her arm.

"Tell me about her birth. What was it like? Did you have a doctor or a midwife? Home birth, or hospital?"

In her suddenly colorless face, her eyes blazed at me. She stopped trying to fight her way out of the booth. "She was born . . ." Her eyes went out of focus; softly, her mouth opened. "I know this, of course I know it." She closed her eyes, and I let go of her arm. "Doesn't my life, this existence of mine, seem pretty stressful to you? When I feel like this, I really can't remember everything. If you give me a second, it'll come back to me."

"All right," I said. "Let it come back to you."

Willy opened her eyes, tilted her neck, and looked at various spots on the ceiling, as if hunting for the answer she needed. "Okay. Holly was born in a hospital."

"Which one?"

She let her eyes drift down to my face. "Roosevelt."

"Willy, you got that from me. That's the hospital my doctor sends me to. How much did your baby weigh?"

She went back to searching the ceiling. A couple of seconds later, she licked her lips. "She weighed a normal amount, for a baby."

"You don't have any idea of how much that would be, do you?"

She made a rapid, inaccurate calculation. "Ten pounds."

"Way too much, Willy. Don't you think it's odd that you can't remember giving birth?"

"But I did give birth, I had a daughter."

"Willy, the little girl who was murdered was a version of your childhood self. She was you. Do you know why you're named Willy?"

She shook her head.

"In my book, your real name was Lily—Lily Kalendar. You couldn't pronounce the letter **L,** so you called yourself Wiwwy, and people thought you were saying Willy. And the name of your hero, your incredibly brave, smart, inventive boy, was Howie Small. Howie equals Holly the way Willy equals Lily. That's how I got these names—from a little girl's lisp."

"My father's name was Kalendar. You said that was someone's name. What was his first name?"

"Joseph."

"Tell me about him."

"If you look into what you already know, Willy, you'll find everything you need to know. Lately, Joseph Kalendar has been in my thoughts a great deal."

"I don't know anything . . ." She began to protest, but her voice died away. Whatever surfaced in her mind, on loan from mine, disturbed her greatly. The initial look of shock on her face gradually melted into sorrow, and tears filled her eyes again. "Oh, my God," she said. "How many women did he kill?"

"Six or seven, I can't remember which."

"And my brother. And my mother."

"Probably. No one ever found her body."

"Can we get out of here now?" Willy asked.

We stepped outside into strong sunlight and moved slowly toward the car. It was like walking someone out of a hospital. She looked at my face. "This is what you know about my father."

I nodded. Before Willy got into the car, she said, "He built secret hallways and staircases into our house." She was still stunned. Her face was all but immobile. "And he built . . ." She stared at the fact she had just conjured and could not speak.

"He built an extra room at the back of the house. Get in now, Willy."

Like a child, she climbed in. Her eyes were glazed. "He built that extra room. It had a slanting roof that came right down to the ground. It had a huge big wooden bed in it. My father did things there, things I can't remember. And that was the real night room."

I closed the door and went around to the driver's side. Despite the shade I had found, you could practically have cooked a pot roast in the interior of the car.

"There were no lights in that room. And it didn't have any windows."

Willy was doing nothing more than parroting what she found in our shared memories. She wasn't even close to responding to them, for they were not yet part of her emotional life. She had been overloaded with information, and what she had learned had exhausted and numbed her.

Her next question surprised me. "What were you going to do with me at the end of your book?" A little wall-eyed, her head back against the cushion, she spoke as though about someone in whom she had once taken an interest.

"You were going to walk into your old house at 3323 North Michigan Street, in Millhaven. That's where Joseph Kalendar lived. You were going to go into the night room, meet the Lily who became Willy, and understand that she was the child you wanted to rescue. Or something like that. I was still working it out. The only reason you wanted to break into that warehouse was that it had MICHIGAN painted on its facade. What really drew you in was the part of your childhood you had blotted out."

I started the car and turned up the A/C. Cool air streamed from the vents, lowering the temperature layer by layer, from the floor mats up.

"Was it going to be beautiful, your ending?"

"I think it was, yes." I backed out of our space

beneath the tree and headed toward the exit. "When I thought about it, it seemed very beautiful."

"And I screwed it up for both of us."

"No, I did," I told her. "In the book that's just about to be published, I implied that Joseph Kalendar had killed his daughter. His spirit, or whatever you want to call it, has been after me ever since he found out. He's enraged."

"What does my father want? What is he looking for?"

I got us back on the road out of Willard and moving toward 224. What did Joseph Kalendar want from me? I remembered the name of the little Ohio town where Willy and I had stumbled across Mr. Davy's splendid Lodge and within Room 119, overlooking the parking lot, first fallen into each other's arms. "Restitution," I said. "That's what the old madman is looking for."

"Well, I want it too. What was the story about my husband's murder? Did Mitchell kill him?"

"I'm not absolutely sure. I hadn't worked it out yet."

"Well, did Mitchell take those pictures?"

"Probably."

"How come a man at that hotel in Nanterre told me he was checked out, and ten minutes later another man said he was still there?"

"I was going to figure that out later."

"Would a banker really ever transfer money like that, without a signature?"

"Probably only in Hendersonia," I said.

Neither one of us noticed the mud-slathered Mercury Mountaineer that had been trailing us, always six or seven cars back, since we'd left the restaurant.

27

From Timothy Underhill's journal

About an hour east of the Indiana border, an enormous building surrounded by acres of parking lot loomed up on the right side of the highway. We could see it coming long before we got close enough even to make out any details. I took it for an enclosed shopping mall until I noticed that the building was a giant box with no ornamentation but a sign that read SUPER-SAVER KOSTKLUB.

"This is it, Willy," I said to the silent, drooping woman beside me. We were down to our last half dozen candy bars. "We can buy enough candy here to see you through to Christmas." The huge store would have ATM machines, too.

Willy said nothing. She had not spoken since I'd answered her question about the banker. I knew she was reacting to everything she had learned in the restaurant, all that overwhelming information that had descended upon her after she'd made her great, shining leap into the dark. It must have felt like the single greatest capitulation of her life, for in effect her surrender had been to absolute and unknowable mystery. And after that I had taken her child from her, and in its place presented her with one of the darkest, most painful childhoods ever endured. The fact was, though, that Willy **had** endured it, because her father had not, after all, murdered her— Joseph Kalendar had loved his daughter at least enough to let her go on breathing. To that extent, Willy had been right about her earliest years: righter than I had been willing to admit.

I turned in to the huge parking lot and drove down the aisles, looking for an empty spot. She surprised me by breaking into my thoughts and saying, "Get me some good dark chocolate. With lots of cocoa in it, and not so sweet. The usual stuff, too, because that works better, although I don't like it as much. And get a couple of boxes of confectioner's sugar, some Coke, in the really big bottles, and some plastic glasses."

I pulled in to a parking place that seemed about a quarter mile from the building and made the mistake of asking her how she felt.

"How are fictional characters supposed to

feel? The hummingbird wings are beating away like crazy, and I think I have about half an hour before parts of me start to flicker out. This sucks. This is a really crappy deal. I was happier before you explained everything to me."

I tried to say something that would have ended up leaking a soupy, self-conscious semi-profundity. Willy saved us both by speaking over me.

"Go on, get me my chocolate. I'll wait here and brood about how miserable and uncertain my life is. I'm not real, I'm a fantasy of yours."

"Who says my fantasies aren't real?"

With a feebleness that was only partially feigned, she raised one hand. Then she let it drop back into her lap and wilted her upper body against the door, her head leaning on the window. Cool air flowing through a vent ruffled the bottom of her sweater. "Just go, Tim. I'll be all right."

A geezer with a red vest and a name tag directed me down through the vast space to aisle 14, where I loaded my shopping cart with boxes of Mounds bars, boxes of almond M&M's, boxes of Hershey's and Kit Kat and 100 Grand bars. A little farther along I encountered trays of dark French and Belgian chocolate, and I pretty much filled the rest of the cart with boxes of French, Italian, and Belgian chocolates—

Droste, Perugina, Valrhona, Callebaut. On the
way back to the front of the store, I circled
around the back of the bakery section, cut
through aisles piled to the ceiling with cake
mixes and vats of frosting, and discovered six
shelves and whole flats devoted to sugar. I tossed
four boxes of confectioner's sugar onto the can-
dies and proceeded to the rank of ATM machines at the back of the building, where I
withdrew five hundred dollars.

Willy started digging into the bags as soon as I
got them in the car, and in minutes candy bars
littered her lap and the seat well in front of her.
"Oh, my God. Perugina and Valrhona dark
chocolate. And here's some Belgian!" Her head
snapped up, and she stared straight ahead. Her
clean, breathtaking profile should have been on
a coin. "I have an idea. By the way, I'm not talking to you, I'm talking to myself."

    She took a box of sugar out of a bag, placed it
her lap, and ripped two plastic glasses out of
their container. Then she half-filled one of the
glasses with confectioner's sugar and filled the
other with Coca-Cola from a two-liter bottle.
First she dumped sugar into her mouth, then
she washed it down with Coke. She repeated
the process a couple of times. Powdered sugar
lay scattered over her lap and across the seat.

"That's your idea?"

"No, but this is by far the most efficient way of handling the lightness problem. It just gets in there and does the job. Chocolate tastes a lot better, of course. But this stuff, I can feel it working."

She gave me a glance that said this, too, was not a conversation, merely a form of Q&A, and crawled over into the back seat and began throwing the useless money out of the white duffel bag. (Willy is wonderful, and I love her, and most of the ways in which she surprises me are far more pleasant than not, but she is a slob, and there's no way around it.) In seconds, hundred-dollar bills that appeared perfectly legit until you looked at them closely were floating down all over the back seat and onto the little shelf in front of the rear window. I asked her what she was doing, and she told me to shut up. When the bag was empty and fake money lay all over the place, mingling nicely with the spilled sugar, I could hear her transferring the contents of the grocery bags into the duffel. Then she dropped the grocery bags on the floor and tramped them flat, her idea of housekeeping. After that, she climbed back into the front of the car, dragging the white duffel with her, and began pitching into it the loose candy bars and chocolates that were scattered around her.

Every now and then she popped a chocolate candy into her mouth.

"I don't actually need this now, but I might as well live it up, right?" she said. "While I can?"

I told her to feel free.

"At least now I can bring my stash with me when we go places," she said, hefting the bag. "It's not as heavy as before, either."

Willy fell asleep about an hour after we crossed the Indiana state line, and she stayed that way until the outskirts of Chicago, where she began thrashing around and whimpering. I shook her shoulder, and she came fighting back into wakefulness, thrusting her hands out before her and muttering unintelligible, panic-driven words. After a couple of seconds, she calmed down and looked around, and her eyes came back into focus.

"Are you okay?"

"I guess." She swallowed and, acting almost entirely on reflex, pulled a Kit Kat from the duffel and took a bite. She eyed me, and I saw her decide to trust me again. "I was having this horrible **dream.**"

"No kidding," I said.

"Did you ever have one of those dreams that keep coming back?"

"A recurring dream? I have three or four, and

they keep recycling." Then I remembered writing Willy's recurring dream, and I knew what she was going to tell me.

"Mine is about a boy standing in front of an empty house. I'm looking at him from behind. The boy is always wearing one T-shirt on top of another, and he looks sort of graceful. I'm attracted to this boy, I like him a lot, and I know that he looks a lot like me."

Oh God, I thought, I didn't even know I was doing that, but she's right. I gave her Mark's face!

"This boy, of whom I am very, very fond, takes a step toward the house, and I realize that the house isn't actually empty—it is, and it isn't. Something filthy lives in there, and it's **hungry.** If the boy goes in there, he's gone, he's lost, he'll never come out again. And the place wants him so badly it's practically trembling!"

"You're dreaming about 3323 North Michigan Street," I told her. "That was Joseph Kalendar's house."

"Michigan. Like Michigan Produce. Where I wanted to break in."

"I didn't even know what I was doing when I gave you that dream," I said. "Not consciously, anyhow."

"Isn't that a comfort," Willy said. "According

to you, you **never** knew what you were doing in my book. Anyhow. This dream. It's like I'm watching everything happen in a snow globe. The air that surrounds the boy is magical air, sacred air, but it won't do him any good once he walks through the door. I feel such dread that I actually understand the word—like, Oh, yeah, this is **dread.** And my dread builds up so much, I can't stand watching that wonderful boy walk toward a horrible doom, and I kind of sail toward him—it's like we're connected by a silver cord, and I'm flying down the length of that cord—and just before I hit him I realize that I'm not going to knock him over, I'm going to sail right inside him."

Willy collapsed against the back of the seat and placed her right hand over her heart. Her eyes and her mouth were wide open. "Oh, no," she said, and gave me a look in which horror predominated over defiance. She shook her head. "Oh, no. That's what this is about! I am going to have to walk in there, aren't I? Like the ending you thought you would write. And guess what, I don't come out."

I remembered Cyrax warning me of a terrible terrible thrice-terrible price and knew she was right. But what I said was "I don't know if that's true."

"Is that the best you can do?" she yelled at me. "You DON'T KNOW?" Willy hit my shoulder, hard. "You don't KNOW? Can't you do better than that?"

"I'm going in with you," I said.

At that point, I looked in the rearview mirror and first became conscious that for the past hundred miles I had been seeing a muddy SUV following along behind us. I thought it was a Mercury Mountaineer. The only reason I noticed it was that the Mountaineer always stayed at a distance from us of about six cars.

"I know, I see, I get it. I'm going to go into the real night room." She looked at me in a kind of disbelieving wonder. "That's it, that's the deal. I have to do what I was going to do in your lousy book, where nothing was figured out and you can't explain why anything happened! I have to go in there. And then what happens? I can't meet the Lily I used to be, can I? How could I? I didn't used to be her!"

"Well, actually, we have to look for the real Lily," I said, sneaking another glance at the mirror. "That's one of the ways I'm supposed to make things right."

"Why? I can't meet the person I was supposed to be!"

"Sure you can. You're a separate person—you

have your own identity, the one I gave you. I'm supposed to find out Lily Kalendar's real fate—aren't you interested in that?"

"You **want** to meet her. You're in love with her, aren't you? You were writing a whole book about Lily Kalendar. Of course you love her."

"I think I'm just supposed to see," I said. "To understand. To see what I got wrong."

"That's going to be a big job." Now she was sulking again, and I couldn't blame her.

"Try not to be afraid," I told her. "Whatever I'll see, you'll see, too."

"Some crappy consolation." Despite her words, she seemed a bit reconciled to whatever her fate might be.

"We're going to have be on the lookout for a character named Jasper Dan Kohle—he's Joseph Kalendar and Mitchell Faber kind of rolled up into one person."

The SUV still hung behind us. I thought it would probably trail us all the way to Mill-haven.

Willy jolted me back into engagement with her. "Jasper Dan Kohle isn't a real name."

"Kohle isn't what you would call a real person."

"No, I mean it sounds like a made-up name. Give me a pen."

"Are you kidding?"

"Pen."

I handed it to her. She groped around in the mess at her feet and found a candy wrapper that was blank white on the other side. "Does Kohle start with a **K**?"

"Yes."

She printed JASPER DAN on the wrapper. "That doesn't even **look** real," she said. "Now spell his last name for me." As I spoke the letters she wrote them down.

"Now watch this, but don't steer us off the road." Beneath JASPER DAN KOHLE, Willy printed JOSEPH KALENDAR. "Right?"

"Right," I said, looking back and forth from the highway to the paper in Willy's hands. Every now and then I checked the rearview mirror.

With my pen, she drew a line from the J in JASPER to the J in JOSEPH. Then she drew a line from the A in JASPER to the A in KALENDAR. "Do you need more?"

"It's an anagram," I said. "His name was an anagram for Joseph Kalendar. And I never saw it."

"People with verbal sensitivity can always tell when something's an anagram. There's something a little off about anagrammed names. It's like they almost always have the same taste, a little tinny."

"Okay," I said. "Enough punishment."

"But you should have seen it."

"Yes, you're right. I should have seen it. I was feeling so clever about inventing Merlin L'Duith, too."

"Now, there—see? 'Merlin L'Duith' has a perfect tinny flavor. No one in his right mind would mistake that for a real name. You'd know right away it was an anagram."

Forty miles south of Millhaven, Willy demanded to eat again, and pointed at a billboard depicting a long white structure with ships' wheels embedded in the plaster and nautical lamps hung beside the entrance. "I want to go to the Captain's Retreat," she said. "I'm sick of all this meat. I want to have seafood. Please, Tim. I'm starving again."

He turned off at the next exit and followed, at a speed of sixty to seventy miles an hour, the directions painted on the billboard, which led him toward Duckvale, a little town he had heard of but never visited. Willy asked him why he was driving so fast, and he said, "I didn't tell you this before, but I think we're being followed."

Willy looked over her shoulder. "That pickup?"

The pickup truck was the only other vehicle on Route 17, the road recommended by the billboard.

"No, it was an SUV, all covered in mud. Just in case it's our boys, let's make sure we've lost them."

Tim spent the next twenty minutes dodging down side streets, cutting through vacant lots, and doubling back on himself without so much as glimpsing the Mountaineer. "Of course," he said, "we don't know that Coverley was driving the thing. We don't even know if it was deliberately following us."

"Take me to the restaurant. Please."

He managed to find the Captain's Retreat with only a little difficulty. When he pulled in to the parking lot, he went around to the side, where big concrete planters bordered a narrow rectangular space containing no other cars, and parked next to the building. The planters would hide him from traffic on the street. Willy gathered up her duffel bag, walked in silence beside him, permitted him to open the door for her, and carried the long bag into the restaurant. She steadily devoured candy bars while she read the menu. When the waitress came, Willy asked for blackened redfish, fried clams, a dozen oysters, the shrimp special, and the fried catfish.

"In any order," she said.

Tim asked for a shrimp cocktail he had to force himself to eat.

After their meal, Willy wandered ahead while Tim was still getting out of his chair, and he watched her heft the white bag as she pushed the door open and walked outside into brilliant sunshine. Through the window in the entrance, he could see her striding off to the side of the building. He went outside and followed, pondering the difficulties of introducing Willy to his brother, which he supposed he would shortly be doing. When he rounded the corner into the side lot, he found Willy staring off into the distance with a vacuous expression on her face. Tim supposed she was thinking about how soon she would need another couple of Score bars, and he opened his mouth to tell her to hurry along.

The sight of the slender young man in a black T-shirt and black jeans leaning against one of the concrete planters froze the words in his throat. Here was the real Mr. Halleden, WCH-WHLLDN himself, watching over his charge. He wore sunglasses as black as his shirt, and his hair gleamed in the sun. He appeared to be profoundly irritated, but when had he not?

Tim realized that Willy still stood where she had stopped, and that she had not moved her gaze from the side of the lot. Then he noticed that a conspicuous silence filled the parking lot. Fear sparkling along his nerve endings, he turned and saw Giles Coverley and Roman Richard Spilka standing, in the shadows at the back of the building, on either side of the mud-encrusted Mountaineer. They stepped forward and into the light. Their faces looked pinched and washed out, and even Coverley's clothes were rumpled and dirty. Both men needed a shave. The nose of the pistol in Roman Richard's hand twitched like a metronome from Willy to Tim and back again.

"This is just us now," Coverley said, and Tim realized that he could not see WCHWHLLDN. "Nobody else is going to come around to park here—why would they? And the staff has no reason to wander around to this side of the building. So I want you to know that you will die, both of you. That is the most solemn promise I ever made in my whole life. But before we kill you, you are going to explain what the hell is going on here."

Willy actually laughed. "Have you had any luck getting in touch with Mitchell? Been getting any assistance from the Baltic Group?"

"It's not THERE anymore!" Coverley shouted. "And we can't find Mitchell."

"The only person we can find is you," said Roman Richard, who looked confused and furious. Both of them had the hollowed-out, slightly spectral appearance of the seriously hungry. "But we sure are good at that. We could find you anywhere, because we just know where to go. How does that happen, you asshole? What did you do to us?"

"How come your face is on our money?" Coverley screamed. "How come I think I went to school in Millhaven and my second-grade teacher was Mrs. Gross? I'm **English**!"

"Why do I know all this shit about jazz and poetry?" yelled Roman Richard. "I hate jazz and poetry! I don't like that shit, I like . . . well, whatever it is I like." He thought about it for a second. "The Ramones. That's what I like."

"How did you pay for your lunch, you asshole?" Coverley asked. "Does your money work here?"

"I put it on a credit card." Tim glanced back over his shoulder, and WCHWHLLDN was still leaning against the planter with his arms crossed. He looked as furious as Roman Richard, but a lot more bored.

"Our credit cards get turned down, because there is no Continental Trust of New Jersey. And there's no HENDERSONIA!"

"Would you like a candy bar?" Willy sweetly asked them.

"Christ, we've been stealing those things," Coverley said. "Candy bars are too expensive to pay for, the way we have to get money. I'm not killing people for candy bars anymore."

"I'm crazy about your scruples," Tim said, watching Coverley and Roman Richard stare at Willy's bag.

She knelt down and partially unzipped it. As if they could smell the chocolate, the two men stepped closer. "Do you really want to know what the secret is?" she asked.

"If you don't tell me, I'll blow your damn head off," said Roman Richard, aiming the pistol at her. Tim moved up between them.

"Get away, or I'll shoot you first." Roman Richard stepped sideways and kept the pistol aimed at Willy.

"The secret is," Willy said, "you're in a book. You used to be in a book, and I did too, but something happened, and now we're here. Where we don't belong. And you know why you can always find him? Because he's the author." She looked over at Tim. "What happens to them if they kill you?"

"I think they'd stay here, in this world, until they disappeared. After that, there's nothing left of them. From the looks of you guys, disappearance isn't all that far away."

"This morning, my left foot disappeared for about five seconds," Coverley said. "Did you do that to me?"

"Reality's eating you alive," Tim said.

"Shove the bag over here, and stay put," said Roman Richard. "Do it. Do it."

Willy gave the bag a halfhearted shove. Unable to control his hunger, Roman Richard moved toward it, his eyes fixed on the heap of candy bars visible through the opening Willy had created. He began to make a strange, guttural humming sound deep in his throat.

"Roman—" Coverley said.

Roman Richard bent down and thrust a hand into the bag, and Tim found himself hurtling toward the man's body before he was aware that he had made a decision to attack. The big man grunted in surprise and was still trying to get his gun hand into position when Tim barreled into him. The force of his impact and Roman Richard's awkward stance sent them both thudding, in a sprawling collapse that included the snapping of Roman Richard's plaster cast, onto the asphalt, where their arms and legs waved like the limbs of a spider tossed into a low flame. Tim was on top of his opponent when they hit the ground, and he instantly reached for the pistol. Roman Richard punched him in the side of the head. It was like being hit by an anvil.

His vision fuzzy, Tim closed his hands around the barrel of the pistol. A big, brutal hand swam toward him. Coarse black hairs sprouted beneath the knuckles. The hand battered his skull again and retreated, giving him a good view of Roman Richard's meaty, stubbled jowl. The pistol twisted in his hand. After the next blow, Tim drove his fist into Roman Richard's neck and yanked at the pistol, and it came out of his enemy's grip as easily as a flower is plucked from a country garden.

Tim could hear Coverley bellowing; he felt a sharp, absurdly painful kick in his back. Aware that Coverley was bending over to snatch his prize from him, Tim rolled away and clutched the weapon tight against his chest, like a football player protecting the ball. Coverley kicked him in the side, again with amazingly painful results, and Tim got the grip in his hand and his finger on the trigger. Roman Richard swarmed over him, roaring like a bull. As if by itself, Tim's finger tightened on the small, curved bit of metal beneath it.

Then he understood that, in something like contemptuous boredom, WCHWHLLDN had opened Roman Richard's hand.

His index finger completed the gesture it had begun. The unforgiving object in Tim's hand flew up with the force of the explosion, and Tim saw that the man he had shot had vanished. Big Roman Richard, who had been immediately before him, looming like a wall equipped with hair-encrusted hands, was no more. From behind him came a high-pitched sound of desperation.

Thinking that the sound came from Willy, Tim got to his knees and spun around. Willy was standing about three feet in front of her duffel, looking down at him with a complicated expression on her face. Giles Coverley had stopped moving. Tim guessed that he had lowered his foot about a second before. The expression on Coverley's face was not at all difficult to read. He'd had enough, this was over-the-top too much, he surrendered, hoping only for due process and treatment under the Geneva Convention.

"Back up," Tim said.

Coverley stepped backward. He held up his hands, his palms out. "Look," he said. "Forget the explanations. What are you going to do now? You can't call the police, you know. They're still after her." His tone made it clear that he blamed Willy for his baffling series of misfortunes.

"No, they're not," Tim said, and got to his feet. "In this world, they never were. The bank doesn't exist, remember?"

"You still can't use the police. How the devil could you explain what went on here?" Keening slightly, he bent over to look at his left foot, which faded abruptly into invisibility and sent him toppling to the surface of the parking lot. From his mouth flew a great many inventive curses. The lightness feeling made him utter a high-pitched humming sound while his foot flickered in and out of view for a short time. At last, it reappeared without disappearing again, and he slumped, panting, over his belt, his legs stuck out before him.

"Throw him a candy bar," Tim said.

"Are you kidding?" Willy stepped back toward the duffel bag as though to defend its contents.

"If you don't, I will. I don't like seeing people suffer."

With obvious reluctance, Willy retreated to the bag, knelt down to reach in, and plucked out the foil-wrapped disc of a York peppermint pattie. She threw it at Coverley as if skipping a rock across the surface of a lake, and it skimmed straight into the center of his chest. Coverley disrobed the patty and thrust it into his mouth in a single movement. His face relaxed into momentary ecstasy.

"Do it again," Tim said.

Willy picked out an Oh Henry! bar and hurled it at Coverley, who caught it with both hands and shucked the wrapper in the second and a half it took him to carry the bar to his mouth.

"I shouldn't blame him," Willy said. "He was only doing what you made him do."

"I have to admit," said Coverley around a wad of chocolate-peanut mush, "it was pretty difficult to threaten this guy. Basically, all I really wanted to do was work for him instead of Mitchell. But, you know, I had this job. Would you mind if I stood up?"

"Stand up," Tim said. He glanced at Willy, who, without complaint, bent down and tossed a Mounds bar at Coverley with an underhand pitch.

Coverley took more time with the Mounds bar than he had with the others, turning it into more of a meal. "I don't suppose you'd consider taking me with you."

"Sorry," Tim said.

"I didn't think so. Tell me this. Where did Roman Richard go?"

"He didn't go anywhere," Tim said.

Willy bent down and picked out a candy bar for herself.

"Are you telling me to go off and kill people to get their money?"

"God damn," Tim said. He took three hundred dollars from his wallet, leaving him with two. "No, I can't do that. Take this money and live on it until you can get a job. Go to Milwaukee and say you'll wash dishes."

Coverley held out his hands like an infant, and Tim placed the bills in their cupped palms. "To tell you the truth," Coverley said, "we didn't really kill those people. Roman Richard shot their dog to show them we meant business, but that's all."

"Why did you tell me you killed people, then?"

"I wanted to scare you. Well, at that point I would have killed you, that's true. How about another Oh Henry! Could you manage that?"

"Get out of here," Tim said, and Coverley dipped the money into his pocket and moved toward the SUV. He would leave it on the street in Milwaukee, and in a day the police would be hearing from its terrified owners.

The rest of the way to Millhaven, Tim sped along a series of roads and highways he had known all his life. Willy went through candy bars at the rate of approximately one every twenty minutes. Tim thought Willy grew more beautiful, more translucent and lit from within, with every mile, and when he considered what lay before them, his heart hurt for her, and for himself, too.

She said, "What happened to Roman Richard, that's what's going to happen to me, isn't it?"

"Let's hope not," he said.

Half an hour from Millhaven, Willy fell asleep beside him, her slender hands limp in her lap, her knees sagging to one side, her head on the seat rest so that he could see only the short blond shag of her hair, which had without his noticing become nearly white-blond and seemed to possess, beneath a healthy shine, its own internal radiance. She uttered a few whiffling sounds that sounded like the lost echoes of unspoken words, then fell again into perfect silence.

The next time Tim checked his rearview mirror, he almost drove onto the shoulder of the road. In her blue dress and no doubt wearing a pair of red slippers, his sister, April, was looking at him from the center of the back seat. April's regard had little of the childish in it. The look in her eye, the expression printed into her unsmiling nine-year-old face, spoke of a steady, familiar impatience. As ever, April hungered to be free, to get out, to be on the other side of all this frustration. More than Cyrax, she was his guide. As he watched, April leaned forward, extended a slightly grubby nine-year-old arm, and, with surpassing gentleness, patted his shoulder.

When Tim Underhill cruised along the overpass from the exit and in the near distance saw the outline of Millhaven rising up, heavy clouds too dark for both the hour and the season hung above the southwest quadrant, far from the granite towers and pillars near the Pforzheimer. He thought, **The Dark Man knows I'm home.**

The Woman
Glimpsed
at the Window

PART FIVE

28

At the Pforzheimer's front desk, a young clerk who had fallen in love with Willy the moment he looked at her confirmed that Tim had a fifth-floor junior suite in the old part of the hotel. An hour earlier, a suitcase had arrived for him from New York. Underhill preferred the old wing to the more modern tower on the other side of the hotel. The rooms were warmer in tone, and in the mid-eighties he, Michael Poole, and Maggie Lah had spent three memorable nights on that same fifth floor. Plastered with FedEx labels and strapped shut with yellow tape, the suitcase was produced in the care of an old friend and schoolmate of Tim's, a five-foot-two bellman named Charlie Pelz.

In the ascending elevator, Charlie Pelz smiled at Willy and said, "Welcome to the Pforzheimer, miss. We hope you enjoy your stay with us." Having dispensed with the preliminaries, he turned to his old acquaintance and said, "Peddling another book, huh? I see this time, your title's all lowercase, like some beatnik wrote it. You gonna give me a copy, or do I have to buy one?"

"Oh, you don't want to read this one, Charlie," Tim said. "Hardly anybody gets killed in it."

"You must be outta your mind," Charlie said. "Who wants to read something like **that**? You should write a book about me. I got stories, they'd make what hair you got left fall out."

Charlie Pelz escorted them down the wide ocher corridors and over the rose-patterned carpet and around a corner to Room 511. Tim experienced a rush of nostalgia he explained to Willy only after Charlie had been pacified with a ten-dollar bill and sent back to his station.

"In 1983, I wrote about four pages of the book I was working on in this room."

"Which book?"

"Mysteries."

"I liked that one," Willy said. "Can you remember which pages?"

"Of course." Yes, he could remember what he had written in this room. And he could remember what he had seen while writing them: a dark lake ringed with expensive lodges, and a boy walking through dying sunlight to a clubhouse overlooking the water. He remembered how he had felt at each moment of the boy's progress.

"Good. You **should** remember them."

"In the next room down, my friends Michael Poole and Maggie Lah went to bed together for the first time, and they've been together ever since. They love each other. It's marvelous to be with them. They don't exclude you; you're part of the circle."

"**We** love each other," Willy said. Then, heart-breakingly: "Don't we?"

"Oh, Willy," Tim said, and put his arms around her. A wave of emotion ignited by the mingled losses and gains of both the past and the present blazed through him, and he was not sure that in the end it might not be more than he could really handle. For a moment it was ex-actly that, and he wept, shamelessly, holding her, also weeping, as closely as he could.

It was Willy who returned them to a state in which they could do things other than cry and hold on to each other. She moved a fraction of an inch away, ran a hand beneath her nose, and for all time proved the immensity of her worth by saying, "You should write books that Charlie Pelz wants to read, or your career's down the drain."

"From now on, I'll send Charlie everything I write, so he can give me his critical opinion."

"Actually," Willy said, "nuts to Charlie Pelz. Could we go to bed now? I know it's not very late, but I feel sort of wrung out and exhausted. And I want to **be** with you."

They undressed; like newlyweds, they brushed their teeth side by side before the sink; they went into the bedroom and, first naked Willy, then enchanted Tim, mounted the three wooden steps that, as in a fairy tale, led them upward to the surface of the bed, into which they fell, open-armed and open-hearted. Locked in motionless embrace, great figures on stone friezes gazed down through a tangle of vines; a panther's eye gleamed, and wing beats troubled the air. They had passed over, Tim felt, into another realm altogether, where miracles were commonplace but fleeting, leaving behind echoes of things lost and half-remembered.

At six o'clock in the morning, Willy said, "I feel different. Something's happening." She could not be more specific.

Later that morning, showered, dressed, and still feeling enveloped in the atmosphere of Willy Patrick, Tim called his brother. After a little thought, he made a second telephone call, to the Millhaven Foundling's Shelter. Soon he found himself speaking to Mercedes Romola, the shelter's matron, who confirmed the idea that had entered his head a moment before: that the real Lily Kalendar had probably passed into the same hands and endured the same process as his dear Lily. Both Philip and Ms. Romola invited him to visit them that afternoon.

29

Willy had swallowed something like half a pound of confectioner's sugar and washed it down with a nice, sugary soft drink while Tim made his calls, and as they drove south and west through the city, she was in a relatively unruffled frame of mind. Tim, however, seemed to grow darker and more troubled the closer they came to his old neighborhood. By the time he turned on to Teutonia Avenue and homed in on Sherman Park, he was actually driving with one hand and propping up his chin with the other, as if he were leaning on a bar.

"What's wrong?" Willy asked him. "Are you upset with your brother, or are you ashamed to introduce me to him?"

"No, of course I'm not ashamed. But I am always upset with Philip," Tim said, considerably shading the truth. He did have wildly conflicting feelings about introducing Willy to his brother. In some ways, it seemed like the worst idea in the world.

"That I'm always upset with him is what makes us a family. I think he's comically selfish, way too cautious, and unbelievably hidebound, and he thinks I'm a flashy spendthrift who turned his back on him."

"I bet he's proud of you."

"Somewhere down in that grudging heart of his, maybe, but I wouldn't bet on it." Tim removed his hand from his chin and reverted to driving an automobile instead of a bar. He wished not to continue this particular conversation, and he was getting dangerously near Philip's house. The tidy green space of Sherman Park floated by on his left; the unhappy little house at 3324 North Superior Street filled with his parents' shabby old furniture lay only two blocks away. He regretted bringing Willy into the former Pigtown. Some disaster would inevitably occur. Also, he dreaded the possibility of meeting China Beech. She was a catastrophe that had already happened.

Tim found a parking space two doors down from his brother's house. He and Willy left the car simultaneously, and Willy immediately reached back in to pick up half a dozen Baby Ruths.

As she ducked into the car, Tim looked idly

up toward the next corner, which was located on a little rise, and saw something he first took for mere eccentricity. A large man built like a plow horse and wearing a long black coat that fell past his knees stood up there, silhouetted against the pale blue sky and staring down at him. He was the sort of man who looks like an assault weapon, and he appeared to be holding his hands over his face in an ugly, complicated pattern that allowed him to see through his fingers while concealing his face.

The knowledge of this bizarre figure's identity came to him almost immediately, and Tim was never sure if his sense that the world had stopped moving began with him seeing the apparition or at the moment he realized it was Joseph Kalendar. Either way, the world froze in place: birds hung motionless in the sky, men turned to statues in midstride, a pot falling from a mantel stopped in midair, and a frozen cat watched it not fall. Willy's head and torso hung motionlessly over the front seat. Kalendar was playing his new book back to him, as he had done on Crosby Street, and the old monster had all the success he could have wished for. In life, Joseph Kalendar had gotten a great deal of pleasure out of frightening people; he must have been immensely pleased at how thoroughly he had succeeded in scaring Timothy Underhill.

Without seeming to change in any obvious way moment by moment, and certainly without moving so much as a finger, Kalendar then demonstrated that Cyrax had known what was coming. Inch by inch, cell by cell, and hair by hair, Kalendar mutated into a sleek, smooth black-haired man with a gambler's mustache and extremely white teeth. Kalendar hated showing his face, and good old Tim had kindly stepped in to provide a handsome alternative. Faber was wearing a tuxedo, but he looked nothing like a headwaiter. Grinning like a dog, Mitchell Faber took a step toward Underhill, whose foremost response was the impulse to turn and run. **Make haste make haste . . . the Dark Man cometh,** he had written in his last book, and here he was, a literally Dark Man. Against Faber's burnished, olive-complected skin his onyx eyebrows shone, the whites of his eyes gleamed. He looked purely carnivorous. In his wake floated many more corpses than Joseph Kalendar had created. If you gave Faber fifteen more years, a run of bad luck, and a stretch in prison, he would wind up looking a lot like Jasper Dan Kohle.

Tim refused to give him what he wanted, a show of fear, although fear now occupied the entire center of his body. He was incapable of speech. Faber advanced another gliding step and then was gone, leaving an insolent vacancy where he had been. The air moved again. Willy came up from out of the car and closed the door. When she saw his face, she said, "You **really** don't want to do this, do you?"

Tim ground the heels of his hands into his eye sockets. "I was a little dizzy. Let's meet the groom."

With a sudden desire for a show of ceremony, he took Willy's arm and escorted her down the sidewalk to his brother's house. The attention made her happy, and she leaned her head against his shoulder.

A second after Tim rang the bell, the door flew open upon a transformed Philip Underhill. In place of a boxy suit, cheap white shirt, and deliberately nondescript necktie, a uniform Philip had worn nearly every day of the past twenty-five years, he had on a blue button-down shirt and khakis—hardly a revolutionary getup, but pretty radical for Philip. The rimless glasses had been replaced by tortoiseshell frames; his thinning hair was parted on the left and had grown long enough to touch the tops of his ears. He had lost at least thirty pounds. Most amazing of all was that he appeared to be smiling.

Although Tim had been prepared in advance

by their recent telephone conversation, his first response to this transformation was to think, **That woman ruined my brother!** His second reflection was that the effects of ruination had been entirely beneficial. The immediate result of these changes in style had been to make Philip Underhill look more intelligent. He also appeared to be a good deal friendlier than his earlier incarnation.

"Boy," Tim said, holding out a hand. "You aren't even recognizable."

Philip grasped his forearm and pulled him into an embrace. Well past the sort of phenomenon described as "astonishing," this verged upon the miraculous. So did his greeting.

"Good, I don't want to be recognizable. I'm so glad you're here! That's the perfect wedding present, Tim."

"I'll come to all your weddings," Tim said.

Philip drew him into the house and demanded to be introduced to "this beautiful companion of yours."

Tim's efforts to think of some way to account for Willy disintegrated when he took in what had happened to the living room. "You changed everything. Where's the old furniture?"

"Goodwill or the junk heap. China helped me pick out this new stuff. I want to know what you think, but, please, first introduce me to your friend."

Tim pronounced Willy's name and stalled, unable to think of what to say next.

"I'm one of your brother's fictional characters," Willy said, shaking Philip's hand. "It's a wonderful job, full of excitement, but the money's no good."

"My brother should pay you just for spending time with him."

Another amazement—Philip had made a joke.

"Oh, he's easy to spend time with. I'm quite attached to him."

As Philip dealt with the possibilities suggested by Willy's statement, Tim let his initial impression of the living room separate itself out into the details of what had stunned him. The transformation was so great that Philip might as well have moved to a different house. Prints and framed photographs hung on the walls. The floor had been sanded and waxed and polished to a warm gleam shared by the pretty little table before the window and the curving arms of several chairs. There were low lamps beside a soft, patterned sofa, a handsome leather chair of remarkable depth with a matching footstool, stacks of books, and vases with cut flowers.

"Philip, this room is beautiful," he said.

"We're happy with it. Won't you please sit down? Can I get you a glass of wine or anything?"

Willy asked for a Coca-Cola, and Tim reeled before the evidence that this formerly fanatical teetotaler had alcoholic beverages in his house and was willing to serve them to his guests.

"I'll have a Coke, too, Philip. We have an appointment for an interview at the Foundlings' Shelter in about an hour, so it's better if I don't drink. But you're one surprise after another."

"Pop might have been an alcoholic, but there was no reason I shouldn't let myself and my guests enjoy one of life's simple pleasures. Why are you being interviewed at the Foundlings' Home?"

"I'm not. I'm interviewing someone for a new project."

"You'll have to tell me all about it when I get back." Philip smiled at them, let his gaze linger on Willy for a moment, then smiled again at Tim before he left the room.

Tim smacked his forehead. "That's not Philip. That's one of those pod people from **Invasion of the Body Snatchers.** Do you know the shit he used to put me through about drinking?"

"Dimly," Willy said.

"She got him to change this room," he said,

musing. "That must have required brain surgery and a heart transplant. He would **never**
have done anything to this room."

"Who is 'she'?" Willy asked.

Philip, carrying a tray with two glasses filled
with ice and Coca-Cola into the room, had
heard this question. "She, dear Willy, is China
Beech, the woman who rescued me from grief
and depression and made a human being of me.
I wish she were here now, but she had some
business to attend to. You'll meet her at our
wedding, though. I know you'll love her. Everyone loves China."

"What kind of business?" Tim asked.

"I'm not too sure. Something to do with one
of her buildings, probably."

"Her buildings?"

"China has buildings here and there, all over
town."

"What do you mean, she has buildings?"

"She owns them. Some are commercial, some
are residential, but the apartment buildings are
more trouble than they're worth. I tell her she
should cash out, let somebody inherit the worries, but she's a little sentimental about those
apartment buildings. They were where her father started, you know."

"Your fiancée inherited property from her father?" Tim felt as though he were trying to run uphill through a muddy field.

"Well, yeah, Bill Beech."

Apparently, land mines dotted the muddy field.

"China's father was **the** William Beech?" William Beech had once owned half of downtown Millhaven.

"Didn't I just tell you that? Willy, how did you and Tim get together? Were you a student of his? That's how I met China—she was one of our student teachers, and I was, well, her mentor, I guess you could say."

"We met at a reading of his," Willy said. "When he learned that I was from Millhaven, too, we decided to drive out here together."

"You **drove**?"

"All the way. I thought you told me that your girlfriend was an exotic dancer."

"That was kind of an in-joke. She's a tango dancer. So am I, although I'm not nearly as good as she is. She makes me look okay, though. We're thinking of entering contests one day."

Philip not only made jokes, he made in-jokes. He danced the tango. He was thinking of entering **contests.**

"You took me seriously, huh? That's pretty funny. An exotic dancer is really a stripper, isn't that right? China's going to love that. I hope she gets back before you have to go."

"How long have you known her?"

Philip looked a bit embarrassed. "I met China in September of last year. She helped me deal with my grief. I should say, she helped me to feel my grief."

He paused. For a short time, it seemed likely that he would start crying. "I never dreamed a woman like that could want to marry me. It's unbelievable. She let God into my life, and everything has been getting better and better ever since."

"It seems to have done you no end of good."

" 'No end of good,' " Philip said. " 'No end of good.' What a beautiful phrase." He hesitated. "I don't suppose you'd like me to talk about my faith, and salvation, and Jesus Christ, and all that?"

"I want you to talk about anything you feel like talking about."

"**I'd** like to hear you talk about God," Willy said. "The god I know never explains any-thing."

Philip smiled. "Tim, you're just being polite. And Willy, one of the main problems with gods is that they seldom feel the need to explain themselves. If you have any genuine interest, ask me about it later. All right?"

"Certainly," said Tim, impressed by Philip's display of restraint.

"Now that that bit of awkwardness is over, will you tell me about this project of yours?"

"Yes," Willy said. "Please be as explicit as possible. I'd love to know more about your project."

"You're full of curiosity today," Tim said. "Unfortunately, I can only describe what I know at the moment. I can't predict the future."

"Why would you want to do that?" Philip asked.

"I mean," Tim said, "that I can't describe what hasn't been created yet. No doubt God had the same limitation."

"All right, describe what has been created."

"Before he does, could you please get me another glass of Coke? I'm awfully thirsty."

"Of course, Willy," Philip said, giving her a slightly curious look, and made the round-trip to the kitchen in less than a minute. He handed her the glass and said, "Please, Tim."

"Okay," Tim said. "I hope you won't object to this, Philip. I've been trying to write a book about Joseph Kalendar's daughter." Remembering the appalling figure that had glared down at him from the top of the street, Tim felt the necessity to employ a considerable degree of caution in what he said.

"She's dead, isn't she? That's what you said in **lost boy lost girl.**"

"Your neighbor Omar Hillyard led me to think her father murdered her. Hillyard was just making inferences based on what he saw at the time. But he wasn't watching the Kalendar house full-time, and he could have missed a lot."

"Wait a second. Is this book fact or fiction?"

Willy laughed. "That's the question I always want to ask him."

"Philip," Tim said, not very kindly, "anyone who believes in the virgin birth and the performance of miracles, not to mention walking on water, shouldn't be so quick to make that distinction."

Philip immediately retreated. "I suppose that's an excellent point." Then he changed the subject. "By the way, you might be interested in hearing that Mr. Hillyard passed away two days before Christmas, last year." Philip stared at Willy, who was tilting the last of her second drink into her mouth. "Anyhow, Kalendar had a real daughter—you're sure of that."

"Oh, I know he had a daughter," Tim said, failing to mention that his primary source of information was Cyrax, a citizen of Byzantium who had been dead for six hundred years. "I just assumed she was dead, so I never bothered to do any research about her. In my book, she had been killed; that's all I cared about. In real life, she was taken into the child-care system, and she wound up at the Foundlings' Shelter. The question is, what can she be today? Is she even still alive? Was she ever put into foster care? Did she ever go to college? Is she in prison? A mental hospital?"

"I bet she never broke into any warehouses," Willy said, darkly.

"I mean, what kind of life can you have after a childhood like that? How healed can you be?"

Philip shook his head and regarded Tim with what looked a great deal like fond resignation. "You never give up, do you?"

"What do you mean by that?" Tim found himself unreasonably rankled by his brother's words.

"Childhood, healing, childhood trauma . . . sound familiar?"

"I'm not writing about myself, Philip," Tim said, irritated.

"I didn't say you were. But you're not exactly **not** writing about yourself, either, are you?"

"You're not my brother," Tim said. "My real brother is hiding in the attic."

"I know why you say that, believe me. I wish I could have been more like this—like the self

China let me discover—with Nancy and Mark. Those regrets are astoundingly painful." Philip seemed to travel inward again, and he clasped his hands and lowered his head, perhaps in prayer. "Yes. They are." Then he looked back up at Tim. "Did you know the Kalendar place is going to be torn down next Wednesday? The view from my backyard is going to improve by a hundred percent."

"The Kalendar place is in your backyard?" Willy asked. "**He** didn't tell me that."

"It's across the alley," Philip said. "Ever since Ronnie Lloyd-Jones got arrested, people have been coming over here to look at the place. Some of them take souvenirs, can you believe that? Souvenirs! Well, the taxes aren't being paid anymore, and the neighbors stopped cutting the lawn, and now you get these disaster ghouls wandering around. Because of all that, there was a petition to raze the place, and it went through."

"How do you feel about that?" Tim asked.

The grim satisfaction visible in Philip a moment earlier hardened into a darker, flintier emotion that had nothing to do with pleasure. His face tightened; his eyes fired darts. Every bit of grief and rage he had been holding down leaped upward within him, and Philip became a little frightening. "You know how I feel about that? I'd like them to demolish that place, turn it into splinters, set the splinters on fire, and shoot the ashes into **outer space.**"

He glared at Tim as if awaiting a challenge.

"After that, I'd like guys with shovels and nets to dig up every inch of ground over there and sift through it, just in case they might have missed anything. They'd dig right down to the subsoil, six feet, eight feet, and sample **everything.** Then you'd have this big rectangular hole in the ground. It would look like a mass grave, which is exactly what it would be. I'd fill it with gasoline and set fire to it, that's what I'd do. I'd have a big, purifying fire, a tremendous blaze. When it burned out, I wouldn't care anymore— they could bulldoze all the earth back into the scorched hole and turn it into a gerbil farm."

Philip stood extremely still for a moment, contending with the emotions he had just unleashed. A little stiffly, he turned to Willy. "Excuse me, young lady. My son's body was never found. It might have been buried over there. It probably wasn't, but it might have been. God is helping me through this time, but every now and then the situation gets the better of me."

"I'm so sorry about your son," Willy said. "I thought I lost a child, too, so I have some idea of what you have been going through."

"Your child was returned to you?" Philip asked, his interest engaged. "Unharmed?"

"Yes," Tim quickly said. "Willy was very lucky."

"**My** god wasn't very helpful," she said. "**My** god seemed to make things worse." She patted the pocket where she had stuffed the candy bars. "Is there a bathroom on this floor?"

Philip told her how to get to the bathroom next to the kitchen. When she had left the room, he turned to Tim with an expression that seemed poised between appreciation and accusation. "Tim, how old is that girl, really?"

"Thirty-eight," Tim said.

"That can't be true. She's somewhere between nineteen and twenty-five."

"That's how she looks. She's still thirty-eight."

Philip appeared ready to dispute this assertion, but he let it go. "You met at a reading? And you **volunteered** to drive her here? You don't do things like that. What did she say to you?"

"It wasn't anything she said, Philip. Call it a whim." Tim regretted bringing Willy to Superior Street. He had known introducing her to his brother was a terrible idea, yet he had done exactly that, and now he had to deal with the results.

"I can't ignore the evidence of my senses. You show up here with this stunning young woman who acts like a kitten around you, and with whom you, supposedly a middle-aged gay man, obviously have some kind of erotic connection, and I'm supposed to ignore that?"

Tim improvised. "Okay. Willy is Joseph Kalendar's niece—she was his brother's daughter. That's why she went to my reading. And I thought I should bring her here for a lot of reasons. Something happened, and we clicked. Right away, there was this great attraction between us."

"You're actually sleeping with her?"

Tim could not tell if Philip was aghast or thrilled. "Philip, in all honesty, this is none of your business."

Philip was not to be deflected. "I work with teenagers. I can tell when people have been going to bed together. You're having sex with Joseph Kalendar's niece. You and Willy, you **remind** me of teenagers."

"We're very fond of each other."

"I'll say," said Philip.

Both of them heard the closing of the bathroom door. "Have you any idea of what you intend to do with this relationship?"

"I wish I did."

Entering the room, Willy sensed a measure of the intensity that had just flared. "Hey, guys, what's going on?"

"I was just telling my brother that he'd better take good care of you," Philip said. "If he doesn't, you let me know about it."

"Don't worry about me. I think I'll just disappear."

Tim said that they'd better be going.

"Oh, I almost forgot," Philip said.

Tim looked up, bracing himself for another assault on his character or his morals.

"Would you like to borrow Mark's laptop? I know you're an e-mail demon, and I can't use it—it reminds me too much of Mark. The thing is just sitting up there in its case. Let me get it for you, and you can use it in your room."

"That's a great idea, Philip. Thanks." According to an entry in Tim Underhill's journal, Mark Underhill's computer had once shown him a miraculous vision—a vision of Elsewhere—and he loved the idea of once again putting his hands on the object, so imbued with his nephew's memory, that had given him his treasure.

Philip went upstairs and came back down holding a black computer case by its handle.

"These things are so small, and they hold so

much. Mark spent hours on it, sending messages back and forth, looking up I don't know what . . ." With a dense, compacted facial expression, Philip thrust it at Tim. He was not loaning out his son's computer, Tim saw; he was getting it out of the house by giving it away.

Philip rubbed his palms on the sides of his trousers. For a moment he looked almost as adolescent and self-conscious as one of his charges. The direct, probing look he gave Willy erased this impression.

"Come with me, Willy. I want to show you something."

"Show her what?"

Already on her feet, Willy looked from brother to brother.

"Willy ought to see the view from my backyard, don't you think?"

Tim glanced up at Willy. "I explained to him why you said you were a fictional character of mine. Philip knows you're Kalendar's niece. From his backyard, you can see your uncle's house."

"I guess I should see it before they tear it down and scorch the soil it rested on," Willy said.

"Excuse me," Philip said. "I can't avoid asking this one question. Did you ever meet your cousin?"

"Never even knew she existed."

"As sick as he was, he must have wanted to protect her."

"I think this is going to have an uncomfortable effect on me. Would you mind if I had a candy bar?" Out came a Kit Kat and a Mars bar. After a moment's contemplation under Philip's fascinated stare, she shoved the Mars bar back into her pocket, broke the Kit Kat in half, unpeeled one of the halves, and bit into it. She held the other half in her left hand. "Lead on."

In the moment of uncertainty Willy had brought him to, Philip glanced over at his brother.

"Go ahead," Tim said. "I'm curious about what the place looks like now."

"It's a dump." Philip turned, strode off into the narrow kitchen, and opened the back door.

Willy and Tim stepped through. Philip joined them at the top of the steps down to his barren backyard. The fence Philip had tried to erect between his property and the cobbled alley still drooped over the patchy lawn. However, on the other side of the alley, nothing remained as it had been. Joseph Kalendar's massive wall had been bulldozed away, revealing the jungly profusion of his old backyard, from which rose the rear wall of his appalling house. The kitchen door through which Mark Underhill and his friend Jimbo Monaghan had broken in could still be made out through the weeds. The crude, clumsy slanting roof of the added room reared up out of the weeds like a huge animal dangerous to awaken.

Willy inhaled sharply.

"The place seems to get uglier with every passing week."

Because he was looking across the alley, Philip did not see Willy flicker like a dying lightbulb. Tim had turned to her when that sharp, sudden sound escaped her, and before his eyes Willy's entire body stuttered in and out of visibility. She slumped against the back of the house. Somehow, he managed to catch her before she slid down onto the worn surface of the yard.

"Eat the rest of that candy bar, fast," he ordered her. "Philip, do you have any sugar?"

"Sure, I guess. I don't use sugar much anymore."

Tim asked him to fill a coffee cup with sugar and bring it outside with a glass of Coke.

"Is she a diabetic? She needs her—"

"Get the sugar, Philip. Now."

Philip vanished inside in a flurry of elbows and knees. Cupboard doors and cabinets opened and closed. Muttering to himself, he came through the door and handed Tim a cup filled with sugar.

"Aren't you likely to throw her into some . . ."

Tim was seated on the ground, his arm around Willy, pouring sugar into her mouth.

"We had this girl go into insulin shock last year, and—"

"She's not diabetic, Philip. She has a very unusual condition."

With a flash of his old, mean-spirited self, Philip said, "Must be restricted to fictional characters, I guess." Then, seeing Willy take the cup into her own hands and wash another mouthful down with the soft drink, he added, "Seems to be working, anyhow. Should we get her to the hospital?"

"No hospital," Willy said, a little thickly.

"Tim. You know she belongs in an E.R. Please."

"I know she does **not.** Back off, Philip."

He did so, literally, holding up his hands in conspicuous surrender. A few seconds later, Willy stood up and, knowing what was required of her, did her best to look abashed. Gently, almost convincingly, she told Philip that her "condition" could not be treated in an emergency room and that she was grateful for his concern.

"Well, if you say you're okay . . ." Baffled, he looked back and forth between them, half-understanding that he had missed something important and explanatory.

"We're on our way," Tim said. Philip did not acknowledge him. His gaze had settled on Willy, and he looked as though he was capable of standing there for the next couple of hours.

Willy thanked him for the sugar.

"I'll see you at the reading," Philip said, without taking his eyes from her.

30

From Timothy Underhill's journal

She told me what I wanted to hear and she
wanted to believe, that the shock of seeing that
house had pushed her deeper toward disappearance than she had ever been. She meant that
what had happened to her was an exception and
that she had her "condition" under control.

Willy passed the next moment that might have
tested her, our arrival at the Children's Home,
with perfect equanimity. It looked exactly as she
remembered it: a hideous building with a dirty
stone facade, narrow windows, and stone steps
leading up to an arched doorway. It matched
her memory because I had driven past the massive old building a thousand times in my youth.

A couple of candy bars, no more; she was
pleased by the harmony between the building
and her memory of it.

The interior was a test of another kind, for I had invented Willy's memories out of a generic muddle of institutions I had seen largely in movies. She kept saying things were "in the wrong place" and giving me unhappy glances, as if I had neglected a hypothetical duty to create accurate representations of things that existed outside of fiction. The lounge where she'd dealt with Tee Tee Rowley was on the wrong floor; the Ping-Pong table we glimpsed on our way past the game room was on the wrong side of the room; the dormitory was all wrong, since it had individual rooms instead of being a big communal barrack.

And the "real" Children's Home in Willy's mind had no matron, because I had neglected to supply it with an administrative staff. The Children's Home on South Karadara Street, however, came splendidly equipped with the regal, kindly Mercedes Romola, who welcomed us into her spare little office, sat us down, and spoke the magical words "Mr. Underhill, it appears you are in luck."

The very sight of Mercedes Romola told Tim that Lily Kalendar's life could have been very little like the one he had fashioned for Willy

Patrick. The matron exuded warmth, practical-
ity, and common sense; she had iron-gray hair,
a comfortable skirt and jacket, and a level, intelligent gaze. She was like the perfect fourth-
grade teacher, a woman whose natural authority
did not inhibit a sense of humor that, in its sly
appearances, hinted at the existence of a private
life more raucous and freewheeling than could
be revealed in the public one. The matron instantly conveyed a sense of solidity and speci-
ficity that transferred itself to Lily Kalendar.
Her life had contained no missing transitions
or amnesiac passages: it had been lived minute
by minute, in a way that made a pantomime of
fiction.

"In fact," she told him, "you are in luck in several ways. As you would expect, we do not release information concerning our present and
former charges without obtaining permission
beforehand. And in this case, the special circumstances surrounding the child's transfer to
the shelter, especially the notoriety of her father,
make us wish to proceed with a great degree of
caution."

"She was here, though," Tim said. "Lily
Kalendar."

"She had literally nowhere else to go. As I told
you on the phone, she was taken into care at the
age of nine. According to her father, the girl's

mother had run off two months earlier, and he could not cope with raising two children. The son was being trained as a carpenter, but the girl gave him problems he couldn't solve. The case-workers agreed, and she came to us. Later, we thought he'd sent her away to save her life. And maybe it was the only way he could stop abusing her."

"I **knew** he loved her," Willy said.

"What exactly is your role here?" asked the matron.

"Willy is my assistant," Tim told her. "She's been very involved with this project."

"And you say the project is a book about Lily Kalendar. My first question is, will it be fiction or nonfiction?"

"Probably some combination of the two."

"Excuse me, Mr. Underhill, but what is the point of mixing genres? Doesn't combining fiction with fact merely give you license to be sloppy with the facts?"

"I think it's the other way around," Tim said. "Fiction lets me really get the facts right. It's a way of reaching a kind of truth I wouldn't otherwise be able to discover."

She smiled at him. "Maybe I shouldn't admit this, but I'm a big fan of your work. I love those books you wrote with your collaborator."

He thanked her.

"Let's go back to the subject of your good fortune. As you will surely understand, I have to be very scrupulous. We make our records open to the public, which includes researchers like yourself, only if the person in or formerly in care, or the legal guardian, gives us permission to do so. Your first bit of luck was that one of your readers is the head of this institution. I made two phone calls on your behalf. I don't know about you, but I think that's worth two hundred dollars to our Big Brothers Big Sisters program."

Tim nodded, forcing himself to appear relaxed.

"As a result of these calls, I can give you the following information." She opened a folder on her desk. Then she put on a pair of reading glasses and peered down. "The Kalendar girl was first taken into care in 1974. The matron in those days was Georgia Lathem, and she made some unusual notations in the girl's file. It seems Miss Lathem found the girl exceptionally closed off, emotionally numb, prone to acts of violence against the other children, liable to nightmares. She also observed that the girl was extraordinarily intelligent and strikingly beautiful."

She looked up. "Now, you see, Miss Lathem and all the rest of the staff would have been quite aware of the Kalendar girl's background. I don't mean murder, because in 1974 no one knew about that, but the site inspections had made it pretty clear that the child had been raised by a very disturbed man.

"We are always looking for good foster parents for the children in our care, and Miss Lathem eventually came upon a couple that seemed perfect. Guy and Diane Huntress had successfully fostered three children some years before—they seemed to specialize in turning around some of our most damaged children. Miss Lathem arranged a meeting, the Huntresses agreed to take Lily into their home. Things went on, lots of ups and downs but mainly ups, until 1979, when Guy Huntress unexpectedly died."

Mercedes Romola looked directly at Tim. "And what else happened in 1979, Mr. Underhill?"

"Joseph Kalendar was arrested for multiple homicides. The police found only a few fragments of the bodies, because he burned most of his victims in his furnace."

"The Kalendar scandal exploded. Mrs. Huntress feared what might happen to the child in school. It seemed to her that Lily would fare better back here in the shelter. But children can be so cruel—she went through two really lousy years. It's no fun being an outcast. She was humiliated over and over. Face in the toilet, things like that."

"What school did she go to?" Willy asked, with the air of one sticking an oar into a swiftly running river.

"While she was with Diane Huntress, Grace and Favor Elementary School in Sundown, Slater Middle School, and Augment High. Why?"

"I was under the impression she went to Lawrence Freeman."

"The elementary school down in what they used to call Pigtown? Why would you think she went there?"

"Sorry, sorry, my mistake," Willy said.

The matron looked back at her papers, then glanced up with the suggestion of a smile on her face. "At this point, an unusual event took place. Diane Huntress came in for a talk with Miss Lathem and said she wanted Lily to come back to her as a foster child. In my considerable experience, this kind of thing is more or less impossible. Foster relationships are terminated for all kinds of reasons, some worse than others, but they are never resumed."

"But she went back," Tim said.

"She went back. And in her way, she flourished. And when I spoke to her an hour ago, she told me that although she would not assist you in any way during the writing of your book, she would not obstruct you in any way, either. She says she'd be willing to talk to you, on one condition, if you wish to speak to her. On the whole, she'd prefer not to, but the choice is up to you."

"What's the condition?" Tim asked.

"That first you meet with Diane Huntress, so that she can decide the next step. Mr. Underhill, do you know what this means?"

"I'm not sure."

"It means that Lily Kalendar trusts Diane Huntress absolutely. In **spite** of the fact that Diane had returned her to us, and left her here for two awful years. Lily knew why she had done it, she understood. And when she went back to Diane, it was with the feeling of coming home to a mother who had been ill, but now was well again. People like Lily Kalendar, not that there are very many, seldom trust anyone at all. You realize, what happened to that child was immense. **Immense.**"

Underhill felt the word sink into him, widening out as it did. The comprehension of that immensity seemed the point behind everything that had happened since his sister had thrust herself through the mirror to shout her silent command. Even getting close to understanding Lily Kalendar's experience was the other half of fulfilling Kalendar's demand: he would acknowledge the bizarre mercy Kalendar had shown his daughter, but he also had to wrap his imagination around the price Lily had paid for his mercy. For a moment, it felt like the task of his life. Then he looked at Willy, and his heart moved at the recognition of her plight. She was listening to a woman talk about the person she had been supposed to be. What could that be like?

"It's an immensity for me, too," he said. "How can I arrange the meeting?"

Mercedes Romola's smile may have been small, but it illuminated her entire face. "I spoke to Mrs. Huntress right after calling Lily, and she is prepared to meet you anytime this afternoon. In fact, this will be your last chance to have her look you over for two or three months. She's leaving for China with a tour group tomorrow, and after that she's going to stay with some old friends in Australia. Do you see what I mean about luck, Mr. Underhill?" She wrote something on a white card and slid it toward him. "This is her address. It's in an interesting part of town. I'll call her and tell her you're coming."

Tim yielded to the impulse to kiss her hand,

and she said, "We don't do much hand kissing in Millhaven, Mr. Underhill. But I'm glad to see you have some idea of what is at stake here. If you're going to write about Lily Kalendar, you'd better make it the book of your life."

31

From Timothy Underhill's journal

Willy cried steadily as I drove to the address the matron had given me. She also ate half a box of Valrhona chocolates, more for the comfort of it, I thought, than in response to her "condition." She kept her head turned from me, and now and then held up her left hand as a shield to protect herself from my gaze.

"It's not the way you think it is," I said. "You're not **nothing;** you do exist. If I love you, you have to exist."

"You're a liar. You love **her,** and you never even met her. But she's real, and I'm not. You think she's immense. She's what I was supposed to be." I got another angry peek. "You're sick. You're twisted. Other people's pain makes you feel good. You must be in pig heaven right now."

"Willy, other people's pain does not make me

feel good. It's that I don't want to overlook it or pretend it doesn't exist. I want to do it justice. That's why you liked reading me when you were depressed, remember?"

She made a dismissive **mmph** sound.

"Do you want to know what I really do like?"

"Lily Kalendar, Lily Kalendar, Lily Kalendar."

"I like the space between," I said. "The space between dreaming and wakefulness. Between imagination and reality. Between no and yes. Between is and is not. That's where the interesting stuff is. That's where you are. You are completely a product of the space between."

"Between **is** and **is not**?"

"Where they both hold true, where they become one thing."

Evidently, this struck her. She faced forward and she kept her eyes on the windshield. She wasn't going to look at me, but at least she had stopped looking away.

"That's so stupid it might actually mean something. Still, I thought I was a real person, and it turns out all along I was only a bad Xerox."

"That's completely wrong," I said. "You're not even close to being a copy. You're unique. Willy—"

"Holy shit," she said, looking ahead.

I snapped my head forward again and, as we

drifted through a turn, saw what Mercedes Romola had meant by "an interesting part of
town." The road we were on, and the houses
that sprouted up on either side of it, went down
into a huge, long, descending spiral that resembled the interior of the Guggenheim Museum
on Fifth Avenue. The top of the spiral must
have been about two hundred yards across, and
down at its bottom lay a grocery store, a movie
theater, a bar, a library, a Gap, and a Starbucks
around the edges of a little square with a bandstand. It brought to mind a Hobbit world; it
was also very pretty. At night, it would have
looked extraordinary, with the lights shining
around the great swooping curves of the spiral.
From the top, the scene suggested a terraced
landscape with houses instead of vineyards.
That the name of this area was Sundown I had
always attributed to its location in the city's far
western reaches. Now I thought that if you lived
even a little bit down on the curve, the sun
would vanish early every evening.

The Huntress house, about a third of the way
down, could have been in any older section of
Millhaven. Three stories, dark wood, cement
steps leading up to a small porch with a peaked
roof: it was no more than a modestly upscale
version of the houses on North Superior Street,

but the setting gave it a slightly Brothers Grimm aspect.

I parked in front of the house and walked around to Willy's door. "Admit you're interested."

Instead of responding, Willy rammed a Three Musketeers bar into her mouth. I hadn't seen her pull it out of her pocket, which she must have filled when I was walking around the front of the car. A bright wrapper fluttered to the ground.

"Oh, Willy," I said, and picked it up. "That's beneath you."

Around a mouthful of Three Musketeers, Willy said, "Do you think this lady is going to like you? This lady is not going to like you."

I hauled her up onto the porch and pushed the bell. A minute later, a stocky woman with a purple cloud of hair and sharp eyes in a big, foursquare face that gave full justice to the mingled pains and joys of seventy-odd years opened the door and released the ghosts of a thousand cigarettes. She reminded me of the Pigtown women of my childhood who had worked on the line in one factory or another, down in the Valley.

We said hello to each other and spoke our names, and I introduced Willy as my assistant.

Diane Huntress said something nice about Mercedes Romola's approval and invited us into her house. It was not what I had expected, nor was she. What that woman said—for the ninety minutes she spoke of Lily Kalendar, it felt like she stopped time. Like Joseph Kalendar, Diane Huntress froze the cars on the street and the kids playing ball and the mailman puttering along in his cart, and anybody else who was in the reach of that smoker's voice and the things it said. She certainly froze me. Willy never moved, either.

Tim Underhill walked amazed into a setting that declared its inhabitant a dedicated traveler of great taste and curiosity. Treasures adorned the walls and gleamed from the depths of cabinets: African masks and tribal figures; Chinese vases and Greek amphoras; Japanese scrolls; small, ornate rugs; a thousand little things that had been lovingly accumulated over decades. Part of the effect was the implied knowledge that, for all their worth, these objects had been obtained at the lowest possible price by travelers who'd never had a lot of money to draw out of their purse.

On the way to the sofa where Mrs. Huntress

wished them to sit, Willy set aside her unhappiness long enough to admire a small tapestry
panel shining with silken threads.

Tim wandered past a group of photographs
depicting Diane Huntress and a large man with
a genial face dominated by a slablike chin standing in jungles, in deserts, before great monu-
ments, beside canals and rivers, at the feet of
snowy mountains, in hookah cafés, in crowded
bazaars.

He turned to Mrs. Huntress. "Did you ever
take Lily Kalendar with you on your trips?"

"As often as possible," she said. "Here. Take a
look." She brought him to the far end of the
group and indicated a photograph that must
have been taken by Guy Huntress, for he was
not in it. His wife, perhaps thirty years younger
than the woman beside Tim now, stood planted
in a meadow rimmed with hills that might have
been in Africa. A little blond girl of ten or
eleven peeked out from behind her legs with an
expression of mingled fear and pleasure on her
intense, radiant face that flew straight to the
center of Underhill's heart. To him, the child
looked like an exposed nerve—the sensitivity he
saw in her dark gray-blue eyes, the planes of her
face, the tilt of her head, in even her sunburned
skin, moved him nearly to tears.

"Lily hated to have her picture taken," said

her foster mother. "She simply refused, she wouldn't do it. Maybe she inherited that from her father, because he was the same way."

"I know," said Tim, thinking of the black-coated figure silhouetted against the sky at the top of North Superior Street. "I hope that's all she did inherit from him."

Something shifted in the way she took him in: it was as if she were imitating the forthright stance in the photograph. "You really want to write a book about Lily, do you?"

Willy wandered up on the other side of Tim. She craned her neck forward and scanned the photo. When she spoke, her voice contained a slightly defeated tone. "She was amazing. I should have known."

Mrs. Huntress gave her a bemused smile. "Well, you're very lovely, too, you must know that. In fact, you're so pretty, it almost hurts to look at you." She turned again to Tim. "Sit yourselves down, I'll get you some tea or coffee, and you can tell me about your book."

In the end, seated on the firm Huntress sofa with a cup of excellent coffee before him, unhappy Willy steadily sipping from a glass of Coke, he could never be sure what Diane Huntress made of his confused description of the book he claimed to be researching. The word "tactful" turned up, as did "respectful." As he blathered, he began to think that this was a book he could actually write, forgetting that he had no patience for the kind of detailed research it would involve. If he tried to write such a book, it would consist mainly of leaps into the dark, a number of them noticeably ungainly.

"I'm sure it'll come into better focus when you've worked on it awhile," Mrs. Huntress said. "I have to be completely honest with you and tell you that I don't think you or anyone else should write a book about Lily."

"Then you're being very generous, letting me talk to you."

"Lily isn't going to do anything to stop you, so I think it's my duty to see that you understand her as well as possible. If you want to talk to her in person, which she is willing to do under certain conditions, you'll get an idea of the life she has now, but that idea won't be good enough—it won't be enough, period. She asked me to tell you that she's willing to meet with you for an hour, but that nothing she says to you can be quoted in your book."

"You don't want me to meet her, do you?"

"Let me tell you about Lily Kalendar."

Hearing those words at last, Tim sensed a movement on the other side of the room and glanced past Mrs. Huntress to see what it was.

His heart stopped. In her Alice dress, April lay
on a vibrant rug no larger than herself, her
cheek resting on a hand, looking intently at
him. Having been seen, she pushed herself upright, got to her feet, and stepped backward,
never taking her eyes from him. Tim knew that
it was she who had led him to this place, that he
might hear out the woman who had known Lily
Kalendar best. She wanted him to do more than
hear: she was commanding him to **listen.**

You have to know a few things about me first,
Diane Huntress said. My father built the Sundown Community, which is what we used to
call this area, in the forties, and he placed it in
this basin because he wanted it to be at one remove from the outside world. He graded Sundown Road himself and he built that little plaza
and the bandstand at the bottom. The whole
thing was his idea. We never had any money,
but that didn't bother us. My father really didn't
care about money. Originally, all the people
who lived here knew one another, and we used
to have these communal meals, and there'd be
singing, and people would play their instru-
ments, and we'd dance. We had this sense of
shared ideals, a shared vision. Nothing ever
stays the same in this world, especially commu-
nities like Sundown. A lot of new people were

moving in by the time Guy Huntress and I got married.

We were busy—Guy was a housepainter, and I came along and did the detail work. I worked as a waitress, too. We started going places together, spending what little we had on things we came across and liked instead of on hotels and fancy meals. We discovered we couldn't have children, and that was a blow. And Guy didn't want to adopt. But one day he said, You know, we could give back to the community by taking in a foster child. That way, at least we'd have a kid around the house. I thought it was a great, great idea, the greatest. We got in touch with Social Services, they put us in touch with Georgia Lathem, and that's how we got our first three foster children. One after the other, not all together.

Sally, Rob, and Charlie. Wonderful kids. Screwed up as hell when we first got them, but basically okay. A little antisocial, you know, shoplifting, mouthing off, testing the rules. All the normal stuff. What we did with those kids, we thought was what everybody would do. Now, to Georgia Lathem and them, what we did was **special.** So when they had an unusual case come in, I guess they thought of us first. We go down to Karadara Street, we go into Miss Lathem's office, and sitting there like a little wet cat is this child named Lily Kalendar. What we didn't know about Lily and her background would fill volumes, let me tell you.

This one is going to be trouble, Guy said. This one is going to break your heart, he said. Are you sure you want to do this? Her first day in the Foundlings' Shelter, Lily peed on the floor and tried to stab another kid with a pencil. Her second day, she lit a fire in the game room. She barely talked. She was like a little **savage.** Sure I'm sure, I told my husband. This kid Lily, this little monster, she's going to be my project, because you know what? I love her already.

And I did. I did love that child. I saw something in her, maybe what you saw in that picture, Mr. Underhill. I saw a terribly damaged little girl who felt everything that happened everywhere. Do you know what I mean, Mr. Underhill? The spirit in there, it might have been scared and angry and half-poisoned, but it wasn't **selfish.**

She was **angry.** Lily was the angriest child I ever met—no, the angriest person I ever met. The first thing I had to do was let her know that she could have all that anger and still feel safe. Once we got through that stage, I was pretty sure we could begin to make a human being out of the girl. She still talked in baby talk half the time, and she pronounced her name Wiwwy, because she couldn't say the letter **l. Wiwwy hate, Wiwwy bite.** You know how many times I heard that? Other times, she rolled out curse words so terrible a superstitious person would say she was possessed. She **was** possessed, but by herself, not the devil.

When she got wild, I'd roll her up in a blanket and lie down on the ground with her and hold her until she stopped screeching. I had to toilet train her, the way you do a three-year-old. We had messes I won't describe, but they were awful. And, of course, she'd never been to school a day in her life, but when she came to see that I was going to stick with her no matter what she did, or how terrible she acted, she calmed down enough for me to get some textbooks and readers. The point was, I wasn't going to leave her, and I wasn't going to hurt her, I was just going to do everything I could to make her feel better.

At first, she was always running away! She'd slip out of the house when my back was turned and take off, but she was so terrified of everything, everything **meant** so much to her, that she could never get very far. I found her hiding behind the bushes, lying flat under cars. Weeping her head off. Terrified to go any farther, terrified of coming back. She'd scream her head off when I carried her home, but she clung tight, she didn't struggle. **No night room,** she said, **no night room for Wiwwy,** and I'd tell her right back, **Honey, we don't have a night room, you don't have to worry about it.** So what was a night room?

Separately, Timothy Underhill and Willy Patrick felt a succession of shocks like that of an electrical pulse zigzagging through their bodies and, like a pinball, lighting up whatever it touched.

I called up Georgia Lathem, **said Diane Huntress,** and asked her, and what she told me just about peeled my scalp off. That terrible, terrible man built a horrible room onto his house, and he didn't put any lights or windows in there, all he put in there was a big wooden bed! With, like, handcuffs on it, restraints. And to be frank, Mr. Underhill, he raped his little girl on the bed—that was his punishment for her leaving the house. Well, I knew she'd been abused, but I hadn't known it had been as bad as all that.

You see, he didn't want her to leave the house because he didn't want anyone to know about her. She had no birth certificate, which gave us problems I'll tell you about later. Officially, Lily Kalendar didn't exist. He kept that child as his toy, Mr. Underhill, and he beat her and starved her, because that was his version of love. When I learned that, I knew I was in for a long siege, and so I was.

After a while, I discovered the one thing that calmed her down. I read to her. It was like I had a charm, like I waved a magic wand over her. When I sat down next to this raging little thing and started to read, it never took her more than a couple of minutes to quiet down, stick her thumb in her mouth, and listen to the story. Oh my God, she was so adorable then. I must have read the same ten books over and over a thousand times, **Goodnight Moon** and **Ping** and **Make Way for Ducklings** and **The Runaway Bunny.** I can still see her, lying on the floor with her chin in her hands, drinking in every word I said. Concentrating, concentrating, concentrating. When I saw that, I knew hope—hope can just about strike you dead, so you have to take care with it, but Lily's ability to concentrate made me feel that sunlight had just entered a very, very dark room.

And the other thing was, she was smart. She remembered everything we read, word for word, and once we moved past those ten books, she really demanded that what we read was stuff worth reading. I tore through that little library my father established down there on Sundown

Plaza. Six books every week, and Lily was pretty vocal about what she wanted me to read to her and what she didn't. We had about six months when all she wanted were murder mysteries and horror stories! Now, I'm not saying that any of this went smoothly, because it certainly did not. Lily could spend days doing nothing but pouting or screaming or breaking things—she even screamed in her sleep. There were days Guy came home from work and looked at the mess and listened to the uproar, and I could see on his face he was wondering if I could really take it much longer. But talk about saints, Guy never said he'd had enough, that we could maybe hand this wild animal back to the city. Never.

Dickens was our big breakthrough, Charles Dickens, may God care for him forever through all eternity. When we got started on Dickens, Lily didn't want to stop! I started on **A Christmas Carol,** and she loved it so much she made me read it three times. The next one was, I think, **The Old Curiosity Shop.** But the miracle, what I call the miracle, happened near the beginning of **A Tale of Two Cities.** She crawled into my lap! This was a girl who couldn't bear to be touched when she first came into our lives, not unless she was wrapped in a blanket first, and then there was a fifty-fifty chance she would crap in the blanket. Never said a word, just squiggled in between me and the book and plunked herself down on my lap. God bless you, Mr. Dickens, that's all I can say. See? It still makes me cry. Because, you know, everything good flowed from that one thing she did, that willingness to be close, that **consent.**

From that, she learned to read. I'd say I taught Lily to read, but really she taught herself. With Dickens! Sidney Carton and Charles Darnay, **they** taught Lily how to read. We'd already taught her the alphabet, and she had memorized those ten children's books we'd read over and over, so it was just a matter of making the connection between the letters and the words. I almost have to say that little girl memorized **A Tale of Two Cities,** because that was her method, all right. I said the words, and she looked at them, and then she said the words, and that's how she learned to read.

And did she read! Like a wolf! Those books, down they went! Social Services had been keeping in touch, of course—we had a weekly visit from Adele Spelvin, Willy's social worker—and one day Adele Spelvin says to us that in her opinion Lily was ready to start going to school, which was a big moment for us, and a big decision, because it really felt like losing her, you know? You send a child to school, you give her to all these other people.

She still had emotional problems, too. That should go without saying, but I'll say it anyhow. You have to think hard about sending a kid to school if you can't be certain she won't lose it and decide to wipe her feces all over the walls of the girls' room or slam some boy's head onto the playground because he upset her in some way. Actually, she was pretty well over the bodily fluids phase, and she really was learning to manage her anger, but she still felt everything everywhere, and she was still wounded and she walked around in a blur of pain. . . . But she was coping!

So I said, Okay, we'll send her to Grace and Favor, which is the grade school right here in Sundown, but you people better know that there will be days when this child will simply not **be able** to come to your school. There will be days when she will show up but won't be able to come out of the cloakroom, and you will have to bring her home. She may cry a lot, for no reason you can see. Well, let me tell you, I said, this little girl has plenty to cry about, and if you'd gone through what she went through, you'd be living in a rubber room and wearing a straitjacket.

Everybody listened because I **made** them listen, Mr. Underhill, and off to school my girl went—oh, so terrified that day, and the next, and the next. After a long while she got used to the idea of walking down to Grace and Favor all on her lonesome. And by reports, because I insisted on reports, she got on well—after a while, I mean—with the other children, although to her they were just **children,** you see, not people she could make friends with and be comfortable around. I'm not sure she ever understood what a friend was supposed to be, and how to act toward one. None of her classmates ever came back here with her. The whole situation was a tremendous success, I can say that. We never **expected** her to bring friends home. Lily only got into a couple of fights, and she didn't do any permanent damage to her opponents, which means that even when she lost it, she could manage a little bit of self-control.

Those were the summers we took her abroad with us, to Kenya, where Guy took that picture after wheedling Lily for about an hour and telling her she could hide behind me, and the Black Forest and the Rhine, and Amsterdam. She didn't have a birth certificate, but in this state there's a document they can make up, called an extraordinary birth certificate, for times like that. The information on it isn't necessarily accurate, because who knew the exact date of Lily's birth? No one, not even her horrible father, I bet. And the hour? And her weight? Please. But there **is** information on her document, and that document is part of the record. So it's fiction, and it's true at the same time. Getting the document took a little doing, but it came through, and we could start going on our travels again. Lily spent every possible minute with her nose in a book, but every now and then we got her to look up from her page and see a cathedral, or a castle, or a good painting.

But right then, when she was fourteen, two terrible things happened. My husband died, very suddenly, no warning at all. Pop, and there he was, dead in a heap on the ground. I thought I was going to go crazy with grief, but I couldn't, for Lily's sake. She took Guy's death in her own way, and she took it hard. By dying, he betrayed her trust, which she'd only just learned to give. He'd abandoned her, and she turned wild again. There were days when I had to wrap her in her blanket all over again and hold her until she could feel some peace. And not long after, here came the second terrible thing: her father was arrested, and his terrible crimes were printed all over the newspapers. She couldn't go to school anymore. I didn't even try. Some of the children in her class came over here and shouted things at her from the front lawn. Every day! They painted things on our front door.

Without Guy, I couldn't handle it. On top of everything else, I had to go back to work, because we had no money coming in anymore. Getting a job was no picnic, but I finally landed a spot at the Dresden, more a cocktail lounge than a restaurant, but they serve food, too. Lily and I cried ourselves to sleep, because we could see it coming. She couldn't stay here anymore, that was it. We both knew it. I was a wreck, she had to stay in all day, those children were calling her "monster baby" and all kinds of things, they were driving us both crazy. . . . And I was losing my grip! So I did the worst thing in the world, the worst thing possible, which I had no choice but to do. I put Lily back in the shelter.

And they tortured her there. I thought they'd protect her, but they can only do so much when the kids are in those dormitories and they turn off the lights. They **tortured** her. I can't bear to think of what happened to my dear girl when she was fourteen and fifteen years old. And do you know the most unbearable part of all that? Lily pretended nothing was wrong. She told me not to come, I thought because she was mad at me, which she was, but believe me, what she was actually doing was protecting me from the knowledge of what her life was like. In those days, Lily went wild—she smoked, and she drank, and she took drugs, because in her old age Georgia Lathem began to slip, and she couldn't see what was going on under her own nose.

By working at the Dresden, and learning to live on my own, I gradually began to put things together, and I realized that more than anything else in the world I wanted to get Lily back. I thought I **had** to get her back with me, if I was going to call myself a human being. So I astonished Miss Georgia Lathem by telling her I wanted to be Lily's foster mother again, and what's more, that I wanted to adopt her. Because that's what we should have done the first time.

Young woman, you appear to live on candy bars.

Anyhow, my darling girl came back, and we lived together in this house, and I adopted her, and we had tons of work to do, academically, personally, psychologically, but we got through it. I managed to scrape together enough money to get tutors for her, but she was so smart that she didn't need them for long. Academic work came so naturally to her, and she turned out to be a whiz in science. The mental problems were a lot more difficult. At one time, **both** of us were seeing therapists. I see you nodding your heads, so you know how much a person can get out of therapy. Guy never understood, and I wouldn't have if I hadn't been forced to do it, but I doubt that Lily would have gone as far as she has without it.

I think Lily is remarkable. She's the best person I know, and in some ways, she's really and truly the worst. I love her. She became so beautiful, I think Helen of Troy was based on **her.**

College? Oh yes, she got a wonderful scholarship to Northwestern. They paid for everything, textbooks, tuition, housing. Her grade point average was something like 3.98, because she got a B in something once, I forget what. Statistics, maybe. And when she got into Columbia medical school, a bunch of Northwestern alums, people who knew nothing about her background or her life story, pitched in and paid her tuition and all her other expenses. She got her M.D. in 1992, and specialized in pediatrics, and now she's back in Millhaven, working as a pediatrician. That's what she does. She takes care of other people's children. She's a great doctor, a brilliant doctor, and her patients adore her. So do their parents. You could have looked her up in the phone book, didn't you realize that? Of course, you'd have to know her name. Lily Huntress, M.D.

That is by no means everything Diane Huntress told Timothy Underhill and his beloved creature Willy Patrick as they sat entranced upon her sturdy sofa, but it covers most of the high points. When time unlocked and resumed its flow, and the cars once again spiraled up and down Sundown Road and mailmen again jolted forward in their carts, Tim felt as though, unlike the journey that had brought him to Mercedes Romola, Diane Huntress's had concluded in a completely unexpected place.

"Is she married?" he asked.

"Married? Good Lord, no. She'll never marry. She'll never write a book, either."

"Is she happy?"

"I don't think Lily understands the concept of happiness—it's like a foreign language to her. She suffered greatly, and now she helps children, that's her life. I think she thought of it as the most beautiful thing she could do. That's the way her mind works."

"Does she work with other doctors in a practice?"

"She works alone. Her practice is in two rooms

of her house. She still has days when everything overwhelms her and she has to cancel all her appointments and reschedule her patients. She locks herself in her private rooms and deals with it. She knows I'd come in a second, but she doesn't call me. She doesn't call anybody."

"What you did," Tim said, "was like a miracle. It **was** a miracle. You rescued her."

"She let me rescue her. I'll tell you what I did, and I'm very clear on this. I hung in there. That's what I did. I hung in there."

From Timothy Underhill's journal

"Well, you got some things right," Willy said.

"I didn't really get anything right," I said. We were driving back toward the hotel, ringing with the emotions that had flowed through Mrs. Huntress's living room. "Except you, I guess. I missed the boat with Lily, but with Willy I did just fine."

"That's nice of you."

"How do you feel?"

"Light. Full of honeycomb spaces. It's okay. I don't mind. It doesn't really hurt anymore."

"It used to hurt?"

"Your whole body feels like one big funny bone, all over."

"You never complained," I said.

"I wish I were like **her,**" Willy said. "She sounds absolutely amazing."

"No," I said, "you don't want to be like her. It's much too complicated."

"In contrast to the simple, sunny history you gave me."

"You had the same childhood, with the same father," I said.

"You should have made me a pediatrician. And you know what else you did? You made me pretty, but in a stupid way. You saw how she looked as a child. Imagine the way she looks now."

I thought of the face Lily had had at eleven, compact and alive with a complex, glowing density of feeling, and could not imagine what she must look like now.

Willy unfolded the paper she had been holding since we'd gotten into the car. I didn't have to look at it to know what was written there in Diane Huntress's surprisingly calligraphic hand: **3516 N. Meeker Road,** Lily Huntress's address.

"Do you want to go there? I guess I could stand it, if you thought you had to see her, at least. I'd have to stay in the car, though."

"I don't know what I want to do," I said.

"Good. Then let's go back to the hotel. You have to get ready for your reading."

"Oh," I said. "My reading."

32

From Timothy Underhill's journal

I don't want to write anything here about my reading at the New Leaf bookstore; the memory is embarrassing enough without reliving it. I stumbled through the stuff I'd selected, the Q&A was all right, I signed a pile of books. China Beech turned up, and I liked her. She's a small, nice-looking woman with a face in which underlying honesty is at war with its superficial prettiness. That's the only way I know how to put it. She is younger than I had expected, about forty, and extremely nice looking, and it doesn't matter. **She** doesn't give a hang, and after a couple of seconds you're so aware of her basic warmth and goodness that you don't really notice how she looks. She wears a little lipstick, that's all. When we were introduced, China took my arm and said, "Philip told me you believed him when he wrote you that I was an exotic dancer. Meaning a stripper. You must have had horrible visions of me!"

"Well," I said, "it did seem an unusual choice for Philip."

"It would have been. But the only man I intend to strip for is your brother."

For some reason, that remark left me in a state of mild shock. Then I went ahead and gave the worst reading of my life, unable to think about anything but Lily Kalendar, Lily Huntress.

After the disaster had ended, Willy and I went out for drinks and dinner with Philip and China at an old hangout of mine called Ella Speed's. The only memorable thing that happened during dinner was something Willy said after I told Philip that she was a writer: "In an alternate universe, I won the Newbery Medal."

Back in our hotel room, I thought Cyrax might have some last-minute instructions, so I plugged Mark's computer into the hotel's online service and discovered that although my gide had nothing new to say to me, my in-box was jammed with messages from the newly dead. I deleted them all without reading them. Willy pretended to read **A Far Cry from Kensington,** which she had picked up at the bookstore—literally picked up, I fear, because she had no money of her own and had not asked me for any—while keeping her eye on me. I paced from the living room into the bedroom, stopped off in the bathroom to see what I looked like in the mirror, and paced back into the living room, where I paced some more.

"I can't take it anymore," I said. "I can't stand it."

"I can't stand watching you act this way," Willy said. "What's **it**?"

"Do you still have that piece of paper?"

Her face went soft and vulnerable. She knew exactly what piece of paper I meant. "I stuck it in this book."

"Do you think she might have deliberately given us the wrong address?"

"Diane Huntress? Why would she do that?"

"I don't know. To protect her? Is there a phone book in the desk drawer?"

Willy uncoiled herself from the sofa, moved to the desk, and found a Millhaven directory in the drawer. "Do you want me to look it up for you?"

I knew how little she wanted to do that, and I loved her for making the offer. I held out my hand for the book. "She's probably not even in it."

She was, though, as I should have known. A pediatrician can't have an unlisted number, not even if she's like Lily Huntress. There she was,

on page 342 of the Millhaven telephone directory, at 3516 N. Meeker Road, with a telephone
number anyone could dial. It was staggering,
like looking through a window of the house
next door and seeing a unicorn.

Willy dared to rest her hand on my shoulder.
"You want to go there, don't you? You want to
talk to her."

"I don't know what I want," I said, "but I have
to go there, at least. I have to see her house, get
some idea of how she lives."

"Why don't you call her? It's not that late."

"I can't call her." If I called Lily Kalendar, and
she answered the phone, I thought, the sound
of her voice would reduce me to a heap of
smoking ashes. This was not something I could
say to Willy. "I guess I'm too shy."

The untruth disturbed her, and she held the
novel in her hands and seemed to look at the
blank screen of the television. "Do you know
where that street is?"

"I can find out," I said.

"Were you going to invite me along? I don't
know if I'd be willing to come, though."

"Will you drive over there with me, Willy?" I
asked.

Gently, almost reluctantly, she slid the Muriel
Spark novel onto the desk and, without raising
her eyes to my face, moved slowly toward me.

An inch away, she turned sideways and stepped into me like an uneasy cat in search of comfort, brushing her shoulder against my chest and leaning her head sideways on the base of my neck. I could feel the candy bars in her pocket.

"I don't want to be here alone," she said. "But I want you to know, I don't like any part of this, either." She turned to face me and looked up, right into my eyes. "Why would you want to talk to her? You're not going to write a book about her, that was just a story, a pretext. Do you think you can **help** her? You can't, you can't help Lily Kalendar. She doesn't want your help. She doesn't even want to see you, really, she just agreed so you'd leave her alone afterward."

"I might write that book," I said, knowing I was fudging the truth again. "I don't know what I'll do until I get there."

Meeker Road turned out to be a short cul-de-sac tucked behind the Darnton Woods golf club on the city's North Side. To get there, we got on the expressway that leads into Milwaukee and stayed on it, hurtling along in a cluster of other vehicles like a wolf in a wolf pack, headlights stabbing and shining out, for about twenty minutes. In the face of Willy's silence, I turned on the radio and found the local jazz station. The sound of a very familiar alto saxophone playing "Like Someone in Love" in Copenhagen in the year 1958 soared from the speakers, filled with the hand-in-hand mixture of joy and sadness, happiness and grief, that great jazz music conveys.

"We love Paul Desmond, don't we?" Willy said, and for a few bars sang along with the solo.

I turned off at Exit 17, and tried to remember the directions from the expressway. There are no streetlamps in that part of town, and dense clouds blanketed the night sky. More or less aimlessly, I swung the car past big houses set far back on perfect lawns. Eventually, I saw the sign for Darnton Woods and kept moving along beside the course on Midgette Road until I reached the extensive stand of oaks and poplars that marked the boundary at its back end. The road wandered farther north, and I thought I had somehow missed my turnoff in the darkness. I told Willy we were going to have to turn around, and she told me that it was too soon to give up. "Distances always seem longer in the dark," she said.

Five minutes later, I saw an old street sign half-submerged by a gigantic azalea bush and knew I'd found Meeker Road. An extraordinary tumult, caused by the most divided feelings I had ever experienced, erupted in the center of my body. I wanted to turn in, I needed to see where Lily Kalendar lived, and I wanted with equal force to keep on driving until I got back to the Pforzheimer, where I could make love to Willy Patrick. She peeked at me out of the side of one eye, and when at the last I turned in to Meeker Road, she braced herself by sitting up straighter in her seat and staring a bit glumly at the windshield.

On Meeker Road, thick trees half-concealed the spacious houses that had grown up at wide intervals between them. Windows glowed yellow. TV sets, some of them wall-mounted plasma screens, glowed and flickered in empty-looking rooms. The basketball hoops above the garage doors wore nets that looked like off-center beards. The numbers on the mailboxes, some of them as big as Santa's sack and painted with ducks in flight, windmills, sailboats, tennis rackets, went by: 3509, 3510.

Down at the far end of the cul-de-sac, a Bauhaus-influenced house seemed to emerge from the giant trees behind it like a yacht cutting through thick fog. White, bare except for the nautical details, solid and functional, beautiful in its unforgiving way, this had to be Lily Huntress's house. A plain metal mailbox stood at the end of the driveway, and when my headlights picked it out, we saw, unaccompanied by a name, the number 3516.

I stopped the car and turned off the headlights. Light shone from an upper window on the left side of the house and in a ground-floor window on the right side of the front door. Dimmer light appeared in a round window like a porthole directly above the front door.

"Look what she did," I said. "Her back is protected by the wall at this part of the golf course, and facing forward, she can see anyone who comes down the street. It's like taking the farthest seat in a restaurant and watching the door. I bet she has the best security system you can buy."

"So what?" Willy asked. "She's scared?"

"She's dealing with it," I said. "Like you. She has her whole life brilliantly controlled, so that she can feel safe without turning into a recluse. I know guys who bought houses in the middle of the woods in Michigan and rigged up perimeters of barbed wire and floodlights. Plus a couple of tormented dogs. They had terrible experiences, but Lily Kalendar's were worse."

"Are you going to knock on the door, or ring the bell, or whatever?"

"I'm going to sit here and think about it," I said.

"I hope she doesn't walk past the window or anything."

I realized that what Willy dreaded was what I

had driven to Meeker Road to see. It would be enough; it would be all I needed. I thought of Lily Kalendar watching out for her patients' arrival, waiting for her receptionist to confirm what she already knew, then treating the children who came to her by giving them the generosity and mercy her early childhood had never known. Diane Huntress had said, **"Now she helps children, that's her life. I think she thought of it as the most beautiful thing she could do. That's the way her mind works."** That last sentence offered an implied touch of criticism, to be taken up or not, in the observation that Lily had aesthetic motives for her moral decisions. I saw it the other way around, that her choice of profession was beautiful in a moral sense.

Then the world changed. A woman with bright blond hair that fell to within two inches of her shoulders walked past the window holding an open book in one hand and a cup of tea in the other. She appeared to be slender; there was a slight stiffness in the way she slipped through the air. The tumult I had experienced when we came upon Lily Kalendar's street reawakened, amplified to an internal earthquake. The woman's face was turned from us, and all I could glimpse was the side and back of her head. She wore a dark green blouse, or maybe it was a light cashmere sweater. It was still warm, though not as warm as it had been during the day, and her air-conditioning was running. She liked cold rooms anyhow, I thought. A moment later, we were looking at an empty window.

The thought came to me that I was the one man in the world who could restore what was missing, and make Lily Kalendar whole as she had never been. In the next second I realized that many, many men had known the same impulse, and that none of us could offer her anything commensurate with her beauty, her pain, or her history. To the extent that these had been overcome, it had been done by her own efforts: she had so thoroughly absorbed the cruelty and wickedness visited upon her that they had been rendered all but invisible, and she paid for what she had absorbed with a hundred daily acts of kindness and generosity. I could not rescue her. When devotion still had an effect, she'd had Diane Huntress; after that, she had simply rescued herself, and done it, with her magnificent intelligence, as thoroughly as she could.

Then I remembered the slight stiffness in her gait, the way she had held herself, deliberately turned from the window, and even my bones went cold. Like her father, she hid her face whenever she could; certainly, she wanted no one to look in and see that face. The cruelty and wickedness she had absorbed, and for which she paid with service to her patients, still lived in her—Diane Huntress knew it, she had always known it. That was why she had told us that Lily was the worst person she had ever known. Diane had not rescued Lily; by dint of tireless, selfless, unending devoted work she had **half-tamed** her. That Lily's new name was Huntress sent icicles through my bloodstream. Her father, who had loved her, loved her still: it was only by a closely monitored borderline that she restrained herself from going out hunting exactly as he had.

I thought I could hear Jasper Dan Kohle cackling and howling from beneath the trees at the end of the country club.

"All right," I said. My voice sounded breathy and battered, and I cleared my throat. "I'm going back to the hotel."

On the way to the Pforzheimer, Tim stopped at the Fireside Lounge, a restaurant he had always liked for its old-fashioned red leather booths and low lighting. Willy said, "I was so preoccupied back there, I forgot how hungry I was." When she ordered a tenderloin for herself, the waitress pointed out that it was intended for two people. "I'm eating for two," Willy said. "What kind of potatoes come with that?"

She devoured her enormous meal in no more time than Tim required to eat his hamburger and half of the French fries that came with it. The other half wound up on Willy's plate. When the worst of her hunger had been satisfied, she asked, with the air of one entering extremely dangerous territory, "What do you think about what just happened, anyhow?"

"I think she's more like her father than anyone has ever recognized," he said. "But what she's done with it is extraordinary."

"I bet you wish you could have seen her face."

"To tell you the truth, Willy," he said, "the thought of looking upon that woman's face fills me with terror. What do you think about what happened?"

"I'm scared," Willy said. Her face rippled, and her cheeks turned chalky and white. "I'm lost, and I'm frightened. She was scary, but you are, too."

His heart and stomach both quivered. "How could I be scary to you?" he asked, fearing that tears would erupt from his eyes, from even his pores.

"You had to see her, didn't you?" She could bear to look at him for only a second longer.

When they returned to their little suite, Willy

went immediately into the bedroom and closed the door.

Tim sat down before Mark's computer, downloaded his e-mail, and discovered another twenty messages without domain names. Their subject lines said things like Need to Hear from You and Explain What Is Happening! and This Is All Wrong!! These, too, he deleted without remorse or hesitation. These sasha would have to find their way without him. A message from Cyrax remained. When opened, it offered him this rigorous and mocking consolation:

deer buttsecks,
with every step 4-ward, every step up,
something new is lost or forsworn.
this IS a process of loss
reed 'em & weep, LOLOL
(foul & flawed & week tho u r,
u must face yr loss 2 come!)
do not FLINCH! do not QUAIL!
do not BACK AWAY! the PRICE
must bee PAID!!! u have luvd,
now u must looze yr love & bid
gud-bye, old soldier. this 2 is death.

33

Brian Jeckyll had rescheduled all of Tim's drive-time interviews for 6:30 to noon on Thursday morning, and at 6:00 A.M., Tim reluctantly un-peeled himself from sleeping Willy, rose from their bed, used the bathroom, and, freshly showered, dressed himself in Gap khakis, a blue button-down shirt, and a black, lightweight jacket. With ten minutes to spare, he went downstairs, bought two Danishes and a cup of coffee, and returned to his room. He had polished off the first Danish by the time the telephone rang, right on schedule. Ginnie and Mack were calling from their radio station in Charlotte, North Carolina, and the first thing they wanted to know was if he'd ever had any supernatural experiences.

"I don't really know how to answer that, Mack," Tim said. "How about you?"

After Ginnie and Mack came Zack and the

MonsterMan of Ithaca, New York, who wondered aloud how weird you would have to be to
write a book like **lost boy lost girl.** "How weird
do you have to be to call yourself Monster-
Man?" Tim asked. "We're all in this together."
There was Vinnie the Vinster of Baltimore,
Maryland; Paulie's Playhouse of St. Petersburg,
Florida; the Owl and the Fox, otherwise Jim
and Randy, of Cleveland, Ohio ("You really
want to make us quiver in our jammy-roos,
don't you, Tim?"); and many more, the Bills
and Bobs and Jennys of morning talk radio,
each with their seven-minute segments in which
they chaffed with each other, updated the traffic reports, and handed off to newscasters with
stories about mangled children, traffic acci-
dents, municipal graft, and homicidal snipers.
Tim ate his second Danish during a run of com-
mercials in St. Louis, Missouri, and by the time
he started to get hungry again had arrived in
California, where drive time was particularly intense. ("You're a well-known writer, you live in
New York—tell me, what do you think of our
governor?" "He's a peach of a guy," Tim said.)
At seven minutes past 12:00, he finished his ses-
sion with Ted Witherspoon and Molly Jackson
of Ted and Molly's Good Gettin' Up Morning
Show, broadcast from downtown Bellingham,
Washington, and staggered over to the sofa,

where Willy was sailing around London with Muriel Spark.

"Are they always like that?" she asked.

"You see why they're so much fun to do."

"They always ask the same questions, over and over?"

"It's more like I give the same answers, over and over."

"Why do you do that?"

"They're the only answers I know," he said. "I have to go back to bed now. I need some sleep."

"Sleep for half an hour, and I'll order a room service lunch."

He looked down at the white bag, into which her right hand was dipping. It seemed to be less than a third full.

Forty-five minutes later, when the waiter rolled his cart into the room, Willy quietly opened the bedroom door and found Tim writing in his journal.

From Timothy Underhill's journal

During lunch, I tore a page out of my notebook and wrote out, in block caps, WCHWHLLDN, and asked Willy if it meant anything to her. Chewing, she looked over, thought for a second, and said, "Sure. It's simple."

"What does it mean, then?"

"Just put in the vowels. I'm not going to do it for you."

"Is there supposed to be a Y in there?"

"Hah! You decide." Her mood changed, and her eyes, looking a bit swollen, swung toward me. "I sense that today is a big day for the home team. What are we going to do?"

I took a couple of slow breaths. "Could you stand to look at that house again?"

"The one behind your brother's, where I had Lily Kalendar's childhood?"

Willy knew exactly which house I meant. She closed her eyes and made internal judgments I could only guess about. Maybe she measured the spaces in the honeycombs and counted hummingbird wings. Her eyes opened, and she said, "Yes. It's not going to shock me, this time. Actually, we have to go there. I know what I'm supposed to do."

"I hope you're going to tell me. I've never really understood what you could do, much less were supposed to do."

"I'm sure that's the truth," she said, taking up my confession with a kind of forgiving bitterness that lifted me off the hook even as it sank the barbs deeper into me. "You never understood what I was going to do, but you should have. You even wrote it, you idiot."

"Where?"

"As if I'd tell you. No, it was in what you **didn't** write."

What I didn't write? This baffled me, but I kept my mouth shut.

Willy knew perfectly well that I had failed to understand: that I had failed **her.** "Do you remember our conversation in that restaurant in Willard with the nosy waitress?"

"Of course I remember that conversation."

"Then remember what you told me. I was going to be healed."

Even more baffled than the first time, I asked, "Did I say that?"

"No. I said it, just now. But it was what you meant."

And she was right, that was what I had meant—that Willy Patrick was to be healed. I understood it now. Willy had perceived what I had not said about what I was never going to write. That seemed perfect for our situation; it was a kind of summation.

"Only I don't think it was true," she said. "It was just what you wanted to believe. You were lying to yourself, because you didn't want to lie to me. I'm through. I was a mistake to begin with, lucky me, and now I'm going to be turned back in like a counterfeit bill. I'm some kind of

price. You made this mistake, and I'm how you pay for it."

"Maybe it won't have to be that way," I said. "**My** Lily Kalendar went to a place I called Elsewhere. Elsewhere is no distance at all from Hendersonia."

"I just want you to understand that I'm very, very frightened. It's worse for me if you're glib."

"Let's drive over there," I said.

When we pulled over to the side of the road a little way downhill from the house Joseph Kalendar had transformed into a likeness of his own mind, it was as though great plumes and ribbons of darkness streamed from the chimney, the windows, the crack beneath the front door. I could see it that way, as a monstrous wickedness engine, polluting the atmosphere around it with its own substance.

"It looks like the evil twin of your brother's house," said Willy, drawing on the soap operas I had made her enjoy.

"It's not as different as all that," I said, thinking of Pop and the wasted hours in the Saracen Lounge, and April's deep unhappiness.

"Is that a burn mark on the front there, beneath the window? The top steps look scorched, too."

"Twenty years ago, someone tried to burn it down. I think it was the old man who lived across the street and one house up."

I explained that after Kalendar's arrest and incarceration, his neighbors had taken turns mowing the front and side lawns, the parts visible from the street. New arrivals to Michigan Street, unaware of Kalendar's crimes, had refused to participate, and, like Omar Hillyard and his dog, the custom had died. Now the front lawn looked like a parched meadow where brown, waist-high grasses cooked in the sun.

"And all those hidden corridors and staircases are still there," she said. "And the stuff in the basement."

"All of it," I said. "Until next Wednesday, anyhow."

We knew that we had to be there; we knew that 3323 North Michigan had been our goal from the moment we'd left the bookstore on Eighty-second and Broadway.

A little girl in a blue-and-white dress peeped out from behind the house, made sure that I had noticed her, and pulled her head back. Or no such thing happened, and I had merely printed an image from my inner world onto the landscape in front of us. When I worked at my desk, installed within the space between, they were more or less the same thing. April's appearances had always signaled Kalendar's presence, and I was not about to ignore her now.

"Let's get out of the car," I said.

"Is something going to happen?"

"I think so."

We walked up the street where Mark and his best friend, Jimbo Monaghan, had so often coursed downhill on their skateboards, and with every step, I knew, we entered deeper into Kalendar's realm. The house watched us with its multiple eyes. It gathered its breath, its heartbeat pulsed, and all the while it pretended to be no more than an empty, unappealing building, a structure almost everyone would walk past without noticing—a building the eyes slid over too fast to see. I felt a subtle pressure pushing us back, keeping us away: that, too, was how Kalendar's house protected itself.

A car drove past, and a kid on a bicycle, and although Willy and I were walking in the street instead of using the sidewalk, neither the boy nor the woman driving the car bothered to glance our way.

We reached the point on the street where in my imagination Mark had stood in amazement as the Kalendar house had seemed to rear up before him, more or less out of mists, fogs, and suddenly retreating cloud banks. In a common impulse, Willy and I joined our hands.

The broken walkway; the dead grass; the fire-scorched cement steps to the hunched-looking porch beneath the heavy, drooping brow of its roof. The rusty holes next to the door frame where the numerals had been. Someone had supposed that if the number 3323 was pried off the front of the house, its identity would change, its aura would shrink. I had the feeling that those metal numerals had probably been cleaned out of Omar Hillyard's basement. The front door, heavy, almost deliberately ugly, and a little out of plumb. The living room window, where apparitions had or had not appeared.

"This is an awful place," Willy said. Her grip tightened on my hand. "I take it back. I changed my mind. I can't go in there."

With Willy's refusal, I understood what she had to do, and how I had prepared her for it. Better than Cyrax, I knew why she was beside me. At least I hoped I did. "You don't have to, not now. What we have to do I don't think can be done in daylight. And later on, you won't really be going into it—you'll go through it."

"How do you know that?"

"I don't," I said. "It's just what I think could happen."

An oily cloud seemed to gather and thicken behind the window, then disperse into shadow and darkness.

"What are we supposed to do now?"

"We're going to stay together as long as we can," I said. "I can't bear the thought of letting you go."

As the afternoon moved toward evening, an odd, flickering life seemed to take place on the other side of the big, dusty window. I had not known what to expect, only that it was necessary for us to be where we were, and I was glad for any confirmation of my belief. Probably anyone who does what we did then—stand thirty feet from a dirty window and stare at it for five or six hours—will be likely to dream up a thing or two to make the task more interesting, and it's possible that's what happened to us. And I say five or six hours, but actually I have no idea how long Willy and I stood there. Time contracted and expanded at the same time. It felt more like thirty minutes; in that thirty minutes, afternoon gave way to evening.

Most of the time, Willy Patrick and I saw the same things.

An indefinite figure seemed to melt forward from the rear of the room, take us in, and fade back again. The dark, oily haze assembled itself before us now and again, and I thought that, no less than the hovering figure, it had eyes. Once, before the air began to darken, Willy and I both saw a dim, phosphorescent glow stutter like a firefly from a position beneath the windowsill. Another figure, much larger than the first and obviously male, swelled into half visibility and advanced nearly far enough to display the features I knew he had, the beard, the hands held crooked before his face, the long hair and black coat. Before I could register the terror he caused in me, the Dark Man, Joseph Kalendar, vanished into the grit and dust he had roused floating through the empty room.

Much of what we saw amounted to no more than animated shadows, shadows that sometimes barely moved, like Morton Feldman's music, offering one tiny variation only after an endless series of repetitions. A darker patch creeping over or out of a distant wall, itself barely visible, then creeping back was riveting, because what animated it had no connection with anything that existed outside that room. What gave it life was the raw hunger that Willy had sensed in her dream.

People walked past without looking. Cars veered around us without honking, moving as if their drivers had accidentally twitched the wheel. We went beyond hunger without ever experiencing it. When it first began to get dark, I noticed that Willy had not so much as taken a bite out of one of her candy bars in over half an hour, and I asked, "Don't you need them anymore?"

"I like feeling this way." In demonstration of exactly how she felt, she took two Clark bars from her pocket and threw them at the porch. "Feed the animal," she said. I thought she had given it an offering.

Then the cars turned on their headlights, and the windows of the other houses on the block lit up and cast yellow light onto their lawns. Something enormous moved toward the other side of Kalendar's window.

"I didn't know until we got here," I told Willy. "I'm still not sure."

"It's not important. It was all in your mind, somewhere."

"You're not being sacrificed," I said. "It's just that I have to pay for what I did."

"This is what I was created for. I came into your life exactly at the moment in the book when the girl shows herself in that house. Anyhow, my whole life is a sacrifice. I don't mind. I'm not angry anymore." She let her head drop and half-mumbled, "If I wanted to make you pay for something, I'd make you write a book."

Her fingers dug into my hand.

"Are you scared?"

"Ask a really stupid question, why don't you?"

"Me, too. My heart's beating like crazy. I don't know if I can go in there."

"Then don't. It's my night room, not yours."

I thought of my night room, the lightless basement of a tenement on Elizabeth Street where madness in the form of a onetime comrade in arms, therefore a kind of brother in the imaginative space, had stabbed Michael Poole and myself. Our survival had made us giddy.

With every bit of energy I had, I hoped that Willy was going to a place I had already established for her; in a sense, I had already placed her there. More than Hendersonia, far more than the baffling world into which she had been propelled, it was where she belonged.

"You're not leaving me behind," I said. "Not until the last moment, anyhow."

"You're so full of shit," Willy answered, in the sweetest declaration of love I had ever been given.

A bloated cloud of bad intentions and sick desires swarmed up to the window and hung before us, darker than the darkness behind it.

"So that's what's in there," Willy said. "I always wondered."

I told her, "It's not the only thing in there."

Second by second, the light had been dying around us, and I think that both of us noticed that it had gone altogether as soon as I had spoken what I hoped were words of consolation.

Willy needed no consolation. She simply started moving up to the curb, across the sidewalk, and onto the cracked cement of Kalendar's walkway. Taken by surprise, I hung back for a second, and realized that she was acting in accordance with the frightening dream an ignorant author had devised for her. Willy was flying on her own silver cord toward the boy who shared her face. I started after her, watching her slender little body move confidently through the darkness toward the terrible house. The front window swirled with a pattern like oil on a huge puddle, and a muted flash of illumination made the colors briefly shine.

Four feet ahead of me, Willy asked, "What's that light?"

"How the hell should I know?"

She moved up the steps and waited for me. "Do we ring the bell or something?"

"And ask for a cup of sugar?"

Even in the darkness, I could see her frown. "Sorry," I said, and went up the steps. Willy moved sideways to let me get at the door. "If I **had** a cup of sugar, I'd throw it away. The lightness is so good now, it's like having music inside me. I can almost forget how afraid I am. Are you still afraid?"

"You have no idea." Most of the inside of my body felt as though I'd swallowed dry ice. My heart had gone into triple time, and my knees, those cowards, trembled violently enough to shake my trousers. I placed my hand on the door and, hoping for some kind of excuse to procrastinate, glanced across the street. I jumped about a foot and a half.

Leaning against a tree in a posture that perfectly expressed his customary mood of bored hostility, WCHWHLLDN was glaring at us through nighttime shades that made him look like an old-school hipster. He lifted one arm and made an impatient, sweeping gesture with his hand.

"Who is that?" Willy asked.

"He's a Cleresyte, whatever that is," I said, "and he'd just as soon kill you as look at you."

More forcefully, the angel repeated his whisk-broom gesture. Before he could slip off his glasses and melt us into grease stains with the force of his gaze, I grasped the doorknob, turned it, and pushed the door open. The hinges squealed like hungry cats. A seared, unhealthy odor of dust, mold, and tormented lives streamed out of every room, along the corridors, down the staircase, through the entry hall, through the door frame, and outside, coating us with its residue. Holding my breath, I stepped inside, Willy following so close behind that I could feel the charged inch or so of space between us the way I might feel her breath on my neck.

34

The reek of death and abandonment that had enveloped Tim and Willy in its outward journey still hung in the atmosphere. Boldly, Willy moved deeper into the entry and peered up the stairs. Grit and fallen crumbs of plaster crunched under her feet. The staircase ascended into an utter darkness that soon resolved into a fainter darkness surrounding a turn of the banister rail at a landing with a lifeless window.

"We should have brought a flashlight," she said.

"We'll see everything we have to see." Tim advanced into the gray territory between himself and the staircase. A little bit farther ahead and on his right was the door to the living room, firmly closed. Somewhere off to his left, one of Kalendar's concealed, spiderweb passageways led to a hidden staircase. The rubble on the floor had crumbled off the ceiling and the walls, and a thousand generations of rodents had scampered through it, leaving printed on the dust the graffiti of their passing. The entire structure seemed surprisingly flimsy to him. At the first nudge of the bulldozer, the whole thing would collapse into itself and turn to splinters and plaster dust. If he touched one of those pockmarked walls, here and there bearing tat-toolike images of florid roses, he knew the stench of the place would come off on his hand.

"I suppose we go in there," Willy said, her voice shrunk down to less than a whisper.

"Uh-huh." Tim was now almost too fright-ened to speak. "Yeah." He forced himself to move to the door to the front room. He touched the knob, and his hand shook so vio-lently that he could not grasp it. "Oh, God," he groaned. "I don't want to do this."

"Do it for me," Willy said. Then, more firmly: "For **me.** I'm just passing through, remember?"

He looked back at his dear creation and saw her left arm flicker into nowhere and jerk back into visibility. Willy looked as though she might faint again. "Okay, Willy," he said, and wrapped his trembling hand around the brass mushroom of the knob, turned, and pushed. The door swung open on a narrow chamber where a huge bole of black particles and swirling dust like a gigantic hornet's nest pulsed like a living thing in the middle of the room. In the instant it was revealed, the vicious thing whirled, he was sure, to look at Tim Underhill and take his measure at last; in the next, it dispersed in a silent explosion that sent wisps and rags and shadows of itself to the corners of the room. Underhill's fear refined itself into a column of mercury stretching from the top of his bowels to the base of his throat.

Beneath the window, an electrical wire that disappeared into the wall writhed and thrashed like a captured snake, shooting out sparks that showered to the floor; it collapsed in loose coils, then whipped back into life and disgorged another fireworks display before dropping again to the floor.

"There's no electricity in this house," Tim said.

"He's **telling** you to go in," Willy said. "He's letting it happen. He's even making light for you. He knows that guy is out there, and he's afraid of him."

"How do you know that?" As he asked his question, Tim crossed the threshold with slow steps and looked into the corners, rubbed smooth with darkness. That he could speak surprised him; that he could walk was an astonishment. Already much greater than in the entry, the stench flared, stinging his eyes and settling on his lips.

"He told me. When he looked at us."

"In words?"

"Did you hear him say anything?" Willy spun around, seeming to attend to those unheard voices. "This isn't where it happened, is it? I didn't meet Mark in this room."

"He was on the staircase at the back of the entry, waiting to hear you moving down the hidden stairs behind the wall."

"Where is the night room?"

"On the other side of the kitchen."

"Will we go there? We will, you don't have to tell me. We'll go there and cleanse the room of its crimes, we'll wash them away." She gave him the most tender smile he had ever seen. "Because that's what **you're** doing, you old writer. You're washing away his crimes, and you're doing it through me."

"So it seems," Tim said. He was too frightened to cry. "Why would I want to do that?"

"Oh, you," she said, with the implication that he had asked a question with an obvious answer. Then she placed her hand on her chest and gazed at him with a wonder entirely unconnected to him. "Those hummingbird wings, whoo, they're beating faster and getting bigger. . . . This is an amazing, amazing feeling. It's like I'm going to float right up off the ground."

"I don't think it's going to take long."

"It **can't.** I'm Lily Kalendar—your Lily Kalendar."

It was precisely the recognition she had been supposed to attain at the end of the book that was her book. As soon as she had spoken, the lunatic electrical wire beneath the window spouted fiery apostrophes and commas, and it seemed to Tim Underhill that the fabric of reality, already sorely strained, rippled around them.

The overtone of a sound too distant or quiet to be identified entered and hung in the air, a single note that had been played on an upright bass, plucked a moment before by the bassist's finger—

There came the burning metallic hum of a thousand cicadas, greedy, intrusive—

Somewhere above, a door softly opened and closed. Light footsteps on the stairs sounded **hush hush hush.** Tim Underhill's blood seemed to stop moving through his veins. A boy with Willy's face entered by something that was not a door, smiled at him lovingly, then without pause moved toward Willy, who took his hand. They were already, instantly, in the roles he had given them, and he could not follow, he could

watch them no more. Where Willy went, she
went for him.

Clamorous, swiftly moving spirits spun, gy-
rated, sailed through the night air, even in Millhaven.

He was alone in the room, but for the presence
that had offered him illumination in the form
of a wire thrashing like a nerve. His Lily had
joined his Mark, and one day, if he was lucky,
he would glimpse them, as he had glimpsed
the world's glorious, disastrous Lily Kalendar,
through a car window. On these glimpses he
would live; on the hope of them he would do
the work of the rest of his career.

A kind of tragedian's wonder had filled him
during the previous few minutes, and, as specks
of plaster and broken bits of wood and char-
coal-gray mats of dust and tissues of flesh like
old spiderwebs began to rustle and twirl in various parts of the room, his fear returned. It
seemed as jittery and unstable as the wire,
now firing sparks and beating its head on the
floorboards as it squirmed. The filthy material
within the room twirled itself together, piece by
piece, hair by hair, speck by speck, and elon-
gated its substance to a height well above
six feet.

The shivery column of mercury again grew up

through the center of Tim's body, and his knees
began their merry jig. Even his heart seemed to
tremble. To the extent that he could think, he
thought: **I hate being this afraid, I hate it, it's
humiliating, I never want to feel this way
again . . .**

The Dark Man began to emerge out of the
fabric of his unclean substance, first a great
brooding bearded head with eyes the color of
lead, then black-clad arms meshing into a bull-
like chest, the long, dirty coat, and legs that
swelled and lengthened into heavy black boots
planted on the floor. He held his wide-brimmed
black hat in one black-gloved hand to demonstrate his anger. Kalendar wanted Timothy Underhill to see his eyes. Insane fury steamed from
his body, as did a pure and concentrated version
of the stink that flowed through the front door.
Commanded to look, Tim looked. He saw the
murderous rage of the grievously wounded.

"I made a mistake," he said, somehow managing to keep his voice from trembling. "I thought
she was dead. I didn't know you had saved her."

The rage came toward him unabated.

"You loved her. You still do. She is very much
worth loving," Tim said. "I made a lot of mistakes. I'm still making them. It's almost impossible to write the real book, the perfect book."

The voice that Willy had heard spoke in his head, not in words but a crude rush and surge of twisted feelings.

"Because no one knew she was alive. Almost no one knew that she'd ever existed at all."

Another ragged bombardment of rage blasted into him.

"Except the ones who did know, yes. And I could have called the shelter, that's right. But I was writing a novel! In my book, your daughter was **dead.** If she'd been alive, she would have ruined the book—she was just a fantasy, anyhow, a reward I gave my nephew." He stared back at Kalendar, a little stronger for having spoken.

The next wave of emotion tones nearly knocked him over. They seemed to struggle within his head and body, like bats, before dissolving. Tim waved his hands in front of his face, reeling with shock and disgust. "What do you want, anyhow?"

He braced himself for another onslaught, but Kalendar held his hands before his face and glared at him through his fingers long enough to make Tim start to shake all over again. Kalendar's hands clutched at his face and pulled at the skin that was not skin. A transformation began to occur over the width and breadth of Kalendar's body, which became shorter and trimmer, more glossy. It grew a handsome tuxedo and a starched white formal shirt and a black bow tie before its hair and features consolidated, but by that time Tim had long known the name of the figure taking shape before him. It was the second time Mitchell Faber had materialized out of Joseph Kalendar's raw materials.

Closer to Faber than he had been the first time, he was able to see how dramatically he had gotten his villain wrong, too, how greatly he had underestimated this creature's capacities, as well as Willy's. By a considerable margin, Mitchell Faber was the scariest, the most frightening, of these apparitions. Faber had produced himself out of his own most savage impulses, and the result was crazier and more feral than his author had understood. At least Tim had not permitted this shiny predator to marry Willy Patrick. This man would willingly rip a foe apart with only his teeth. After he had washed off the blood, he would slip into his tuxedo and proceed to charm the wives and widows of his monomaniacal employers. (He was what you got when you asked for James Bond, Tim realized—you got a beast like this.)

"It's no good if I **tell** you what you have to do, you miserable turd." Faber grinned in a way

that Willy had undoubtedly once found winning. "You have to come up with it by yourself.
Let me say this: it should be obvious, even
to you."

"I'm too scared to think," Tim said.

"You have to make amends. What do you
have to offer, you moron? How can **you** make
amends? Let's see, how did you wrong me in the
first place?"

"Oh," Tim said, realizing what was being
asked, and that it was exactly what Willy had
proposed for him. "I can't do that."

Faber slid an inch nearer. His teeth gleamed,
and so did the whites of his eyes. He had the
most perfect mustache humankind had ever
seen. "But isn't that exactly what you do? And
you must realize that if you refuse, our friend
Mr. Kohle will make your life an utter horror
for the brief period of time you will have left to
you. That is certain. And all we ask is that you
do a good job, the best you can manage."

"I can't restore your reputation," Tim said.

"Of course you can't. I have exactly the reputation I earned. What I want you to do—what
you are **going** to do, if you want you and your
precious friends on Grand Street to go on en-
joying your lives—is to do justice to my case."

He stepped forward again, crushing pellets of

plaster beneath his gleaming shoes. "We're through. Get out of here. And tell that blasted **thing** out there to leave me alone. I'm just as good as he is."

From Timothy Underhill's journal

Mitchell Faber/Joseph Kalendar snapped out of visibility with a contemptuous abruptness, leaving me alone in the filthy room. Though I didn't know it at the time, I was about to learn what a Cleresyte is, and that, as with artists and detectives, its identity is inseparable from what it does.

When he saw me coming out of the house, WCHWHLLDN pushed himself off the tree and straightened up. By the time I got to the bottom of the steps, he was already striding along the walkway. The black lenses of his sunglasses gleamed silver with moonlight, and under his tight black T-shirt, his muscles stood out like an anatomy lesson. He looked like pure purpose encased in pure impatience. As I drew nearer, I felt the coldness of his disdain and thought, **He hates me because I'm not pure!** I wasn't sure what it meant, but I knew it was right. When we passed, I took a half step to the right, expecting him to do the same. Instead, he deliberately shifted with me, and for the briefest of moments, his right shoulder brushed my left. I felt as though I'd been hit by a truck.

The impact knocked me off my feet and sent me flying six feet over the dying meadow of Kalendar's lawn. I came down with a thump on my side. From the pain that blazed from shoulder to elbow, I thought my arm was broken. I propped myself up on my good arm and watched the menacing angel move up the steps. He got onto the porch and turned around—because I was watching him. He opened his mouth, and again I knew the concentrated terror I had felt when I'd opened the living room door. I understood with absolute certainty that the angel's voice would ruin my hearing and drive me madder than I had ever been at Austen Riggs. There I had been merely a basket case, not a hell-for-leather, mush-brain lunatic. He chose not to speak. That's all it was: he didn't want to waste his time on me.

He spun around and passed through the front door without bothering to open it. Even his boot heels looked pissed off. A moment after he had entered the house, an explosion of light turned all the windows brilliantly white, and his great wings creaked open and penetrated through the walls without breaking them. Glowing, glowering, WCHWHLLDN reared up through the roof and into a wide column of light that now circled the house. Each of his hands held something slithery, shapeless, and dark, from which depended a long, apronlike robe in which I thought I saw a thousand glittering little eyes and a thousand screaming mouths.

I thought I knew what he was carrying—not the evil that had been done in the house but the pain and sorrow of Kalendar's victims. All along, that was what had made the little house so ugly, so elusive, so avoidable: Kalendar's real trophies—not the corpses of his victims but what they had felt in his presence. WCHWH-LLDN was the night crew; he did the cleaning up and clearing away. The giant angel flew higher and higher, mounting the sky, and the dirty fabric trailing behind him unreeled and unreeled from the house. When the last of it went snapping upward and disappeared, the angel came battering down from the heavens and did the same all over again, repeatedly, bearing away the scraps and residue of that stinking darkness and that sacred charge until the house was cleansed. The burn marks had disappeared from the front of the house.

I think WCHWHLLDN would have made Philip very happy, for in his way the angel followed his wishes to the last degree: he burned down the house, dug a six-foot-deep pit where it had been, filled the pit with gasoline, and set it alight. His job, his task throughout eternity, had been purification, and he had been assigned this case. He cured infection and eliminated pollution. In his eyes, I, along with every other human being, represented a vast irritant. We carried pollution and contamination wherever we went, and we were far too imperfect to be immortal. We didn't have a chance of understanding what was going on until we reached zamani. (Come to think of it, this is pretty much the way Philip used to feel, back in the days before his rescue by China Beech.)

The light no one could see left the Kalendar house and the star realms above it; the work no one had seen had been concluded. I pushed myself upright and staggered back to my car, bruised and aching and almost too numb to feel.

When I let myself back into what had been our room and now was mine, I felt Willy's absence the way you feel a phantom limb. She had been amputated from me, and although I had performed the surgery, I wanted her back. I missed her vastly, oceanically. Her face appeared wherever I looked, on the windows, in the wallpaper, in the air above the bed we had shared. The

Cleresyte's touch, and the fall it had given me, still pounded throughout my body. In a funny way, I didn't mind, because the pain helped take my mind off Willy.

I filled the tub and soaked in a hot bath until my fingertips were wrinkled. Hunger returned to me as I toweled myself off, and with Willy's voice in my ear, I called room service. Sheer longing tempted me to order two steaks, two orders of onion rings, and a dozen candy bars, but when the waiter answered, I settled for tomato soup and roasted chicken, the kind of meal my mother used to make.

In my mind, I had changed so much that I was surprised my shirts and jackets still fit. When the food came, I took a couple of bites and thought I was going to throw up before I could get to the bathroom, but I did get to the bathroom, and instead of throwing up I stood over the toilet and made gagging noises. **Where was Willy?** I wondered. I had made up Elsewhere, but I couldn't go there any more than I could go to Hendersonia.

Except, of course, that I could—but before that prospect, I stepped back, shivering, unwilling to tamper with those dear shades and phantoms. About that time, while I wandered toward Mark's computer, I remembered, I thought I remembered, that I had agreed to a contract with a sleek character made of cobwebs and mouse droppings. That part of the evening had been knocked out of my head by the angel's bruising touch and the sight of that industrious and furious being at his eternal task: both of these had banged my head against the ground, inducing a mild amnesia.

I sat at the keyboard, clicked on something or other, I know not what, and a familiar blue rectangle claimed the center of my screen. Cyrax had dropped in to make his good-byes and pass on some more of his ominous advice:

underfoot, u hav dun xceeding well & I yr gide now plant a ki55 up-on yr wrinkled brow. 1gnore not yr hart-8rake, u hav earned it, it is yrs! & now u hav another mity task, ol' buttsecks, 1 to test u to the x-treem of yr fond talent (LOLOL)

oho my deer u must follow yr Dark Man Joseph Kalendar through the lost echoes of his nuit sombre profonde! Yr title shall b— KALENDAR'S REALM. u must not gild that lily nor praise it, wht u wrote abt. his dghter struk hom, it did strike hom & he wants onle justthis. Justthis iz next-dor 2 mercy but another country 2 it! UZ yr hart-brake & u will find the way within.

those 2 u love r in yr ELSEWHERE, which is
our EDEN, frum whence they began so long
ago. We watch ovr them in their EDEN,
self-created & beautiful to behold. u gave
them that!

a last word abt the last word (LOL)—u will
behold an IDEEL, & u must pass it by. IDEEL
will des-troy u 4 u r not red-e 4 it, buttsecks,
NOT NOT NOT 4 u r an un-perfect being in a
un-perfect world, that is yr strength & yr lode-
ston & yr compass 2.

35

At five o'clock in the sunlit afternoon of Friday, the twelfth of September, Timothy Underhill took his seat at the end of the second row of metal folding chairs lined up in a sweet, breezy glade in Flory Park, on the far eastern edges of Millhaven. A professor of religion at Arkham University had once told him that it was one of the most beautiful parks in the country, and he saw no reason to dispute the old man's claim. Sunlight fell through the leaves overhead and scattered molten coins across the grass. In front of the rows of chairs, filled primarily with teachers and administrators from Philip's school and congregants from their church, Christ Redeemer, Philip stood a little way before an imposing African-American gentleman wearing a white robe with voluminous sleeves over a shirt with a black banded collar. This was the Reverend Gerald Strongbow, who conducted services at Christ Redeemer and before whom Philip Underhill's lifelong racism had, apparently, left him, as if by unofficial exorcism.

Tim had developed a great fondness for Reverend Strongbow. In a brief conversation at the edge of the glade, the reverend had told him that he enjoyed his books. The man had a gorgeous voice, resonant and deep, capable of putting topspin on any vowel he chose. After the remark about Tim's novels, the reverend inclined his head and said, more softly, "Your brother was a tough customer when he first came to us, but I think we managed to slide some good Christian goose grease into his soul."

A little buzz and rustle of conversation went through the assemblage when China Beech appeared, holding lightly on to her brother's arm, at the far end of the glade and, in a cream-colored dress, pearls, and a pert little hat with a veil, began to make her way up the aisle. The expression on his dour brother's face when China Beech joined him in front of the clergyman astounded Tim, for it contained an emotional sumptuousness that would never before have been within crabby Philip's reach.

Tim thought of Willy Patrick coming toward the signing table at Barnes & Noble, fear, fatigue, and fresh, amazed love shining in her wonderful face; and he thought of Lily Kalendar, stopping his heart as she carried a book and a cup of tea past a Bauhaus window. At that moment, if he could somehow have married both of them, he would have linked arms with his Lilys and joined his brother at Reverend Strongbow's portable altar.

He thought, **Can I really write a book about that monster Joseph Kalendar?** Immediately, he answered himself: **Of course I can. I am Merlin L'Duith, old soldier, old killer, man of conscience, magician, and queer comrade in arms!**

After the ceremony, everyone drove to one of Bill Beech's old clubs for a reception party in the ballroom, and while the band was playing "Stardust" (for the youngest musician there could remember the Eisenhower presidency), Philip approached Tim at one side of the bandstand and with a touch of his old paranoia said, "I saw you grinning to yourself while China walked up the aisle. What were you so amused about?"

"You make me happy these days, Philip."

He took it in good faith. "Lately, I almost make myself happy. By the way, where's your friend Willy? I thought we'd be seeing her today."

"Yes, Tim," said China Underhill, wandering up. "I hope you know you could have brought Willy. I think she's charming."

"She wishes she could be here, too," Tim said. "Unfortunately, she had to go back to New York this morning."

"Um," Philip said. "Will you be seeing her a fair amount, back home?"

"Answer cloudy," Tim said. "Ask again."

"Willy said the funniest thing to me during your reading," said China. "She asked me if I loved my God. I said, 'Of course I love my God, Willy. Don't you?' You'd never guess what she told me. She said, 'I love my god, too, but I wish he didn't need it so much.'"

"You can't imagine how much I miss her," Tim said.

From Timothy Underhill's journal

So here I am, on tour, in the Millennium Hotel in St. Louis, waiting for my escort to drive me first to a radio station, then to a bookstore for a reading, then to the airport—tomorrow, Phoenix! After a morning-show interview and before lunch with my publisher's rep, I wandered around downtown St. Louis, trying to get the flavor of the city, and when I came across a big secondhand- and rare-books store called Stryker's, I strolled in. I cannot enter such a place without buying a book or two, and I roamed through the stacks looking for anything I hadn't read that might be interesting. In minutes, I turned up a beat-up old copy of H. G. Wells's **Boon,** the book in which he disparaged Henry James, and because it cost only five dollars, I picked it up. In another part of the store, I found an even more battered copy of Charles Henri Ford and Parker Tyler's **The Young and Evil,** with a dust jacket yet, going for the price of a necktie at Barneys. **Boon** and Parker Tyler would certainly see me through Phoenix and on to Orange County. I was winding my way back through the aisles and half corridors when I saw the sign for MYSTERY SUSPENSE and decided, in a moment of authorly vanity, to see how many of my books they had in stock.

On a long, waist-high shelf I found a nice row of my books, two copies of **Blood Orchid,** three of **The Divided Man,** one of **A Beast in View,** and two each of the books I wrote with my collaborator. Ten altogether, a handsome number, and all in hardback. As books will do, the middle copy of **The Divided Man** seemed to call to me and invite inspection. In all innocence, I reached for the book and pulled it halfway off the shelf. Then I noticed that it was roughly thirty pages shorter than the books on either side. I removed it from the shelf and saw that it was in fine condition and had not been vandalized. In fact, it seemed remarkably bright; in fact, it seemed brand-new. What happened next was a moment of recognition, surprise, and terror all jumbled up together. The word "galvanic" was invented for moments like that. I uttered some sort of moan or grunt, as if the book had stung me.

The "real" book of my best book—I realized first how beautiful it must be, then how much I could learn from it. What powers would be mine, were I to read it. I could, it occurred to me, learn how to write the real book, which was the perfect book, every time. I could be the best novelist in the world! Praise, adulation, love, money, prizes would descend upon me in a great wave of never-ending applause. My hands trembled with the majesty of what they held, and I felt a sick love, an addict's love, for the book.

A slight disturbance in the murky light at the end of the MYSTERY SUSPENSE aisle caused me to look up, and I found myself confronted by ungainly, unhappy April Blue-Gown. My sister was glaring at me with eyes that were furious black dots. Her mouth shaped words I did not want to, and did not, hear. This time, I listened anyhow. Only then, too late in the day for it to have influenced me, did I remember Cyrax telling me u will behold an IDEEL, & u must pass it by. I shoved the sirenlike thing back on the shelf and charged to the front of the store. I want no part of the ideal, I want nothing to do with it. I've seen what it does to people. Give me the messy, unperfect world any day.

ABOUT THE AUTHOR

PETER STRAUB is the author of seventeen novels, which have been translated into more than twenty languages. He lives in New York City with his wife, Susan, director of the Read to Me Program.